Amie

SAVAGE SAFARI

Lucinda E Clarke

AMIE: Savage Safari

Cover art and design by Daz Smith
darryl@nethed.com
http://www.nethed.com/book-covers/
Editors:
Prof. Richard Butler – Dave Cantrell – Jo Holloway
Paperback compiled by: Rod Craig

This story is for all my friends who have loved Africa and the captivating beauty of its people and its wildlife; and to those wonderful readers who have supported Amie and me on her continuing adventures.

Also by Lucinda E Clarke

PSYCHOLOGICAL THRILLER
A Year in the Life of Leah Brand
A Year in the Life of Andrea Coe

FICTION
Amie – an African Adventure
Amie and the Child of Africa
Amie Stolen Future
Amie Cut for Life
Amie Savage Safari
Samantha (Amie backstories)
Ben (Amie backstories)

MEMOIRS
Walking over Eggshells
Truth, Lies and Propaganda
More Truth, Lies and Propaganda
The <u>very</u> Worst Riding School in the World

HUMOUR
Unhappily Ever After

Contents

1   HOME INVASION

"Eouww, hold her still!" the heavy-set, black woman shrieked at the two older girls who were battling to pin down the struggling child. The victim was no more than seven years old, and her limbs were flailing and kicking against the women who were about to mutilate her body without benefit of anaesthetic or antiseptic. The parts of the knife that were not rusty glinted in the sunlight as the butchery began. Shrill screams punctuated the air as the blunt steel tore into her private parts. The procedure ensured that she would never enjoy sex and therefore would be faithful to the man who was going to buy her the next day. She was just another female whose young body was up for sale to the highest bidder after enduring the excruciating pain of having her clitoris sliced away.

Amie jumped as a hand touched her shoulder, snapping her out of the nightmare she fell into whenever she closed her eyes, or let her mind wander. It was weeks since she'd attempted to rescue a party of little girls from such a fate, but the grotesque images still flashed before her eyes. She had seen some terrible things at the hands of both women and men and didn't know if the horrors and cruelty she'd witnessed would ever leave her.

One of her co-workers in the office was leaning over her desk.

"You have a visitor. He's waiting in the boardroom and he's very impatient. Said to get you immediately."

Amie had no idea who would be visiting her at work. Her cell phone buzzed and she glanced at the text briefly. It was from Simon. *Just landed in London. Wish you were here. Missing you. xxx.*

As Amie approached the boardroom, the door flung open as the security officer, with a sweeping device in his hand, came out. "All clear, I don't know who he is but he's in a foul mood." He loped along the corridor and disappeared into the main office.

"Come in Felicity. Don't loiter in the doorway."

She groaned. She hated the name Felicity. Some faceless person in some faceless London building in the bowels of the Secret Service had decided it was the perfect name for a spy. No one of course had thought to consult her for her opinion or choice.

"Felicity."

Amie snapped out of her musing and came face to face with Ian Fleming. What was he doing in Durban, South Africa?

"Sit down."

The words were terse and for a moment Amie wasn't sure if she'd heard correctly. The last time she saw Ian, he was in Apatu, the capital city of Togodo miles to the north, where he'd been charming and friendly. Today, his whole demeanour was quite the opposite. His balding head with its thin wisps of fair hair framed a round, chubby face with dark piercing eyes. His lips were thin, and he was running to fat where his stomach was hanging over his belt. Amie couldn't imagine anything further from the James Bond of an earlier Ian Fleming, or a more unlikely name for a real spy.

Her Majesty's portrait stared down on Amie as she slid into a seat halfway along the highly-polished boardroom table, but Ian Fleming shook his head and pointed to the chair closest to him.

"We have another job for you."

"Look, Ian, I'm sorry but I'm quite happy where I am. I'll work for Her Majesty's government here in Durban for as long as you want me. However …"

"I don't think you quite understand Amie. We own you, we decide where you will and will not go, and we decide what you will do and will not do."

A rush of anger coursed through her. She stood and began pacing across the green carpet. "No! No! No! I've put myself into danger, fought to survive, slogged miles across Africa, lost a husband, tried to rescue children from female genital mutilation and I've even killed people. I've had enough. I want an ordinary life with marriage, kids and school runs, the whole works. I'm done being a spy. I never know who I can trust, so I trust nobody. I mix with people I don't like, and get into things that I don't want." Amie ran out of steam and slumped back into her chair, head in hands on the table.

Ian Fleming didn't flinch. He sat still for several minutes not uttering a word, not moving a muscle. He picked at an imaginary piece of lint on his trousers, re-crossed his legs, sat up and leaned forward. When he spoke the tone of his voice sent chills down Amie's spine.

"I'm sure we both agree on one thing. You're not a good spy."

Amie jumped in quickly. "Exactly, so there's no point in using me. I'll just continue as normal."

"Life will never be normal for you again, Amie-Felicity. You're way beyond that point."

"Nonsense. I'm sure the great British Institution of SIS won't miss one small, bad spy."

Ian's smile sent more shivers down her spine. "Frankly, none of us expected you to last this long. You were on the expendable list right from the beginning. Come on Amie, you didn't really think that a very basic six months' training in Scotland, with no preliminary aptitude tests, would give you all the tools necessary to be a proper spy?"

Amie thought this very unfair. She had uncovered a double agent that no one else in the Service had even suspected.

"No, I'm sorry my dear," Ian continued, "you were in the wrong place at the wrong time and it was just too good an opportunity to pass up. I'm afraid we're stuck with each other and that's all there is to say on the matter."

"Let's be reasonable here, Ian. You can't possibly force me to do something I don't want to do. Not any longer; I've had enough." She stood up and walked towards the door. She turned to look back at him. "So, I'll need to find another job, I understand. It's a shame, but it's worth it to be free and independent. I'm sorry, but that's the way it's going to be."

Back at her desk, she was still shaking. She gripped the edge of the keyboard, the spinning figures on the screen made no sense. The coded letters swirled round and round in a frantic dance, and she found herself breathing heavily.

Pull yourself together, she told herself. You've faced worse things than a man sitting in a boardroom making threats. He'll just walk away and accept defeat – won't he?

She stroked her lower belly. Pregnant! She couldn't believe it. She should have given Ian this powerful reason for keeping herself safe. It would give her the excuse she needed to walk away from what she knew would put her and the unborn child in the path of danger.

It was early days, but she and Simon had talked for hours about names, where they should live, how much time off she would take for the confinement, and whether she would return to work after the birth. As soon as he got back from London, they planned to marry and be as normal a couple as his job allowed.

It suddenly dawned on her that Fleming had appeared in Durban when Simon had told her he'd been ordered to meet up with Fleming at HQ in London. This didn't make sense, what was going on?

She did her best to concentrate for a while, then accepted defeat. She was unproductive and unable to work. One moment she experienced a blinding rage, the next extreme anxiety about her untenable position. She had no idea how safe she would be now. SIS did not mess around, and she had defied them.

She emptied the cache, powered down her computer, collected her belongings, and signed out. The hot sun hit her as she left the building and the heat radiated shimmering waves off the tarmac as she walked towards her car. Where *was* her car? It wasn't in its usual bay.

She squinted round the parking area but it was

nowhere to be seen. She stopped to think. Nobody could have stolen it from inside the compound, not without authorisation.

She went to the guardhouse.

"Afternoon Madam," the friendly African greeted her.

"Hello, Gabriel. I can't see my car anywhere. Do you know…?"

"Ah, no Madam, yes Madam, it was driven out of here just a little while ago. The man I do not know, but he had the proper papers. There was no reason to stop him. You did not know?"

"No. No I didn't know, Gabriel."

"I am so sorry Madam, sorry Madam. He told me you had agreed and I could not stop him – he had all the right papers – so sorry Madam. And he had the keys." His forced smile looked a little lopsided.

"Never mind, I'm sure you're not to blame."

Amie turned and stared at the one-story brick building housing the British Consulate in Durban. She was loath to go back inside. Only this morning, it was a warm, familiar place full of friends. Now, it loomed large and menacing; it was a place where she'd been threatened.

One of the office workers came out and waved. "Hi," he called. "Problem?"

"Yes, you could say that. Someone has borrowed my car and left me behind."

"Need a lift home?"

"Yes, please."

"Hop in; it's not far out of my way."

Amie inserted her key in the downstairs door and took the

lift up to her flat. Her head spun and her heart thumped. All she wanted to do was have a cool shower, climb into bed, curl up and hide from the world. She needed time to think things through and make plans.

The first thing she saw when she opened her door was Ian Fleming reclining on her couch. He'd raided her drinks cabinet, the half-full wine glass sat blatantly in front of him on the coffee table.

Her feet were rooted on the doorstep, her muscles frozen.

"Don't just stand there Amie, come in and sit down. You're making the place look untidy."

"How, dare you!" she gasped kicking the door shut behind her. "This is *my* flat, *my* place! You have no right."

"Calm down." There was a menacing sharpness in his voice. "My dear girl, I have every right. Who leases this flat, provides you with a car and employs you?"

His use of the present tense wasn't lost on Amie as she flung her bag on the table and stalked into the kitchenette to put the kettle on.

"I'm terminating my employment as from this moment," she said as she grabbed her favourite mug. She opened the coffee jar and scooped out two heaped spoons of granules, throwing them into the mug. Her hands were shaking.

Fleming watched her. If he was fazed by her behaviour he didn't show it; his laid-back demeanour and infuriating calm made Amie see red. He sat quietly as she made herself a cup of coffee. She was playing for time and hoped he'd give her some space while she considered what to say and how to react.

She poured the boiling water, splashing scalding drops on her hands as she concentrated on trying to steady them. This Ian was not the man who'd helped her when she returned to Apatu a few months ago. He'd arranged a comfortable hotel room, cleared up the dead bodies and joked with her about the low standard of hotel housekeeping. This was a stranger who'd invaded her flat – the small, one-bedroom apartment she was so proud of, her sanctuary. It was where she felt safe, even though these days the crime rate was high in South Africa. But it held precious memories of many wonderful nights spent with Simon.

She stirred her coffee and walked over to the large window that overlooked the back gardens and the large, communal pool.

"I can see you're going to make life difficult for me," she said.

"No, Amie, not difficult – impossible."

"Why can't you just leave me alone? Put me in witness protection if you like. I promise not to contact my parents, nor any family members. They have no idea I'm still alive," she lied. "I'll never set foot in Britain again. No one need ever know I exist. Give me new papers, another life and I'll be out of your hair once and for all. You said yourself, I'm a rotten spy. I'm useless with guns and I hate violence." She'd run out of arguments.

"Yes, you're all of those things Amie. You have no idea how aghast I was listening to your debriefing, at the mistakes you made, the people you *didn't* kill that you should have terminated. You have, I admit, on occasion shown a little initiative, but to be honest, you are the last person I'd want to send out on a job. You're a liability.

However, this time we have no option. It's most unfortunate you're the only suitable person we have."

"I'm glad you think me suitable for *something*," Amie snapped back. She hated being a spy, but being deliberately called inept wasn't pleasant either.

"Frankly, I'm not in favour of using you at all, but we don't have anyone else and time is of the essence. You will be leaving early tomorrow morning."

"But – but I can't." Amie was horrified. She grabbed a cushion from the couch and tugged at the fringe as she paced back and forth across her small lounge – her coffee forgotten on the windowsill.

"And," he continued ignoring her distress, "you will tell no one you're going. I'll smooth things over at the office. You will remain here this evening; pack. I'll be here at six tomorrow morning to take you to the airport."

Amie felt her world fall apart. How could she disappear and not contact Simon? Well Mr bloody Fleming, that was one instruction she had no intention of following.

And the baby, what about the baby? Some instinct told her not to mention it. She wouldn't put it past him to march her to a local clinic to dispose of another unwanted encumbrance.

She fought back the tears threatening to spill down her cheeks. She would not cry in front of this man. Her mind raced. There had to be a means of escape.

Fleming stood up, strode over to her handbag, blatantly removed her cell phone and put it in his pocket. He took her laptop from the dining room table, her last line of communication.

Amie was too stunned to stop him. Had he been an assailant, an ordinary burglar or a total stranger, she would have attacked him, fought for what was hers and given him a good kick in the balls or a poke in the eye. But he was her boss, one of the few she'd met. The man she'd liked and admired so much was now cold and calculating.

With the laptop under one arm and her keys in his hand, he gave her a slight nod as he made for the door.

"Remember Amie, not a word to a soul, and believe me, I'll know. Don't even think about doing anything stupid." He opened the door and walked out, locking it behind him.

She stared at the space on the table where her laptop had rested,   then shuffled into the bedroom. Nothing looked different. The clothes she'd worn last night were still flung over the chair in the corner; the odd bumps in the duvet where she hadn't made the bed properly this morning; her slippers resting by the chest of drawers where she had left them, all told her that life was normal – they lied.

Everything in her wardrobe and in all the drawers looked the same, yet there was something not quite right. She couldn't put her finger on it. She checked out the bathroom, flipping the lid closed on the toothpaste tube as she looked around, even lifting the top of the toilet cistern to see if there were foreign objects lurking in the water. There was nothing out of place, but she felt uneasy. Her training had taught her to follow her instinct. So, what was it?

She examined the lounge from all angles. There was nothing hidden behind the pale green, floral print cotton curtains that blew slightly in the breeze from the open windows. They had told her again and again during her training to look up.

At first, she couldn't see anything, but then she noticed that one of the inset ceiling lights didn't match the rest. The silver ring around the edge was a fraction wider and a little shinier. Dragging a dining room chair over, she climbed up and stared at the light. There were several holes in the steel ring. A microphone? Camera? Or both?

Amie jumped down and raced back into the bedroom, but here the light fittings all looked the same, and to her relief the bathroom lights had not been tampered with either. She went back into the bedroom and flung herself on the bed. She needed to slow down, think, work this out, and make a plan. What were her options?

There were only two possibilities, go along with what they wanted or run away. Running away wasn't feasible. She had very little money to hand, and she'd need her passport … her passport! It wasn't in her bedside cabinet nor in her spare handbags. Somehow, she knew she wouldn't find it.

She sank down onto the bed. If she was going to make a run for it, she needed to pack, then get out of the apartment – but with limited funds and no transport where could she go? She couldn't ask anybody at work for help. She couldn't allow them to put their own jobs – or lives – at risk and after today, she wasn't sure who she could trust.

Her flat was on the third floor with a three-storey drop straight down to the concrete pavement below, with no balcony or a drainpipe to hang on to. There were pipes outside the bathroom window, but there was no exit from the inner well formed by the adjoining apartments.

Just in case her ears had deceived her, she tried the front door but it was locked, and impossible to open without the key. Her beloved flat had become a prison. There was no concierge to call, and Amie had no idea who the building administrators were. Besides, how would she explain she had locked herself inside her flat? There was no way out and even if she could escape, she had a feeling that she would not survive for long. Besides, Ian took her phone.

Ian's change in attitude had shocked her more than she'd realized. When they had met in the Embassy in Apatu, he was warm and friendly, joking, and sympathetic to her tale. Not for one moment during her debriefing had he given any hint that she had performed badly or made mistakes.

If escape wasn't possible, she had no option but to obey. Perhaps she could pretend to go along with whatever wild scheme they had in mind, then make a run for it later. At some point, they were bound to return her cell phone and laptop as she would have to keep in touch with the guys in London. Would they assign her to Maddy again? The faceless, sexless 'friend' who sent her coded emails pretending to be backpacking around the world while he or she was most likely bunkered down in a basement cubbyhole in Whitehall. Maddy would blithely send Amie into danger and grumble when things went wrong, while the most dangerous situation the handler encountered was getting stuck in the tube doors as the train left the station.

Amie sighed, stood up and went to her closet to get a rucksack. She dropped it on the bed and stared at it. Ian Fleming had not given her any idea where she would be sent, or what they wanted her to do. Did she need to pack summer or winter clothes? How typical of a man. If she was going to make a run for it, she needed to travel light. She flung in two pairs of cargo pants, six t-shirts, a thick jersey, basic underwear, and toiletries. She packed her Kindle, too, after unsuccessfully attempting to download a pile of new books. Ian's lot had disconnected or jammed her internet access. They'd thought of everything.

She picked up the small framed picture of Simon and her taken recently at a function at the City Hall in Durban and slipped that into a side pocket.

Thoughts of leaving without being able to tell him where she was going, or even how long she was going to be away brought tears to her eyes, and this time she didn't try to hold them back. There had to be a way of contacting him.

Opening the lounge window wide, she peered out. She thought the walkway was empty, until she saw a man right below her window, tucked in close by the wall. It wasn't anybody she'd seen before and he seemed out of place in the heat of a Durban summer, dressed in a suit and tie. He looked up at her and nodded, leaving her in no doubt that he was there to ensure she didn't leave.

She made herself another mug of coffee. Usually the caffeine calmed her nerves, but not today. Why hadn't Ian briefed her in private, in the consulate, where they swept for listening devices? It was all a mystery.

The only possible act of defiance was to tape over the light fitting to give her some privacy for the evening. She crisscrossed masking tape over the light and the metal rim. It was a fire risk, but if it set anything alight, at least the fire department would have to come to her rescue. Let the Service talk their way out of that one.

The evening dragged on. Every time Amie checked her watch the hands had barely moved. By seven o'clock it was getting dark, and her guard was still there – she guessed there'd be a change of shift, but somebody would be out there all night.

Supper was a frozen dinner for one and the whirring of the microwave echoed round the flat as it cooked. It felt inappropriate to put on the TV or the radio or to play music. She took her food into the bedroom where it felt more private. There may be more bugs, and if she found them she could bash them to little pieces with her rolling pin on the chopping board but then the Service would take the cost of them from her salary, for damage to Her Majesty's property.

After clearing away her dinner things and dusting around, as she didn't want to leave the place dirty, she fell into bed. She slept fitfully. Her dreams were peppered with fight or flight situations. One minute she was racing to escape, the next she was battling hand-to-hand with a half-seen adversary who evaporated when she tried to get to grips with its wraith-like form.

She woke bathed in sweat and exhausted. She staggered towards the bathroom and paused seeing herself in the mirror. Her shoulder-length fair hair framed a pretty oval face, but there were dark shadows under her grey eyes. At five-feet-five, she took an average size in clothes and was neither too thin nor too fat.

Huh, some fighting machine, she thought to herself before turning on the shower.

As she stood under the scalding water, her thoughts ran riot. She couldn't make up her mind what to do, but, in the end she did nothing, because there was nothing she could do. She had to escape, but didn't know how. There must be places where the tentacles of Her Majesty's government didn't reach. But even if she ran to a country with no extradition treaty, they wouldn't be bothered about such minor details. The 'system' would send somebody to dispose of her. They would never take the risk of her turning up in Britain to a barrage of cameras and microphones to tell the world that she hadn't been killed after all, and that SIS, MI5 or 6, or whatever numbered department it was, had coerced her into taking her husband's place, and then forced her to kill and spy for them.

Amie may be a very poor spy with only a basic training, but she had already seen first-hand how ruthless any country could be when it came to protecting its secrets and its reputation.

She stepped out of the shower and towelled herself dry. Even now, a little after dawn, she could feel the warm air wafting in through the windows. The temperature seldom went below nine degrees Celsius in Durban; she had never needed to buy a winter coat. She hoped they would not send her anywhere cold and wondered if it was true that years in a hot country thinned the blood, making it more difficult to withstand cold weather.

Fleming rang the bell at precisely 6:00 am, before unlocking the door from the outside and walking right into the lounge. He gave her a sharp nod before striding over to stare out of the window.

"I expect your pet Rottweiler is still out there on guard?" She sneered.

"Are you ready? We need to leave."

"I've not finished my coffee."

"You have fifteen minutes; we've a plane to catch." he walked out locking the door behind him.

Amie fought back the tears, this may be the last time she saw these rooms; she felt so helpless. She had scribbled notes for Simon and secreted them away where she hoped he'd find them, but she wasn't too sure he would ever get to see them. It was more than likely that Fleming's minions would sweep through the apartment and destroy them before she even reached the airport.

When Ian returned fifteen minutes later, she picked up her rucksack and reluctantly followed him out into the corridor. He took hold of her arm, keeping a firm grip on her all the way down in the lift and onto the pavement before ushering her into the back of a black luxury car waiting at the kerb.

A man Amie had never seen before left the plush leather passenger seat and threw her rucksack into the boot. Ian slithered in next to her, nodding at the driver to pull away. She hadn't expected he'd be travelling with her.

Amie wondered if they would go to the new King Shaka airport on the north side of town, or make for the small airfield at Virginia. Looking out of the heavily tinted windows, she marvelled at the normal life going on around her. Minibus taxis wove in and out of the traffic on the highway, screeching to a halt to pick up passengers standing on the verge or the central reservation. A coach, filled with school children bouncing up and down on their seats pulling faces through the windows, was left behind as Amie's sedan threaded through the dozens of commuters making for the businesses and offices in and around Durban and the industrial area to the south of the city.

They drove into the short-term parking area at the main airport. The driver manoeuvred into a bay before he and the man in the passenger seat got out and walked away. She tried to open her door, but nothing happened.

"Childproof locks are so useful," Ian said.

She wanted to slap the self-satisfied smirk off his face.

"Now, admit it, you must be curious about your destination?" he continued.

Amie didn't reply but her stony face had no effect on him.

"You and I are bound for Togodo – Apatu to be precise, your old stomping ground, so it will all be familiar."

"You're coming too?" His words jolted Amie into replying.

He leaned back against the black leather seat and smirked. "Now you see why we have to use you. You're the only one who can get close to our target – you already have an 'in', as they say."

"But I don't know anyone there anymore." Well, that was true if you didn't count Mrs Motswezi who ran the orphanage or Ouma Adede, her witch doctor friend – but she wasn't going to remind Ian about them.

"Oh, but you do. An old friend of yours Ben Mtumba?"

"Ben," gasped Amie. "But it's been ages."

"Yes, but we'll arrange for you to connect up again. You'll be working in the Embassy; there'll be plenty of occasions when you're likely to meet. You know of course he's now president of Togodo?"

"Yes, I've heard." Amie wasn't feeling comfortable about this, something wasn't right.

"We need information and, depending on what you learn, we'll tell you what action to take."

2   SIMON LANDS IN LONDON

As soon as Simon stepped off the plane an official had appeared on the tarmac to welcome him and usher him into the baggage claim from a separate door off the airside apron. He'd relieved him of his mobile phone the moment he sent his arrival message to Amie.

Simon made to take it back but the young man, who looked barely old enough to be let out of kindergarten on his own, merely smiled, and whipped out a small black box from his pocket. "Just need to scan it, Sir." He swiped the phone on both sides before handing it back and then took Simon's laptop and passport on the pretext of lightening the load and being helpful. Simon felt more harassed than welcome but was not surprised after he claimed his suitcase, to be ushered through another service door, avoiding customs and immigration. He was taken out the side of the building and into a waiting car with the engine already purring.

The rain poured relentlessly from the grey clouds that hung low over London and Simon swore when he was evicted from the car and escorted along the Embankment, then down a side street and through a small door leading to a single flight of steps. It was dark and dingy inside and he assumed that spending money to tart up government offices wasn't high on the priority list these days, but even a coat of paint wouldn't have gone amiss. At the top of the uncarpeted wooden stairs a door led into a small reception area. His guide motioned to him to sit on the cracked leather couch. The young man – who had not thought to introduce himself – disappeared through a door behind the counter, wheeling Simon's case behind him. Simon had no option but to sit and wait.

He smiled at the middle-aged woman behind the counter. She only gave him a brief nod in reply and turned back to her computer, her fingers flying over the keyboard like lemmings dropping off a cliff. The walls were devoid of pictures, the coffee table in front of him held no newspapers or magazines, and the moment Simon got to his feet the receptionist, if that's what she was, shook her head and indicated he was to remain seated. She was quite immune to his well-built six-foot frame and his friendly blue eyes under the blonde hair that fell boyishly over his forehead.

Simon sat back down and sighed. He had no idea why they'd summoned him to headquarters in such a hurry, barely giving him time to drag out his warm clothing. If it was so urgent, why had they left him sitting here, watching a typist pounding computer keys and answering the telephone?

The airport welcoming committee reappeared and made some vapid excuse about the party Simon was supposed to meet having been called away; but that was hours ago. Although a few people had come out of the door behind the counter and nodded to him briefly before disappearing down the stairs, nobody talked to him or asked if they could help.

It was all cloak and dagger and he could see no reason for it. He had travelled on a passport in a different name, not for the first time, but they were keeping close tabs on him. Why? He took his phone out intending to send Amie another message, but the screen was blank; the kindergarten kid had disabled it and now he couldn't contact friends or family in Durban, or in England. There was nothing he could do to alert anyone that he was in Britain and not thousands of miles away in South Africa.

After hours of kicking his heels in the drab reception area, he was escorted through the door behind the counter, where they pointed to a desk and gave him a battery of forms to fill in. 'Updating' they called it, but from the basic questions on the papers in front of him Simon was convinced that all the answers were already securely lodged in his personal files. There was nothing new to add. He was up to date on the routine reports from Durban – there was precious little to account for anyway – life had been quiet lately.

At lunchtime they gave him a mug of disgusting coffee in a paper cup the size of a small bathtub – and a plate of wilting sandwiches.

In the middle of the afternoon a door at the far end of the large office opened and an elderly man approached him.

"Simon Peterson?" he asked, although Simon was pretty sure there weren't any other visitors in the office. He nodded.

"Martin McClusky, Deputy Chief." He extended his hand. "Sorry to keep you waiting. It's all go, go, go here. There's never a moment to spare. Come on through."

Simon was about to make a sarcastic comment about them having wasted almost a whole day of his life, but decided against it. As they walked into McClusky's office, Simon noted the greying hair and large paunch that suggested the Deputy Chief was going to seed from sitting behind a desk all day. Simon couldn't imagine him out in the field grappling with bad guys or running for cover with bullets flying all around him.

The first things he saw as he entered the office were his suitcase and laptop standing next to the wall and it crossed his mind they had probably been through both with a fine-tooth comb while they kept him waiting. How paranoid were these people?

McClusky's office was no brighter than the rest of the building, and to Simon, after the bright African sun, it was dark and dingy. Thin net curtains hung over the tall windows on one side of the room, while floor to ceiling bookcases stuffed full of dusty books and box files took up two more walls. A solid government-issue desk occupied most of the space in the room. It was piled high with mounds of papers and dog-eared files some of which were covered in dust.

Walking behind the desk to sink into the overstuffed leather swivel chair on the far side, Martin waved Simon into the visitor's chair facing him.

"Tea, coffee?"

"No thanks," Simon said, remembering the earlier cup they'd served him.

Martin pushed piles of papers to one side and opened a file.

Simon caught a brief glimpse of his photo attached to

the front, and watched Martin quickly flick through the pages.

"I see you've been asking to go out in the field for some time now?"

"Yes. Yes, that was my plan." Simon needed to put this delicately. While Amie was an active operative, he'd wanted to be out there with her, but now that she was pregnant it wasn't a good idea. A secure job in a British Consulate, moving every few years, should provide enough excitement for them along with the two children they planned. It would be a good life, but he wasn't about to tell McClusky that. Fraternisation between employees was frowned upon if either was in the field and Amie wanted off the active list too.

"Actually, I've decided that I'm settled where I am right now. For a while I was considering it, but circumstances have changed."

McClusky gave him a look that made him distinctly uneasy. He was one of those people you felt sure could read what you were thinking. Simon shifted on the rather uncomfortable chair and crossed his legs.

The Deputy looked down again at the file. "I'm afraid that your earlier request has been granted and I am now authorized to send you for a refresher course."

"Is there no way out? We can't cancel that?"

"No, *we* can't. The wheels might turn slowly, but once they do turn there's no turning back, if you get my drift."

"How long will the training take?" he asked.

"Two, three months, depending on your personal progress."

"But what about my work in Durban?"

"All taken care of. You begin as of now." McClusky initialled a paper in Simon's file, closed it, and stood up to indicate the interview was over.

Simon got to his feet. "About my cell phone – mobile, it seems your guy at the airport wiped it clean."

"Don't worry about that, you'll not be using it where we're sending you. As far as I remember there's no reception in those parts anyway, so it wouldn't be of much use. Oh, and don't forget your case and laptop." He smiled but it didn't reach his eyes. His expression reminded Simon of the sharks he watched in the tank at Durban Sea World.

There was nothing he could do but stretch out his hand to return a crushing handshake, collect his belongings and leave the room.

A different minion hovered outside the door, and escorted him through the front office, back down the stairs and along the street in the pouring rain to a waiting car parked at the end of the road. He did not offer to help Simon with his luggage.

As the driver left the kerb, Simon took out his laptop and powered up. As he suspected, it had been wiped too, defaulted to factory settings and wouldn't connect to the internet. He felt a flash of fear. He was out of touch, nobody knew where he was. Something didn't feel right, but he couldn't put his finger on it. Most of all he was worried about Amie. He had promised to keep in touch. He was anxious to know how she was and how the baby was doing. He couldn't even tell her it might be months before he saw her again.

3   MATHILDA

The ceiling fans creaked as they turned in the midday heat, irritating Ben as he rifled through one drawer after another looking for a clean pair of socks. Damn Mathilda. She had a slew of servants to boss around and she couldn't even check if he had enough clean clothes to wear.

The door to the bedroom burst open and slammed as Matilda marched into the room. She was having another temper tantrum. She flung past him without a word and walked into the *en suite* bathroom slamming that door too. Now was not the time to complain about missing socks. Ben sighed. His marriage was a mistake, a big mistake, but he had yet to acknowledge it even to himself. He was overawed by her stunning looks.

Mathilda had long blonde hair that fell past her shoulders, her large, brown, almond-shaped eyes, and her toothpaste smile displayed perfect teeth – the stuff of beauty queens. And that was where he met her, on one of his rare trips to London. He was wined and dined as befitted his status, and the entertainment laid on included front row seats at the Miss World Pageant.

The moment Ben saw Mathilda, he knew he had to have her. From his earliest days, even back in his native village, he'd sworn to marry a girl who was educated, sophisticated, quick-witted and charming. Not for him the rough village maidens who simpered and fawned over every male because they saw themselves as second class citizens. There were many such females who gave him sly glances, dropped broad hints and giggled every time he walked past. He ignored them all. He had loftier ambitions. He could do better.

London felt a million miles away. He remembered how he wangled a visit backstage and asked for an introduction to the woman who intrigued him and left him breathless. She was having a meltdown, she was only placed fourth in the competition, and, in her mind, first place was the very least she deserved. But on hearing this tall, handsome, black man was a president, albeit of a small African country, her mood turned full circle.

She deigned to be his guest at dinner, rightly guessing it would be somewhere expensive and thus began their whirlwind courtship. He extended his overseas stay and wined and dined her every night, taking her on trips to Britain's most famous tourist destinations: The Tower of London, Madame Tussauds, the Changing of the Guards at Buckingham Palace; then further afield to Stratford-upon-Avon, the Beatles Museum in Liverpool and a night of bliss at a sixteenth-century manor house hotel in the Cotswolds.

He was besotted with her; she was everything he had ever dreamed of, in and out of bed.

She was not so interested in him but in the lifestyle he could provide. He spent huge amounts of money on her in all the best shops as he plied her with shoes, bags, coats and dresses. While he did not tell her of his humble beginnings as the son of the chief's brother in a rural

African village, she in turn did not admit to being born in a caravan park on the outskirts of Newcastle, to a mother who was permanently drunk and a father whose name she never knew. She had counted on her looks to get her this far and being First Lady in a country – any country – was now within her grasp.

Within two weeks they were married at Caxton Registry Office which, Ben had been informed, was where all the celebrities promised to love, honour and obey till death – or lawyers – they did part, and shortly after they were winging their way back to Africa as the sole passengers on Togodo Airways' one and only plane.

Mathilda's first culture shock was the traditional African wedding ceremony. After the palatial home Ben had taken her to on her arrival, which met with her full approval, he carted her off to the countryside and a village in the middle of nowhere. She was expected to sleep on a thin mattress on an earthen floor in a mud hut, and introduced to groups of women clad in vivid cotton turbans and matching dresses. It was all so, primitive.

She was forced to wear horrendously garish outfits, sit only with the women listening to a cacophony of their wailing ululations, and watch in horror as a group of cackling men slit the throat of a white bull right before her eyes. As the blood spurted out, a few flecks flew onto her shoulders and chest and she thought she'd be sick. Everybody else saw this as a sign of good fortune and the prompt arrival of lots and lots of healthy babies. Mathilda viewed it as utterly gross and would have rushed off for a scalding hot shower and change of clothes, except they insisted she wore the blood-spattered garments for the rest of the day. For good luck they said.

There followed three full days of 'feasting', which consisted of drinking indescribably appalling still-fermenting beer, gnawing on over-roasted bones using nothing but her fingers and watching long, boring dances as several dozen men pranced around like idiots flinging and stamping their legs in the firelight.

This was not what she had signed up for. First Lady or not, a huge presidential palace and a small army of servants to do her bidding did not make up for the fact that she was now stuck in some hellhole of a backwater with no way out.

Ben was oblivious to how she felt. He was madly in love, still pinching himself that this beautiful woman was in love with him, and he was filled with pride every time he showed her off. He was the envy of his old school friends and admired by his current colleagues and ministers. It was his belief that if he gave her all the material things she demanded and ask for nothing more than she appear on his arm at social and state occasions, and they regularly roll around together between the satin sheets, she would be both happy and satisfied.

He still couldn't believe his luck.

Mathilda became bored very quickly. There was nothing for her to do. The mansion was swept, polished and scrubbed with no input from her. Her days were spent lounging by the pool, taking walks in the extensive grounds of the presidential palace, and spending hours preparing herself for the next public outing.

She ordered a driver to take her out into Apatu, but the

sights of the beggars scrounging for money, the children sitting on the pavements sniffing glue, and the chaotic traffic, horrified her. She saw no charm in the street sellers or their beads, carvings and cloths: or in the brightly clad shoppers, the sturdy little donkeys pulling carts loaded with dirty sacks of fruits, vegetables and old bits of wood, nor in the bustling crowds that darted in and out of the traffic from one side of the street to the other. She wrinkled her delicate nose at the smells: a mixture of stale spices, rotting vegetables, fragrant fruit and sweaty bodies.

If she had expected shops similar to the ones Ben had taken her to in London, she was sorely disappointed. There wasn't one smart department store in the whole of the city – only small cubbyholes behind steel shutters, some of which were pulled down against the heat of the day. They were crammed full like miniature Aladdin's caves and it was impossible to sort the good quality garments from the locally produced cheap goods.

There was the rubbish and dirt in the streets. Did anybody ever think of using litter bins, she wondered – conveniently forgetting how often she'd thrown trash out of her own car window.

While she expected to be given a car, preferably one costing thousands, Ben explained to her it was not the 'done thing' for a First Lady to be seen driving around on her own. It wouldn't be safe. Didn't she enjoy being chauffeured wherever she wanted to go?

At first it was a novelty, but that soon wore off. She missed her sense of privacy, with two bodyguards occupying the other seats. She was unable to leave the palace grounds without her faithful watchdogs behind her.

The burly Africans Ben had assigned for her safety frightened her; she could never tell what they were thinking. She prided herself on being able to read other people's reactions from facial expressions and body language and her expertise had paid off in the way she was able to manipulate the large number of men she'd encountered in her murky past. But these thugs were inscrutable and had no sense of humour. She hated them, and would have given them the slip if she could, but they were eagle-eyed and never gave her the chance.

All her machinations had led her to was a life in a gilded cage. She wanted for nothing, yet she was now bored out of her mind. She often thought about escaping, but she had no access to money; the goons settled the bills when she was out shopping or simply signed for things. She was discontented, but she had no intentions of reverting to her previous poverty levels. Once she worked out how to fund her escape she would be out of here. If she left Ben with a broken heart, that would be just too bad.

4   RETURN TO TOGODO

The flight to Togodo was uneventful. To Amie's relief they were not seated together. Ian Fleming was several rows back, and she could feel his eyes boring into the back of her head. He was only a couple of inches taller than Amie, and the first time she saw him with his ruddy cheeks, sparse hair and rotund figure she'd wanted to giggle. He was hardly a person to catch your eye, but that was probably what most spies relied on; getting lost in a crowd. She doubted many people on the plane even noticed him. He blended into the upholstery.

The moment they landed and opened the doors, Amie took in a deep breath of the hot and humid air. While South Africa was still Africa, it was now built up with so many modern cities and highways and up-to-date infrastructures in place that it wasn't quite Africa, not like Togodo with Ruanga to the south and Budan further north on the east coast next to the warm Indian Ocean. It was good to be back in the real Africa, as she walked down the steps and onto the hot tarmac.

There was the usual chaos in the large tin shed that served both customs and immigration for domestic and international flights and there was little point in hurrying. The luggage would be unloaded manually, then wheeled over to the conveyor belts which, likely as not, wouldn't be working.

Amie flashed back to the first time she'd arrived in this airport and remembered how scared she'd been to see the gun carrying soldiers lined up along the walls, as if they were waiting for the order to open fire. Now she took such things in her stride. This was the way it was in Africa.

She felt a firm hand rest on her lower back, reminding her she was not alone, or free, as Fleming guided her away from the long queues to one side of the line of booths. He flashed his diplomatic passport at the bored official who leant back in his chair with his eyes closed.

Ian tapped his passport irritably on the counter to attract the man's attention and the official slowly opened his eyes, and leaned forward to peer at the document, and then nodded before settling back in his chair.

Ian and Amie were met by an official from the Embassy who was waiting for them. They had just settled in the back seat of the car when a young man raced over with her backpack and Ian's case, leaving Amie to wonder how he'd identified them – had they been tagged with some device? More flashbacks to the tracker she'd had in her boots on a previous assignment which pinpointed her exact location for weeks and she hadn't a clue. As soon as she had a moment, she was going to examine every square centimetre of everything she owned to find even the smallest device. She rotated her ankles to help the blood circulate, thinking they wouldn't need real live spies in the future. It would all be accomplished by using the latest high-tech gadgetry. For her it couldn't come soon enough.

As the Embassy car sped along the highway into the centre of the city Amie saw that nothing much had changed – but then it had only been a couple of months since she left. She'd told Ian she didn't know anybody in Apatu, and she wracked her brains trying to remember if, during her debriefing, she had ever mentioned Mrs Motswezi at the orphanage. She would take the first available chance to visit her and see if there had been any more progress on the rebuilding.

She didn't think that she'd ever mentioned Ouma Adede. Ian Fleming would doubtless sneer at a friendship with a witch doctor. Most modern westerners would be reluctant to believe in ancient tribal beliefs, seeing them as primitive rituals with no substance in today's world.

Amie couldn't remember exactly where Ouma Adede lived, but it was somewhere in a maze of makeshift shacks like the ones they were passing now. Some dwellings were constructed from earth packed down between upright poles, while others had used sheets from broken packing cases for the walls. Most had roofs of corrugated tin, weighted down by old truck tyres to keep them in place. They stood in ragged rows, with a water standpipe at the end of each walkway. It was impossible to drive a truck down the paths and the area was a fire hazard. On several occasions whole families had been burned to death trying to escape while the fire engine idled on the edge of the township, its hoses too short to reach the flames. Most years there was a fire, accepted with the African sense of fatality, and almost as soon as the fire had run its course, they'd rebuild in exactly the same places using the same highly combustible materials.

Amie smiled at the number of satellite dishes mounted on the roofs. Priorities were different here; each shack would be furnished inside with three-piece suites bought on credit, a wall cabinet to display the photographs and sports trophies for all to see, and the largest television the family credit rating could afford.

Most families would live on the earnings of one or two members in full employment who would be expected to share their hard-earned cash on payday. The elderly and the younger siblings would be tended by the children, while the mother was out working. Here and there, groups of men could be seen lounging against a wall or tree, puffing on their pipes or playing cards. If there were to be any future for Africa, it was in the hands of the women who worked from dawn until dusk or longer, raising the children of their frequently absent fathers.

The car sped past the outer suburbs – with rows of neatly built brick bungalows, their gardens surrounded by wire fencing, through which Amie could see sparkling blue swimming pools. She spied maids sweeping the verandas and garden 'boys' watering the lawns and she wondered where she'd be staying. She prayed it wouldn't be in the Embassy, or even the compound where most of the clerks lived. She longed for some privacy and space.

As they swept through the gates of the Embassy, Ian undid his seatbelt and jumped out of the car the moment it came to a stop. Amie didn't even bother to try and open her door, she'd guessed that the childproof locks were on, but the chauffeur hurried round to let her out. Her feet crunched on the newly-laid gravel as she retrieved her rucksack from the boot.

Walking up the steps, Ian looked back to call out "Coffee in the dungeon in ten minutes. Tanya will show you where to leave your stuff." Then he disappeared through the front door.

Amie glanced at the queue over by the far wall where a long line of hopeful visa applicants was waiting by a side door. *What was the lure of wanting to visit Britain?* She wondered. *Would they arrive only to disappear into the crowded London streets looking for work while keeping themselves under the radar? Did they watch the television programmes and believe they would find a better life in those cold, wet climes? Many of them would be sadly disappointed.*

Inside the building, a young girl rushed over to greet Amie.

"Welcome, Amie, isn't it? We're so glad to have a new face here. Have you been to Apatu before?"

Amie wasn't sure how to answer – Ian hadn't briefed her on what to say – but she needn't have worried; the eager young lady didn't wait for a reply but rushed on without pausing for breath.

"I can guess it must be a bit of a culture shock. I've only been here a few weeks myself, and I'm still getting used to the heat, and the crowds, and the noises, and smells. I miss my local coffee shop and the chain stores, but they have promised that a few of us can go out on safari soon, to see the wild animals – I'm looking forward to that."

As she chattered, she led Amie through the building and out into the back garden. Despite the scarcity of water, the lawn glistened a bright green beneath the sprinklers, sending out a rainbow mist over both the grass and the path. The borders were a riot of colours with impala lilies, ice plants, freesias, leopard orchids with their variegated leaves, and African daisies all jostling for space.

"It's so convenient," her guide chattered away. "They have just built this walkway. It connects the Embassy to the compound at the back with all the staff bungalows, so it takes two ticks to get into work. You know there was a civil war here a few years ago? That's when they decided to buy up extra land and build living quarters for the staff so they would still be in British territory. Great idea, huh? Apparently when the balloon went up last time, the personnel were scattered all over the city and evacuating them was a nightmare. Yours is the one at the end here, all mod cons, and I sent a maid over this morning to make sure it was nice and clean."

"Thank you," Amie said as she followed her in through the door.

"Oh, that's awful, I've not even introduced myself yet. It's Tanya." She held out her hand and gave Amie's a firm shake. "If there's anything you need, just give me a shout. My office is the second on the left past the reception desk. But I heard Mr Fleming say he'd meet you in the dungeon."

"Yes."

"Just drop your bags and I'll show you the way. It's not as scary as it sounds. We call it the dungeon because it's underground and all the conversations there are private – no one can listen in – if you know what I mean." She winked and held a finger against her lips.

Amie nodded as she followed Tanya who marched into the main building, along a carpeted corridor, and down a set of stairs – she was obviously unaware that her new guest knew the way and had been in the safe room many times before.

Fleming was waiting, sitting at the head of the table that stretched the length of the room. He drummed his fingers leaving smears on the polished surface.

As she sat down, Amie noticed that since her last visit, they'd added portraits of Winston Churchill, Margaret Thatcher, Theresa May and John Major to that of Her Majesty. She wondered if anybody had suggested displaying any Labour Party Prime Ministers on the walls. Maybe the next time the Labour party won an election all the pictures would be replaced?

Ian telling her to sit down jolted her out of her daydream. He nodded to the pictures.

"The new Ambassador is a rabid Conservative, so you won't see Gordon Brown or Tony Blair adorning the walls." It was the first sign of levity he'd shown. Maybe he felt more relaxed having got Amie this far without any problems. He leaned forward to pour her a cup of coffee, leaving her to add her own milk and sugar.

"First I want you to run through what you know about Ben Mtumba and what dealings you've had with him in the past. Take your time." He leaned back in his chair cradling his coffee cup.

There was little point in holding back any information, so Amie explained how Ben had first acted as her cameraman when she'd been filming new social projects for a Colonel Mbanzi, then later how he'd come to help when the rebels were in force; and how he'd saved Amie's life when they'd fought together against the extremist forces, who had taken not only her foster child but her late husband, too.

"He's my friend," she concluded. "I'm sorry Ian, but I

won't do anything that could harm him. He's always been a good man and I admire him. When I was with him, I had no idea how well connected he was, but that wouldn't have made any difference. He got me out of more than one bad situation."

Ian leaned forward and replaced his cup on the tray.

"That's the word – difference. You've heard the saying, 'Power corrupts, absolute power corrupts absolutely'?"

"Of course, I have. But I know Ben. He isn't the corrupt type. He's good and kind and honest."

"And this is Africa. Give me the name of one country on this continent where the elections are free and fair, where presidents step down when they are voted out. No, they ensure their party wins every election – even if it means killing off the opposition candidates and beating any citizens brave enough to cast their ballot for the other side. And to make doubly sure, their chosen parliament endorses them as President for Life. That's democracy in Africa Amie, that's how it works. So, why should Ben be any different?"

"He went to the International School here in Apatu. He probably even studied the same syllabus I did." Amie protested.

Ian snapped his fingers. "That means nothing. Idi Amin fought with the British Colonial Army, King Mswati of Swaziland went to an exclusive British public school, President Nkrumah studied in London, Thabo Mbeke studied at the University of Sussex. The list is endless. Your Ben has only travelled to the UK a few times; he still thinks like an African."

"You say that as if it's something bad."

"It's different, I'll grant you that. But what you're forgetting Amie is your first loyalty must be to England, the land of your birth. People have 'gone native' in the past, but I don't think it's too late to rescue you. You're here to act in any way that is the best for England, for Britain, and you will follow orders. Is that understood?

"Don't think for a moment you could find peace in England again Amie. The storm that blew up after your last mission wasn't pleasant. A cabinet minister resigned because his wife was thrown in jail after you exposed her. I can tell you, you would not be the flavour of the month. So, you will follow orders. Do you understand?"

"I'll follow them as far as my conscience allows, but I can't turn on an old friend, Ian." She felt her anger spiral almost out of control – she wanted to hit this obnoxious man.

Perhaps he realized he'd pushed her too far too soon, for he changed his tone.

"Amie, I'm sure we won't ask you to do anything you couldn't agree with. But surely there's no harm in listening and letting us know what's going on."

"And that's all you want?"

"Yes of course. What were you thinking?"

Amie didn't believe him. She suspected he wanted her to kill Ben.

5   OPERATIVE TRAINING

The car carrying Simon didn't stop once it left the London office, but made for a small airport in the south of England. From the back, the tinted windows were too dark to make out the road signs and after the first few miles trying to figure out which way they were going, Simon gave up. Since landing he'd not had an opportunity to take a shower, change his clothes or have a decent meal. He was irritable, and the irritation was turning to anger. He was a Deputy Consul for heaven's sakes and expected more respect. They were treating him like a raw recruit entering the army for his basic square bashing, cannon fodder to be whipped into shape, and trained to blindly follow orders.

He could do with a refresher course – it was a few years since he'd had any physical training – but there was a lack of deference, or even camaraderie. He wished he could work out what bothered him. It was something he'd seen but each time he tried to concentrate, it slipped from his grasp. It would come to him when he wasn't trying to remember.

The car came to a halt next to an aircraft hangar and sitting outside was a Piper M350, the engine rumbling, the single front propeller spinning. Simon was helped up the steps. The goon pushed him into one of the six seats, and pointed to the seatbelt. It had not escaped Simon that his minder had not uttered one word since escorting him out of the London office, and it didn't look as if he was about to start talking now.

Within a couple of minutes, they were airborne in the fading light. Although Simon tried to lean forward to see which direction they were heading, the pilot was blocking the instrument panel.

He put his head back and closed his eyes.

He was jarred awake by the wheels bumping on a grass landing strip, lit by flares on either side. The moment the plane rolled to a stop, the flares were extinguished. Simon was hustled out into a blast of wintery air, the rain falling in sheets, soaking his coat and running down the back of his neck. His shoes squelched on the wet grass.

The goon took his suitcase, and Simon followed him into a waiting Land Rover. A couple of miles later he was man-handled out at the side door of what looked to be a sizeable manor house. There were no lights close by, but he was so eager to get out of the rain, he barely noticed how isolated it was. They marched him up a flight of uncarpeted back stairs and along an empty corridor before flinging open a door and ushering him inside. The goon pointed to the bed and *en suite* bathroom before closing the door behind him. Simon heard his footsteps grow faint as he retreated down the stairs.

The room had only the bare essentials. A bed, which looked none too comfortable, a wardrobe, chest of drawers and a single ladder-back chair. He was pleased to see he had a bathroom to himself, and stripped off before stepping into the shower. While the water wasn't icy cold, it wasn't hot either, and he lost no time in towelling himself dry and dressing in the warmest trousers, shirt and sweater from his luggage, in preference to the clothes they had put out for him: several sets of t-shirts, sports shorts, and a pair of running shoes that looked as if they would fit.

Just in case, he tested his phone again, but McClusky hadn't lied when he said there'd be no signal. Simon sighed. He searched for his passport, but couldn't find it. He didn't remember his 'meet-and-greet' guy handing it back at the airport. He went through his case, laptop carrier and every pocket. More disturbing was the absence of the passport in his real name, which he had slipped under the lining in his computer case. As soon as he got back to London, he would put in a complaint at the highest level. A refresher course was one thing, but isolating him from the rest of the world – and theft – were quite another.

As soon as he was dressed, he made his way downstairs. The place was deserted. He'd expected there would be other operatives from the army and other services around; it was unlikely he'd be the only one here.

The kitchen was warm, lit by a cast iron stove set against one wall. A large scrubbed wooden table occupied the central area with benches on either side, and a Welsh dresser holding a set of willow pattern plates stood against the left-hand wall. There were pots on the stove and the waft of fresh vegetable soup tempted Simon to lift the lid and inhale the aroma.

He hesitated, but since there was nobody to ask, he helped himself. Grabbing a soup plate and a ladle he filled the bowl and sat at the table.

They might be lousy hosts, but they employed a great cook.

By the time he'd finished and had a second helping, he

was still sitting there on his own. Feeling bolder, he investigated one of the other pots and dished up a serving of stew. Searching through the cupboards he found a bottle of fruit juice, and purloined that as well.

Despite a day of relative inactivity Simon felt exhausted and after waiting for another half hour without seeing anybody, he went to bed. In the morning he would find out who was in charge here and have a serious talk with them.

He had slipped into a deep sleep when abruptly he was roused from his bed and marched down the stairs, still in his pyjamas, and into a room next to the kitchen. They tied him to a chair and shone a bright light in his eyes.

Disorientated, he struggled against the cable ties binding him tightly. "What the hell's going on?" he shouted.

He sensed the two men who'd brought him here standing behind him, then the door opened and another person entered the room. The new arrival stayed well back behind the light and it was impossible to see who it was, but Simon was sure it was McClusky.

"Name?" the disembodied voice asked.

"You bloody well know who I am. You had me sent over from Durban and I haven't been out of your sight since I landed."

"Name."

"Simon Peterson."

"Real name."

"That *is* my real name, it's Simon Peterson. I'm not lying to you. Why would I?"

"Who do you work for?"

"This – this is insane. I work for *you*. We're on the same side, dammit."

"And what side is that?"

"The British of course. I work for the government. The same government you work for."

"And how do you prove that?"

"What? How can I? You've disabled my phone, wiped my laptop and taken my passport away. How can I prove anything?"

"If you can't then you will have to tell us who can vouch for you. Names, addresses."

Simon paused. None of this made sense. He was here for a bit of toughening up, running around a few mountains with a rucksack full of stones, slogging across marshland following a compass, that sort of thing. No one had suggested interrogation techniques. They had specialists who did that, not basic field operatives.

He sensed a trap and said nothing.

"Names and addresses – now."

He refused to say anything. It didn't take a rocket scientist to look up the location of government offices in London and elsewhere and if they wanted to track any of the employees as they left work to return home in the evening, that didn't require too many brain cells either.

The questions were relentless, hour after hour until Simon could barely keep his eyes open. The same questions, over and over and over again. To his surprise they used no force at all. At any minute he expected one of the goons to attack but they didn't touch him – expecting blows at any moment to rain down on his body was almost as bad as receiving them.

The first rays of grey light were slipping through the cracks where the shutters didn't quite meet before they cut the plastic ties, hauled him back up to his room and left him to sleep. As he lost consciousness, he remembered what had been bothering him and hoped he would be able to recall it in the morning.

6   TANYA

Amie woke and stretched before rolling over and peering at the bedside clock radio. She'd deliberately not set the alarm. She owed it to herself to sleep off the jet lag – which was a bit farfetched, since there was little longitudinal difference between Durban and Apatu. Her other excuse for having a lie-in was Ian talking for hours in the Dungeon, which constituted overtime in her book.

She'd smiled when he realized that she would have to go shopping for suitable clothes. She reminded him that he'd given her no idea what to pack, and she could hardly attend Embassy and government functions in cargo pants and a t-shirt. She would need several dresses, and shoes and bags to match, and evening wraps, and several smarter outfits to wear for work as well, not to mention makeup. His face was a picture when she'd reeled off her list of requirements.

There was one good thing about this mission – she would not have to invent a cover story, so there would be no need to communicate with the obnoxious Maddy. Amie had not spoken to her since her handler had hung up on her in a huff several months ago, so that was another irritant removed for now.

There was the question of her name. She'd first met Ben before all this spy nonsense had started, and he knew her as Amie. He would easily accept that she was now working here as a clerk in the Embassy but he wouldn't understand why she would change her name. Ian had to agree that she could use her real name, at least for now, so there'd be no more Felicity. That was a real plus.

She was less convinced that all they wanted was a look, listen and report back. That's what they'd said last time, and look where that had ended up. For now, she would take one day at a time. That had always been her motto, but, she decided as she crawled out of bed, *I'm more decisive than I used to be and a whole lot more assertive.*

The bungalows included a small kitchenette and somebody had filled the fridge with yogurt and fruit and stocked the tea and coffee jars. There were three cereals for her to choose from, and a large can of powdered milk in the cupboard. She ate breakfast, and after clearing everything away, she lay back on the bed with her Kindle. They would come to fetch her when they needed her. If she was coerced into this, she was going to do as little as possible, besides they probably wouldn't even pay her salary.

Did she still have her account in the Royal Bank of Togodo? Would it be possible to check that out? They might have closed it down after her 'death'. But she had discovered the Service didn't think of everything, and that might be one thing they'd overlooked. That's what comes of letting men run the show, they lacked a woman's attention to detail.

She was reading the second chapter when there was a

knock on the door and, at Amie's invitation, Tanya bounced into the room.

"Good morning, I've been sent to take you shopping. Isn't that fun?"

"Uh, yes," Amie replied wondering if her new companion was always this bright and breezy. *She couldn't be more than early twenties*, Amie decided as she observed the slim girl with her long dark hair, dark brown eyes and a nose that was rather too large for her small face. She wore jeans with a sleeveless top and trainers, or *takkies* as Amie now called them. She'd dressed for a shopping trip rather than a day at her desk.

"Give me a moment to brush my hair. Did anyone mention what we use for money?"

"Oh yes, really cool, look." Tanya pulled out a wad of Togodian dollars from the bum bag she wore around her waist. "We can get a heap of stuff with this." She handed it all to Amie, who took it wondering how much she could hide away and keep after the shopping trip.

An Embassy car waited for them at the front of the building and, as they hopped in, Amie said, "The mall in Brianwood, please." Then mentally kicked herself for forgetting she was supposed to be new in Apatu.

Neither the driver nor Tanya appeared to notice her mistake. Driving out to the suburbs, Tanya chattered all the way. She had joined the Service straight from school and because she had a gift for languages they'd fast-tracked her; this was her first overseas posting. "I've picked up a bit of the local lingo already, so, if we run into trouble, I can help you out."

"Thank you." Amie looked out at the Jacaranda trees

with their bright purple flowers in full bloom. She had yet to meet a Togodian who didn't have at least a smattering of English and was ashamed that she'd picked up very little of the African languages, but they were notoriously difficult to learn.

Parts of the mall had been destroyed during the civil war. It had been ages since Amie had last been there, but she was pleased to see it had been restored to its former state and even extended. While they had repaired and rebuilt the shops and hallways, they had neglected to re-tar the parking area and they were thrown around like rag dolls as they bumped over the potholes.

"Tell me, is there an expatriate club or something like that here?" Amie asked rubbing her head and feigning ignorance.

"No. There was one once, with proper tennis courts and a swimming pool and they held dances and parties. But not anymore. I've only been here a couple of months, and there is nowhere to go. It gets boring."

"So, there aren't many British nationals living and working here?" Amie thought it unlikely she would run into anybody she knew – Ian would not let her loose if there was a chance that might happen.

"I don't think so, but you'd have to ask someone else. It's not my section. It's mainly single men – no wives and families, which makes it lonely. I'm so glad you're here now to talk to."

But only if you don't talk too much. Amie's head was already spinning.

The driver, a friendly Togodian who told them his name was Moses, parked under a black wattle tree and told them he'd wait for them there.

"Won't he get bored all by himself?" Tanya asked as they walked towards the mall entrance.

"I expect he'll sleep until we come back. The Africans have a lot of patience and will wait for hours if necessary."

"So, you know a bit about Africa then?"

"Not really, just bits and pieces picked up here and there."

"Mr Fleming told me this was your first official overseas posting, so I was to take good care of you." Tanya's smile showed how proud she was of her new task.

I bet he did. Thank you Ian. Amie shook off her irritation and concentrated on the job in hand. A new wardrobe at her tormentor's expense was too good an opportunity to pass up.

They walked into one of the few air-conditioned public complexes in Apatu, and Amie considered giving Tanya the slip, grabbing a local taxi and going out to see Mrs Motswezi at the orphanage at Tamara. Then she remembered somebody else – Sohanna Reddy, the matron at the hospital. It would be lovely to meet up with her again.

No, it wouldn't be fair to Tanya to run out on her; she was so proud of her responsibility, and it would be a huge black mark on her file if she lost her charge even for half a day. But Amie was determined to lose her for at least a short time to pick up a new cell phone. She had to get in touch with Simon one way or another, and Ian had not returned hers. She eyed the phone shop as they walked past, planning to double back at the first opportunity.

7　THE CABINET MEETING

Ben checked the figures again and frowned. He looked round at his top six ministers and their deputies, gathered for their weekly cabinet meeting.

"These do not add up. I thought we put in fifty million for the new housing development, and the money has been allocated, but according to these documents, nothing has been done. They have not even cleared the land."

"There must be some mistake, I sent the instructions through weeks ago," Kirimu Nashele replied. "Do not worry about it. I will make sure everything is put right." He leaned across the table, collected the papers and files and swept them into a pile, which he stuffed in his briefcase.

"That is not the only problem. I had a call this morning from the hospital. They have not received any new medicines for three months. I have checked and the payments have been authorised. What do you know about that, Kirimu?"

"That is indeed a mystery. It is possible that the money went into the wrong account. I do not trust these suppliers. You know how greedy they are in the West. They think they can take the money from new countries like ours. They think we are stupid and primitive and they look to make fools of us. I am sure they have the money and now they tell lies about it."

"No, Kirimu. I do not agree. There is corruption in many of the major corporations, but I do not think they would take our money and not send the supplies. This will need to be thoroughly investigated. You are the finance minister. Who signed the payments?"

Kirimu opened another file and slowly drew his finger down a list of names. "That would be Gilbert Msomi. He is the chief in the payment department. But my brother, you do not need to worry about such things, that is why you have me to sort out the finances for you."

Ben chewed his thumbnail. "These problems need to be solved, and quickly. I am not happy with the way the affairs are being managed."

"Yes, yes of course. We will soon find out where the problems are, but I have something to show you which will take all such worries away. Look – I have here the plans for the new football stadium and they are magnificent."

He stood, walked to the end of the table and unrolled the architect's drawing, anchoring down the four corners with the water bottles placed in front of each minister. He jabbed at various points with his finger as he explained.

"Here is the Presidential Box, where you will sit. It is big enough for your whole family and your distinguished guests. It will be in the very best place to see right across the pitch." He slid his finger over the plans. "Then here, we have seating for ninety-thousand of your most faithful supporters, and here – kitchens for the food, and the toilets here and here, and we have not forgotten beautiful quarters for the players. When they come to play football against Togodo they will be amazed at the luxurious splendour of our facilities. We will have only the very best."

"It will indeed be a place to be proud of." Samuel Suma, the Minister of Sport had a broad smile on his face. "These must be the hospitality suites yes? There will be one for each of us too? I would like to choose my one now please." He chuckled. "My wife's sister is an interior designer and I know she will make it quite beautiful."

"And maybe we can bid for the Football World Cup," the Interior Minister added, his voice trembling with excitement.

"It will put Togodo on the world map and bring in thousands of fans who will spend lots of money. The people will be very happy." The Foreign Minister was hopping up and down on his seat.

Ben looked at the blueprints. "I don't remember us deciding that we needed a stadium this big."

"But it needs to be this size, for the international games. FIFA will not look at us unless we have a main stadium this size, and we will have to build others in the smaller towns … but there is time for that. I have here all the papers from the World Cup Association and we can meet all their requirements, I know we can." The Minister of Sport was grinning stupidly.

"Look too," Kirimu's finger jabbed on the plans, "there will be a wonderful media centre, because we must not forget that every country in the world will be sending their announcers and camera crews."

"And where" Ben asked, his voice laced with sarcasm, "will all these people be sleeping?"

"We will need to build a new hotel or two," the Interior Minister waved his hands theatrically, "and then the airport as well. We must ask for plans for that. It will need a new runway."

"Stop," Ben shouted. "This has gone far enough. When I was elected, it was not to build fancy stadiums and prestige projects. I promised my people houses, water and electricity, schools and hospitals, and I intend to keep those promises."

The Finance Minister shook his head. "My President, you do not understand. None of those things will bring us money. It is better to build what will generate income, then, when the tourists have brought in the foreign currency, we can provide those services. Do our people complain about their houses? No. Do they need electricity? No. For centuries they have lived without these things, and when we put them in place they will be of the highest standard."

"And," the Interior Minister added, "by then more of our people will have an education and they will be properly trained to run successful businesses."

Ben looked at the ten men sitting round the table and sighed. Was this the best that his country had to offer in governance? They were all close friends, men he'd thought he could rely on, who had hopes for uplifting his people, but he could see that each and every one of them was in it for himself. Glancing at the plans he noted that the architects were all related to Kirimu. He was sure that every contract would be awarded to family and friends of the Ministers in this room.

He sighed. It was going to be an uphill battle to overrule them, and the moment he did they would become mortal enemies and set out to depose him. He was in a bind and could see no way out.

His thoughts were interrupted as the door to the Cabinet room flew open and Mathilda burst into the room.

"How dare you. You can't keep secrets from me. How dare you go behind my back."

Ben rose swiftly and, grabbing her arm, hustled her out of the room.

"I have told you before. You do not interrupt government meetings and make me look a fool in front of my ministers."

"You and your bloody ministers, having your schoolboy meetings. Don't think you can hide behind them, because you can't. I know what you've been up to. You can't keep secrets from me. I know you've been meeting with her thinking I wouldn't find out."

Ben manhandled her along the corridor and up the stairs towards their private apartments.

"Who the hell are you talking about? I do not know what you mean."

"Don't play the innocent with me. Nogo or whatever her name is, that's who, Mr Innocent. You've been sniffing around her again."

"Ngonicansaga? That is pure nonsense. All I know is she has a job in the palace. I am not even sure where."

Mathilda didn't let him finish. "Well I want her gone. Today. Now. Send her back to whatever little backwater village she came from and forbid her from entering the city."

"I will do no such thing! She has done nothing wrong and neither have I." He pulled his wife further along the corridor, ignoring the curious looks from the servants as they passed.

Mathilda rushed on. "I know what you're up to. All you little tinpot African dictators have dozens of wives, and I bet she's lined up to become Number Two. But I'm not having it, understand?"

As they reached their private rooms, Ben flung open the door and pushed Mathilda inside. "You need to keep your nose out of official business, stop listening to gossip and get a grip. I am not planning on taking another wife. One is more than I can handle, so behave yourself."

He let go of her arm and Mathilda flung herself on the couch wailing. "I'm so bored, I've nothing to do and you're never around to keep me company."

"I have more important things to do than entertain you," Ben replied unwisely. "I have a country to run, in case you have not noticed."

"You and your bloody little country. That's all you ever think about."

Ben sighed and went over to sit beside her. He reached for her hand, but she snatched it away and stalked into the bedroom slamming the door behind her.

Ben sat there for a moment and then returned to the cabinet room and his bunch of greedy ministers. Becoming President was more trouble than it was worth. If he didn't care so deeply about his people, he would resign tomorrow.

8   CROSS COUNTRY

The sweat ran down Simon's back as he scrambled up the steep slope. He was close to exhaustion. From early morning they had kept him moving without a break. After a minimal breakfast, he'd been kitted out in sports gear and ordered to run around a field too many times to count; then one of the goons had arrived on a motorbike and instructed Simon to follow him.

They kept up a brisk pace across country, through streams, over hilltops and along the valleys. At no point did Simon see a house, road, or farm track. Whichever part of England – or possibly Wales – he was in, it appeared to be deserted. He had no idea there was this much open country. From what he could see, from one horizon to the other the area was uninhabited.

As they crested another rise, he collapsed on the ground, the stones in his backpack bumped against his spine and he gasped for breath. His heart raced and he felt disorientated.

"Get up," his tormentor shouted looking back over his shoulder. "Keep moving."

Simon couldn't summon enough breath to reply. His chest heaved, the landscape swam before his eyes and his legs felt like jelly.

The man turned the bike round and approached him.

"Come," he commanded, but all Simon could do was shake his head. If he didn't rest, he'd have a heart attack. The man could shout all he liked, Simon wasn't moving until he'd recovered.

"We have many more miles to go."

"Not yet," gasped Simon. "You will just have to wait."

The man muttered something that Simon didn't catch. It didn't sound like familiar English words, but he was too fatigued to take notice.

This was the seventh day in a row that they'd had him out running without a break. By the time the light faded each night, he could barely prop himself up at the kitchen table long enough to eat his supper before falling into bed exhausted. He wondered when the nightmare would end.

9 AMIE IS TRAPPED

Amie smiled as Ian entered the dungeon and settled comfortably in the chair at the head of the table.

"You look very cheerful this morning, Amie. You've decided that being a spy isn't the end of the world after all?"

"Wrong." Amie couldn't stop smiling. "I've just realized that you've gone to all this trouble for nothing. Your scheme won't work."

"Oh, please enlighten me. I'm all ears."

Amie wanted to stand up and punch Ian in the face, but that would not achieve anything, and he was not going to spoil her mood.

"Fact – my house was blown up. Everyone was killed right?"

He nodded.

"The Embassy here held a funeral for Jonathon and me. But the truth was you, or SIS, locked me up, told the world I was dead, and then you forced me to become a spy. Right so far?"

He nodded again.

"You gave me a new name, Felicity Mansell, so I wasn't Amie anymore. Now, you want me to be Amie again when I just happen to meet up with an old friend. Ben knows who I am, he knows I was married to Jonathon and he'll know about the explosion, so the truth will come out."

Amie was pleased with her reasoning. They hadn't thought it through. SIS wasn't as clever as they thought they were.

So why was Ian still smiling? No, smirking was a better description.

"I'm so sorry to burst your bubble, Amie, but you have overestimated your importance and your newsworthiness. You've probably had wonderful daydreams of landing at Heathrow and proclaiming to the world. 'Look, here I am, alive and well. They told you I was dead and then forced me to become a spy, now I'm here to tell you the truth about these ruthless people.' Am I right?"

Amie didn't reply, but her cheeks were red and she picked at a hangnail on her thumb. The wretched man could read her thoughts, and the way he told the story made it sound so insignificant and tawdry.

"Let's look at the facts differently, as they really are, Amie. It's unlikely Ben or his cronies ever got to hear about the explosion. We researched that he was up-country at the time. Even if the incident reached his ears, there was very little publicity here about which family members died. It will be so easy to explain that your body was thrown some distance away and you wandered for days with no idea of who you were. I'm afraid the accident wasn't made public in Britain, either. I understand there was a small memorial service for you both in your hometown, possibly covered by the local rag, but certainly no mention on any of the national news channels. Frankly, the pool of people who know you died is very small, and I don't think your parents will consider questioning what they were told. Oh, and that documentary showing you crawling to freedom during the civil war? They used a look-alike in that, and it was filmed in Spain." Ian chuckled at his explanation, which covered all possible objections.

Amie flashed back to the meeting with her parents in the Johannesburg hotel, and remembered they'd accepted her death as the truth – government officials didn't lie, did they? She wondered if the 'life insurance' pay out to her parents and in-laws, had been an extra incentive to encourage them not to investigate further.

"It's all quite simple. You will tell Ben, if he ever mentions the explosion, that you escaped. You were deeply traumatized, found by us and have been away recuperating. The British government took pity on you, all on your own and so far away from home, and they offered you a job in the Embassy here in Togodo. We realized how much you love Africa and England held too many bad memories for you."

Amie sat stunned. They *had* thought of everything. Mrs Motswezi and Ouma Adede both knew the truth, but they were hardly a threat to the spooks in the British Secret Service. She would keep that knowledge to herself. There was one other piece of proof she had, and ... somebody somewhere else said something ... who was it?

Fleming leaned towards her. "Will you just stop fighting us? We're not asking you to do anything dangerous, just to look and listen."

"Yeah, like last time."

"Quite different. You were way out in the bush, countries away. This time you're safe here in the Embassy, surrounded by friends who'll be there to watch your back."

Ian's tone was so persuasive that Amie wondered if she was making too much of everything. She had a roof over her head, a comfortable bed, presumably they would be paying her a salary, and she had just spent a fortune on new clothes for state occasions. Maybe it was time she relaxed and agreed to cooperate. Do what they asked her to do. She was tired of fighting an enemy with tentacles all over the world. She was unlikely to win, so why not sit back and go with the flow?

"I don't seem to have much choice, do I?"

"Frankly, no you don't. Now, let's order in some coffee and talk about getting close to Ben."

"I *won't* harm him. He's my friend, and he saved my life."

"Let's take this one step at a time Tea? Or your usual coffee?"

10 DISCUSSION IN A LONDON CLUB

The rain lashed against the window panes and there was a distant rumble of thunder as four men took their seats next to a blazing fire in a discreet corner of a famous gentleman's club in London.

"Any further news?"

"No, nothing. Simon Peterson seems to have disappeared off the face of the earth. We've discovered that the request sent to Durban telling him to report to Ian Fleming here in London did not come from us. When we contacted Durban to summon him, they told us he had left the day before."

"But he flew out of Durban?"

"Yes, on the 17th. The plane landed with no problems, but that was the last piece of information we have."

"He must have passed through immigration and security?"

"He was probably using another passport. He could have been any one of the hundreds in the queue. He's average looking, nothing special, and we've had our chaps check the footage from that day – and there's no one resembling him coming back in."

"I can't believe he vanished into thin air. That's not possible in this day and age," said the eldest of the gentlemen.

"Really? Can you tell me where those hundreds of illegal immigrants have gone to ground? Hell, we can't even keep tabs on the known terrorists right under our damn noses."

"Any ideas?"

One by one they all shook their heads. Where did you begin to look for a lone operative who'd disappeared over a week ago?

"What's his grade and how dangerous is he if left loose?"

"Nothing too serious. Mostly office stuff … been on a couple of missions in Africa, but they wouldn't get much out of him under torture."

"That's one thing less to worry about. No operatives he might be forced to shop?"

"The only one I'm aware of, is that woman Amie Fish, the one we grabbed after the explosion. I'm reliably informed they were buddies, and spent a lot of time together. It could be awkward if he let that slip."

"So where is she now?"

"We've moved her back to Apatu, under Ian Fleming's wing. He's setting her up to deal with Ben Mtumba. He's not playing ball with us, and the Russians and Chinese are sniffing around. It'll be part of her job to get him to cooperate with us or finish him off. He could be replaced though. The Finance Minister, Kirimu Nashele, might be a better fit as President from our point of view."

"Why on earth are the Russians and Chinese interested in Togodo? It's only a two-bit African country on the east coast, isn't it?"

"Charles, you've not kept up to date with dispatches,

have you? There have been enormous finds in the north – lithium, rhodium and uranium."

"I've heard of those, but have no idea how important they are."

"Rhodium in particular is rare and we all know the dangers of letting irresponsible people get their hands on uranium or any of those other dodgy minerals."

"To get back to this Peterson chap…" The oldest man in the group took a sip of his brandy. "Are you honestly telling me that we have an operative running around somewhere that we can't trace?"

"Seems so."

"Well I can't say I'm happy about that."

"Me neither." One of the group glanced briefly at the large portrait of Winston Churchill that hung over the marble mantelpiece. "But it beats me as to where the bloody hell we start looking for him."

"I'll have some of our people go over the CCTV airport footage again. He's got to be on there somewhere – and I'll get the passenger list rechecked."

"That's all we can do for now. I'm loathe to plaster his face all over the media as 'missing.' It would be the end of his career as far as field work goes."

"True, but as long as he can't upset any apple carts then he shouldn't be too much of a problem. Now you'll have to excuse me, I've got a meeting with the PM at three, and you know how she hates to be kept waiting."

The youngest member of the group had a nasty feeling in the pit of his stomach as he returned to work. He hadn't been completely honest. Simon Peterson did have information that if shared with a foreign party, would do England no good at all.

11 THE COCKTAIL PARTY

Amie groaned as she struggled with the zip on the back of her new cocktail dress. Of course, she hadn't tried it on in the shop. Tanya, the watchdog, had disappeared into the next cubicle and Amie took the opportunity to dart back out along the mall to the phone shop, something far more important than taking time to try on a stupid dress. Now, she was paying for it. The damn thing was too tight. She'd automatically grabbed her usual size, quite forgetting that for the last two months she'd been wining and dining with Simon and devouring the amazing steaks that only South Africa could serve, and she'd put on pounds.

No. She was fatter because she was pregnant. Her life had been a whirlwind. There were times she almost forgot she was going to have a baby before the end of the year. It was Ouma Adede, the witch doctor, who'd told her she was pregnant – probably the day after conception and from experience, Amie had no reason to doubt her.

Back in Durban, she and Simon had kept it a secret. She had one appointment confirming her pregnancy, and a second visit to check both mother and baby were healthy. She'd been due another visit but Simon was summoned to London, Ian arrived and she'd been whisked back to Apatu. She didn't dare think about what the future held for the small person growing inside her. She should tell Fleming, beg off the career path he had planned for her, but still she held back on 'wait and see.' She knew she would protect her baby, and if necessary give up her life for it, but until she was positive that it was too late to be forced into an abortion – and she wasn't exactly sure how many weeks that was – she'd keep it a secret. She didn't trust Ian or any of his colleagues one inch.

She wriggled and squirmed and finally managed to pull the zip up. It looked too tight, but it would have to do.

As she brushed her hair, she wondered where Simon was and what he was doing. The moment she'd returned to her bungalow, she'd tapped his number into her new mobile, holding her breath as she heard his phone ring. But there was no answer. She'd tried a second time, holding on until a disembodied voice told her that the person she wanted was not available and to call back later. That was strange, where had Simon's voicemail gone? She couldn't even leave him a message.

A knock at the door announced Ian Fleming's arrival to take her to the palace.

The ballroom was crowded by the time Ian and Amie arrived. As she walked through the grand entrance, she gasped. It was surreal, a miniature version of the Hall of Mirrors at Versailles she had only seen in books, but the highly sprung wooden parquet flooring, the tall windows, carved angels supporting lighting fixtures, the glittering chandeliers above her head hanging from a gold-painted roof, and the floor to ceiling mirrors could only be a poor carbon copy. It was out of place in the middle of Africa. Fans, or at least decent air conditioning, would have been more appropriate than a cheap copy of French grandeur. Even with the windows wide open, the men in their tuxedos and traditional outfits and the ladies in either western dress or brightly coloured African *Kitenge* with matching turbans, were all sweating profusely. Waves of sickly air, laden with perspiration mingled with aftershave and perfume, wafted past, and Amie had a hard time not wrinkling her nose.

In one corner a string quartet was playing Schubert, as far as she could tell, but she didn't have a chance to think about it before Ian tightened his hold on her arm and propelled her forward towards the receiving line.

Amie's idea of a cocktail party was people milling around with a plate in one hand and a glass in the other, nothing as formal as this.

The ministers standing to attention in the receiving line were dressed in tuxedos, with snowy white shirts and an interesting range of ties. She recognised Ben immediately. He was wearing brightly coloured robes in green, red and blue – the colours of the Togodian flag. Standing next to him, and towering over him, was a rather sulky-looking woman with long blonde hair and a toothpaste smile, only she was not smiling. Amie could feel the woman's brown almond-shaped eyes bore into her. A shudder ran down her back. She smiled at the tall girl but her gesture of friendship was not returned.

They shuffled up the line, shaking one hand after another. Several of the ministers clicked their heels in the old-fashioned German manner, but few met her eyes or even looked at her – it was another reminder of a woman's status in Africa.

A young man preceded them, murmuring out one name after another, but Amie wasn't concentrating. The sounds of raucous laughter and chatter made it difficult to hear the names and titles, and she automatically nodded and shook the limp, damp hands. She found herself in front of Ben while the valet droned out a long list of titles and praises. The President of Togodo had his hand out, briefly shook hers and then glanced towards Ian standing behind her. He paused, looked back at Amie and his face lit up.

"Amie. It is Amie, isn't it?"

"Yes. Ben, Uh, Mr President, it is."

"But I thought there was an accident. This is amazing. We have so much to talk about and catch up on. It's wonderful to see you." He withdrew his hand a second before Ian could shake it, and instead reached out and took Amie's hand again. "How long has it been? Years, now. What has been happening my friend?"

He was interrupted by a white hand with talons long enough to groom an orangutan, which slid onto Ben's arm, effectively pulling away his grip on Amie's hand, while a piercing voice said, "Darling, I'm not sure this person should monopolise your time."

Ben frowned and glanced at Mathilda. "Allow me to introduce Amie, a very old and dear friend."

"Charmed, I'm sure." Mathilda's limp sweaty hand briefly brushed Amie's, with insincerity oozing from every pore.

"Very pleased to meet you." Amie radiated her best smile. "You must be Ben's new wife?"

"Her most Excellent, Right Honourable wife to our beloved President, Mrs Mathilda Mtumba," the minion standing behind her replied, his voice reproachful.

The line of guests bunched up behind Amie as Ben reached back and touched her arm. "We'll get together very soon, take tea and talk about old times, yes?"

"Love to," Amie replied as she tried to escape, but not before hearing Mathilda hiss, "No you bloody well won't! Forget it."

Amie breathed a sigh of relief, anxious to move on, but Ian Fleming was in no rush. She could hear him telling Ben that the British government was taking great care of Amie and had sent her to recuperate by the sea and had employed her at the Embassy. She wished she'd been wearing stilettos so she could accidentally step hard on his foot. The Embassy was playing the 'angels of mercy' role.

The moment Ian broke free, he again held her by the elbow and manoeuvred her towards a quiet corner while sweeping the room with his eyes.

"See how easy that was?" he whispered with a self-satisfied look on his face. "It's all falling into place."

Amie longed to wipe the stupid grin from his face as he steered her to a group of men who were laughing at some joke.

"Good evening, gentlemen. Gordon, Bill, Frank, so nice to see you here. Allow me to introduce Amie Fish, she's new to the Embassy but we have high hopes for her future."

They turned and politely shook hands, while Amie smiled and nodded feeling the seams of her dress straining across her hips, her new shoes were hurting, and she felt a headache coming on.

Small talk was not Amie's favourite thing, but she stood and listened and nodded in the appropriate places. They were a delegation of businessmen here from the mining companies, attending in the hope of securing at least part of the action for their government of origin.

Her mind flashed back to a conversation she'd overheard in the Expat Club years ago. Some prospectors had joined them for dinner one evening before they flew back to Europe. There were whispers about finding huge deposits of important minerals in the far north. It was supposed to be a big secret, but it was impossible to keep anything like that under wraps. She could only guess that there would be plenty of countries willing to help the Togodians dig the precious ore from the ground. It may be one of the reasons they wanted her here on the inside, and close to Ben.

Amie swivelled to grab a drink from a passing tray. There was nobody she recognised – which was a relief, but they'd worked out a cover story so it wasn't a problem. She wondered who or what was in those coffins that had been laid to rest. The explosion had blown everything to bits.

Amie backed away against a wall and watched the crowd. She noticed Fleming talking to a very fat African man, he was one of the ministers.

"Hello. Tell me why such a beautiful lady is standing here alone? We've not been introduced. Please tell me your name."

Amie looked up to see a tall, brown haired, blue eyed man with sun-darkened skin, dressed impeccably, and who was taller than her by at least six inches. She smiled.

"Amie Fish, and you are …?"

"Vladimir Petrovnikov, Russian delegation." He extended one hand to shake hers while with the other he plucked her empty glass out of her hand and replaced it with a full one he snatched from a passing waiter.

"Pleased to meet you," Amie murmured, thinking that he was the first Russian she'd ever met and he wasn't what she expected. Russians were always portrayed as short, fat, brutal looking thugs, this man was anything but. "You don't look Russian," she said without thinking and then blushed. *Now you've done it*, she thought.

He didn't take offence but put his head back and laughed. "Ah, you've caught me out," he chuckled. "I'm only half Russian. My mother was Polish."

"You speak excellent English."

"A few years studying in Britain. You have some fine universities."

"So how did you guess I was English?"

"I saw you walk in with Ian Fleming, so you had to be on the Embassy staff, no?"

"Very clever. So, who is Ian talking to now?"

Amie noticed the muscles around Vladimir's mouth tighten as he stared at her boss across the room. "That," he replied slowly "is the esteemed Minister of Finance, the Honourable Kirimu Nashele. He and the President are close. I hear they grew up together in the same village, and when Ben Mtumba came to power, he invited Nashele to serve in the cabinet. It caused a big fight between the President and some of his old friends who were unhappy about it, or so the rumour goes."

"Oh, do you have any idea why?"

"Possibly some tribal conflict. Who can tell? You seem to know His Excellency well?"

"Oh, we have met once or twice, way, way back."

"He looked delighted to see you, and of the hundreds of people he must meet, he remembered you."

"He probably has an excellent memory for faces and names."

"Now that is a puzzle. You knew the Togodian President years ago, yet countries rotate their Embassy staff every few years? You have been here a long time then?"

Amie's mind raced. This was another example of the trouble she could get herself into if she didn't watch what she said. "No. I can only think that the few times we've met at official occasions, he's remembered my face. What can I say?" She gave him her most beguiling smile. "I've heard he's a good President, so what is your opinion of him?" She attempted to steer the conversation away from dangerous ground, but Vladimir was not so easily deflected.

"How long have you been in Togodo?"

Amie explained that she had been here previously with her husband and after an accident, she had remained and was now working at the Embassy. "I love Africa," she concluded. "I love the people, and the wildlife and the feeling of being alive. Have you felt the drumbeats under your feet when you are out in the bush?"

"I've uh, not had that pleasure."

He looked over at a group on the far side of the room and excused himself, but if Amie hoped she'd be left in peace, she was mistaken for immediately the space he'd occupied was taken by another middle-aged diplomat, this time from the American Embassy. Amie gave him the same story and managed to turn the conversation round, plying him with questions about his home state of Texas, where, he'd drawled predictably, everything was bigger, and better and greater than any other state in the USA.

He was mind-numbingly boring, and Amie wondered

how many of these awful receptions she'd be required to attend. Her dress felt as if it was about to part at the seams, and the sparkly material was scratching her skin. She was desperately hungry – the finger food looked so unappetising that she'd refused it all – and the only drink on offer was the champagne. She'd already had three glasses, more than her normal limit, but she guessed it was good quality, it slipped down so easily. Her feet ached, it felt as if her new shoes had shrunk. She looked round in desperation for Ian to rescue her.

Instead it was Ben who wandered over, nodded at the American, and steered Amie to one side.

"When can we meet and catch up on old times?"

Amie smiled at him. "I'm free most of the time. You're the one who must be busy these days, Mr President."

Ben laughed. "That is an understatement, but I will make a plan. If I send a note to the British Embassy, it will get to you?"

"Yes, I'm sure it will. I'll look forward to it." Amie turned away as she spied Mathilda bearing down on them and managed to slip between the guests before Mathilda could say a word, but if looks could kill, Amie wouldn't be walking across the fake hall of Versailles with its mirrors that needed a damned good clean.

"Well done." Ian grabbed her elbow. "Excellent, this is going to make life so much easier."

Having met Ben again, Amie was more determined than ever not to cause him any harm.

12 SIMON'S BID TO ESCAPE

Simon was uneasy about the training centre, the people running it, and even the food. He'd never been in the army but he'd assumed that they served typical British dishes, while the fare he'd been offered was unfamiliar, more foreign. He had no idea what flavour the soups and the stews were. Although they tasted good, they contained odd herbs and spices that were unfamiliar. Something was wrong.

He'd tried to voice his concerns but the only man who ever spoke to him waved away his words, saying that he was following orders and as soon as Simon was fit, he would be sent back to London. It was not reassuring, and Simon was frustrated. He hadn't been allowed off the property by himself, and whenever he was walking or running, the goon on the motorbike accompanied him and only ever told him to keep up or run faster. On occasion, Simon wondered if he even understood what Simon said to him.

Falling into bed one night, after weeks of torture, Simon decided he'd had enough, and it was time to leave. He had no idea what security measures they had in place, but he had to get back to London and talk to the people there – not the office where he'd been taken from the plane, but one he'd visited before. He needed to meet up with people he knew. There was no point in hanging around. He'd pack up and go. He'd hit the nearest road, flag down a motorist and get a lift to a hotel.

The thought of walking out hadn't occurred to him before. At the end of each day, all he'd been able to do was collapse into bed after another back-breaking marathon running and climbing, wriggling under netting, and flinging himself over badly constructed walls, but subconsciously the idea had been growing in the back of his mind for days.

Despite feeling tired, he scrambled off the bed, gathered his things, slipped out of his room and padded down the corridor. When he went to open the door leading to the stairs it wouldn't open. He rattled the handle, pushed, pulled and wriggled, it but it remained shut.

He walked the length of the landing looking for any other way downstairs but there was only the one exit to the floors below. He couldn't believe they had locked him in. What a ridiculous state of affairs. He couldn't get out. It hadn't occurred to him that he might be a prisoner.

He returned to his room, flung his case on the chair and sat on the bed. If he'd been suspicious before, now he was sure. There was no reason to lock him in at night or to keep him under close surveillance during the day. If he couldn't leave of his own free will, then he would escape – and his best chance was while he was out running.

Maybe he should talk to them first, to try and sort out the problem logically, but nobody had answered his earlier questions, so he wasn't hopeful. There was also the possibility he would alert them, and they would keep an even closer eye on him.

He'd take his chances. When they sent him out running tomorrow, he'd try and lose his minder. That was a better idea – he was exhausted and even if he could get out, he wouldn't get very far in his weakened condition tonight. One more night on the uncomfortable bed wasn't the end of the world.

At some point in the early morning somebody unlocked the door, for when he grabbed the handle to go downstairs for breakfast, it swung open.

They offered him coffee, biscuits, cake, ham and cheese. He hid some food in his pockets. He had no money, but he'd only have to travel as far as the nearest village.

"You run again today," his minder said with a faint smile on his lips. He was leaning against the kitchen cabinets and from the size of his paunch, Simon guessed that he didn't do much running himself, if any.

"How many more days? I am fit. Is this all I'm supposed to do, run and race around the obstacle courses?"

"You will get fit. You are not fit yet. We will make you tough. Today you run two extra miles."

The sky was grey and overcast with a persistent drizzle, which suited him just fine. It wouldn't make him invisible but it could work in his favour.

Each time they'd left the shelter of the manor house, they'd handed him a fluorescent yellow jacket to wear. After half an hour, he'd handed it to the goon on the bike as it got too hot. The first time he did it, the thuggish creature sitting astride his motorbike refused to take it, indicating that he should put it back on, to make his prisoner more visible. Running long distances, with a heavy backpack, was difficult enough without wearing a coat as well, so Simon sat down and refused to budge until it was taken from him and slung over the front of the bike. While it was cooler, the downside was the straps on his backpack chaffed his shoulders. Today he was in luck; he was handed the garish safety jacket but the backpack didn't appear.

They followed a track at the back of the house running downhill, towards the valley surrounded by the hills and shrouded in mist. The raindrops bounced off the pebble-strewn path, making it slippery as Simon's feet pounded over the loose surface. His plan was to make a break for it and then hide at what he guessed was the farthest point from the house. Large rocks scattered on the valley floor would provide temporary refuge until he could make a run towards civilization.

He kept his senses keen and was observant as he ran, wondering which direction he should go. Each time he'd been taken out he'd looked for signs of life, a house, a signpost to a village, even a shepherd's hut, but he hadn't seen anything from the outside world. It was surreal that in Britain there were still areas devoid of human habitation. How they managed to cram seventy million people onto such a small island and still leave space was a conundrum.

Half an hour into his run, he put his plan into action. He said he had an upset stomach and had to stop to relieve himself. He waved the toilet roll he'd brought to show his mute captor what the problem was.

They had reached the valley floor and were ascending the hill on the far side and Simon had stopped four times, setting a pattern. He didn't hurry, peering out to see what the goon did. Each time he took a few minutes longer.

During the first couple of stops his guard sat on his bike with the engine idling; then he got bored and rode up the road to check the route.

Simon chose a particularly large rock for his final stop and disappeared behind it and slipped off his fluorescent jacket and placed it so that a flash was visible from the road. The bike roared further up the track. Ducking, Simon slithered down the slope. The rough surface scraped his hands, his knees, and even his face as he rolled over always falling away from the path. The low-lying damp mist and drizzle prevented any dust from rising, which would have given his position away. The elements were with him. Glancing back, he could no longer see the road, and the sound of the motorbike swirled around with the natural echoes making it difficult to gauge which direction it came from. He heard muffled shouts. His minder had discovered him gone, but it had taken him more than five minutes to realise it.

Keeping his head down, Simon ran, crouching behind a line of rocky outcrops. He hoped they were not too far from the area around Snowdonia, if they were in Wales at all. It was only a hunch, but it was his best bet. There may even be tourists or hikers nearby.

He took a chance, stood upright and ran. He was fitter than he had been in years. His feet pounded the ground, his ears flaring as he tried to identify the sounds of the bike engine, hoping that the rough terrain would hinder his pursuer. The sweat poured down his face. He could feel his joints protest. The muscles in his legs were on fire. His shoulders ached but still he ran.

At one point, he dived for cover behind a rock,

convinced the roar of the motorbike was close. He huddled under an overhang, scraping the skin from his bare arms and legs as he wedged himself in as deep as he could get. He watched the vague outline of the man on his bike, weaving his way in and out of the low-lying boulders, wiping the drizzling rain from his eyes as he turned his head from side to side.

Simon was scared to breathe, worried that his warm breath would be visible in the cold wind. The moment he'd stopped running he shivered and the hairs on his limbs rose in a futile effort to keep the warm air close to his skin. He listened as the roar of the motorbike ebbed and flowed.

Time stopped as he crouched under the low-lying rock, the rough ground below made indentations on his legs. It sounded as though the rider had seen him, he came too close for comfort. Simon held his breath. The engine idled, and he was too scared to look up, afraid that the goon would see his eyes peering through the mist.

His pursuer hadn't seen him and roared away, the sounds growing fainter until Simon could no longer hear them. Still he waited, in case it was a trap and the goon had killed the engine, to lull him out of his hiding place.

He counted to a thousand and made a break for it. The mist had lifted, no longer his friend, but he couldn't stay there risking hypothermia and had to take a chance.

He inched from under the rock, crouching as he massaged his aching legs. He whipped his t-shirt off, worried the white material would highlight his position. His tan would provide better camouflage against the green-brown grassy slopes and the grey rocks. He mopped the sweat off his face with his shirt and rubbed dirt over himself. He realized he was still wearing his watch. If that reflected, he'd be a sitting target. He eased it off his wrist and slipped it in his pocket. He took deep breaths, filling his lungs with fresh, clean air, and looked around. He was alone. He ran.

13 THE RUSSIAN EMBASSY

Vladimir Petrovnikov smiled as he walked into his office in the Russian Embassy in Apatu.

"You met the woman?" asked the man sitting in front of Vladimir's desk.

If the Ambassador's visit had surprised Petrovnikov, he didn't show it.

"Yes, I did, Mr Ambassador. We had a long chat. She's quite charming." The Cultural Attaché walked round his desk and settled himself comfortably in the large leather, revolving chair. "I think this is one assignment I might enjoy."

"As long as you don't lose sight of our objective."

"Not for a moment. I saw the bond between her and Togodo's esteemed President. They have history, those two, I'm sure of it. He'll be happy to avoid an international incident. They are putty in our hands."

"I hope you're right. What about the wife? She's a jealous harridan, or so I've heard."

"A veritable hellcat, she was shooting hate lasers from both eyes when they were introduced."

"Then I think it's important she does not take the trip north."

"I agree. Leave it to me, Sir. I have friends inside the palace and I'll make certain she is indisposed at just the right time."

"And who is the prime target for President after Mtumba's removal?"

"The Finance Minister, Kirimu Nashele. I would think him the best and most cooperative."

"And the other options?"

"There is Samuel Suma, Minister of Sport; Blessing Ochido, Minister of the Interior; and Royal Papele, who is Foreign Minister. They are equally corrupt."

"And greedy?"

"Oh yes, very greedy and ready to make as much money as they can. They all have many relatives to support – and enemies to hurt. None of them got into power without foul play."

"Good, it seems you have plenty of fertile soil in which to plant your seeds. Don't let me or Mother Russia down, Petrovnikov. I have been called back to Moscow urgently, so you will take my place until I return," The Ambassador stood up and walked out of the room, closing the door quietly behind him.

14 COFFEE WITH BEN

The letter from the palace arrived the following morning. Tanya rushed into the office waving it at Amie. Its heavy-duty paper was embossed with gold and the seal on the back bore the Togodian Royal coat of arms, even though there was no longer a royal family.

"Wow. It's addressed to you. It's from the palace and looks really important." She leaned over Amie's shoulder waiting for her to open it.

"Thanks." Amie smiled as she put the envelope in her in-tray and continued to type.

"Aren't you going to open it then?"

"Yes, of course, but not now."

Tanya hovered then flounced out of the room.

Amie had no desire to upset the young clerk, but she doubted that Tanya could be discreet about anything, and the less she knew the better. The moment the door closed, Amie prised open the envelope. *Could she meet Ben in his office at 2:00 pm?* He said there was no need to reply if the time was convenient.

She had no choice but to tell Ian why she was leaving the Embassy and where she was going. She'd ask if she could sign out a pool car because it would give her the chance to visit the orphanage as well. Ian would have orders for her and a list of questions to ask the President, but betraying Ben was not on her agenda. She felt a closer affinity to her friend than she did to those representing the country of her birth.

It took some time persuading Ian to let her drive herself to the palace. He was adamant that he send a driver with her but Amie hinted that it would be more discreet if she slipped in quietly, and he finally agreed. He gave her a list of things to find out. She was to grill him on his policies, talk about his plans for future development, discover how well he got on with his ministers, who might assassinate him, and which ones were waiting to jump into his shoes.

Amie stood in Ian's office nodding, hoping he believed she would be ferreting as much inside information as she could, with no intentions of doing any such thing.

Amie chose the smallest car from the carpool, a Mini. It may have been manufactured in Oxford, she thought as she drove it into the main street, but these days Germans owned the plant. However, most people still thought of the Mini as a quintessentially British car, and it was a small way of flying the flag abroad.

The streets were crowded as usual. Pedestrians weaved through traffic without bothering to look where they were going, stepping off the pavement to avoid treading on the wares spread out on cardboard sheets across the pavements. Taxis stopped as and when they had passengers to pick up and drop off, and donkey carts, piled high with anything from mealie cobs to old tyres, plodded along the roadside labouring under the heavy loads. Most of the vehicles sported dents and scratches, and Amie noticed one door held on with bits of string as she manoeuvred the Mini between an ancient bus, spewing black smoke from its exhaust, and a Citroen C1.

She saw a group of boys sitting on the central reservation of the dual carriageway. They were passing a brown paper bag from one to the other, burying their heads and sniffing hard. *So sad,* she thought, *if only Mrs Motswezi could take them into the orphanage at Tamara.* But there was a limit to the numbers of lost souls she could accommodate, and occasionally those she had rescued ran back to the streets again. The gangs were their family, most had lost parents to AIDS and had nobody to care for them.

Ben's instructions were to enter by the back gate, and as Amie drove past the front of the palace, she wondered which insane architect had worked on the building. The older part bore a resemblance to Disneyland, with round turrets topped by pinnacles. Tacked on to one end, were new concrete walls inset with huge glass panels that would not look out of place next to the Shard in London. She guessed the administrative offices were housed there.

Two guards at the rear entrance leaned on their guns, half asleep. Amie had to beep the horn to get their attention. One ambled over, his boots covered in dust, shirt hanging out from his trousers, while his jaws worked rhythmically as he chewed a betel nut. As he came to the car and smiled at Amie, his teeth and lips showed bright red. She was tempted to tell him how dangerous the habit was, but decided against it.

"Amie Fish." She showed him her ID card from the Embassy.

The guard nodded and meandered over to the guard hut, reappearing a moment later with a clipboard and pen attached by a piece of dirty string. He pushed it through the window and Amie signed her name. He waved to the second guard whose job, and sole purpose in life, was to open the large heavy metal gate. The first guard did nothing to help, and watched as his colleague panted in the heat. He opened it barely wide enough for Amie to squeeze the Mini through.

Inside the high walls was a dramatic change. Wide lawns swept up to the building, and a pond in the middle was home to ducks. Palm trees were dotted around, providing shady patches and the occasional flowerbed was a riot of colour. Amie saw three gardeners pottering around, although they did not appear to be doing anything useful.

She followed the small gravel driveway and stopped outside the only door she could see, but before she was out of the car, Ben bounded down the steps to welcome her.

"Amie, it is so good to see you again," he smiled. He grabbed her hand between both of his before giving her the more usual three-directional African handshake. "It has been so long."

"It's great to see you too, Ben, and in such different circumstances."

"Life throws us many curves." He beamed as he led the way inside and along a passageway to a small sitting room.

It was simply but tastefully furnished in pale blue, with matching sofas and chairs. Several occasional tables were scattered about, and an impressive modern art collection adorned the walls. The floor-to-ceiling windows overlooked the gardens but cut out the glare of the bright sunlight, making Amie wonder if the glass was one way.

A tray of tea with an array of small cakes waited for them as Ben waved her to a chair opposite him. As she sat down, Amie studied his face. He'd aged considerably and looked as if the weight of the world sat on his shoulders.

"Are you well, Ben?" The words were out of her mouth before she could stop them.

"What makes you say that? Let me say life is not too easy." He indicated that she should pour the tea.

"I can only imagine being president is a nightmare," Amie said as she handed him a cup. "I doubt you get much time off."

"No, but it is mostly a question of trust. When you are in a position of power those around you are not your friends. They wait on the sidelines to take for themselves and their families. They tell you what they think you want to hear, not the truth. They are full of false words and praise, but I trust you, Amie. We were friends before I was President."

"Thank you. We have been friends for a long time and have seen much together."

"Yes, and you saved my life."

Amie frowned.

"At Dirk's camp remember?"

"That was nothing, you would have done the same for me."

"But it was Dirk's man who wanted to kill me. And then you rescued me from that fundamentalist group."

"Ben, enough. You came to rescue me, too, and you were my friend right back when we were filming together."

Ben put his head back and roared with laughter. For a moment he looked ten years younger. "Oh yes, yes, I remember those upliftment projects which were a total disaster."

The next few minutes were spent reminiscing about the various scenes they had recorded, until the massacre was mentioned.

"Those were dark days," Ben said.

"But everything is okay now, isn't it? The city is busy. You were chosen in a free and fair election, you have your ministers, and I believe you have the best interests of your people at heart Ben – or should I call you Mr President?"

Ben laughed again. "You can call me Ben, Amie – I'm still just Ben. I have big plans for my country. I will not make the mistakes that many of my fellow Africans have. I will work for the ordinary people to make their lives better with schools, more clinics and hospitals, good roads and factories where they can work and earn money to keep their families happy and healthy. I have big ideas, big plans."

"I'm sure you do, Ben, and I think you have the wisdom to make it happen."

"But it will take money. Big money – and that is why the north is so important."

"The minerals they've discovered up north?"

"You know about this?"

"It's an open secret Ben. I heard rumours years ago, there were whispers all around the Expat Club even before we filmed for Colonel Mbanzi."

"Today it is hot news. I have people snapping at my heels for the permission to mine them. Applications are coming in from all over the world Amie. I don't know who to trust. And I must keep an eye on the Luebos – the minerals are on their tribal lands."

"Weren't they part of the Free Togodo rebels that overthrew your uncle's government in the civil war, because they were afraid they'd get no benefit from the mining?"

"Yes, for a short while they made friends with the M'untus, but we pushed them back and now I rule Togodo. I will let them share in the new wealth, they must trust me."

Amie wasn't convinced that the Luebos would agree to that, or the M'untus either. Africa was riddled with tribal politics and nobody trusted anybody else, even within the same tribes. She remembered Helen, her friend at the game lodge telling her that the Luebos were a peaceful tribe, so maybe it could work.

"I need your help, to see which of these countries I will give the mining rights."

Amie was appalled. "I'm not sure I would be of much use. I'm not worldly Ben!"

"You have lived in the West, Amie, you understand what they are thinking in their heads. Not what words they are using. I need some guidance. I asked you to come and see me, because we are planning a safari to the north, a visit to the area where we will entertain the representatives from overseas. I want you to help organize it and then, when everyone is there and we talk, I want your thoughts on what you see and hear."

"Goodness Ben, I don't know what to say."

"You will say yes." For a moment Ben sounded like a president. It was an order not a request and Amie bristled.

"I will have to ask at the Embassy, they employ me."

"That will not be a problem, I will tell them they must allow you."

Amie had no doubt that Ian Fleming would be thrilled to hear the news and would agree with alacrity. She wasn't sure she was capable. The biggest event she'd ever organized was a dinner party for friends, and a couple of parties at the Expat Club with the management and the other wives. And how was she supposed to advise Ben on which country to favour? She wasn't equipped to give her opinion on huge multi-national decisions. She would be expected to push for Britain, yet her feelings towards her country were raw and angry.

Ben stood up so suddenly, Amie wondered if she had upset him. She'd been eying a chocolate brownie, but Ben had not offered her a cake and she was hesitant to appear too bold. He relieved her of her half-drunk tea, and walked her to the door.

"I will expect you tomorrow. Be here at eight – and remember to be my eyes and ears. We leave for the north in a few weeks."

"But – but how many are we catering for, and for how long?" Amie was appalled at the responsibility he'd placed onto her shoulders.

"Ask to see Gaga Medwewe. She has all the details. Do not fail me Amie, I am looking to you for help."

They had reached the door. Ben opened it, steered her into the corridor; then turned abruptly and marched out of sight without a farewell. Amie was left, presumably to see herself out. She cast a longing look back at the chocolate brownie but decided it was best to leave it where it was.

She walked outside and a quick glance at her watch told her she would have time to take a trip out to the orphanage; it would give her the opportunity to think. She'd landed between a rock and a hard place, in essence working for both sides, and she was damned whichever side she chose.

15 COFFEE AT THE GRAND HOTEL

To Amie's bitter disappointment, Mrs Motswezi was not at the orphanage. Her cheerful secretary, a new one Amie hadn't met before, told her the headmistress had taken a taxi into town to collect supplies. All she could do was leave a note telling her elderly and dear friend that she was back in Togodo and would take the next chance to pay her a visit.

On her way into the city, she made the decision not to return to the Embassy immediately. She would stop off at the Grand Hotel and treat herself to a good cup of local coffee. At work they were always offering her tea, which she disliked, or the bland coffee imported from UK, which had little or no kick.

She was surprised to see her favourite coffee shop had been revamped. The tables along the wall had screens between them giving them privacy. She stopped by the counter to place her order and looked for a quiet table in a corner. She needed to think.

She'd been served when she heard a couple approach the next table. She couldn't see them and wasn't interested. Well-connected men would often bring girls here to impress them, and she assumed it was one of those occasions.

Amie's concern was organizing a safari for foreign delegates way out in the bush. It was a nightmare. She wondered how helpful this Gaga Medwewe would be, and if she had any experience in such events.

"One day you will be pleased and proud to be my wife. It will be so much better than a marriage to Ben Mtumba."

The mention of Ben's name broke into Amie's thoughts making her sit up. The voice was familiar but she couldn't place it.

"No, I do not deserve such an honour," was the quiet reply.

"I am going to be a wealthy man, with more money than you can dream of, and then you will not be able to say no. I will buy you such clothes as you have never seen, and I will take you to many places all around the world. It is just a matter of time. We will always go to fine restaurants, far better than this to dine. We will have the best of everything."

"Thank you, but no."

"Do not be so stupid, girl." The voice was angry. "You have always wanted him, from the day you gave him that silly love letter. Well, you can never have him. He is married. And who did he choose? A white beauty queen from across the sea, a white woman. A woman bought and paid to enhance his public status. It is too late for you. And even if he takes a second and third wife, I would not like to be one of those. His English wife would make life very bad for them."

"I will never love another."

"Do not waste your love on him. His days are numbered. He will not live long, so accept your state."

"You did not put a spell on him?" The girl sounded shocked and angry.

"It is no business of yours, but soon you will see him become sick and then Ngonicansaga you will be crying out for a dead man." There was a pause. "Who brought you to the city?"

"You did."

"And who got you a job at the palace?"

"You did."

"And who is going to take you on a grand trip to the north of our beloved country?"

"You."

"So you see, I am the one who has given you good things. It is to *me* you should be grateful. Do you want to go back to the village and live in a mud hut fetching water from the river? You would spend all your days working in the fields and you would have many children, one after the other. You will never have the President, so is that the life you want to carve for yourself?"

"No."

"Then you must do as I say. Soon the one you think you love will be no more."

Amie heard a chair scrape and the sound of coins rattling on the table. She tried to look, but she was too late to see who the man was before he hurried out of the café. She could hear muffled sobs from the table behind, and for a moment was tempted to go and comfort the young Ngonicansaga (if that's what her name was), but she had problems of her own and it was none of Amie's business. She was sad for her but was distracted by the waiter bringing over the bill.

Amie pressed some coins into his hand and stood up. At the same time the guest at the next table rose to leave.

Their eyes met, and Amie saw a beautiful Togodian girl, in her mid-twenties, with large brown eyes, high cheekbones and a slender figure. It was not surprising that her gentleman friend wanted her – she was stunning.

Keeping her face neutral, as though she had not heard their conversation, Amie gave her a brief smile and made her way out to the lobby. She was curious to see if the man was still around, but there were several well-dressed African men wearing western suits in the reception area so she couldn't be sure. She heard him say that Ben's life was in danger. He *was* talking about Ben, wasn't he? Who in particular would want to kill him and why? She had heard that voice before, but couldn't recall where and when. It wasn't unheard of in Africa for those in power to be disposed of. Should she warn Ben, tell Ian Fleming or say nothing? Was the man being serious, or only showing off?

She bit her lip as she stepped out of the air-conditioned hotel into the baking sun and walked back to the Mini at a loss as to what she should do.

16   THE WELSH FARMHOUSE

Simon ran, his legs pumping as he raced over the slippery grass. He dragged air into his lungs, gasping. The sweat dried on his body, sending cold shivers down his spine. The rain fell, slowly at first and then in larger drops. Still he ran, faster, with no idea where he was going. He must reach a town or village soon.

He found tracks but guessed they were made by animals for there were no tyre prints. In the pouring rain his chances of bumping into a party of hitchhikers were slim, and still there was not so much as a bothy to be seen.

He ran up an incline, pausing only to listen for the sound of the motorbike engine. He stood on the top of the rise and looked around.

There was a small hamlet; he could see smoke rising from several of the houses. His heart leapt, and he made his way down the slope.

A black dot in the sky caught his attention – what was it? His numbed brain didn't recognize it as a drone at first, but the moment it did, he dived for cover behind the nearest rock, rolling himself up in a ball on the sodden ground. If it had heat-seeking capabilities it would only be moments before they found him. Despite feeling cold, he knew that the machine would still record his body temperature and pinpoint his hiding place.

He glanced around and almost laughed as a few sheep ambled past him, stopping to nibble at the long grass. He prayed the drone would be fooled.

The craft came closer, skimming above the treetops as Simon scrambled closer to the nearest ewe, grabbing her hind leg and pulling her towards him under the overhang. She baaed and struggled, but he held on fast, keeping her between him and the drone. It hovered for several seconds and then took off, flying over the hill and out of sight.

Simon had no idea if he'd been seen, but he wasn't going to hang around to find out. He released the animal, patted her woolly back and set off for the village. From his sighting at the top of the hill, it hadn't looked very far – a couple of miles at most.

He crested another rise and dropped down into another valley, losing sight of the houses. Hoping he was still taking the shortest route he ran on, his muscles painful, legs aching, shoulders burning and chest heaving with every step he took. It was impossible to get into an even rhythm on the rough ground. He had to weave to avoid the rocks half buried in the ground. Several times he stumbled, landing on the spongy grass and scraping the skin on his arms and legs. The food he'd stuffed into his shorts pocket was wet and mashed to a pulp, and despite all the rain, he was desperate for a drink.

He saw a hedge, a well-manicured privet hedge. A pruned hedge meant a garden, a garden meant a house and a house meant people. The moment he reached it he sank to his knees, desperate to get his breath back.

A dog barked, and a Welsh Collie bounded towards him, snuffling on the other side of the hedge, then barking again.

"What you seen then Chaser?" A male voice called.

Simon stood up and jogged along the boundary, and the dog followed, barking, bouncing up and down and keeping track of him. He reached a gate and paused. He knew little of Collies and if they were likely to attack; and he hadn't the strength left to fight off the animal.

Seeing Simon, the farmer shouted to his dog. "Stay Chaser. Down."

The dog obediently sank down, and put his head on his paws without taking his eyes off the intruder.

Simon couldn't get enough breath to say anything, and seeing his distress, the farmer opened the gate, grabbed his arm and guided him into the farmhouse.

The heat from the Aga stove in the corner of the kitchen made Simon dizzy, and he fell rather than sat into the chair by a roaring fire in the grate. The room was like a sauna, but he shivered uncontrollably.

"You one of them young squaddies on the training exercises then?" asked the farmer, picking up the kettle standing on a hot plate. "A nice cup of tea should go down well then."

Simon nodded, taking deep gasps, and trying to steady his breathing. He grasped the mug the old man handed to him, the surface burning his hands. Looking round the spotlessly clean kitchen he guessed there was a Mrs Farmer around. A moment later there were footsteps outside and the Norfolk latch on the door rattled.

Simon dropped the mug on the floor and dived through the nearest door into what he saw was a sitting room.

The farmer stared at his behaviour in amazement, then

turned to his wife who entered carrying a bowl of new laid eggs.

"There's sommat going on here. You stay over by the door my dear."

"Bert, what is it? Who was that?"

Hearing a woman's voice, Simon sheepishly came back into the kitchen in. "Look I can explain," he said.

"I think you better had, young man, and be pretty sharp about it." The farmer didn't look as friendly now.

As Simon sidled into the chair by the fireside his mind raced. What was he going to tell them, and would they believe him?

"Wait," said the farmer's wife staring hard at Simon. "Look at the mess you be making of my kitchen." Then her face softened. "Poor dear, you look all done in." She placed the bowl of eggs on the table, prised off her wellington boots and put them on the mat by the door. She looked at the shattered mug with the tea trickling over the shiny kitchen tiles. "I think you need a good hot drink, something to eat and ..." she eyed Simon standing shivering in his dirty, wet shorts, his shirt dangling from his hand, "... a shower. Then we can sit down and you can tell us what yer running away from and why yer here."

"Thank you," Simon mumbled.

The farmer's wife waddled over and threw open the door to the bathroom. She pointed to some towels and gave him a shove. "I'll look out some of Bert's old things for now. You get yourself clean."

The water at the mansion was lukewarm at best and trickled out of the shower head like a leaking tap. The hot water cascading down Simon's body now was both soothing and painful. He was battered, bruised and scratched all over, but it was heaven to feel warm again as the feeling slowly returned to his fingers and toes.

He had turned the water off, after rinsing out his filthy clothes and was hanging them up on the rail, when he heard a loud thumping on the outside door and an angry voice demanding they open up.

Grabbing a towel, Simon wrapped it round him and bolted into the kitchen intent on racing up the stairs to find somewhere to hide.

The farmer's wife moved swiftly across the room, grabbed Simon by the arm and dragged him into the sitting room, closing the door behind her. She steered him to the huge open fireplace that dominated the room. She pushed him into it and indicated he should climb up.

Simon hesitated, then, hearing the farmer open the outside door into the kitchen, his hands shot up to feel rungs set into the walls on the side of the chimney. He hoisted himself up until his feet were out of sight, and hung on for dear life in the dark. Even in his fear, he was intrigued by the ladder inside the chimney. Then it came to him, the cottage had to be at least three hundred years old, and in those days, they would have sent small children up to clean the soot away. He'd often wondered how they were able to climb inside the chimneys, and now he knew.

He heard angry voices coming from the other room, doors being flung open and protests. He heard the sitting room door creak, footsteps pacing round, the curtain rings protesting as they were flung to the side and the squeak as furniture was moved. He could hear the visitor breathing and muttering as he paced the room a second time, then walked out, slamming the door behind him. He heard the thump of boots from above, clattering down the stairs, and the farmer's voice raised in anger, his wife adding her protests as they shouted at the intruders.

Simon felt as if he'd been holding his breath for hours and gulped in large mouthfuls of air. He tried to relax his hold on the rungs, but his fingers cramped. The sharp metal dug into his bare feet and he twisted from side to side to relieve the pain. He wasn't sure how much longer he could hold on. It felt like an age before the front door slammed and all was quiet.

He didn't dare move. His hands were frozen around the iron bars and his feet were numb as they balanced on the narrow metal.

Minutes passed before the farmer's wife came to rescue him.

She took him back through the kitchen and into the bathroom on the far side of the room. She laughed when she saw his face and so did Simon when he caught sight of it in the mirror. He was covered in soot, his blue eyes shining out of a black face.

"Yer look just like them chimney sweeps of olden days. Yer better have another shower and get yerself clean again. I've put some of hubby's old clothes here on the chair." She saw the blood on Simon's hands and feet. "Oh Lordy, I'll see to them as soon as yer get clean. Looks nasty, and you don't want to be getting tetanus or some other horrible disease."

She went out, closing the door behind her.

He patted himself dry – it was too sore to rub his skin hard – and eased into his host's clothes. The man was several sizes bigger than Simon, and a lot rounder, but he wasn't complaining. He was ready to face his rescuers, not sure of the best story to tell them. If they turned him over to the police, they would be doing him a favour, but that might delay his return to London.

He went back into the kitchen, still towelling his hair dry.

The farmer pointed to the chair by the fire and stood with one hand on the mantelpiece.

"Now, young man, you'd best explain yerself, and it had better be good."

He was holding a shotgun and looked prepared to use it.

Simon stared at the farmer and his wife, his mind racing. What did you say in a situation like this? I work for the British Diplomatic Service, but I was brought up here for a refresher course as I'm also a spy?

While he was still hesitating, the farmer's wife bustled over from the Aga and passed him a mug of hot tea – the British answer to all situations.

"Yer escaped from that big house over in the next valley?"

Simon nodded. "Yes. I was supposed to go for some army training, a refresher course, but they locked me in. Something wasn't right, so I made a break for it."

"Told you them lot was up to no good, didn't I tell yer?" She glared at her husband. "I'm Mags and this is my hubby Bert. I can tell yer a proper gentlemen and English, not like that rude lot there," she waved her thumb in the air. "Ever so rude they is, well the one that comes into the village shop. Never says a word, just points to the things he wants and stares if you wishes him good morning. Always the same one too, though we's seen several of them driving past in big cars. Told you they was up to no good, didn't I Bert? No good will come of that lot. And how dare they burst into our house like that, no manners at all, traipsing mud all over my clean floors."

"How long have they been there?" asked Simon. He was going to report them the moment he got back to London.

"Ow, now yer asking. Must 'a been at least a good few months now. Yer not the only one we seen running up and down them hills with the man on the motorbike upsetting our sheep."

"I've got to get back to London as soon as I can. You've both been an amazing help, but can I trouble you for more? I promise you will be amply rewarded."

Mags beamed, but her husband didn't look so sure. He lowered the gun but still maintained a firm grip on it.

"My superiors will recompense you in full, you have my word," Simon added.

"And who did yer say yer superiors are?" Bert asked.

"Ultimately the British government."

"Of course, we'll help yer," Mags said. "As I told yer, I've had my eye on that lot for some time and maybe yer superiors can root them out. My Bert here went and complained to our local constable, but he were worse than useless, he weren't the slightest bit interested. Waste of space he is."

"And what was Constable Hopkins supposed to do? Go racing in there all alone and unarmed against a house full of men?" Bert shot her a disgruntled look.

"He could have done something," she snapped back at

him. "So, young man, I guess yer need new clothes. I can see there's not much belonging to my Bert as fits yer too well. Tell yer what, I'll get our Henry to bring some over tomorrow. Thursday's his day off, and then we can take yer to the station and put yer on a train for London. How's that?"

"Thank you. The sooner I'm on my way south the better. Uh, not that it's not beautiful around here, but I need to get back to work."

"Then that's all sorted then. Put that bloody gun down Bert, if he was gonna attack us he would 'a done it by now. 'Bout time yer had a rest, young man. I'll put clean sheets on the bed upstairs and yer can go sleep in Henry's old room. Yer look exhausted."

"I am," Simon smiled. He would have preferred it if Henry could arrive in the next five minutes with fresh clothes, but tomorrow would have to do. He'd attract a lot of attention dressed in Bert's ill-fitting clothes, and that was the last thing he needed.

As he wriggled under the blankets and lay his head on the pillow he wondered where Amie was and what she must be thinking. He'd thought of asking to use the farmhouse phone, but he decided it was best not to leave any trail of his whereabouts. He needed to get through to the correct department in London, in person. In the meantime, for one night he could relax and sleep peacefully in a really comfortable bed.

All of them had forgotten the running clothes Simon had left on the rail in the bathroom, but someone had noticed.

17 AMIE MEETS GAGA

Amie was at the palace gates before eight the following morning. She guessed she should use the back gate, but when she stopped the Mini next to the guard house there was nobody there. She beeped the horn and waited. The guards appeared, one zipping up his trousers as Amie caught sight of a couple of giggling girls slip away among the piles of rubble and rubbish that were strewn around the back of the surrounding wall.

Those girls aren't more than twelve or fourteen, thought Amie. *They were willing to allow the men to use their bodies for a few Togodian dollars, and if they got pregnant, it was the end of their school days and any chance of further education. They would probably take the baby back to mother and the whole cycle would repeat itself. If only they would think to the future. Was it worth it for the few trinkets the dollars would buy?*

Her thoughts were interrupted by one of the guards tapping on the window. Amie held up her Embassy ID.

The guard demanded she lower the window and the pass was snatched out of her hand. She watched him disappear inside the small hut.

Amie was tempted to jump out of the car and keep a close eye on her document, but while she was dithering, he came back to the car and thrust it into her hand.

"I will be coming many times," Amie informed him.

"Then you need pass," was the abrupt reply.

"Yes, of course, I will ask for one. Thank you."

The guard took his time opening the gate, and Amie had to take care not to scratch the paintwork on the Mini as she drove in. Ben did not rush down the steps to greet her – in fact, there was nobody in sight at all.

She parked her car at the entrance and walked up the steps. The moment she rang the bell next to the imposing double wooden door, it was flung open by an armed soldier, who stared at her before reaching behind him and picking up a clipboard from a nearby table.

"Name?" he barked.

"Amie Fish. I am here to meet Gaga Medwewe. We will be working together. And, I understand I need a pass."

The soldier glanced at his clipboard; running his finger slowly down a column of names. He nodded and indicated that Amie should follow him. She doubted he had found her name on the clipboard. It was possible he couldn't even read. Sometimes being a white person in Africa had its advantages; it was assumed you were important.

They walked down a narrow corridor with large windows on one side and a row of office doors on the other. The guard stopped so abruptly that Amie ran into the back of him, and he turned to glare at her. He opened the door and ushered her inside to where a large black lady sat working at a desk. She looked up, frowning at the interruption.

"Miss uh…" The soldier looked again at the clipboard, brow wrinkled as he tried to find Amie's name.

"I'm Amie Fish, here to work with Gaga Medwewe," she said smiling.

The lady scrambled to her feet.

"Ah, yes. I am so pleased to meet you." She extended her hand as she walked over. "It is much work. It will be good to have help, yes, good indeed." She waved an imperious hand at the guard, dismissing him and turned back to the desk.

"She not have a pass," he muttered, not budging an inch.

"I will get a pass for her. You may go."

The man glared at her but shuffled out of the room, slamming the door behind him.

"These men, they are so stupid. That is why they need the women like us to plan this big trip. Come, sit." She pointed to an empty chair on the opposite side of the desk. "There is much to do and not many days."

Amie perched on the chair and put her bag on the floor.

"Just tell me what you want me to do."

"Here is the list of invitations to go in envelopes. We must send them." She passed the pile over to Amie, along with a list of addresses.

Gaga reminded Amie of Mrs Motswezi at the orphanage. She was short, round and big breasted, with a large bottom that flowed liberally over each side of her chair. She had kind, brown eyes and wore her hair in its natural state, with tight black curls close to her head. Her smile was open and friendly, and like Amie's friend at Tamara, she wore a polyester suit which was stretched to the limit over her generous frame. Amie warmed to her immediately and happily set to work, sure they were going to get on well.

A few hours later, Gaga looked at the clock on the wall. "Time for lunch," she announced.

Not knowing what the routine would be, Amie had brought a couple of sandwiches and some fruit from the kitchen at the Embassy, but Gaga rose to her feet and propelled Amie out of the room, and down a bewildering number of corridors and into a large room that served as a canteen.

From the moment Gaga opened the door, the noise was deafening, as dozens of men dressed in various uniforms, office workers and cleaners talked at the tops of their voices as they queued at the food counter. Gaga pushed Amie to the end of the queue.

As they shuffled forward Amie looked round. The bare metal tables were set out in groups, most with four chairs around them and all of them could do with a good clean.

"We get a big meal here in the middle of the day," Gaga yelled in her ear grabbing a tray as they reached the counter. The queue was slow moving as most of the workers demanded more food on their plates. Amie's eyes widened as she saw the tin plates stacked high, some of them so full the food was in danger of falling off.

"How can they eat so much?" Amie gasped.

"Ah, you wait and see. It is not all for them."

Amie watched in amazement, as the workers balanced their plates and set them on the tables, before delving into their bags and dragging out a variety of plastic containers, plastic carriers, and in one case a brown paper bag. The diners scraped the majority of the food off the plates and returned the containers to their bags. Of course, food for other family members. The gravy seeped out of the paper bag and onto the floor, pooling around the chair legs unnoticed by the diner, who was shovelling food into his mouth as if it was his last meal before walking to the electric chair.

"I do not look at these people," Gaga sniffed. "They are peasants. I went to proper school, the one where they teach you English, and I know how to behave."

Amie nodded, but was amazed at the amount of food that was piled onto her new friend's plate. She had to stop the server from putting an equally massive amount on her own dish.

There was little small talk at the table as they ate. Gaga was itching to get back to work; there was so much to do and little time to do it. They only had a few weeks to arrange everything for all the dignitaries, their retinues and the construction materials for the grand *boma* they were building. Somebody had suggested they build traditional huts inside the perimeter fence, but this was turned down as not suitable for foreigners. They would have tents, and a large marquee for dining and as a venue for the auction. Most times, she explained to Amie as they walked back into the office, this could never be done, but it was on the order of the President, so the suppliers would work fast. Amie wasn't convinced but nodded encouragingly.

They worked far into the night and it was long past dark before Amie, new pass dangling round her neck, crawled back into her car. As she drove to the Embassy compound her thoughts turned to Simon. She'd gone through the whole gamut of emotions, including anger, that she had not heard from him. She pictured him in London, dining in clubs with old friends from work. She saw dim lights, heard the pounding music and pictured the hostesses pulling Simon to his feet and rubbing themselves against him on the dance floor.

Her anger then turned to worry. What had happened to him? Maybe they'd told him he was being re-assigned to another posting and he was not sure how to tell her? Scenarios raced round and round inside her head. The only thing she knew for certain was she had not heard from him since he'd landed at Heathrow. When they'd said goodbye, he'd given her no indication he wanted to break up. And why now, when she was expecting their baby? She was miserable just thinking about it.

18   PLANNING THE SAFARI

Amie wanted to hit Ian Fleming. She squared up to him in the dungeon, her voice shaking with anger.

"You don't know Ben like I do. He only wants what is best for his country and his people. He's genuine, he's not like the other African tinpot dictators. He's pushing for upliftment, connecting water, electricity and sewage. He's fighting for education for all."

"Cut the crap Amie, we've heard all the rhetoric before. How do you explain this?" He pushed a newspaper across the table and Amie read the headline.

LARGEST FOOTBALL STADIUM IN AFRICA FOR TOGODO
Below was an artist's impression of the finished building while the copy underneath waxed lyrical about the seating, private boxes, media centre, luxurious changing rooms, even down to a description of the parking areas lined with trees.

"Does your precious friend think building football stadiums a priority? More important than schools, clinics and hospitals?"

"I can't explain this, but it's not what Ben told me, and I believed him."

"Now will you come to your senses and understand that the best person to rule this country is one who will listen to the voice of reason?"

"No. Wait Ian, I'll talk to him about this."

"You'll let him fill you up with more lies and he'll get you to believe him again. Amie, when will you wake up and see life as it really is? There is not one African country that has been a success, and all of it is down to corruption and power play."

"So, what's your answer? Rule behind the scenes? Make sure that the guy at the top answers to Britain?"

"Yes, if it will improve the lives of millions of people."

"That's no different than colonialism – only this time nobody's being open and honest about it." Then the penny dropped. "Of course! This is about those mineral rights in the north isn't it? Britain wants to mine and control them."

"Amie, grow up. If it's not us then it'll be another power. These minerals are vital in sensitive industries. What if the Russians get their hands on them, or would you prefer the Saudis have access? Take that a step further and let in a radical extremist group. You want those people to hold the rest of the world to ransom?"

"No, of course not, but it doesn't mean we have to twist Ben's arm. Any dealings should be fair and above board and what's best for Togodo and her people. The 'important' minerals are under *their* soil, after all."

"How about North Korea, Amie? Did you know that a delegation arrived last month and they have set up their Embassy in the suburbs? Should we allow some madman like Kim Jong-un to get his hands on them? He's threatening to blow everyone to smithereens!"

Amie paused, horrified at the thought. "I think you need to give Ben a fair hearing. I can't believe he's lied to me."

"It's vital for the free world that we, or at least our allies like the Americans, are given the mining rights. We will not let them fall into the hands of the wrong people – people who cannot be trusted to hold that amount of power."

Amie had known for years that the African mindset was not the same as that of the West. Ben seemed so sincere, but on the front page of the newspaper on the table were the designs for a super, unnecessary, and expensive project which went against everything he'd told her.

"I didn't call you in here to fight with you. What have you got to report back? Which countries are going on this safari – or mining auction?"

Amie sighed. "We've sent out invitations to the French, Russians, Americans, Chinese, and us of course."

"Are you sure it was China, and not North Korea?"

"I'm not sure. Possibly both. Gaga has the full list."

"Really Amie, you need to clarify things. First thing tomorrow you will find out exactly which countries are being invited. You're in position to get us way ahead of the competition. And I want you to find out what you can about Kirimu Nashele, the Finance Minister – his likes, dislikes, family, aspirations and anything else of use."

"Why?" Amie asked.

"Because I'm telling you to. If I had my way you wouldn't be the person I'd have chosen for the job."

And I wouldn't choose me either, thought Amie.

"Ian, I'm not a good spy, I accept that, and I don't know a lot about business or high finance either. I don't understand the reasons for the safari. I thought deals like this were conducted in offices between representatives of the buyers or leaseholders, and papers had to be signed. Is this kind of trip usual? It must be costing the government a fortune."

Ian leaned back in his chair and steepled his fingers. "It's highly unusual which is why I want to get to the bottom of what's going on – there are ulterior motives in the undercurrents. I suspect Mtumba has two objectives. He will meet all his prospects at once and can observe their interactions, especially as many of them will be out of their comfort zone. Secondly, I do think he has an auction in mind. If he can pit the countries against each other on the spot, he will get the best price for permission to mine. The minerals in question are not benign, like gold or even diamonds; their uses are far more dangerous. I admit, it's a novel idea – and it just might work."

"I told you Ben isn't stupid," Amie repeated. "Were the British the only ones to prospect in the area and locate the deposits?"

"What makes you ask that?"

"You forget how closely knit the Expat community was. The engineers had dinner at the Club before they flew out. It wasn't difficult to work out what they'd been up to – at least they let on they'd found something."

"You already know more than I'm happy for you to know. That's all for now." Ian stood up to show the meeting was over, handing the newspaper to Amie as he walked round the table. "And read the details, maybe it will help change your mind about Ben's intentions for his fellow Togodians." Ian strode out of the room, leaving Amie holding the damning report.

Back in her bungalow, Amie paced the floor as she

often did when she was thinking. So, she *was* naïve, Ian was right. She'd never taken that much notice of world politics, there was little she could do about the decisions taken by people in power so she left them to it. Why was Ian taking an interest in the Finance Minister? Was he earmarked as Ben's successor? Would he be malleable and do what the British government told him to do? They would not be above bribing Kirimu Nashele with a luxury home in London, money in the bank, and any other trinket his heart desired. The only difference was that today the cost was a lot higher than in the past.

There was no earthly reason for Amie to distrust Ben, he had never lied to her as far as she was aware.

Seething after her meeting, Amie drove to the palace and rushed to the office to explain why she was late, but Gaga's chair was empty.

Looking at the piles of paperwork strewn around she wondered how they would ever get everything ready for the safari north.

There were tents to organize, beds and bedding, a catering team, transport, lighting equipment, water supplies and mosquito nets, the list was endless. Amie had noticed how stressed Gaga Medwewe looked, as Amie mentioned several necessary items the African woman had not even considered. You could hardly offer important foreign representatives food and drink on tin plates and mugs, so they must source china, glasses and cutlery which would need to be packed and transported with care.

As the necessary requirements grew, listing them was the easy part. Sourcing everything would be the biggest headache. This was not Europe or America where companies dealt on a daily basis with corporate clients, this was Africa, and it was the first international event several hundred miles from the capital that had ever been attempted.

Amie consulted with every safari company she could locate in and around Apatu. There were several new ones now the political scene was stable, and they gave her as much advice as they could. She phoned Ruangan companies in the hope they could make up the shortfall in supplies.

"Anti-mosquito spray," she mentioned to Gaga as her friend bustled in through the door.

"They need that?"

"Yes, some of the representatives might not bring their own, so we will need some to give them."

"But why? I have never used such a thing."

"I know Gaga, but you've lived in Togodo all your life and the mosquitos don't bother you. But the foreigners will get bitten. Which, reminds me, we will need First Aid kits and medicines as well. Have we invited a nurse and a doctor as part of the crew?"

Gaga shrugged her shoulders, straining the polyester fabric on her business suit to bursting point. Despite the heat, against which the slowly turning overhead fan brought little relief, she refused to remove her jacket even in the office. The white blouse which she wore under it looked fresh and crisp when she arrived first thing in the morning; now it looked wilted and sweat stains had appeared under her arms and spread across her bosom.

In contrast, Amie was wearing a light, loose-fitting,

cotton dress with short sleeves, and had pinned her hair back to help keep her cool.

"Why are we planning for three nights? Surely, we drive up in one day, look at the mining or whatever there is to see the next day, sleep over and then drive back? That's only two nights."

"There is the one day for the hunting," Gaga replied rising to collect more brochures from a side table.

Amie's heart sank. "They are going to hunt wild animals?"

"Of course, that is the point of safari. It is why people come to Africa, for the wildlife. We learned this at school."

"But if the hunters kill all the animals, there will be nothing for the tourists to see. It's fine to take photographs of them, but not kill them."

In reply Gaga shrugged again. "Minister Suma, he tell me the guests they will hunt on the second day, but the army, they have the guns and so that is not for us to do. That is good, yes?"

"No, not good," Amie muttered under her breath. "And which minister is Suma?"

"He is the Honourable Minister for Sport." Gaga smiled. "He is a good and important man. He has four wives and many children. But the greatest of them all is Honourable Minister Nashele, he is in charge of the money and he works very hard. I have much respect for him. He too likes to hunt."

"Does he now?" Amie wasn't the slightest bit impressed and wondered if Ben knew about the plans to slaughter their magnificent African wildlife. She would take the first opportunity to ask him. The thought of being involved in a hunting expedition took all the joy away for her. She had been looking forward to going back out into the bush, but she wasn't sure she'd be able to keep her mouth shut if she saw men assuaging their bloodlust on defenceless animals. She was committed to accompanying Ben and Ian Fleming on the trip north and there was no way she could get out of it.

19 LANDMINE

It was the farmer's wife who noticed the wet running shirt and shorts that Simon had left over the shower rail.

"I think they know yer was here," she announced as she walked back into the kitchen and threw the wet clothes on the back of a chair.

Simon's heart sank as he looked at the farmer standing with one foot on the hearth lighting his pipe. He puffed away sending clouds of fragrant-smelling tobacco smoke wafting through the air.

"Will they come back tonight?" The farmer's wife sounded nervous.

"Not sure if they'll take the chance. Up till now they've kept a low profile."

"Well there's plenty in the village what doesn't like them. Surly lot."

The farmer closed his eyes, lost in thought. "Best to keep watch. And bring Chase and Bessie indoors, they'll kick up a racket if they hear anything."

"Good idea," agreed his wife, but Simon could tell she was nervous. The worst they could expect way out here in the middle of nowhere was the odd bit of sheep rustling every now and again.

Simon had been looking forward to a good night's sleep in a comfortable bed, but he lay there in the dark on high alert. He'd checked the window catch in the bedroom twice and agreed he would take a turn keeping watch with the farmer.

The old man had taken his place in the rocking chair by the kitchen Aga, with his shotgun across his knees, and his sheepdogs curled up at his feet. He dozed off, relying on his working companions to alert him, but upstairs, Simon was too on edge to relax. Every time he closed his eyes, he heard a thump, a bump, or the moan of the wind through the trees outside. Several times he climbed out of bed and peered through the gap in the curtains. It was pitch dark and impossible to see anything.

He was unaware that downstairs Bessie growled and got up to sniff at the door, the hackles standing up on the back of her neck, but she didn't bark and after a few moments she lay down again.

Simon went to relieve the farmer, and found him sound asleep in the rocking chair, hands locked around his gun. It seemed a shame to wake him only for him to go back to sleep. Simon settled in the paisley patterned armchair opposite and waited. He was scared. In movies and books the heroes were always calm, decisive, meeting danger head-on, but it was different in real life, very different. His stomach clenched up, his mouth felt dry and he couldn't stop shaking. They wanted him back, and he had no idea what their agenda was. He doubted they were a British government department, but who or where they came from was a mystery.

It was a long night but eventually the lighter streaks in the sky heralded the false dawn and little by little the room came into focus. Simon had dozed off, and when he came to, he saw the farmer's wife adding logs to the Aga, and there was no sign of the farmer or his dogs.

"So, it was quiet after all. After a good breakfast my Bert will see yer safe and sound with the right people."

"I can't thank you enough. I need to get to London, but I don't have any money for a train. I would leave you my name and address but – if they come back, then it could be…"

"Don't yer worry about a thing, my Bert will have thought things through. Yer just leave it all to him." She took a frying pan off the hook and threw in some bacon and eggs. "Just lay the table, will yer? This'll be ready in a jiffy."

Bert, with his dogs running around him, came in from outside. "No sign of them, so we'll be off as soon yer've had your fill." He smiled at his wife, as she piled his plate with food.

"If yer going into town, give me a moment and I'll come too," Mags said. "Give me a chance to get something for the christening next week. I'll change while yer finish up here." She disappeared up the stairs.

"How far is the nearest town?" Simon asked.

"'Bout forty minutes."

Mags was back in five minutes and announced she was ready. As the farmer struggled into his coat, he handed Simon an old anorak.

"Not a lot of warmth in that Son, but it'll do until we can get yer to safety."

"Thanks."

Bert locked the gun in the safe, put the keys in his pocket and looked around the farmyard. Seeing the dogs placidly sniffing near the henhouse, he opened the garage doors and climbed into an old Daimler V8 250 which started at the first turn of the key. Mags clambered into the passenger seat and Simon got in the back. He was admiring the walnut finishes on the dashboard, the wide rear-view mirror and the absence of seat belts in the back, which by Simon's reckoning made the car a classic or vintage model. Peering over Bert's shoulder, he noticed the odometer registered less than a hundred thousand miles.

As if reading his mind, Mags looked back over her shoulder. "This is Bert's baby. We don't use her very often, and when he's not out with the sheep, he's out there," she indicated the garage with her thumb. "He's out there tinkering with his girlfriend." She laughed.

Simon smiled. The car was in pristine condition and he guessed that Bert wasn't above showing off by taking him into town in his pride and joy rather than the bent and battered old Land Rover left behind in the garage.

As they approached the yard gate, Simon jumped out and opened it to let the car through.

"Thanks lad; there be four more of those before we hit the road." Bert nodded.

"Quite a treat for me not to have to get out," Mags smiled.

They bumped along the rough track, the Daimler swaying in the ruts and the tyres squelching in the mud. As Simon jumped out to open the second gate with the farmer's ill-fitting clothes flapping around him, he hoped he would be able to keep a low profile on the trip down to London. He looked like a tramp, but it wasn't a good idea to wait for Henry to turn up bringing more suitable clothes. He needed to get to head office as soon as possible.

As he grabbed the gate, he noticed there was a large puddle he couldn't avoid, so he didn't push it outwards but pulled it back towards the car. Bert reversed to allow the gate to open fully. With a smile, Simon bowed and touched his forelock as the grand old car swept past him.

The blast sent him reeling backwards and his ears rang as he sailed through the air and landed flat on his back against the grass bank.

There was very little left of the car. Its mangled metal was twisted out of shape, like a surrealistic modern sculpture. A strong smell of charred flesh floated through the air and a pool of petrol ran back down towards the gate. The ground was sprinkled with shards of glass, pieces of the bodywork were strewn in all directions, and a trickle of blood poured down Simon's cheek where a sharp piece of metal had pierced his skin.

The air resounded as the shock waves passed over him. It had to be a landmine, dug in beyond the gate and concealed by the puddle. Simon had no idea how far the sound of the blast spread, but he wasn't going to hang around to find out. There was nothing he could do to help Bert or Mags and his heart ached for the friendly couple who helped him. They were innocent and didn't deserve to die.

Shaking himself out of his stupor, he raced back to the farmhouse, half running, half stumbling, looking around for signs of his captors. He was still deaf in both ears; all he could hear was a loud buzzing – trucks could be racing towards him and he would never know.

He grabbed the handle on the kitchen door. It was locked. He pushed against it, but it was solidly built and there was no way he could break it open. Darting round the side of the house, he picked up a rock and smashed the bathroom window, chipping away the loose shards of glass. He threw himself in, landing awkwardly in the bath just as the dogs raced over, barking wildly.

"Chaser. Shut up," screamed Simon, but neither animal obeyed.

There was no dial tone on the telephone in the kitchen. These guys took no chances. He flung open cupboards and drawers, searching for a cell phone, money, anything that could be of use. He riffled through the coat pockets hanging on the back of the door, but only found a wad of paper hankies.

He bounded up the stairs, ransacking the main bedroom, wrenching at the wardrobe handles, lifting the mattress, throwing the clothes aside in the chest of drawers. He struck lucky. In Mag's bedside drawer, right at the back, was a roll of fifty-pound notes bound by an elastic band. Not stopping to count them, Simon shoved the money in his pocket and went downstairs. He raced from window to window, peering out to see if anybody was coming but there was no sign of life.

There was no sign of anyone as Simon inched the front door open and peered out. He clutched the bunch of keys from the hook next to the coat stand and sprinted over to the lean-to garage. He scrambled into the ancient Land Rover and fumbled with one key after another but none of them worked. There was an old motorbike leaning against the wall and, jumping out of the car, his shaking fingers flicked through the key ring again until he found one that looked promising. He flung one leg over the bike, pushed it off its stand and inserted the key. The engine broke into a noisy roar. Putting his foot down, Simon raced out of the barn nearly flattening Chaser, who lunged forward trying to grab his leg.

The dogs chased at his heels as he roared out of the farmyard, taking care to avoid the middle of the wide track. What were the odds there was only one landmine? He manoeuvred the bike next to the first gate, lifted the latch and eased his way through, not bothering to shut it behind him. To his relief the dogs didn't follow, but stayed in the yard, it was their job to guard the house.

As he approached the second gate, still swinging open on its hinges, he took a deep breath. He could feel the tears prick the back of his eyes. As he shot past the tangled wreckage, he saw the remains of Bert's burnt body slumped behind what had once been the steering wheel. The stench of burned flesh hovered in the air, and Simon gulped. How he was going to explain this, and to whom, he had no idea.

To his horror he saw the needle on the petrol gauge was just above empty. He had no idea how far that would take him, and didn't know which way to turn when he reached a tarred road. He hoped and prayed there would be a signpost.

He put his foot down and kept going, the wind whistling in his ears, the loose clothing flapping round his body, eyes watering in the cold air. He was still tossing up whether to find a police station in the nearest town or make for the train station and go straight to London, when something made him look behind.

The guard who'd accompanied him on his running

marathons – was right behind him and gaining fast. Simon's bike gave a splutter and the fuel gauge light winked at him. He wasn't going much farther.

20 THE UNITED STATES EMBASSY

The US Embassy in Apatu was in the leafy upmarket suburb of Brianwood, well away from the centre of town. The previous staffing levels had only included the Ambassador, a chargé d'affaires, an assistant attaché and a couple of secretaries.

Edward Keller, the new Ambassador in Residence, was smarting from his recent eviction from the White House. It wasn't his homosexuality that had infuriated them, but the knowledge that his boyfriend was ex-KGB, which called more than his loyalty into question. He was a loose cannon and not to be trusted. He would have been thrown out except for the fact that he had powerful connections in his home state of Texas, and the President didn't want to rock the boat in a state that gave him a huge voting platform. The answer was to pack him off somewhere unimportant where he couldn't do any further harm.

Keller was furious when he heard he'd been exiled to Togodo, a two-bit African country he couldn't even find on the map. What the hell, he hadn't given away any state secrets. His frantic letters to the President were ignored and they sent a minion to tell him that his only other option was to return to his ranch in Texas and round up his cattle – that or the Embassy in Apatu. He chose the latter, although he missed his boyfriend more than he liked to admit, but he couldn't face his friends and neighbours probing into his affairs. Some parts of the world accepted homosexuality, even same-sex marriages, but not in his home state.

He'd been appalled, on arriving in this hellhole, to find that homosexuality was a crime and carried with it the death penalty. His wings were well and truly clipped.

He sat behind his desk raging against the injustice, when his secretary showed Ian Fleming into his office. He rose to his feet and held out his hand.

"How ya doing, Ian?"

Ian gripped Edward's hand firmly, possibly too hard, and the US Ambassador winced as he pulled his fingers away.

"Take a seat." He waved Ian to a comfortable wing-backed chair opposite his desk.

Ian glanced around the walls lined with bookcases and a series of cupboards which likely housed a television and a full range of drinks. He was right, for no sooner was he seated than Edward opened one of the doors to reveal an impressive array of bottles.

"What'll yours be?"

"A nice cup of tea would go down very well, thank you." Ian pinched the material on his trousers, realigning the perfect crease, while not bothering to look up to see Edward's reaction.

The American slammed the cabinet door too hard and picked up the phone to order a tea and coffee.

"I invited you over for a brief chat. I thought we might be able to do a bit of horse trading, seeing as our two great nations are so close."

Ian doubted Edward thought of Britain as great. He would be well aware that Texas was three times the size of the British Isles.

"What did you have in mind?" Ian asked.

"Well it's about this little shindig."

"You mean the safari?" Edward was the kind of man he despised: no class, no presence and, as far as he could tell, pig ignorant to boot.

"Sure do. Burning daylight if you ask me. A heap of us ridin' hundreds of miles out of town to look at a bit of land that is said to conceal a pot of gold."

Ian's grunt was non-committal.

"You've seen the plans then?"

"Plans?" Ian played dumb.

"The geologists' report, the findings. I understand there were both Americans and Brits in the survey team, so it seems to me we should have first dibs on things, don't you agree?"

"For permission to mine, you mean?" Two could play the stupid stakes.

"Yeah, 'course. But I heard there's gonna be a whole crowd of us. All this is on a need to know basis, you understand?"

Ian nodded in agreement. He guessed every word they said was being recorded by equipment concealed behind the doors to one of the other cabinets.

"So, how can we fix this?"

Ian gave Edward a puzzled stare.

"We gotta get the contract, no question. What I want to tie up now is that we don't go up against each other, and if only one gets it then we go into partnership. Agreed?"

"I'm not in a position to speak for my government so it's not possible for me to give you my word."

"Come on. We can't let the Chinks get their paws on all this. They've made enough inroads into Africa as it is, and as I hear it, we're talking about minerals that are pretty handy for nuclear bombs and the like. Dangerous stuff."

Ian leaned forward in his chair and ticked off on his fingers as he replied.

"To my knowledge, the US, UK, Russia, France, and China are already known to have nuclear weapons. And beside those five, so have India, Pakistan, and North Korea. Israel is presumed to possess them. Add to that Belgium, Germany, Italy, the Netherlands, and Turkey – they have access to them through NATO. I'm not sure I see your point"

The look on Keller's face was satisfying. Ian had no idea what he'd been up to in the White House, but he considered that watering the pot plants would have been onerous for him. *What an idiot they've sent to represent their country*, Ian thought with disgust.

"Hot damn. That many, eh? Well I never would have believed that. Yer sure now?"

Ian nodded.

"Well you heard who'll be traipsing south …?"

"North." Ian interrupted.

"Oh, north is it? Well any idea who'll be entertained at the President's expense so he can ramble on about this two-bit hellhole's newly found wealth?"

"We will probably find out when we arrive," Ian responded.

"Humph … You're going, of course?"

"My Ambassador has received an invite, and as his *chargé d'affaires,* I may be going, but I'll wait to see."

"Hmmm. OK. So, what do you think his take on all this is?"

"Our Ambassador?"

"Yeah. What's he like?"

Bearing in mind that every word would be on tape, Ian replied blandly: "Decent sort of chap, does a good job, no complaints." He lifted his cup and tried not to wince as the hot brown dishwater masquerading as tea hit his taste buds.

"Yeah, well as I said, thought I'd have a word with you, as I know your Ambassador is away, and I guess that makes you in charge?"

"Only until he returns." Ian forced himself to smile. He was well aware that Sir Humphrey had been called back to discuss the trip north. Years earlier when word had got out about the mineral deposits, London had been quick to upgrade the status of its Embassy in Togodo and put a competent civil servant in charge.

"I'd like to keep this between ourselves for now," muttered the American.

"Of course."

"But we must make sure this mining deal doesn't get into the wrong hands."

"There is a fair amount of competition. I've heard, on the grapevine the North Koreans might be on the guest list." Ian stood.

Edward Keller turned white. "Hot damn! You don't say." He scrambled to his feet. "Now that's serious and a real good reason for us folks to stick together. Agreed?"

Ian Fleming only bowed his head, which he hoped

Keller would take as acquiescence, and besides, the Yanks might be recording this in full Cinemascope.

He shook Keller's hand and left the office. He couldn't fathom why a nation like the United States would send an idiot like that abroad; even Amie had more suss than their Ambassador to Togodo – and that was saying something.

21   AMIE'S INSTRUCTIONS

A few weeks later Amie was called into the dungeon for a meeting with Fleming. She'd had a long think and given herself a good talk. She was in no position to fight Ian, or any of the employees at the Embassy, and the rest of the staff were easy to get on with. She could see no way out, so she would make the best of it. She was looking forward to getting out of the city for a few days and back to her beloved bush.

"Sit down. I'd like to run through things one more time, as this will be the last opportunity we have to speak privately."

Amie nodded.

"You'll be travelling up with Gaga Medwewe as I understand it, and as such not part of our Embassy contingent. I expect you to be my eyes and ears and to report back discreetly. You know what that means?"

"Yes, of course."

"I've told the people who will be in my party that you are working for the palace, so they won't be trying to fraternise with you. I'm sure you understand."

Amie had no problems with what Ian was telling her – it made sense, but she didn't think the rest of the guests would believe she was totally divorced from her own countrymen.

"I want you to keep your ear to the ground – for informal chats between various parties and possible on-the-side deals and alliances. It will be useful to know who gets on with whom. My colleagues will be keeping eyes and ears open, but you will have more freedom to float about, so to speak."

Amie thought it highly unlikely she would hear anything even remotely useful, but Ian droned on, and she had to pinch herself to stay alert. His voice had a soporific effect as he reiterated the importance of finding out as much as they could about their opposition.

"Will the agreements and licences be signed in the bush?" she asked when Ian stopped for a microsecond to take breath.

"It's not the usual way to conduct business, but who knows how your friend Ben operates. Many a deal has been made after several drinks and a drunken handshake. We guess he's planning to get as much as possible in down payment and the highest percentage of the pickings."

"Makes sense for Togodo. They need all the money they can get to spend on infrastructure."

"Britain needs money, too. With an aging population, benefits flying out of control, zero hours contract work, Brexit, the Snowflake Generation and the NHS mired in debt, we need all the help we can get."

All the problems in her old country were so distant they didn't feel relevant to Amie and she stopped listening until the word *Simon* pierced her thoughts.

"What?" she asked, startled.

Ian cleared his throat and glared at her. "I said, have you heard from Simon? Simon Peterson."

"No. He was called away to a meeting in London just before you hijacked me. I thought he was going to meet you."

"He didn't turn up and no one knows where he is. He said nothing to you?"

"No. Did he arrive in London?" she asked, to make sure she'd heard Ian correctly. Her hands were tightly clasped beneath the lip of the desk to stop them from shaking.

"I'm not at liberty to say more. Please focus on the job in hand. There are six countries involved – the United States man is Edward Keller. The Chinese contingent is led by Xiao Ping Wang. The French representative is Francois Dubois – and we've heard that the North Koreans have somehow succeeded in getting in on the act. No idea who their man will be. Last but not least, the Russians have got their foot in the door with Vladimir Petrovnikov. You might need to watch out for him. I've made notes with as much information as possible on each delegate. I want you to learn and inwardly digest this information. Understand?"

Amie nodded. "So, in order of preference the UK first, then the US, France, China or Russia, and lastly North Korea. Have I got that right?"

"Put simply like that, yes, but the bottom line is that *we* need to wrap this up," Ian said as he shuffled the papers on the table in front of him.

"But, if the UK is so broke, how can we possibly afford to outbid countries like America, China and Russia?"

"Leave that to the professionals Amie, no need to tax your brain with matters that don't concern you. That's not your brief. All you have to do is listen and report back to me – or one of my guys up there – with anything that might be useful."

Well, that put me firmly in my place, Amie thought, *but at least I'll be safe on this trip, and that will make a change. I have two people to look after now, so I'm taking no risks.*

Ian left Amie in the dungeon studying the file and walked back upstairs to his office. She felt that Ian had drip-fed her only what he wanted her to know and left out important details. He was more interested in the competition than in learning what Ben wanted. Why? At the moment though, her biggest worry was to find out where Simon was, and if he was safe.

22 SIMON UNDER ARREST

Simon weaved the motorcycle frantically in a bid to avoid any bullets that might be flying towards him. The skin on his back tingled, anticipating a hit from behind. Through the sweat pouring into his eyes, he thought he saw a thin strip of shining grey ahead and prayed it was a main road.

The bike spluttered several more times as he urged it to keep going. "Please, please," he whispered. "Please get me as far as the road and please let there be a lot of traffic." It was his only hope, but as he approached the tarred road there were no other vehicles in sight.

Right or left? Simon didn't know which way to go, but his mind was made up for him as he skidded off the dirt track onto the rain-wet tar with the bike pointing to the right. He put his foot down and sped dangerously up the road. As the bike gasped for fuel it leapfrogged forward in short hops, making his progress erratic.

He chanced a look over his shoulder and saw that his pursuer was closer and gaining on him despite having a less powerful machine.

The farmer's motorbike was going no further; it slewed across the road and sailed into a ditch, slipping sideways and trapping his leg underneath it. He struggled to free himself and make a run for it.

Neither the guard nor Simon heard the police car as it

accelerated up the road behind them. It had its lights flashing and siren shrieking over the deserted landscape.

The goon turned abruptly and veered off the road, on to a track and away across the open countryside. The police car came to a stop next to Simon, who was struggling to extricate himself from underneath the heavy bike.

"Whoa there," the young policeman said as he came over to help. "Your leg crushed?"

"No, I don't think so. There's a dip in the ditch and I landed in that."

"That's a bit of luck," the second policeman said as he climbed out of the car. He helped lift the bike off Simon who scrambled to his feet.

"Am I glad to see you."

"You won't be when we throw the book at you for dangerous driving. You were all over the place. Surprised you only hurt yourself and not someone else."

Simon hobbled to the side of the road, rubbing his legs and flexing his arms. As far as he could see he was uninjured.

"Look, I can explain. Can we go back to the station?"

The policemen cast surprised looks at each other; it wasn't usual that offenders asked to be charged.

"You will take me in, won't you?" Simon thought they might drive off and leave him there to the mercy of his captor, who would be waiting to see what happened.

"If you insist," the younger policeman said smiling, "but this means points off your licence, at the very least."

"Gladly, take all you want, it'll be worth it." Simon practised his story as they sped past miles of open moorland, dotted here and there by cottages and farmhouses.

The British Police Force is known for its hospitality and politeness, and before long Simon was sipping a cup of tea in an interview room. A plain-clothed investigating officer walked in followed by a constable. He shuffled some papers and picked up his pen to write notes before he looked up at Simon.

"So, what have you got to say for yourself?" The officer gazed at the dishevelled creature across the table. The suspect was an enigma, dressed in ill-fitting clothes yet apprehended riding a bike that was worth a fair bit – stolen obviously.

Simon paused. "I can't prove anything, and I've no identification on me, but I can explain."

"This should be worth hearing."

Simon tuned out for a moment. He was unsure the raw truth was going to convince even the most cooperative listener.

"I'm entitled to one phone call?" he asked.

"Certainly. But let's hear what you have to say first."

"Am I under arrest?"

"Let's hear what you have to say first, shall we? Your name, for the record?"

"Simon Peterson."

"And you were apprehended for dangerous driving on a motorcycle that you subsequently crashed?"

"Yes."

"And this motorcycle belongs to you?"

"No."

"Did you have the owner's permission to ride it?"

"Not exactly."

"So, do I take it you stole it then?" The officer scribbled notes on the pad.

"This is all very difficult to explain." Simon didn't want to mention the whereabouts of Bert's farmhouse or the death of the farmer and his wife with the possibility that he could be charged with murder.

"Take your time."

"If you would let me make one phone call, I promise you it can all be sorted out very quickly."

"We'll get to that in a minute. We'd just like to hear your version of events first."

"Am I under arrest?" Simon repeated, realising they had not read him his rights, though he wasn't sure of the precise order of police procedure.

"You do not have to say anything. But it may harm your defence if you do not mention when questioned something which you later rely on in court. Anything you do say may be given in evidence."

"Then I'd prefer not to say anything until my lawyer is present." Simon put his hands flat on the table.

"The name of your lawyer?"

He gave them the name of his most senior contact at the offices in Vauxhall Cross, and added that they were to say that Simon Peterson, late of Durban, South Africa, was being held on possible charges of murder.

The officer in charge leant across the desk and stared at Simon.

"You are having us on, right?"

"No. I'm allowed one phone call and this is the one I want you to make, with those exact words."

The policeman shook his head, glanced at the number he'd written down on his pad and stood up.

"London. Well it'll take time for someone to come all

the way up here, and if you are refusing to say anything further…"

"Not one word," Simon confirmed.

"So, what's this about a murder then? Who, and where?"

"Not one word," Simon repeated crossing his arms.

Simon could see they were itching to grill him further about the murder but the law forbade them from probing. The older man shrugged, told the younger one to take Simon to one of the cells, and left the room.

The sound of the cell door slamming echoed along the short corridor and left Simon sitting on a thin plastic mattress laid over a stone bench. They had removed his few possessions and all he could do was sit and wait and hope for the best. He stretched out on his back, stared at the ceiling and wondered where Amie was and what she was doing. He hoped both she and the baby were safe and well.

23 AMIE AND BEN

Amie knocked on the door and waited. She wasn't sure why she was nervous, but the Ben she'd known as her cameraman and then later when they'd saved each other's lives didn't relate to the Right Honourable Ben Mtumba, President of Togodo. In Africa, those in charge could practically do what they wanted: order a death, commute a life sentence, go to war and accumulate public money for their own purposes. She hadn't spoken to Ben since their first meeting. When she'd seen him at a distance, he either ignored her completely or simply didn't notice her. She knew that people in power could blow hot and cold at a moment's notice.

She knocked a second time, and a voice from the other side shouted for her to come in.

Ben glanced up at Amie and nodded for her to sit down.

She slid into a comfortable chair, the plush velvet clutching at her skirt as she wriggled to get comfortable.

The President put his pen down.

"I wanted to check with you that everything is ready for the day after tomorrow."

"But hasn't Gaga given you the itinerary?"

"Gaga Medwewe will tell me what she thinks I want her to say. I'm asking you because you will be honest with me."

"Mr President …"

"Ben."

"Right, Ben. We've been able to source most of the equipment and catering, but I need to chase up some of the suppliers today. I should have brought the list with me, but we are still waiting on confirmation for the crockery, some of the First Aid supplies and, would you believe we're still chasing glasses."

"But the drinks are sourced?"

"Oh yes, that was close to the top of the list."

"I have ordered that we start out early tomorrow in convoy. It will be cooler then."

"Yes. Have the numbers changed?"

"No. Personnel from six countries, plus my government officials, plus drivers, catering staff and workers. The army can fill in any gaps if you need extra labour."

"Is it true there will be a hunting party?"

Ben dropped his eyes and ignored her question.

"How long are you expecting to remain in Togodo?" he asked suddenly.

"I have no idea. It's up to Her Majesty's government, I guess."

"And they employ you now?" The President put a heavy accent on the 'you'. "A replacement for your husband, Jonathon?"

"How, what do you know about my husband?"

"Amie, this is my country. It is my job to know what is happening." He hesitated then said, "I trust you still feel loyalty to Togodo?" Ben's voice had a sharp edge.

"Of course I do. I love Africa – the people, the wildlife and the bush ..."

"Even though they have not always been kind to you?"

"I can see that in the midst of a civil war it's impossible to be neutral, but I have reason to be grateful to the people who were kind to me and saved my life."

"Good. I should hate your loyalties to raise a conflict. Be aware Amie, that the country that will win this contract to mine the minerals may not be your country of origin. I must do what is best for my country, and I will not allow you to interfere in any way. I hope you understand that."

"Yes, I do, Ben. But it could be disastrous for the world balance of power if the wrong country was successful, wouldn't you agree?"

"The rest of the world can sort out its own problems. My role as President is to do what is best for my own people."

"Yes, of course."

"We are old friends, Amie, and I brought you on board as someone who will help to run this business safari successfully. I hope you will not get involved in anything else."

"No, of course not." Amie's heart sank. Ian Fleming was using her to spy on the guests while first the President had asked for her help, and now he was telling her to back off. Had he only recently found out about Jonathon's real job in Apatu and if so, did that mean he didn't trust her?

As she walked back to her office, Amie ran through the conversation in her head. Ben apparently knew Jonathon was a spy, yet he had never mentioned that before. How long had he known? He also hinted he knew that Amie was one as well. He would be watching her very carefully. The other point he'd made quite clear was he would choose the country that promised the most to Togodo, and loyalty to her and her fellow British would not come into the equation.

She would love to beg him not to entertain signing with the North Koreans; they were threatening to let off nuclear bombs against the United States, and if they colluded with China, they could hold the rest of the world to ransom.

Why had there been a shift in Ben's thinking? At their last meeting he'd asked for her help and advice, an extra pair of eyes to help him judge the best candidate. Now he'd turned full circle and told her to stay out of it. Perhaps that would make her job easier because she couldn't work for both sides at the same time.

Gaga was not in the office when Amie returned. She chided herself for letting her imagination run away with her. She was worrying over nothing, and in any case, there was nothing she could do about it. The only certainty was that Ben was President, and although they were still friends, she knew there was a clearly defined gulf between them. She felt she had been put firmly in her place. It was a humbling thought. She picked up the phone to call those companies that had not delivered as promised.

24 OUMA ADEDE'S WARNING

While Amie and Gaga were organizing the logistics of the grand safari, other meetings were taking place. On the other side of the palace Samuel Suma, Minister for Sport, plotted with Blessing Ochido, Minister of the Interior, as to how they could disgrace the President – or kill him.

Closeted in an empty office, Kirimu Nashele Minister of Finance was doing his utmost to coerce Ngonicansaga into becoming his wife, while Royal Papele, the Foreign Minister, was on the phone to a member of the North Korean delegation, listening to the personal offers they were making to ensure their name was on the mining contract.

Across town, the diplomats in the British Embassy had earmarked Kirimu Nashele as their best bet to replace Ben. Kirimu was the perfect puppet since his love of foreign travel and a very expensive lifestyle made him the most susceptible to bribery.

The French in the meantime were keen not to upset the current government, and were discussing any weakness or leverage they could use against their competitors. They were aware of the indiscretions that resulted in Edward Keller being posted to the US Embassy, and were prepared to use that knowledge if it would further their cause.

Not far from Brianwood Mall, in the Russian Embassy,

they targeted Samuel Suma. The Sports Minister's plans for a new football stadium and his desire to put Togodo on the world map by hosting the FIFA World Cup in the near future, told them he would be happy to champion their bid. The Russians were prepared to promise him the earth in return for his cooperation and they were convinced they knew how to manipulate FIFA. They had no intentions of losing this contract, no matter what it took.

There was no indication which way China would jump and in the United States Embassy, Edward Keller talked to his staff about how they could ensure they could get the leverage and be the ones signing on the dotted line.

They all had the same problem. Ben Mtumba had given no indication as to how he would conduct the negotiations. He hadn't discussed it with anybody. Would this be just a 'look see' trip, showing them the exploration sites, or, as the rumours suggested, was there going to be an auction with the highest bidder walking away with the prize?

Amie left the office early to pick up some last-minute shopping. She parked on a side street, hopped out and walked around the corner and was hunting in her bag for her shopping list when she bumped into a lady walking the other way.

"I'm so sorry," she said and then took a step back. "Ouma Adede. How wonderful to see you."

"I see you Amie," the witch doctor replied.

She smoothed down her voluminous skirts with her free hand. She was dressed the same as when they last met: a full cotton black skirt reached her feet, a faded t-shirt which advertised a Madonna concert held in Europe years ago, beer bottle tops threaded round her wrists and ankles clinking as she moved and chicken bladders, bows, feathers, and beads in her hair. The outfit that proclaimed her status and power.

"This is a surprise," said Amie, delighted. "Tell me, how are you? Is everything well with your family?"

"Yes, it is all well. But I know you are here in Togodo. I see you many times."

Amie wanted to ask her friend why she hadn't said hello before but decided against it.

Ouma Adede steered her over to the area referred to as the Park. Once, it had been a well-tended green and shady area with trees, plants and manicured hedges in the middle of the city. Now, it was a neglected expanse of weeds, overgrown lawns, pathways and litter. There were used condoms and empty syringes lying about, and one of the metal lions on the gate post was now missing, possibly sold to a local scrap yard. The second lion head teetered dangerously to one side and probably wouldn't be there after the weekend.

The older lady manoeuvred Amie towards one of the grubby stone benches and pushed her down. Goodness, Amie realized, this was the same bench where she'd waited with Shalima for Ben to collect supplies. It was all so long ago now.

The witch doctor turned to Amie and grasped her hand tightly.

"I am very worried for you. I am most worried for the baby. You must not go north."

Amie gave a start, then remembered the medicine woman had known Amie was pregnant before she knew herself. It was just one of those things about African life that would never be understood by westerners. She had learned long ago not to question it.

"Ouma Adede, I am safe now, please don't worry about me. I am not going into the bush alone. Everyone else will be there, even the President, people from my own Embassy, and Gaga, and goodness knows how many army men as well. There can't be any danger this time." She paused. "Is Ben in danger? Is that why you are trying to warn me?"

"I talk only to you. I do not tell you dangers for other men and women."

"Are you sure I'm going to be in danger?"

Ouma Adede nodded and moved her hand to stroke Amie's tummy.

Amie put her hand over the witch doctor's.

"No, not this time. It can't be true. I will be quite safe. And Ouma Adede there is no way I can refuse to go north – both my Embassy and the President have ordered it. I will be in more danger if I refuse. Are your predictions, always right?" She looked closely at the wise face, trying to read the answer, but the witch doctor sat quite still for several seconds and Amie couldn't even guess what she was thinking.

At last Ouma Adede gave a gentle shrug, which told Amie nothing.

A gang of school children raced into the park, shrieking, pushing and shoving as they ran after a partly deflated football. Amie stared at them and worried for her baby. Images of Angelina, the little African she had fostered, flashed through her mind. Ouma Adede had warned her of danger before she took the little girl on a visit to England, and she had been right that time. Fate couldn't be that cruel, not again.

The witch doctor broke the silence.

"You must go where life takes you but remember my words. Beware of the little ones – and take care of your little one."

Amie stared at her puzzled. "Please Ouma Adede, can't you be a little more specific?" Amie wanted to grab her by the shoulders and shake her and beg the clairvoyant to tell her exactly what to expect and how she could avoid heartbreak.

Ouma Adede gave her a sad smile and shook her head. "The spirits of the ancestors, they speak, but they do not always show me all they know. Take care my Amie." She rose to leave.

"Wait." Amie put her hand out and grabbed her arm. "What can you tell me about Simon?"

The older lady paused and frowned.

"Is he all right? Is he alive? Please, do you know?"

"He is in a bad place. He is far away and I cannot see him clearly." She laid her hand on Amie's head as if in benediction. "You must be brave about your loss."

At least Simon was alive. She let out a long slow breath and looked up but Ouma Adede was gone.

Amie ran over the conversation in her head as she stood up and began to walk towards the shops. Was she going to lose Simon, or the baby – or both?

The witch doctor had always been right in the past. Amie hoped desperately that this time, her predictions were wrong.

25 SIMON'S BRIEF

Simon had no idea how long he was left in the police cell. He'd dozed for a while exhausted from the events of the day. On waking, he counted the tiles on the ceiling and the floor, peered through the fresh paint on the walls trying to decipher the graffiti that had been covered over and tried his best to sleep again. His nerves were jangling, but he was in the best place. He was hopeful that London would act quickly; they must have been wondering where he was. The most reassuring thought was that, now he was safe as a guest of Her Majesty, his biggest problems were sheer boredom and a creeping claustrophobia. His present accommodation assured him that he would not adapt too well to life in prison. Locked up for any period of time, he'd go stark raving mad.

The food wasn't exciting. At lunchtime, they'd pushed a plate through a hatch in the door with two tasteless sausages, a spoonful of lumpy mash, and a collection of mixed green vegetables accompanied by a cup of tepid tea. They'd taken his watch and he guessed it was now afternoon, although there was no way of telling from the little patch of grey sky he could see through the bars high up in the wall. He wondered if anything would happen before the next meal was due. Now that he'd escaped, he was fed up with going nowhere.

He was worried about Amie. He couldn't wait to contact her; he needed to know she was safe in the office in Durban. He could picture her walking along the beach as the sun rose over the Indian Ocean before going into work. In the evening she might have a drink at one of the many bars before returning to her flat in Umhlanga. With any luck, the moment he'd been debriefed, he'd be on the next plane back there.

The light outside faded and the unprotected bare lightbulb high up in the ceiling switched on. Simon heard footsteps outside and the key turned in the lock. A young police officer he hadn't seen before opened the door wide.

"Come along with me, Sir."

Simon stood up, thinking it strange that the police addressed criminals as sir. People behind bars were unlikely to be as polite.

He was taken back into the same interview room and to his relief Sir Gerald was sitting at the table.

"Thank heavens."

"Simon, what sort of trouble have you got yourself into now?" Sir Gerald rose to shake his hand.

"I didn't go looking for it, I can assure you."

The charge officer poked his head round the door. "Need a few moments?" he inquired politely.

"I'll call when we're through," Sir Gerald said.

The policeman nodded and closed the door behind him.

"Give me the brief version of events Simon. What happened? We lost you at the airport. You disappeared into thin air."

Simon described how he'd been taken through a side

entrance to avoid customs and immigration then the visit to the offices where they'd pumped him for information. At that point he paused and swore.

"Now I remember what's been bothering me. The office in London, supposedly one of ours, there was no Queen there."

"Pardon?"

"There was no portrait of the Her Majesty on the wall. I thought it strange at the time but then I forgot and it slipped to the back of my mind. If only I'd remembered sooner."

Sir Gerald scribbled down the street name and number, and told Simon to continue.

He finished his story and then said, "Do you know if they've found the burnt-out car at the farm yet?"

"They haven't mentioned it to me, and I'm not sure they would have connected the dots to you yet."

"The motorbike would have been registered surely?"

"Only if the farmer used it on the road. We forget, things move slowly in the countryside."

Realising he was a witness, Simon's heart dropped. "You can get me out of here, can't you? Now?"

"Yes, no problem there. I've spoken to the Chief Constable. But I suggest you give the police a full version of events, and I'll coordinate with the army to do a thorough recce of where they kept you. I think they'll be long gone by now. You've been lucky; we've had two other agents disappear without a trace in the last few months. Are you sure you were the only one locked up?"

"Quite sure, I only ever saw three of them and I don't think any of them were English. I should have been more suspicious when they asked me to fill in all those forms in London."

"Well, no good crying over spilt milk, but I'd like a list of as many of those questions as you can remember." Sir Gerald stood up. "Unfortunately, we don't have time for a more thorough debriefing. I need you on a plane as soon as possible."

"Where to?"

"Togodo. There's something I need you to sort out for me – highest priority." Then he glanced at Simon, "First, though, I think you need some new clothes."

Simon had forgotten he was still wearing farmer Bert's old clothes. He gave a wry grin. "Yes, the nearest outfitters I think."

Outside the police station, the air was crisp and clear. Simon savoured the freedom as he breathed deeply and relaxed for the first time in days. A slight drizzle fell, mirroring the street lights on the pavement and a damp chill penetrated his clothes. On the plus side, he was a lot fitter than he had been a few weeks earlier and he couldn't wait to get back out in the field in Africa under a warm sun and blue skies. However, if he was going to Togodo he would still be miles and several country borders away from Amie.

In the car, he asked to borrow Sir Gerald's phone. He punched in her number but it patched through to a voice recording telling him the number was unavailable. Before he could say a word, Sir Gerald held out his hand for the phone.

Simon sighed and relinquished it, wondering when he could get one of his own. The cell phone he'd stuffed in his pocket before his escape was lying on some Welsh hillside, soaked through and ruined. The police had handed back the roll of banknotes he'd stolen from the drawer in the farmhouse and he promised himself he would return it just as soon as he could arrange to transfer it from his own account – but for now, he'd hang on to it.

Slumped back comfortably in the government car, and against all Health and Safety rules, Sir Gerald lit his pipe and puffed between sentences as they drove back to London.

"What I don't understand, Sir, is why these guys went to all the trouble of abducting me. I still have no idea what their end game was going to be. The interrogation and the insane running round those hills didn't seem to have any purpose. They could have just rubbed a microdot of poison on my hands or attacked me with the end of an umbrella? That's more usual, isn't it?"

"They wanted information."

"From me? I can't think of anything that would be particularly useful to them. They interrogated me regularly, but always the same damn questions, real name, names of superiors, what work was I doing in Africa? I refused to answer, and I was amazed they didn't hit me, not once."

"That's reassuring. I take it they never mentioned mining contracts?"

"No, never."

"Good. You had what they wanted to know, but you didn't know it."

"You've lost me."

"We're expecting a rather nasty situation in Togodo. It's the reason we called you back for a briefing. We've known about the problem for some time, but now it's coming to a head. The new President, Ben Mtumba, has invited the whole bloody world to come and tender for the mining rights to minerals discovered and reported a few years ago."

"Not the Decker report?"

"One and the same."

"Oh, shit."

"Exactly. Now Ian Fleming tells me they're all about to hike north on a 'look see' safari, and he suspects the mining rights will be sold off to the highest bidder."

"That could be a disaster."

Sir Gerald paused to re-light his pipe, filling the back of the car with clouds of blue smoke as Simon watched the green countryside fly past through the sheets of rain blowing against the window.

His boss leaned forward, opened the cabinet in front of him and removed a bottle. "Whisky?"

"Thank you, Sir." Simon watched him pour a generous measure into two stainless-steel tumblers.

"They've certainly drummed up enough interest; the Americans, Russians, French, Chinese, and North Korea."

"North Korea. How did they get in on the act?"

"Remember they've been cosying up to China ever since Kim Jong-un paid a visit to Xi Jinping, who, as we know, is there for life. If they form an alliance, they will be a considerable force and the US is nervous. We're all nervous, they may have their eyes on South Korea. Working together it wouldn't take too much effort on their part to gather the south back into the Communist fold."

"And we're there as well?"

"For appearances sake, we have to be in there. It would look bloody suspicious if we said thanks, but no thanks."

"But if the truth comes out, all hell will break loose."

"Exactly. And that's why we need you there to scupper the talks in any way you can."

Simon sipped the whisky which flowed down his throat like silk – only the very best for Sir Gerald. "What about Ian? Isn't he already on the ground?"

"Yes, but he doesn't know what you know, and he can be a bit of a loose cannon. He blows hot and cold as the mood takes him. Simon, what you know, and what I know, doesn't go any further. We've managed to keep it under wraps so far and that's the way I want it to stay."

Simon leaned back against the padded leather seat, his mind whirling.

"I don't care what it takes," Sir Gerald took another puff on his pipe before continuing, "just get out there and upset the apple cart. You have to make sure no one signs anything."

"Without admitting the truth?"

"Of course."

Simon pinched the top of his nose and squeezed his eyes shut. He knew what Sir Gerald wanted and why, but he hadn't the faintest idea how he was going to do it.

26 GAGA'S STORY

As Simon boarded a plane at Heathrow Airport to travel south from London, Amie travelled north to the exploration area in Togodo. Unlike Simon, reclining against a leather seat in first class with a whiskey in hand, Amie perched on a cardboard container in the back of a rusty Toyota Land Cruiser, which had seen better days, clutching a bottle of warm designer water. Every time they went over a bump or dipped into a pothole her rear end bounced off the box, jarring her spine.

Beside her, Gaga Medwewe was immune to the discomfort, her wide, bulky hips stayed firmly on the other half of the box. She was in high spirits and chatted as they drove through the Apatu suburbs just before dawn. A cool breeze blew through the open windows, and Amie was glad of the jacket she'd put on. A few purple flowers from the jacarandas at the side of the suburban roads fluttered down, brushing the vehicles as they passed.

Gaga exclaimed in delight as they drove through the Brianwood area, pointing out the large, well-appointed mansions where the important people lived.

Through the early morning twilight, Amie could see some of the gardeners already arriving for work, and maids busy shaking out tablecloths and hanging out washing. Even before the sun was fully up, there was a buzz as the city outskirts awakened to a new dawn with an undercurrent of excitement for the new day.

Further out of town, the houses were scattered and the silver tarmac road stretched out in front of them as far as the eye could see. The truck raced past low-lying shrubs punctuated with acacia trees and open spaces. Now and again, herds of goats or cattle, followed closely by small boys waving sticks, slowed them down, and several times the driver had to swerve to avoid cows that had wandered onto the road quite unconcerned, a danger to traffic and themselves.

They sped past little villages of mud huts, each surrounded by low chicken wire fencing, the bare earth littered with broken beer crates and occasionally an old rusty car. Each village had two or three *spaza* shops, already serving workers catching the local taxis into the city. They were little more than lean-tos constructed of wooden planks, with a makeshift counter in front of piles of goods, from plastic buckets to sacks of mealie meal. Crudely built shelves supported tins of beans next to pilchards and corned meat, stacked neatly beside boxes of crisps. Most sold brooms, hoes, rakes, buckets and sweets, chewing gum and salt. A few of the larger shops boasted cold fridges supplied by Coca-Cola, its name emblazoned on the sides of the glass-fronted cabinets powered by portable generators or gas bottles.

Gaga pointed out a group of Africans waiting patiently by the side of the road. "Every morning my mother was up long before the sun. She would light the stove and heat the mealie porridge for our breakfast before waking us and putting on her good clothes to go and work in the city. She cleaned in a very smart house for some very important people in the government." Gaga laughed. "The thing she did first in the big house was to cook breakfast for that family too, but they had all kinds of good food to eat."

"How many of you were there in your family?" Amie asked.

"There were nine children, we all had the same mother, but we did not have all the same father."

"Your father did not live with you?"

"No. Mama told me he was away working in the mines in Johannesburg, but he never came to visit us."

"That's sad."

"No, it was a good thing because then maybe he would fight with the other fathers. I was the eldest, and the next one, she had the same father."

"And the others?"

"Many different men, I think. Sometimes Mama would go to the city at night, especially close to Christmas or a holiday when her Madam gave her extra money. Later, her tummy would get big and then we would have another brother or sister."

It never failed to surprise Amie. The African way of life, so fatalistic in the midst of what would appear to be a severely dysfunctional family – yet many of the family bonds were strong.

"As the eldest, it was my job to go and get the water every morning, very early. I also had to walk to the river in the evening two or three times for more water. The men, they decide that it is best to have the village close to the road, not near to the river. They do not worry that the women and children must go far to get water and to take the washing all the way to the river."

"How far was it to the river?" Amie asked.

"Two miles. In the summer it was easy, but in the winter time the earth was cold. We did not have shoes. I cut my feet and there was much blood. Being a girl, I did not have to look after the cows, that is work for the boys, but I had many chickens and they gave us the eggs."

Amie remembered an occasion when the hose had broken while she'd been helping her father water the garden. She'd lugged the watering can to the outdoor tap and filled it, not realising how heavy it would be. For a child it was backbreaking work carrying the can down a short garden path.

"We had many men come to the house, too," Gaga prattled on cheerfully. "Then Mama would send us out into the street to play, and said not to come back until she called us. As the eldest, I had to help Mama with the little ones, so I learned early to keep the house clean, and to wash and to cook, as well. But it was hard. Often, we had very little money and our tummies would be empty. The smallest ones would cry at night before they slept."

"Did you go to school?"

"Sometimes. If my brothers and sisters were ill then I could not go, but I learned to read and write, yes, and how to do arithmetic."

"Primary school and secondary school?"

"I did well at my first school, and I was top of my class, but I could only go to the secondary school for two years. It was not close by, and we did not have the money for the fees. I walked many miles to that school, but I got home when it was dark and Mama needed help … and then she was late."

"Oh." For a moment Amie didn't know what to say. 'Late' in Africa meant dead. "I'm sorry."

Gaga shrugged her shoulders. "Many people, they are now late, and Mama was almost thirty."

"Do you know what …?" Amie knew she shouldn't ask.

"They tell me it was her chest. So now I could not go to school, I had to be the new Mama. But the boys were very bad. They did not listen to me, they did not want to go to school, and they did not obey me."

"How did you cope?" By Amie's reckoning, Gaga would have been about thirteen and left with eight younger brothers and sisters to bring up.

"I look after the house just like Mama did, of course," her tone implied the question was unnecessary. "She taught me everything. But we needed money, so I walked to the city, to the house where Mama worked, and told them I wanted to clean for them."

"And you were what, thirteen?"

"I was almost fourteen. I was a woman. Many girls my age get married by then. But I did not want to do that. I saw that so many children were hard work for Mama. I liked the city, and I wanted to get a good job in a smart office."

"So, what happened then?"

Gaga told her story simply, without self-pity or entitlement. She was one brave girl who had beaten the odds and done well for herself. She spoke in that delightful way of many Africans — mixing tenses, ignoring contractions – a nightmare if you were part of the grammar police brigade.

"I was so fortunate. They have in this house a girl

about my age, and she is going to the good English School. When no one is looking she shows me her books and helps me to learn. Sometimes she allows me to take books home, and at night I light the candle and go through all the words and the questions. She looks at my work and tells me what is right and wrong. She is my new teacher, Sibonyana, she is a very kind girl."

"Are you still friends?"

"Yes, indeed. Her parents went to the English school and told them how hard I had been working, and then they take me there and ask me to answer some questions on papers. The teachers were so kind, they tell me I was good enough to go to the school every day and have lessons like all the other students. So now I get a proper education. Then, when I finish they help me get the work in the palace and they tell them how good I am, and I learn they are good friends of Minister Kirimu Nashele. At first, I am working there cleaning, but then one of the men …" Gaga started giggling and Amie had to wait patiently for her to calm down before she continued her story. "He, this man, he thinks I am a clerk and he shout for me to come and write for him." She lowered her voice. "Even though he was an important person in the government he cannot write, except for his own name. So, then I am very brave and I ask him if I can do all the writing for him because I have been to the International School, and he agreed. So, I am not a cleaner any more, now I am a secretary."

"That's an amazing story. You must be so proud of what you've achieved."

"Then when I am working for that man, I learn more at the college, they have the lessons at night in the big school and I pass my exams. So now I am a proper secretary, with the certificates to tell me that."

"And your family?"

"I go to see them on pay weekend, and I take them money and food, but they are happy to live in the farm areas. Many people do not want to work hard, and they will be peasants." She sniffed loudly, reminding Amie of how deprecating Gaga had been about Togodians living in the rural areas. At the time she'd thought it unkind of Gaga having a poor opinion of them, and she wasn't afraid of expressing it either. Now Amie could understand, because Gaga had been a rural peasant herself and worked her way out to what she saw as a better way of life in the city.

"And I take money for my son as well. I want him to grow up to be a big important man."

"You have a son?"

"Yes. He is now almost ten years old." Gaga smiled proudly and rummaged in her bag and dug out a faded, dog-eared, photograph of a badly dressed skinny little boy standing in the doorway of a rural hut. "See he is so handsome."

"Yes, he is." Amie stared at the picture wondering how he felt with his mother away for most of the time. "You must be sad to only see him at month end," she handed the photograph back and Gaga stuffed it into her purse.

"He does not mind. The family, they care for him. I was pregnant also with a little girl, but at two months she was late."

Amie mumbled how sorry she was, and turned to look out of the window. She mulled over Gaga's contradictions.

She'd said she was not going to get caught like her mother, yet she was only in her late twenties and had already experienced two pregnancies. She also had no problem allowing the rest of her relatives to raise her son, and Amie guessed that the next youngest girl in the family had taken over Gaga's job as mother, when she went off to work in the city.

As they travelled north, the villages were less frequent and Amie was spared the constant exclamations from Gaga about how these stupid people were content to live without running water and electricity. Earlier she'd said people were happy with their lives and had little ambition to do anything else, however hard their lot. It was confusing for Amie. From what she could gather, Gaga was the only one of the nine children to drag herself away from the rural life and climb the African version of the corporate ladder. It was a shame that the spoilt brats growing up in the west, who had it handed to them on a plate with no effort on their part, did not appreciate the advantages they were given. It was likely that Mama had contracted AIDS like so many on this continent, especially given the number of boyfriends she'd had. It was also a testament to survival that her nine children still lived. Gaga had not been specific about that and Amie didn't ask. In African culture, Amie had already been very rude, asking Gaga personal questions. She condemned the rural area where her boy was growing up. Did she see her own child as primitive? Yet, she had ambitious plans for him? It was a conundrum. It was Africa.

The sun began to beat down, turning the inside of the vehicle into a sauna on wheels. Amie could feel the sweat trickle down her back, making her shirt stick to her like a second skin. This morning the nausea had not bothered her and she surreptitiously stroked her tummy, sending mental messages of love to the tiny baby growing inside her. As soon as they got back to Apatu, she would have to come clean with Ian and tell him she was pregnant. What he would do, she had no idea, but already she'd had to buy cargo pants in a larger size, with elastic waists and voluminous t-shirts to conceal her condition. When she thought about the baby, her mind wandered to where Simon might be and if he was safe. She didn't know how she would face life without him.

She wriggled, trying to get comfortable. The dust flew up from the wheels and wafted into the car, and they were forced to close the windows. The tarred road leading to Budan had been left behind hours ago as they headed north-west deep into Luebos territory, the same tribe that had risen up with the M'untus tribespeople against the Kawa in the recent civil war. Amie wondered how safe it was for the President, as Paramount Chief of the Kawa tribe, to arrive in Luebos tribal lands along with foreign delegates and armed troops. Were the foreigners and their envoys aware of the danger?

27 SIMON FLIES SOUTH

Simon settled into his seat and fastened his safety belt. The only last-minute ticket available was in First Class, and Sir Edward had to fork out a fortune to send Simon back to Africa in a hurry. He was pleased to see an empty seat next to him; he was not in the mood to talk to fellow passengers. He had too much to think about.

The plane taxied towards the runway, and the cabin crew waved their arms demonstrating the safety procedures. Few people paid them much attention. Even the films showing the bail out instructions on video were ignored. Simon smiled as he remembered the news clip about an evacuation from a British Airways plane where all the passengers had taken time to grab their hand luggage before they disembarked.

As the aircraft gathered speed down the runway before lifting off and climbing up through the dense clouds, he mulled over the strange instructions Sir Gerald had given him. He was not travelling in his own name nor on a diplomatic passport; he was John Smith. Like Amie, he did not have a high regard for the faceless individuals at Vauxhall Cross who assigned names to operatives in the field. He could only assume they had no imagination at all. Perhaps it was a form of revenge or passive aggression.

He accepted a drink from the hostess, who thumped

and bumped the trolley down the aisle, before settling down to sleep, wondering if he dared try using a borrowed phone to contact Amie when he landed in Apatu. He wouldn't put it past the London snoops to have him shadowed and Sir Gerald would be furious if he found out he'd broken his cover.

Simon hadn't realized how tired he was, and even some extreme turbulence over the Sahara in the Boeing 747 was not enough to wake him as the elderly plane transported passengers and cargo south to Africa with its equally turbulent history.

His first task on landing was to connect with a local Togodian named Lucky, who would meet him at the airport. Simon had never met anybody called Lucky, but many Africans were given interesting names by their parents or they used the pet names they acquired in early childhood.

Simon was to avoid the British Embassy at all costs. Lucky would take him to a downtown hotel, where his team would be waiting. They would hire a car, provide arms and a satellite phone, and the four of them would drive to designated GPS co-ordinates to meet with a local chief, and they would stay in his village. Once he'd reported back to London, they would instruct him on what to do next. He was told not to go in the camp where the President and dignitaries were, but to observe and report back via the satellite phone. He would be instructed on a day to day basis. Overall, his task was to do as much damage control as necessary to protect the good standing of Her Majesty's government.

Fact was often stranger than fiction, and the

undercover world was no exception. Growing up, you learned that yours was the only country that was honourable. Great Britain told the truth and could be counted on to do the right thing. It was all nonsense. Countries lied, broke promises, and deceived other countries and their own citizens. They were worse than a playground of squabbling toddlers, and Simon was just one micro cog in the whole game.

Sir Gerald had told him before he'd left England they'd located the manor house which showed signs of a hasty departure. It had been let out over the Internet by an ex-banker now living in the Caribbean, and the trail had gone cold there. The offices where Simon had been taken in London were rented on a daily basis and were now stripped bare leaving no paper trail and not a single fingerprint. SIS wouldn't give up and would investigate until they discovered the identity of his abductors.

28 ZEEBEE

The Land Cruiser drove into camp and Amie's behind was now completely numb. With each passing mile the box she'd been sitting on had become harder and the bumping that threw her up in the air must have caused bruising. She uncurled her legs and shuffled towards the door to ease herself out.

In comparison, Gaga hopped out without any trouble, despite her bulk. She wasn't sweating as hard either.

"So much easier than walking, and so much faster." She smiled at Amie.

Their driver had covered the miles without wasting any time. He hadn't bothered to swerve around the potholes but drove in a straight line like a bat out of hell – and it was the ride from hell.

Amie was surprised to see so much activity. The army, cooks, labourers and camp staff had been busy. A rough hedge of prickly acacia surrounded the camp to which they had attached swathes of green plastic artificial grass reaching four metres high to provide privacy. It looked incongruous in the middle of the bush. The largest structure within the compound was a white marquee. To either side were eleven distinct areas, each pegged out with low picket fences painted white, and each housed three luxury tents. The layout was like a mini United Nations and no expense had been spared.

Amie looked inside one of the tents. The floors were laid with polished wooden tiles, the camp beds looked comfortable, set well off the ground beneath mosquito nets attached to the roof above. A wardrobe, dressing table, a small side table, a desk with chair, and a washstand with jug and basin completed the fittings.

Gaga crowded in beside her. "They have done well, yes?" she beamed. "These are tents good for a king, or a president."

"I'm sure that a few Heads of State would rather be here themselves, than represented by their government officials."

"Let us go now to see that the caterers have everything they need. It is all going to plan. This is very good."

"When are the bigwigs arriving?"

Gaga looked puzzled. "What is this bigwigs?"

"Sorry. I mean the dignitaries."

Amie wondered if she had offended Gaga. She'd spoken without thinking. Africans took their leaders very seriously and treated them with reverence. In some countries you would be put to death for mocking the President.

"They will be coming soon."

"Today?"

"Yes, late today." Gaga marched off to a tent at the rear where Amie guessed the cooks were stationed. She trailed along behind her. The main marquee would serve both as a dining hall and a conference venue. The long tables were set up between rows of chairs with gilt backs and velvet-covered seats. It looked out of place in the African bush. Amie eyed the white tablecloths and wondered how long they would stay so clean.

"Now the ablutions," murmured Gaga, as she scuttled off to inspect the facilities there.

"Where are we going to sleep?" Amie hurried to keep up.

"The spare tents there." Gaga pointed to one side. "You and I are to have one together, that is right, no?"

"Yes, I mean no. Of course it isn't a problem."

"We tell them they bring only three people for each country, so if they bring more there is no bed for them." Gaga chuckled, it was her moment of glory; it thrilled her that everything was in place. Amie had never seen a more organized lady, and she had every right to be proud.

Gaga took Amie's hand and squeezed it tight. "It is all good yes? I think our President will be very pleased."

"I think you've done a wonderful job," Amie smiled at her and then gave her a hug. "No one could have done it better, Gaga."

The lady beamed brightly and, pulling Amie by the arm, they walked back to the Land Cruiser. "Now we make our tent nice to be in."

"And those tents outside the *boma*?" Amie asked her as they made their way over.

"They are for the kitchen people and the lower workers." Gaga sniffed to show her attitude towards the ordinary people. "We do not have them to sleep in here near our beloved President."

Amie thought that if his people loved him as much as everybody said they did, he could be in no danger from them, but then status was everything in Africa, and everybody knew his place. A chief was to be obeyed, given any privileges he asked for and was never questioned.

There were always small mutterings led by the newly educated youth, but it would take many generations to acknowledge that all people are equal despite their tribes and status at birth.

The late afternoon sun beat down on the sandy soil. Small stone chips glistening in the sunshine made Amie wonder what treasures lay undisturbed beneath their feet. She gazed through the *boma's* entrance at the miles and miles of pristine African landscape. In the distance, she could see a herd of what she thought were Thompson's gazelles, with their brown backs, white tummies and the distinct horizontal black strip in between. The two straight horns rising from the top of their heads gave them an exotic look. While one or two kept guard the others nibbled the short grass or browsed on the lower bushes. Amie remembered Dirk telling her they were the most common antelope in Africa and could run up to fifty kilometres an hour, zigzagging to avoid predators. They often followed herds of zebra and larger game such as wildebeest, and she hoped she might catch sight of more animals. At the same time, they attracted predators: cheetahs, lions and hyenas, but it was doubtful they would come anywhere near the camp with so many people around.

She drew in the warm dry air and exhaled slowly. This was the real Africa, not the cities, re-designed to be carbon copies of those in the west with their busy highways and high-rise buildings. Soon, this place too would be spoiled by man. They would erect quarters for workers and supplies, build a mine head, and the peace would be shattered by the noise from the machinery raping the earth of the minerals man required to live his modern lifestyle. She sighed. There was no stopping progress, and diminishing numbers would experience this land and its unique animals in their natural state. She reminded herself she was one of those lucky people, as she turned to grab her backpack from the truck.

Several miles behind them, the convoy of over twenty cars carrying the various government officials and their entourage made its way slowly towards the camp. It would have been sensible to have provided bush vehicles suitable to the terrain, but the members of the Togodo council opted for limousines, as befitted their illustrious guests. While the occupants enjoyed the air conditioning, they suffered the bumps and jolts as the softly sprung cars followed the weather-beaten dried mud roads.

They were preceded front and rear by army and police personnel on motorbikes, each with their headlights blazing and blue lights flashing. The cavalcade looked out of place as it rumbled towards the prospective mining area.

Ben Mtumba rode in the second car with Kirimu Nashele, who was sulking because he'd planned to travel with Ngonicansaga. He'd insisted she be included in the party in the hope he'd persuade her to marry him. If she refused, maybe he would get to bed her before they returned to the capital. She would have no reason to refuse him marriage then.

In the car behind them Samuel Suma, the Right Honourable Minister for Sport, was closeted with Blessing Ochido, the Right Honourable Minister of the Interior. They had agreed that Ben Mtumba should be got rid of, but it had to be done discreetly and with no blame falling on either of them. During the journey, they discussed various ways of accomplishing this. Blessing had already visited one of the best-known witch doctors in the capital, but it wasn't wise to ask outright for a curse against Togodo's most important citizen. He had to pretend he wanted rid of a man who was vying for his wife's affections, but by not giving the medicine man the real intended victim's name it would weaken the effect of the spell. The best he could do was to buy the *muti* (medicine) which turned out to be handfuls of crushed leaves and powder the witch doctor promised him would kill the strongest man. He'd also purchased a small bag containing a variety of bones, herbs, grains and animal hair. He was assured that should he put these beneath the man's pillow, he would not wake the following morning. Blessing hoped the medicine man was right; the *muti* had cost him a fortune.

What neither Samuel nor Blessing admitted was that the moment Ben Mtumba was dead, they each planned to denounce the other. They were friends because they needed somebody to pin the blame on afterwards. As they travelled up north, they discussed ways to dispose of their leader and questioned whether they could involve the head of the army who would be guarding the camp.

In the car carrying the Russian delegation, they were deciding who to support in the event of Mtumba's death. The President's cabinet members thought their assassination plans were a well-kept secret, but they were mistaken. News of their discussions had leaked to most of the diplomatic corps in Apatu, and each Embassy was choosing who to support when the time came. Who would be the most malleable? Who was the greediest? Africa was a more stable place under puppet regimes and this one came with a lucrative mining contract. They could always help out with the assassination as long as they could hide their involvement and escape detection.

Kirimu Nashele was the first choice for both Britain and Russia, while Edward Keller was now instructed by his government to cultivate Royal Papele, the Foreign Minister.

What the Chinese, French and the North Koreans, thought and what they planned to do, was anybody's guess.

Amie stood in the doorway of her tent watching the cars arrive. As the guests climbed out, she grinned when she saw they were all wearing suits. How ridiculous, to follow protocol out here in the middle of equatorial nowhere. The sun dipped low, its heat dissipating across the sky, but the earth held residual heat, and the thermometer showed thirty degrees.

Gaga pushed past her to confer with Ben's chief aide, and Amie noticed that Mathilda hadn't come on safari. That was a relief. She would not have to spend time avoiding her.

She made no eye contact with Fleming as he walked past her with a camp attendant showing the British delegation to their tents. Amie thought that she and Gaga were the only women there, even the cooks and camp attendants were all male. But then she saw the girl from the Grand Hotel coffee shop clamber out of the last car, after two suited gentlemen who appeared to be bodyguards. The girl blinked in the sudden light and looked around fearfully. She was dressed in a bright cotton dress, which looked new, and she clutched a plastic bag which Amie guessed must be her luggage.

While each delegation disappeared into their respective quarters, Gaga ran around fussing, worrying, and getting into quite a tizzy about everything being in order. She rushed over to the girl and there followed a heated conversation. Gaga looked furious.

Amie strolled over. "Is there a problem?" she asked. The new arrival looked as if she was about to burst into tears.

"I was not expecting another female." Gaga was incensed. "They do not tell me this, and now I have no bed for her. This is most inconvenient."

The girl put her head down, muttering, digging into the loose earth with her sandal.

"I'm sure we can make a plan," Amie put her arm around the girl's shoulder and gave her a hug. "She can stay in our tent with us, can't she Gaga?"

"There is no bed. We have only two beds!" Gaga was not letting go without a fight.

A short fat man pushed his way forward and grabbed the girl. "Come. I show you where you will stay."

To Amie's horror, he dragged her away, as she stumbled along behind him looking miserable.

"Who is that?" Amie asked.

"Our esteemed the Right Honourable Minister of Finance, Kirimu Nashele," Gaga replied proudly.

Amie shuddered. *This* was the man Ian Fleming and Her Majesty's government wanted to deal with? And she'd recognised the voice – she'd heard it before, in the hotel coffee shop. This was the worm who was coercing the poor child into marriage against her will, the girl who had loved Ben from childhood. She sighed. It would be unwise to get involved, but if an opportunity presented itself, Amie wouldn't be able to stop herself interfering. She wanted to help the girl.

The safari was running according to plan, and there was nothing for Amie to do. She wandered over to the *boma* gate and, nodding and smiling at the guards, walked through and out into the veld. She usually enjoyed being in the bush and the feeling of her microscopic place in the wide-open landscape that was unpolluted and undisturbed by man, but not this time.

Loud voices floated over to her from the camp, shouts and laughter, dishes banging from the kitchen area, and the odd car door slamming. They drowned out the loud squawks from six majestic grey and purple hadedas as they flew overhead to their chosen trees to roost for the night.

Amie sat down on a rock and gazed at the setting sun, just visible through the thorn trees, then something moving near her feet made her freeze and look down. It was a dung beetle, walking backwards past the rock. Its back feet clutched a huge ball of dung while its front feet propelled it along. It couldn't see where it was going, the dung-ball was much larger than the beetle and she'd once heard that the ratio of insect to dung could be equivalent in size to a person pulling six double-decker buses full of people. The little Taurus dung beetle was capable of rolling a ball over a thousand times its own weight, possibly the world's strongest insect.

It couldn't see where it was going, yet it pushed over the ground in a perfectly straight line. As Amie watched, the little creature reached a dip in the ground and lost its grip on the ball which started to roll away, but at the last minute it managed to hold on and was flipped over the top. Both beetle and dung-ball bowled over and over until they reached the bottom. Another dung beetle, probably its mate, Amie thought, scurried over to guard the ball while the first got back on his feet. Without pausing he took his position behind the dung and continued pushing it towards his goal. Only they knew where they would stop, mate and bury their eggs in the dung to feed the larvae that developed inside. Then they would bury the dung in the ground and find more dung. They rolled dung their whole lives.

Amie smiled and shook her head in amazement at this little contest of nature. To what extent would the mining operations upset the habitat for little insects like this?

A shout made her look up to see one of the guards walking over. He waved at her to come inside the *boma*. She stood up, dusting down her cargo pants, and sighed. This was not a real safari; this was business. As she wandered back to the gates, she spied a group of young boys in the gloom. They smiled and waved at her, and bouncing towards her, they arrived outside the gate at the same time.

Amie guessed they were children of the Luebos who lived in this area, the same tribe that had joined forces with the M'untus and started a civil war, grabbing power from the ruling Kawas. The reasoning behind the conflict had been to gain control of the minerals lying under their tribal lands, so they could benefit from its wealth. But they were no match for the Kawas, and their term ruling Togodo had been short. Within a couple of years, thousands of M'untus were butchered and the Kawas were back in power.

These were children with their white teeth shining out of smiling faces as they crowded round Amie. They held their hands out, but she shook her head. She had nothing to give them, and if she gave to one, she would need to give to all seven of them. She held her hands up to show they were empty and pulled out her pockets.

She put out a hand to ruffle one boy's head, his black curls were shining in the dim light. They followed her towards the gate like a pack of chattering starlings, but that's as far as they got. The guards, who had no compassion to offer this ragtag bunch, shooed them away, waving their guns. One clubbed a boy with the butt of his shotgun.

Amie checked the boy to see if he was badly hurt before rounding on the guards.

"You do not hit children, they are just little boys."

The soldier was taken back by Amie's attack, but gathered himself and pushed the children away.

Amie watched them to ensure the guards didn't hit the children again, but another soldier urged her inside and the gates closed behind her. She heard the men beating the children, and peered through the fake grass hedge, but it was impossible to see what was going on. There were a few cries and sobs, more thumps, and then silence.

Lights shone through the large marquee behind her and she heard the murmur of voices from inside. There was no reason for her to join them, she would collect her meal from the kitchen later. First, she would try to contact

Simon. He was rarely out of her thoughts and she worried about him. Her emotions swung from anger to suspicion and then to despair.

Before she reached the tent that she shared with Gaga, the lady herself jumped out, grabbed Amie and hurried her over to the main marquee.

"Take a look, is everything good? Something will go wrong. I can feel it in here." She thumped her chest with her fist.

"Calm down, Gaga. You'll be a nervous wreck by the end of three days." She squeezed her friend's hand and allowed herself to be dragged over to the smaller entry at the back of the tent used by the serving staff.

"Look inside," Gaga urged.

Amie slipped through the gap and was amused to see groups of men with glasses in their hands. None were interacting,, each contingent huddled like human *laagers*, avoiding contact with any other than their fellow countrymen.

Of the six nations, each had received invites for three delegates only, including any security detail. The invite had specifically stated that security would be provided by the Presidential guard and members of the Togodo armed forces. Bringing more bodyguards would be seen as an insult to the government, and since each country was desperate to win the auction, despite their reservations, they had all agreed.

The limitations did not apply to Ben and his four cabinet ministers. Between them, they had brought twenty bodyguards who were all lined up with their backs to the marquee walls.

Amie counted fifteen from the security detail, and eighteen men from the various diplomatic corps huddled in groups in the space between the long tables, mingling uncomfortably with the four Togodian ministers. Ben was nowhere to be seen.

Waiters, smartly dressed in black trousers and white jackets with unpolished shoes, shuffled between them balancing trays of cocktails and bite-sized pieces of food.

"They are not having a good time?" Gaga sounded distressed.

"I'm sure they will, once they get enough drink inside them. They're here in competition with each other." She nudged her companion. "Can you imagine six football teams all in the same dressing room before the big championship final?"

Gaga giggled, nodded her head, then shook with mirth as she pictured such a scene. Her over-sized breasts and backside wobbled, jelly-like and tears ran down her face.

"Even if they don't talk to each other, you have done an amazing job," Amie reassured her. "They won't find fault with your work."

Amie left Gaga to collect a plate of food to eat in her tent, which was preferable to sitting at the small side table reserved for Gaga and herself in the marquee. She didn't feel like listening to the chatter in the kitchen, most of which she couldn't understand.

Balancing a meal of roast beef, boiled potatoes and vegetables, she sat on her bed. She didn't feel like being sociable. She knew it was quite unreasonable of her to hope that this pristine wilderness would remain unspoilt, but there was no way to halt progress. Like the rape of the

Amazon rainforest, man was hell bent on destroying his world.

There was a scratching at the entrance to the tent and a small head appeared. It was followed by a wriggling body as the youngest of the little boys she'd seen outside the gate wormed his way through the front flap.

"How did you get in?" she asked, but he only smiled at her and shook his head. Of course, he wouldn't understand English.

He looked at the plate of food on Amie's lap and poked one finger in his mouth and rubbed his tummy with the other hand. The language was universal and Amie sighed as she passed over her plate. She didn't need to eat for two, the books about pregnancy warned you about that, and the cook had been generous with the helpings.

The boy grabbed it from her with both hands and bowed his head before scuttling over to the far corner. He slid down, dropped the knife and fork on the floor and supported the plate on his knees with one hand while shovelling in the food with the other.

He was stick thin and very hungry. Most of Togodo's wealth was spent in the urban areas, while little filtered to the tribes in rural areas. The poor kid's t-shirt had several holes in it, the seam on his shorts had split on one side, showing he wore no underpants, and like the majority of children, his feet were bare.

"I wonder how you managed to get inside the *boma*?" Amie murmured. The gates had closed at sunset and she'd noticed there were soldiers on guard with patrols outside as well. He must have burrowed under the fence, he was skinny enough. There were dust particles on his face, and his fingernails were caked in dirt.

He mopped up the last of the gravy with a piece of roast potato, and then licked the plate clean. He looked up at Amie and shuffled over on his bottom, replaced the cutlery on the plate and handed it back to her.

"My name is Amie," she said patting her chest. "Your name?"

"Zeebee," he said pointing at his own chest, and then Amie. "Amieeeee?" he cocked his head to one side.

She laughed and stroked his cheek smiling at him. "Nice to meet you Zeebee," she said. "Are you Luebos?"

Alarm spread over his face and he looked down, but then crawled over to Amie's backpack and opened it.

"Oh no you don't, that belongs to me. It is not for you." She yanked the rucksack away from him and put it on the far side of the bed.

"No, that is bad, you do not take. This, is Amie's, it is mine, not Zeebee's." As she spoke she pantomimed her words, shaking her head and wagging a finger at him. As much as she hated to, she would have to hand him over to the guards and have him escorted away from the *boma*. He was a security risk and should never have got into the compound. She felt mean, but if he riffled through cases belonging to the diplomats and helped himself, all hell would break loose.

Before Amie had a chance to grab hold of him, they heard voices outside and Zeebee leapt to his feet. He slithered out of reach and was out of the tent in a flash. Amie jumped up and followed him, but by the time she had opened the flaps wide enough for her to get through, he had already disappeared into the darkness. She looked at the main gate, which was still closed and guarded. She followed the inside of the perimeter fence and would have missed the hole except for the fact that her foot kicked an empty cardboard box. As she bent to put it back, she noticed that somebody had burrowed under the fence close to the granite rock forming the fourth side of the compound. *So that's how he got in.* She would have to inform the guards, but she hesitated, knowing that if they caught him they would beat him – possibly to death. Who could she talk to?

She made her way back to her tent and found Gaga in tears.

"What's the matter?" asked Amie putting her arms around the distraught woman.

"Oh Amie, the men they fight, they are shouting at each other. What can I do?"

"Hush now, don't let it upset you. Are they hitting each other?"

"No, but they are shouting loudly."

"I'm not surprised, they are in big competition and that's what men do."

"You do not think they are angry that the place is not to their liking? If they complain to our President, then he will send me away from the palace."

"No. I can't think of a single thing you have forgotten. You've organized this safari brilliantly. You mustn't blame yourself. I couldn't have done it half as well."

Amie's heart went out to her new friend, who was beside herself with doubt. Giving her an extra hug, she slid off the bed and peered out of the tent. There were raised voices in a mixture of languages from inside the marquee, and it was too tempting not to creep closer and see what was going on.

Checking to see that Gaga was not following, Amie marched across the compound to the service entrance, and looked inside. She only knew a couple of the diplomats by name: the two she had met at the cocktail party, Vladimir Petrovnikov from the Russian delegation, and the middle-aged, brash Texan whose name she couldn't remember.

Hiding behind the open flap, Amie looked for Ian Fleming. He was not involved in the shouting going on between five of the diplomats. Amie muttered to herself that women would have got the job done without all the hot air.

She was returning to her tent when an arm grabbed her from behind.

"I saw you peeping at us and I am so delighted you are here. We can get to know each other better," whispered a voice in her ear.

Her instinct was to swing round and knee her attacker in the testicles, followed by a sharp blow to the side of his neck. But sanity prevailed. This wasn't a street yob, but a government official with diplomatic immunity, and she knew who it was.

"Vladimir Petrovnikov, we've met before, I think!" She smiled as she spun out of his grip.

"Ah, you remember me. That is good." His teeth shone in the dim lights mounted on poles around the perimeter of the *boma*.

"How could I forget," murmured Amie. "Well it is nice to say hello again, but I'm on my way to bed."

"But no, it is too early for sleep, unless you have something else in mind?"

"I beg your pardon?"

"You like to come with me, yes? I have excellent vodka in my tent." Vladimir made another grab for her but Amie stepped back.

"I am flattered by your offer, but I'm exhausted, it was hard work organizing all this." She backed away as quickly as she dared, then waved towards the marquee. "I'll sort that out for you first thing in the morning," she called out to somebody behind him.

As Vladimir turned to see who she was talking to Amie spun round and dashed towards her tent.

Gaga was asleep, but there was no sign of the young girl. The odious Kirimu must have taken her into his tent. At this very moment, the child was probably being raped and there was nothing Amie could do to help her. All she wanted to do was curl up and sleep. She wriggled out off her clothes, and pulled her voluminous nightshirt over her head. She stroked her tummy to see how much of a bump she had, before crawling into her sleeping bag and turning off the small gaslight. In a matter of seconds, she fell into a deep sleep.

29 ONE OFFER AFTER ANOTHER

Ben lay on his bed exhausted. He should mingle with his guests, but he didn't have the energy. He had met the delegates this evening and was weighing up his options.

As soon as he walked into his tent and put his laptop on the table, Ed Keller pushed his way past the guard outside and stormed in.

"Can I help you?" Ben was hesitant to insult the diplomat for his lack of manners.

"Yeah, sure ya can." The Texan perched himself on one of the chairs. "See here, this auction, just want ya to know how it could upset the balance in the whole world. Ya do understand the importance of what ya got under the ground right here?" He tapped his foot on the wooden flooring."

"I've seen the reports, yes."

"Well see, if we let them Asians get their hands on them, it's asking for trouble. It could put the whole of the West in danger, and I know ya country trades a lot with us. It would put all that at risk can't ya see? Ya can't afford that."

"I have my own country to consider, just as you are thinking of the United States." Keller hadn't even had the manners to remind Ben who he was.

"Exactly, so we can do a deal right? Sweeten the pot a little? We'll guarantee the best price, to mine and export and – in turn, ya suggest what would be good for you, Mr President."

"Such as?" Ben raised an eyebrow.

"Well now, whatever ya heart desires. We'd be mighty pleased to assist in expanding your industries, road networks, helping with ya tourism. Hell, we got a couple a' billion United States citizens just busting to come over and see ya wild animals."

"I'm planning on developing Togodo, yes."

"We have a big pot to play with – bigger than any of these other countries – even Russia. And we're mighty interested in doing some back-scratching with ya, if ya get my drift. But that's not all. We think there should be something in it for you as well, as President. What ya say to a yacht, moored in the Caribbean, ya own little home when ya want to get away for a while? It can be arranged. You just name it and the great US of A will provide. Now, I'm not clever enough for all ya fancy talking and ya treaties and diplomatic garbage. I'm a simple man and I believe in calling a spade a spade. I think we can offer a sweet enough pill for us to be able to shake hands like gentlemen, right now. Whaddaya say?"

Ed Keller looked pleased with himself. There, he'd laid his cards on the table before any of the others had got a look in. Boy he was smart.

"You're offering investment for the country and a bit extra for me personally?"

"Yeah, ya got it right on. Anything ya heart desires and we can make a plan, just as long as we get permission for those metals below us. Money's no object, trust me."

"And you speak on behalf of your government?"

"Sure do, they told me to do whatever it takes."

"Thank you for the offer. I will certainly consider it." Ben bowed and looked towards the tent door hoping the American would take the hint and breathed a sigh of relief when he smiled, grabbed his hand, gave it a shake and bounced back outside.

That was only the start.

Having listened to the American, he instructed his guards to allow the other diplomats in, and one by one the ambassadors beat a path to his tent – the only difference being the Chinese and North Koreans came in pairs, both needing their interpreters. Every nationality offered him his choice of personal bribes if he would favour them. The Russians even came with a briefcase full of money.

If he accepted them all, he would own houses in six countries in the world, an equal number of mega yachts, bank accounts in Switzerland, or the Caribbean and just about every material possession he could dream of.

Ben closed his eyes. From the son of a small businessman and younger brother of a village chief, he had risen to ruling his country and being courted by the super powers who needed the minerals his poor, neglected country possessed. Ben Mtumba had the world's most prominent nations in the palm of his hand with their offers of personal wealth that would turn his life around. He could have anything he had dreamed of. He could satisfy Mathilda and make her the happiest wife in the world, just thinking of her caused a stirring between his legs. He was sad that she was not here, but the stomach upset which caused endless vomiting meant a long car drive was out of the question.

He began to fantasise about all the bribes he'd been offered. A dream that shattered when the first bomb rocked the camp.

30 THE FIRST ATTACK

A couple of kilometres away, a group of men patted each other on the back. The sound of the explosions bounced through the air telling them the strike had gone off exactly to plan, and this was only the beginning. They waited for the rest of the team to join them and went to their temporary quarters, satisfied with a job well done. Tomorrow, they would send somebody inside the camp and assess the damage. Their informant would be in position with precise information on the layout and where each delegation was housed. Then they could target their victims with more accuracy. Not too long to wait. They would be well rewarded for their work tonight.

31 AFTERMATH

The explosion shook Amie out of a deep sleep. She sat up in shock, threw herself onto the wooden floor of the tent and rolled under the bed holding her hands over her ears. All she could hear was a loud ringing and her head was buzzing. She felt, rather than heard, the two following bangs which sent shock waves reverberating through the *boma*.

There was silence for a few seconds, and then shots rang out, and several screams were followed by an eerie silence. She pulled her rucksack closer, fighting to get it under the mosquito net which wrapped itself around everything. Ripping the bag open, she felt inside for some clothes and wriggled into a pair of trousers and a warm jumper which she dragged over her nightshirt. She felt for a pair of socks and pulled on her walking boots. Nothing would protect her against bullets or grenades, but clothes gave her an illusion of invulnerability.

There were no more explosions so she wriggled out and looked over to see if Gaga was hurt.

Her bed was empty.

The ringing in her ears died down, and she heard footsteps running past the tent and people shouting.

Amie didn't know what to do. She hadn't been briefed regarding protocol in the event of attack. As far as the

African contingent were concerned, she was only there as a backup to Gaga who'd organized the event. She should look for Ian Fleming and the other two British guys and see if they had survived the bombing. It was the most logical thing to do.

A fire raged on the other side of the compound. The red glare provided a brilliant backdrop, highlighting the men running around like wraiths in the otherwise pitch-dark night.

There was no order, and nobody taking command. The guards and other military were absent – the soldiers and kitchen staff had been sent out as soon as they'd finished working so the only people left on the inside were the diplomats and the government ministers. How many of those outside the *boma* were left alive?

Keeping low, Amie scuttled to Ian's tent, but ran headlong into somebody who tried to grab her. It was impossible to see who it was in the dark as unseen hands tried to steer her back towards her tent, but she gave her attacker a sharp dig in the stomach with her elbow forcing him to step back. She seized her chance, raced past him, and made for the British tent.

Clouds of dust swirled round, making her cough and splutter. The acrid smell of gunpowder in the air stung her eyes. People were milling about unsure where to go or what to do.

Amie pushed her way through the crowds and bumped into Ian in the semi-darkness then floodlights illuminated the compound and the damage caused by the explosion. Despite the commotion, Amie was amused to see Ian in regulation red and white striped pyjamas buttoned down the front. He'd probably been wearing the same brand since boarding school.

All three of the tents inside one of the designated 'countries' were completely destroyed and one was still smouldered.

"Who was in there, they can't have survived?" Amie looked aghast at the damage.

"I believe the one on the right was occupied by the head of the Chinese delegation Xiao Ping Wang, but I'm not sure if any of the Chinese survived."

"I wonder what will happen now?"

"It's most unlikely that they'll abandon the auction, but we can only wait and see."

"Once news gets out, it will be all over the media. It could be a disaster for Ben."

"He's most probably the one behind this," Ian's voice was deliberately low.

"That's ridiculous Ian, why would he blow up his customers! It wouldn't make sense. What have you got against Ben and why don't you trust him?"

"I don't trust any of them. You can't force democracy and a civilized way of living on a people who are not ready for it."

"We were tribal ourselves once in Britain," Amie replied.

"Yes, a very, very long time ago."

Amie swallowed her next retort, now was not the time to get into an argument. "We should go and see if we can help." Ian held her back.

"Stay where you are. It's best that we don't get involved."

"We are already involved." She watched the chaos and noticed that nobody was taking charge. There were two bodies lying on the ground with no one attending them. There was no sign of either the doctor or the nurse.

Ian held Amie firmly by the arm, but from what she could see, her primitive First Aid skills would be of little help to the wounded lying a few feet away – and the dead were beyond redemption.

"Have you seen Gaga?" Amie asked Ian.

"No. Why, is she missing?"

"I have no idea, but she wasn't in the tent when the blast woke me up. I should go and find her." Amie tried to pull herself out of his grip but Ian tightened his hold and refused to let go.

Edward Keller came towards them.

"Thank God you're both okay," he exclaimed. "What the heck just went down?"

"We're not sure yet," Ian's voice was cold; it was too much effort to be nice to the obnoxious American. "I'm sure they'll tell us when they know."

"Yeah, well I wanna know soon if we're all traipsing back to Apatu. Y' all think they'll cancel this shindig?"

"I wouldn't know." Turning to Amie, Ian whispered in her ear. "Go and see if you can get a quiet word with Ben. If we're lucky he might talk to you, but even from a distance you can gauge his reactions and see what his response is."

Amie glared at him for using her friendship with Ben again.

She was apprehensive as she went to find the President. The last time she'd spoken to him, he was cool towards her and hinted that he knew she was a spy in Jonathon's place. If he believed that, he wouldn't trust her. When she reached his tent, a bodyguard stopped her and refused to allow her any further.

"I would like to speak to the President," she said politely with a smile. "He knows me well and I may be able to help."

The soldier shook his head, lifted his AK47 and pointed it at her. Amie took a step back and tried again. "If you would just tell him that Amie Fish wants to speak with him."

Whether the armed guard understood her or not, she wasn't sure, but he thrust the gun at her until it was only an inch from her chest.

Togodo's president stood in the doorway of his tent and beckoned Amie forward. The guard lowered his weapon and let her pass.

"Ben, are you OK?" Amie asked him.

"I am not hurt." He paused apparently lost for words then continued. "Xiao Ping Wang is late. I do not know what to say to the Chinese delegation."

"And the other two from China?"

"They are alive, they were in the big tent."

"Who would do this Ben? Who would attack the camp? Is it the Luebos?"

The President shook his head. "It could be many people."

Amie wondered if he was hinting that members of his own government were involved. She looked at the layout of the tents. The one recently occupied by Xiao Ping Wang lay on the opposite side of the compound to Ben's. Had the attackers chosen the left-hand row, it would be Ben and not the Chinese Ambassador lying dead only a few feet away. She shuddered and she could see how shaken Ben was. Despite being surrounded by his government ministers and a large army contingent, somebody had either broken in from outside or was already among those inside aiming to kill the President of Togodo. Standing beside him, she felt very vulnerable.

The early light in the east indicated the coming dawn, and above the chaos in the boma, the birds had flown back and were chirping merrily in the acacia trees outside the camp.

A soldier approached. He was wearing sufficient ribbons and medals plus gold braid looped over his shoulders and chest to ensure everybody would know he was important. He looked at Amie and said nothing until Ben indicated he could speak.

"My President, we believe it was a fire grenade. That is why the tents, they burned. We think there were three of them."

"Thank you," Ben said simply and watched as his army general walked away.

"Are you going to send everyone home?" Amie's words were tentative.

"No. That is not possible. We will not be scared by threats or grenades. We have work to do, we need the money to uplift my people. We go on." Ben nodded to the guard who followed him as the President turned away and crossed the *boma* to talk to his guests.

Ian stood with Edward Keller. They were joined by a third man, Kirimu Nashele. Amie was about to report what

Ben had told her, but something made her hang back in the shadows. It was something about the way the three of them were huddled together that made her pause. Did Ian have something to do with the deaths? Did the Americans? Had they tried to kill Ben?

Amie still thought of Ben as her friend and she'd take no part in blowing him to pieces. She slid between two of the canvas structures and worked her way along the back trying to get as close as she could to the whispered conversations. The overhead lights illuminating the compound made her task more difficult and she only overheard a few words, her ears were still ringing and sounds were muffled. "… next time … tomorrow … better luck … well rewarded." It was enough to convince her at least for now, that Ian and Edward were in league with the Finance Minister and the attack had been aimed at Ben.

32   SIMON MEETS LUCKY

The Boeing 747 jumbo jet touched down at Apatu airport and Simon grabbed his hand luggage. Long before they opened the doors, he stood in the aisle at the front of the queue ready to disembark. He was anxious to hook up with his team.

He rushed down the steps, dragging his cabin case behind him. He'd taken the time on the plane to make a list of the supplies he needed to pick up before heading into the bush.

He was surprised to be greeted by name. A young African was just airside and held out his hand.

"It is Mr Simon, yes?" he said.

"Excellent guess. It is indeed."

"I am Lucky."

Simon was about to agree it was lucky they'd made contact so quickly until he remembered that Lucky was the man's name. They shook hands and hurried into the airport, where the fans did little to dissipate the heat. Simon sweated profusely in his winter clothes and couldn't wait to change into something more suitable.

His companion steered him to the far end of the immigration counter, holding out his hand for Simon's passport. He slapped it on the counter and spoke in rapid Togodian to the sleepy official on duty who rubbed his eyes, leaned forward, and studied the document. To

Simon's amusement he held it upside down before turning it the right way up. The immigration officer glanced at the picture, stared hard at the new arrival's face, then nodded and stamped the document several times using a variety of stamps in different colours before leaning back in his seat and closing his eyes again.

Simon was relieved he hadn't been asked questions, even though Sir Gerald had given him a basic background story. He hardly looked like a tourist in the clothes he was wearing, and wasn't confident anybody would believe him. He had no hotel booked and no official safari planned either. There had been too little time to set up a proper cover for him.

He grabbed his passport and walked outside with Lucky to an old Toyota Corolla. Lucky bowed slightly as he held the passenger door open. He flung Simon's case onto the back seat and climbed in behind the wheel.

Simon felt for his seat belt but there wasn't one. The moment Lucky started the car, he was first thrown against the dashboard and then back in his seat as Lucky wrenched the gear stick from reverse into second gear.

Lucky smiled at him. "This one pedal, it does not work so well, so sometimes the car, it jumps."

"Yes," Simon said and pushed himself right back into his seat and held on to the broken roof handle. "You might need a new clutch?" he observed as Lucky attempted to grind the gear stick into third.

"Ah, but it is a good car. It can go many more miles yet. I have it long time."

A bloody long time, Simon thought eying the stuffing leaking out of the front seats, the cracks in the dashboard from the sun's heat blasting through the visible areas not covered by the bright orange, fluffy cover which stretched from one side to the other.

Lucky showed his love for his car with the dangly decorations swinging from the rear-view mirror. Simon observed them: a bald monkey, a furry tiger, a small bag he suspected contained muti for protection, a crucifix, and a small black plastic figure dressed in traditional costume.

The car left the airport and headed into the city, but before they reached the suburbs Lucky pulled over to the side of the road and brought the Corolla to a shuddering halt. He turned to Simon. "The men in London they tell me you have something for me?"

"Yes, of course." Simon pulled out an envelope from his coat pocket and passed it to Lucky who tore it open and scanned the contents.

"Yes, this is what they tell me to do and it is done already. "

Simon raised his eyebrows.

"I am to make the disconnection to the cell phone tower that is near the campsite, where the President takes all the foreigners. This way they cannot talk to anybody, see, their cell phones they do not work now."

"How did you do that?"

"I jam them with radio waves. But I will have to wait until we are much closer to test it. Now, I am to give this to you." Lucky leaned over and picked up a case from behind the passenger seat and dumped it in Simon's lap. Simon opened it and took out a small satellite phone. It wasn't new, but it looked as if it worked.

"With this," Lucky pointed to the case, "you can talk to London when we go to the site."

"We? Are you coming with me?" Simon had assumed that Lucky was just his airport contact. He looked too skinny and frail to be part of an assault force."

"Yes, I am to stay with you. We go together with the others. That will be good, yes?"

"But not in this car?" Simon was alarmed, he didn't want to risk getting stranded halfway to the mining site.

"Oh, no, no, no, no, no," he cried. "London has ordered a nice Jeep for us from the best car rental place in town, and I have put in water and food and the right safari equipment. We go to get it now."

"I need to get a few things like more suitable clothes."

"Ah, yes of course. There are shops near to here, so we go there now, and then we go to get Trident and Bones."

"Pardon?" Simon's face creased in a frown.

"Trident and Bones, Mr Simon. Those are the names of our team members."

"Oh, I see." Only in Africa did you find such amazing names. He thought of asking how they had acquired them, but then decided it might be taken as impolite.

Within an hour Simon, Lucky, Trident, and Bones were on their way, taking the same road as Amie and the rest of the party a short time before. Simon thought his girl was in South Africa and assumed she thought he was in London and was probably worried about him. With the cell masts further north disabled, there was no way of letting her know he was safe but now he had a satellite phone which didn't need cell towers. He smiled.

He also had no idea that the camp was in an uproar.

33 SNAKEBITE

Amie was quite impressed at the speed the soldiers and camp staff – once someone had the courage to open the gates and let them in – got things back to normal, or as normal as they could be after such a disaster.

Ben ordered everybody to assemble in the marquee where he announced that the auction would go ahead, the only difference was there would be fewer bidders because the two remaining members of the Chinese delegation had decided to leave.

What's left of them, Amie thought as she listened to Ben. The two aides were shell-shocked and Ben had ordered some soldiers to accompany them back to Apatu.

There was discussion during the morning about the remains of Xiao Ping Wang. The heat from the grenades was fierce and the plastic tent had melted over the body and all of his belongings. Teeth and bone fragments were found among the ashes and a couple of the camp staff were helping the Chinese delegation to gather as much of the remains as they could. It was a gruesome scene and Amie couldn't bear to watch any longer. She couldn't find Gaga anywhere in the compound and was worried about her. She may be blaming herself; she'd been such a bag of nerves the previous day.

This time no one stopped to tell her to stay within the

boma, so she walked a few metres beyond the fencing and continued to follow the perimeter. A quarter way around she realized that it would be impossible to find any tracks, too many of the soldiers had patrolled and the sand was indented with dozens of footprints.

She had wandered a fair way, when she heard giggling behind her. Turning she saw Zeebee, with three of his little friends.

Zeebee held up his hand in a soldier salute, and Amie burst out laughing, then checked to see that nobody from the camp had heard her. It was neither the time nor the occasion for laughter, or for consorting with strangers. The boys in their ragged clothes were cute. They were happy and carefree as they hopped sideways, ducking and diving as they fought mock battles with long sticks.

The smallest one bounced on the balls of his feet then marched up and down like a soldier puffing his chest out and swinging his stick over his shoulder pretending it was a rifle. He looked so comical that Amie couldn't help laughing.

The little boy stopped in his tracks and glared at her; he was not amused. He shouted something she didn't understand and the others ran over.

He glared at her. "Me Capitan," he shouted and then marched forward, turned and marched in the opposite direction, throwing his shoulders back and lifting his knees in the air, while he held his pretend rifle like a real soldier.

A movement caught Amie's eye and from nowhere a puff adder slid sedately from behind a rock as the smallest boy stepped back and trod on its tail. Amie saw the serpent's head twist and strike, burying its fangs in

Capitan's leg. He screamed, flung himself backwards releasing the snake which slithered from view, not bothering to hurry.

Amie rushed over to the child and picked him up. She'd recognized the snake from the dark brown chevrons on a lighter brown background which provided excellent camouflage against their enemies like the honey badgers, warthogs and the Mozambique spitting cobra. She held Capitan close to her chest as she made her way back to the *boma*. He retched and the poor child would have vomited if he'd had any food to bring up, and his green and yellow bile soaked into Amie's shirt as she hurried towards the gate.

The puff adder causes more deaths in Africa than any other snake as they seldom bother to move out of the way when they sense people approaching, but its venom is enough to kill an adult within a day and Capitan was only a small, skinny child. He was already in severe pain.

The boy weighed more than she'd expected – the soldiers on guard duty waved their arms at her and shouted words she could not understand. She ignored them, but at the gate they stopped her and even pushed her away. They pointed to the child and their meaning was obvious. She could enter. Capitan could not.

The small crowd of urchins had followed her and now stood at a distance waiting to see what happened.

"You don't understand," Amie yelled at them. "He's been bitten, a puff adder, *nyoka, nyoka*. Look." She nodded towards Capitan's leg which was already swelling up and blistering.

To her horror the guards only shrugged their shoulders and refused to let her pass.

"He will die if you don't let me take him to the doctor," Amie pleaded. "Daktari, the doctor. Quickly."

Her pleas fell on deaf ears; she was getting nowhere. She didn't know what to do. She pushed forward again, but the largest soldier sidestepped to block her with his body. She tried to elbow him out of the way, but he was not letting her past. A second guard stood next to him. It was hopeless, the soldiers had their orders and would obey them blindly.

The boy's leg swelled and the poison discoloured the skin. It had been less than ten minutes since he'd been bitten and although the men could see the problem, they shrugged their shoulders and refused to let her inside.

Amie saw Vladimir Petrovnikov and yelled to him. The tall Russian diplomat stopped and squinted at the commotion by the gate.

"Vladimir, come help, I need to get this child to the doctor, quickly," Amie screamed, her eyes filling with tears. The child whimpered from the pain and clutched her, sending shockwaves down Amie's body. He was getting heavier by the minute.

Vladimir hurried over with a look of horror on his face. He pushed past the guards and stared at the damage to the young Capitan's leg. "He has been bitten by a snake?"

"A puff adder, and we need the doctor to inject the anti-venom as soon as possible. It's already blistering, but they won't let me in."

Vladimir turned to the soldiers and rattled off words like an automatic rifle in full spate. One of them objected but a further tirade from the angry Russian, made him take a step backwards. He was reluctant to defy an order from one of the President's guests, but he was also fearful of allowing a local child into the *boma*.

Seeing a gap, Amie pushed past him and made for the tent allocated to the medical team. She ploughed through the flaps and laid Capitan on the bed, rubbing her arms and flexing them to get the blood circulating.

The doctor was sitting on a chair reading a book and looked up in alarm at the sudden intrusion.

"What's the problem?" He rose to his feet and walked over to look at the patient. "Snakebite? Did you see it?"

"Yes, it was a puff adder."

"Are you sure?"

"Yes, I recognised the markings on its back. He stepped on it and it flew back and bit him." Amie couldn't understand why the doctor was hesitating and not doing anything to help the child. He was swaying on his feet just staring at the injured leg.

"Why don't you do something? Don't you have to treat it quickly?" Amie's voice wavered in frustration. First the guards and now this.

"I am not sure. I am here to treat all the foreign people. He is just a local boy and he should not be here inside the camp. You should take him away."

Amie couldn't believe what she was hearing. How could a doctor not treat a patient, and even if he wasn't part of the important entourage, didn't the Hippocratic oath say he had to treat all the sick? She grabbed his arm and shook it.

"You have to help him, or, or I'll tell the President how cruel and callous you are. If you don't help him, he'll die."

Vladimir appeared in the tent doorway and spoke to the doctor. Amie had no idea what he said but he scowled and picked up his case, slammed it down on the bed and opened it.

The nurse, hearing all the commotion came running into the tent. She leaned over Capitan, who was unconscious, the sweat lining his face as he moaned in pain.

"Oh, you poor baby," she cried and immediately opened the medicine cupboard and took out bandages and a splint. She peered at the leg looking for puncture marks and splinted the leg from the knee down lowering it below the level of Capitan's head.

Moving at a slower speed, the doctor filled a syringe and injected the fluid into the child. "I do not have a lot of anti-venom," he said as he pushed the plunger before withdrawing the needle. "I can't waste too much on this child, it may be needed for someone important."

Amie bit her lip to stop herself from screaming at him. She was used to people in power showing contempt for the poor. There was no comparison between the doctor's expensive silk shirt and immaculately pressed trousers with the child's dirty t-shirt and torn shorts, but they were both human beings.

"That is all I can do for now," he said sharply, throwing the used syringe back into his bag, "but, if he survives, he should go and see his local village doctor."

"And how is he supposed to do that?" Amie's voice dripped with sarcasm. "He's out cold, he can't walk."

The doctor simply shrugged and walked out of the tent leaving her fuming.

Vladimir looked at the boy and patted his head. "Maybe he will live, we wait and see."

Amie turned to the nurse. "*You* will help him?"

The young girl smiled. "He will sleep for now but I will watch him. Poor little thing."

With a glance at the unconscious boy, Amie thanked the Russian for his help and went outside and across the compound to her own tent. The events of last night and the drama following the puff adder attack had left her exhausted. She peeled off her shirt, still covered with the bile from Capitan's stomach and washed herself in the basin and bowl which had been refilled by the camp attendants. She pinned her top to the mosquito net rail and fell onto her bed, curled up, and was soon fast asleep but it was not to last. Less than an hour later, in broad daylight, the camp was rocked by a second explosion.

34 THE CHINESE DELEGATION

Simon drew in deep breaths as they left the Apatu suburbs behind. He could smell the dust in the air, feel the sun on his arm resting on the passenger window and hear the cicadas whirring as they rubbed their wings together in the acacia trees bordering the road. There was little game to be seen only the occasional group of antelope grazing in the distance.

"So, Mr Simon, you work for the British government?" Lucky asked breaking into his thoughts.

"Only a minor official, nothing important," Simon was non-committal. "And you? Are you employed at the Embassy in Apatu?"

"Only now and again. Most of the time I am a game ranger out to the north, so I am, how do you say, a part-time Uncle Tom?"

"Uncle Tom?"

"Yes, from Harriet Beecher Stowe's novel."

"Of course," Simon murmured, kicking himself for not expecting an African in Togodo to be so well educated.

As if he could read his mind, Lucky laughed. "Ah you did not expect me to know about such things."

Simon squirmed in embarrassment.

"I will explain. My parents worked on a farm much farther north. The farmer and his family were good kind people and they had a farm school for all the children and even employed a lady to come and teach us. She was a properly qualified teacher. I did well, and they sent me to the International School in the city and there I worked hard and did very well in all my exams and I won a scholarship to a university in England."

"That's amazing. And you speak excellent English. What did you study?"

Lucky laughed. "I take communications because it is a skill not many people have in Togodo. England was very nice, and I lived there for five years, but I missed Africa, and, all this," he said waving out of the window. "And, those of us with a good education must give back, to help our country to grow and prosper."

"So, you didn't go into politics, or a government job?"

"No. I have seen enough and read too that in most of those positions, to do well you have to be corrupt, horse trading if you like. I turned my attention to the land outside the cities, agriculture, and the preservation of the wildlife. Some days I take a few tourists on tours, sometimes I meet with Mr Ian, you know him?"

"From the embassy?"

"Yes."

"We've met a few times."

"He often has a few small jobs for me."

"And do you go back to see your folks at the farm?"

"No, it is not possible. In the first war, when I was away in England, the army came over the land and tried to make people join the fight to attack the Kawa in the city. Those that refused were killed, and then the 'freedom fighters,' set fire to the crops and drove all the cattle away. There was very little left."

"I'm sorry."

"But many survived. They ran away when they heard the soldiers were coming, and when the soldiers left, they returned and rebuilt the houses and planted more crops. My father was alive, though the troops had killed my mother and two of my brothers. But then came the second war, when the Kawas fought to take back power. Again, our farm was a battlefield and this time there was nobody left to start again. Now, the wild animals roam through the fields that are not there anymore."

"And will the peace hold this time, do you think?" Simon guessed he was on shaky ground for it was never a good idea to discuss politics in Africa. Criticizing those in power could lead to terrible consequences.

"I am not convinced it will remain peaceful," Lucky replied slowly. He paused to think. "This mining project has caused much bad feeling. It is in tribal lands, as you know, that do not belong to the Kawas, and the Luebos want to claim the profits for their own people."

"You can't really blame them, can you?" Simon said.

"No. Under the earlier Kawa government all the taxes and aid money went into the government's own pockets or was used almost exclusively in Apatu and there was no one to control it. The tribes outside the capital got very little, no schools, water or electricity, yet in Apatu, up went the high-rise buildings, extensions to the palace and paving the roads to the mansions the officials built with the money they got their hands on. But the peace held as the Luebos are slow to anger, until they teamed up with the M'untus who are not as peaceful."

Lucky slowed the car to allow a herd boy with his

Nguni cattle to cross the road. Neither beasts nor boy were in a hurry; it was too hot to move fast. He continued then slowed again to allow a family of guinea fowl to pass. The little ones looked so comical as their small feet skittered across the hot tarmac in an effort to keep up with their parents.

"And today?" Simon poached on even shakier ground.

"Things have improved. Ben Mtumba seems to have the right ideas, he speaks the right words, but only the future will show if his words hold the truth. It is difficult to explain the costs to the rural people, the enormous amounts of money needed to string electricity hundreds of miles, and drill for water and then pipe it long distances. Nothing will happen overnight, and the villagers are impatient."

"Not an easy thing to explain."

"No. In areas where there are no televisions and few books or magazines, the people are happy and satisfied with their lives. The problems occur when they see pictures of places like England and America and the houses they have there. They want all those things, too."

"And I guess it doesn't help looking at the mansions in Apatu."

"No, it does not. They feel dispossessed. But, the African is changing. Before, he would accept that the chiefs and officials deserved the best and looked up to them and accepted their lot. Little by little, they are asking questions and demanding more for themselves."

"It amazes me how happy so many of the people are, especially in the rural areas, when they have so little."

"There is much to be said for being unaware of how other people live," Lucky paused and slowed a little as they topped a rise and saw a huge pall of black smoke. "What the …?"

"Not a bush fire from that colour," Simon peered through the dusty windscreen. In the far distance they could see the tail end of several trucks as they disappeared on a dirt road leading inland.

Lucky approached the scene cautiously. Already the smoke was dying down, and they could make out the remains of three burnt-out vehicles, surrounded by lumps of blackened flesh, partially burnt suitcases and shards of metal and glass which glinted in the bright sunlight.

They drew up a safe distance from the site.

"What the hell went on here?" Simon stared at the carnage.

"A big car one of those for ministers and two army trucks," Trident said, startling Simon who had forgotten he was there.

"He's right." Lucky jumped out of the car and poked at the remains with a stick. "These bits are, were, from one of the limousines they used for the delegation and this was no accident."

"Someone attacked the President's guests? There'll be hell to pay. Shit I hope this doesn't start another war. Mtumba is going to be furious."

Lucky nodded. "He will be angry, very angry."

"Tribes from the north?" It was the only reason Simon could suggest for the attack.

"You can never trust a M'untu. They are bad men. Our president must go and kill them." Trident had no doubts about who was to blame or qualms about voicing his opinion.

"Who knows." Lucky kicked aside what was once an arm belonging to a foreign official or bodyguard. He bent down to pick up the charred remains of a pendant which had flown on the car. "This country?" He passed it to Simon.

Simon scraped the charred material with his thumbnail.

"Chinese I think, it was red and this looks like part of a yellow star on the edge here."

Lucky shrugged, while Bones had picked up a long stick and was riffling through the remains of the fire which was still smouldering in places.

"I wonder what they were doing out here in the middle of nowhere all by themselves? I expected all the delegates to travel together, surely there would have been a larger party than this?"

Lucky shrugged. "The village chief might know."

Simon looked at him sharply. "Can we trust this chief? Is he behind this?"

"It is where they have told us to go. We are not to go to the camp, those are the orders from England."

"Yes, I know, but if someone is bumping off the foreigners, then we're targets too."

"So, if we are," Lucky gave a wry grin as he headed back to their truck, "there is only one way to find out."

Simon climbed back into the passenger seat and fastened his seatbelt. They had to wait as Trident and Bones kicked through the rest of the remains, bending down to pick up a few small trophies which they stuffed into their pockets. Lucky clicked his tongue in annoyance and pressed the horn startling the raptors already circling overhead. Trident picked up one last remnant and with Bones climbed into the back.

London had instructed Lucky to liaise with a local chief a few miles from the camp and wait for further instructions. *One down, five to go* thought Simon with a shudder as they continued on their journey to an uncertain welcome.

35 SECOND ATTACK

"One down, five to go," giggled Samuel Suma as he slapped his best friend, Blessing Ochido on the back.

"I am not sure this plan of yours is going to work," muttered the most Excellent Minister of the Interior.

"You are not getting scared now, are you?" The Sports' Minister's eyes narrowed.

"No, of course not. But some of the soldiers are restless, I am not sure we can trust them."

"Stop worrying my friend. They know they will be well rewarded. They know which side to support."

"Some may favour Nashele."

"Kirimu Nashele will learn he is of no importance. We have the ear of the North Koreans and the Russians, and if there is less competition that is good for us."

"What if the Chinese come back?" Blessing Ochido was nervous.

"I can promise you comrade there is no chance of that, they will not be back." Suma sniggered. "There was not much left of their chief negotiator, he is with the ancestors now and he can't bid from there, can he?" His high-pitched giggles irritated Ochido who turned away before Samuel Suma saw the fear and contempt in his eyes.

After the chaos dissipated following the first explosion and the departure of the Chinese delegation, a state of stupefied lethargy fell over the camp. Ben, surrounded by bodyguards, was seen approaching each of the leading parties and having a few words, but there was little interaction between the delegates; everybody was viewed with suspicion.

The support staff were brought back inside the fencing, nobody wanted to be on the outside where the danger lurked. Even the soldiers ordered to patrol the exterior perimeter were reluctant and huddled in a group by the main gate which remained open a fraction to allow them to run inside at the first sign of trouble.

As the sun rose high into the sky, baking the earth and everything on it, people went to their tents to rest. Nobody was anxious to take part in talks, most were in a state of mild shock. Birds flew in, searching for food remnants, and a few brave rodents sniffed the blackened area formally occupied by the Orientals. Even the soldiers on guard lounged back against the nearest post and closed their eyes.

Silence reigned.

The stillness was broken by the second explosion at exactly 2:03 pm which once again shook the camp, the shockwaves resounding and bouncing from one side of the *boma* to the other. An attack in the middle of the day hadn't been expected and this time the grenades landed on the tent occupied by the French contingent. There had been a whoosh of flame which shot into the air, and one or two stifled screams then the sound of burning canvas and the odd small popping noises from jars and bottles exploding in the heat.

The soldiers snapped to attention, looked round in fear, and the bravest opened the gates and peered outside, pushing past those on the outside trying to get in. There was nothing to be seen.

The previously quiet compound was now a seething mass of people asking questions, shouting, demanding to know what had happened, the ringing in their ears making it difficult to hear anything.

Amie lay frozen in shock for a moment, then she scrambled to her feet and flew out of the tent and looked round. She could see Edward Keller and Ian Fleming hunkered down by the main tent, so they were safe. Then she remembered Capitan. Had he survived? And where was Gaga? She tried to remember which country had occupied the tent that had been next to the Chinese but couldn't remember. If the British and Americans were unharmed, then it was the Russians, the French, or the North Koreans.

As she approached the tent occupied by the medical team, she could see it was still in one piece, but when she opened the flaps and peered inside, Capitan wasn't there. She looked for the nurse or the doctor to see if they knew where the child was.

A strong arm grabbed her and swung her around and she was face to face with Ian Fleming.

"Where the hell do you think you're going rushing around like a chicken without a head?" he demanded.

"I'm looking for Capitan, the little boy who was bitten by a snake."

"Stay here."

"I thought you wanted me to stay away," Amie couldn't resist the dig.

Ian glared at her. "This is not a situation we were expecting," he hissed at her, forcing her to read his lips rather than hear what he was saying. Her ears were only now starting to clear from the blast

"I sure believe it's time to leave," Edward Keller said as he walked in.

Ian nodded. "I agree. As soon as it calms down, we pack up and go."

"But what about …" Amie began, but one look at her boss's face and she said no more.

It made sense. It was suicidal to sit here like stool pigeons to be picked off one by one. Somebody didn't want them here, the message was very clear.

"Who, who was hit?"

"The Frogs I think," Keller replied. "Poor bastards."

All three of them turned as Vladimir Petrovnikov scuttled over.

"You staying?" he asked.

"No, we're out of here as soon as we've packed up and they open the gates."

The soldiers were totally ineffectual. Their general, or whatever rank he held was screaming and trying to round them up. He was shrieking orders they either could not, or would not, follow. He marched a couple over to the gate flung it open, and indicated they should scour the surrounding area. Nobody wanted to leave the safety of the camp. Despite the two attacks, it felt safer within the boundaries than outside in the open.

The atmosphere was chaotic and surreal at the same time. Amie felt disembodied but put it down to shock. She felt vulnerable and crossed her arms tightly across her chest to stop them from shaking. They should be leaving, but they sat there like zombies.

There was a flurry among the soldiers and suddenly one of them keeled over and slumped to the ground frothing at the mouth.

"What now, for God's sake?" Ian Fleming shouted. "What the fuck's going on?"

They all stared at the young man as he lay convulsing, gave a gargled cry and went still.

"Is he sick or what?" Keller's face went white.

"I think he's dead," Petrovnikov was composed.

There was nothing they could do but watch in morbid fascination as two of his comrades dragged the body to the medical tent. Then another soldier swayed and keeled over into the dust.

"This is absolutely bloody bizarre," Ian exclaimed. "What the bloody hell's going on? We need to get out of here and fast. The whole fucking place is under attack."

"You're right partner. I'm getting out as fast as I can." Edward Keller sprang to his feet and hurried to his tent, yelling for the other Americans to get packing pronto.

Amie turned to look at Ian.

"Shall I travel back with you?"

"Yes, best we keep together. Get your stuff, hurry."

Amie ran to her tent crouching low. It was no safer than standing up and running, another missile could fly over the fence and set another tent on fire, but she felt safer crouching down.

She dived into her tent and rammed her clothes into her backpack, grabbed a torch and her phone, hoping there would be some reception once they were closer to Apatu.

She was about to join Ian when ear-splitting screeches came from the other side of the *boma* fencing.

"Stay where you are. You are surrounded. You will not escape. I say again, stay where you are, we are all around you." The same message was repeated in Togodian and two other African dialects. Whoever was out there had decided they could control those who were left.

Amie saw two more soldiers collapse while many more were being sick. The breeze wafted the stench of half-digested food towards her.

It hit Amie like a bolt from the blue. There was no certainty that those who said they had the *boma* surrounded would allow any of them to live. With no protection from the soldiers, they were helpless, and their enemies would not worry about reprisals. They had declared war, and knowing the President and most of his cabinet were at their mercy, it would be every man for himself.

What was she going to do? She was tempted to leave, to try and run away but she couldn't do that could she? She'd never get away.

She felt her baby kick stronger than she had felt it before, reminding her she had a second life to protect. She patted the bump gently. *What am I going to do little lump? Do we stay here with the embassy people? Or should we leave and try to get back to the city? I have to protect you, I'm damned if I let you die before you're even born. You trust me to protect you, don't you?*

She sank onto her camp bed rocking, her thoughts in a jumble. As if in answer, the baby kicked again. *Are you trying to tell me something? Do you agree we should leave?* The next kick was even stronger. *OK, stop dithering*

Amie, you can never make up your mind. You've always had this problem, what are you going to do?

Like a bolt from above, it all became blindingly clear. She made her decision. She would find her own way out and make for the capital. If it was quiet there, then she would get help at the embassy and if possible, fly out. She'd survived a trek across the African savannah before and she could do it again. She didn't trust Ian Fleming, not when he blew hot and cold, and she doubted he had many survival skills; he'd had too many years behind a desk ordering other people into danger. She trusted Ben more, but he was a target, probably the main target, and she would be putting herself in the line of fire by staying close to him. Much as she would like to be loyal, the new life growing inside her was her priority.

Slinging her backpack over one shoulder, she slipped out of her tent and crept round the back. Keeping a low profile she worked her way around the inside of the perimeter fence to the kitchen tent. When she glanced inside, her stomach turned over. Every member of the staff responsible for feeding the delegates was either lying comatose or retching and convulsing, mouths spewing a dark green foam. Had they been poisoned? Had some unknown hand only contaminated the food earmarked for the staff and army, or would they all get sick? Amie's stomach heaved and the nerve endings tingled on her back. Was this the first sign? She took a deep breath and steadied herself. There was no time to stand and wonder why. She needed to get moving while things were still chaotic.

She grabbed six bottles of water from the gas fridge, checking they were sealed. She would have to take a chance that they hadn't been tampered with. From the shelf next to the fridge she helped herself to four cans of sardines, two of baked beans, and three of corned beef. She looked at the boxes of biscuits but it wasn't worth the risk.

Footsteps were approaching, and she ducked behind a table as two people entered.

"Holy shit, they're dropping like flies." It was Edward Keller's voice.

Through the legs of the table, she could see him bending over one of the corpses.

"We haven't got time to waste on them," Ian responded harshly. "Let's get what we came for. The sooner we break out the better. Water's our priority now."

"Yeah, well, guess yer right, buddy. It's just you and me now."

The footsteps came closer. They were making for the fridge. As quietly as she could, Amie slid back around the corner of the preparation table, nearly gagging as she stumbled over yet another corpse. She was exposed but neither man was aware of her presence. They raided the fridge, emptying it of every bottle of water before throwing them into a discarded cardboard box and leaving.

Were they going to wait for her, to take her with them, or even come and look for her? Ian's words about her expendability came back to her and she knew that she had been abandoned.

She made her way out of the back of the tent and round the perimeter until she was at the edge of the high *kopje* which formed the backdrop of the camp on one side. She pushed the discarded boxes aside and found the hole Zeebee had excavated under the fence. Her sharp Swiss

Army knife made short work of the sticks, which butted up against the sizzling hot grey stone as she hacked at the lower ends to make the hole large enough for her to scramble through.

Satisfied with the size of the gap she had made, she peeped out and saw no one. She tugged a spare t-shirt and wrapped it round her hands to minimise any scratches as she scrambled through. The lightest of wounds could turn septic in this heat. She wished she'd dared to raid the medical tent for supplies, but that would be pushing her luck too far. She'd have to make do with what she had in her backpack.

She planned to creep round the base of the rocks and then take a wide circle in the direction of the capital, but a scruffy looking man with a gun suddenly appeared, pacing along the other edge of the *boma*. He was dressed in a filthy t-shirt and long cargo pants tucked into an old pair of boots which were splitting apart. He had a makeshift turban of dirty linen.

It was true, they'd surrounded the camp. Amie slid her backpack back through the hole and ducked inside, peeping out to see what he would do. The soldier, with his back towards her, sat on a low rock, put his gun down and fished in his pockets for his cigarettes.

Amie crept out and approached him. He was on the point of lighting the cigarette when he sensed her behind him. He turned to face her, brushing the flame over his hand which made him jump.

It gave Amie the extra second that she needed. She sprang forward and chopped him hard on the neck. He fell sideways, his eyes wide open staring at the sky, his hand only inches from the gun. For good measure she gave him a swift kick between his legs, which just might slow him down if he recovered enough to shout an alarm. Her nostrils wrinkled at the odour of stale sweat as she rifled through his pockets, relieving him of a packet of painkillers, a knife, some tissues and a bunch of keys. She doubted she would ever find the door they unlocked, but they might be of use. She undid the buckle on his bandolier rolling him over to free it and wrapped it around herself. Finally, she picked up his gun, a rusty AK47, and grabbing the backpack, ran round the side of the rocks.

She could hear gunshots, the cracks resounded through the air followed by a scream, but she didn't wait to find out what had happened.

The sun sank lower in the sky and it was cooler on the far side of the *kopje*. As she moved away towards the denser bush, she disturbed a troop of baboons who shrieked and chattered. She ducked behind a Mountain Cypress tree willing the chattering monkeys not to draw attention to her. They could also be curious, and if they smelled food, they might attack her for her backpack. She wouldn't be able to fight off an aggressive male and do it quietly. More shots from the camp frightened the primates and they took off shrieking.

There was a loud crash, more shouts and from her oblique angle Amie could see the road leading to the capital. She watched one of the diplomatic cars break through the gates and speed southwards. Amie wondered if she had made the wrong decision, but then the car swerved violently to one side as some well-aimed bullets took out the tyres and shattered the back window. Men waving guns ran over and pulled on the door handles. When they refused to open, they used their rifle butts to smash the glass and dragged the protesting diplomats out.

It wasn't possible, at this distance, to see exactly who they were, but Amie thought she recognised Keller, Fleming, and the Russian. The driver and the passenger in the front seat, were shot. Their bodies spewed blood, they twitched and convulsed, and then stopped moving. The soldier in charge shouted out to one of his men. He ran off and returned carrying three shovels. It was surreal watching three diplomats being ordered to dig a grave for the two who were dead. Amie watched in horror as they laboured to make an impact on the rock-hard ground. One of them, she thought it was Vladimir, picked up a rock and began building a cairn. The attackers nodded and sniggered at their captives' efforts. They clubbed one of the prisoners with a rifle butt to set an example to the others, and the air filled with their raucous laughter.

When the bodies were covered with stones they spun the captives around and frogmarched them back inside the *boma.*

Amie shrugged her backpack onto her shoulders and set off through the dense cover, leaving the carnage behind. She was a survivor and she had her child to protect. She remembered Ouma Adede's words. She'd warned her not to go north, and she'd hinted that the baby would be in danger. The baby had kicked her strongly for the first time. It was a message, reminding her of the life growing inside. She imagined it was screaming to her to care for it, give birth to it, and nurture it as it grew. *Please protect my baby,* she whispered as she plunged through the thick bush.

36   THE LUEBOS VILLAGE

Lucky had turned off the tarred road and they saw more game. A herd of Cape buffalo mingled with families of zebra, each animal with its individual set of stripes. Lucky pointed out the calves and said they were migrating north to an area where the grass was greener. Some of the newly born were having problems keeping up as the animals moved at a steady pace, huddled together for safety.

"Keep a lookout for big cats, they often follow the migration."

"They are difficult to see, the grass is too long," Simon remarked.

"That is the point. The grass camouflages them but there is little goodness in it; it is yellow and dry. The ancient wisdom of the animals tells them where the rains have fallen in places to the north, and every year they will make this journey. There is much we can learn about them, and we must protect them." Lucky sighed. He was aware of the decimation of wildlife from the poaching, not only for food but for sheer greed.

"The people who live in China and Vietnam do not care about our beautiful animals. They think of their own needs for medicine and their belief that rhino horn will make a man produce many children. It is a bad world we live in."

Simon could only nod in agreement.

The open plains were densely overgrown and Lucky slowed down.

"We are close now," he said, "but we must go a wide way around the camp. They must not see us."

"Is the village far from the camp?"

"A few miles, a man can walk it in half a day."

By Simon's calculations that could mean anything from twelve to twenty- four miles. An African half day was sunrise until the sun was at its peak, and Africans covered the ground faster than the average man in the west. He was uncertain though how well they would be received in the village.

"Lucky, are you absolutely sure this chief is friendly?"

"Yes, Mr Simon, he is very friendly. He is a great supporter of our President and he believes he will share the money they make from the mining companies."

"I suppose if he doesn't share out the spoils, then there could be another civil war?"

"Oh yes, most definitely there will be one. We Luebos are a peaceful tribe, but the M'untus? Ah, they are different. They do not love the Kawas and Mtumba is a Kawa. They kicked them out and they ruled Togodo but it did not last for long. Soon the Kawas picked up their guns and took the power back. We do not work together like your people in the west."

"I'm not sure we're much different," Simon responded. "In theory, we can vote a government out if they don't please the people, but whichever side is in charge of the government, the opposition do not co-operate with them at all."

"Ah, it is simpler if you have one man to tell you what to do, then the people must obey."

Until the next uprising by a disaffected populace, thought Simon, *which is a lot worse than some shouting and screaming in the parliaments.* He smiled. "So, Lucky, you think life in Britain too would be better if we only had one leader?"

"For sure. There would not be arguing over laws and delays in changing things. You have a good man in power and he can achieve wonderful things."

Despite having lived in England, Simon realized that Lucky still thought like an African. Democracy as the west knew it was not for him.

They circled to the east, and Simon guessed it was to give the camp a wide berth. The tarred road was miles behind and their route took them across the bushland. The flat plains were bordered by rocky outcrops rising to the lower slopes on the range of hills that separated Togodo from Budan where President Muwaba was in power over his majority tribe, the M'untus.

The truck bumped and rattled over the rough stony ground with Lucky steering around the low-lying bushes and larger termite mounds. There was no road or track to follow so they bush-bashed over the veld.

"Lucky, how do you know this is the way to the village? There isn't a proper road in site."

"Ah, I follow the sun," the African displayed his shining white teeth. "Before, I would go on the track further north that has been worn by many cars in the past, but it goes too close to the President and the diplomats so we need to keep away."

"Of course, just as long as you're not lost."

Lucky tapped the compass on the dashboard. "With this, we can never get lost, and we are close now. You will see."

For several miles they had only seen a few animals, with no people, huts or signs of agriculture – it was deserted.

"Why aren't there any people, Lucky?"

"This is a private hunting area for the chief we will stay with. If the chief says you are not to farm or build your house here, then you do not build."

"He owns all this land?"

"The land is for everyone, but the chief is the one who tells his people where they can go."

It didn't make total sense to Simon, but he'd accept it as the way things were.

The sun sank as Lucky swung the vehicle up an ungraded gravel road leading to the village. It was lined by small huts built from mud and dung topped with grass. Each house was surrounded by a bare earth yard, fenced with sticks. Women tended black cooking pots on open fires by their doors, and stopped and looked up to wave at the approaching visitors. Children ran into the road to shout, holding their hands open in the hope of sweets or cents. There were fenced areas inside where they saw rows of vegetables. Mangy dogs and chickens roamed everywhere along with a few scruffy goats.

Lucky drove slowly through the village until they reached a fence.

"This is where the chief lives. See the smaller huts belong to his wives, and over there is the kraal for the cattle to come in at night. See, they bring in the cows now."

Several boys waving sticks busily herded the animals inside for safety. Their cries rang out in the stillness as they brought the beasts home.

The chief came to meet them and he greeted Lucky with the traditional three directional handshake before giving him a hug. He nodded to Trident and Bones and offered his hand to Simon. He was a short tubby man, the tight curls on his head already turning grey, reflected the deep age lines on his face. He was dressed in well-washed jeans cinched at the waist by a wide leather belt below a smart blue shirt over which he wore a cheetah skin draped across one shoulder. Despite being small, he carried himself straight, a great presence as befitted the leader of his people.

"You are welcome in my village," he said and smiled. "Come."

They followed him to the door of his hut where rough wooden stools had been placed a little way from the fire.

"Sit." The chief turned to Lucky and spoke in the local dialect.

Lucky sat down next to Simon.

"The chief apologises, he speaks little English, so I will translate for him. He welcomes you to his house and hopes your stay will be comfortable."

"Please thank him for me, and that I am sure I will be very comfortable," Simon lied. From what he could see, nothing looked comfortable and he reached to pull out a splinter that had detached itself from the stool and was digging into his leg.

One of the women handed out tea in chipped enamel mugs. Simon tried not to burn his fingers as he took it from her, nodding his thanks. He took a sip and, as he suspected, it was heavily laced with sugar. He glanced up and noticed that Lucky was worried.

"What is it?" he asked as soon as there was a break in the conversation.

"It is bad news. There has been much trouble at the camp. There were explosions and a fire, and many people have died."

Simon was shocked.

"It is chaos there, and some have tried to leave, so the chief tells me."

"That wreck, may have been the Chinese. But who?"

Lucky shrugged his shoulders.

"The M'untus," spat Trident.

"Maybe from over the border in Budan," Lucky added.

"So, they are all leaving? There is to be no auction?"

"No, they cannot leave, they are surrounded by tribesmen."

"How can we find out if these men are from Budan or here in Togodo?" Simon caught the look that passed between Lucky and the chief.

"The chief does not know," replied the African after a pause, but Simon didn't believe him. Whatever they knew, they were not going to share it with him. He was uneasy.

"Simon, this chief is loyal to our President. He will fight with Ben Mtumba to protect the mining for Togodo and all its people."

"That's reassuring, but who has attacked the camp? Are there other chiefs around here? Which tribe does this chief belong to Lucky?"

"Chief Lgego is a Luebos and we are a very peaceful tribe. We do not like to fight."

Which explains why they have been ignored in plans to modernize here in the north. Like the Tswana, they were probably driven north into less fertile areas, thought Simon. *Now, they were sitting on the doorstep of great wealth and you could not blame them for wanting control over their own lands. Their very pacifism in the past might lull the Kawas into a false sense of security.*

"Are there many M'untus in this area?"

Lucky turned to ask the chief.

"He says there are a few, but not many. Most live over the great mist mountains in Budan to the north. Sometimes they come to visit, but not often."

"You think the people who attacked the camp are from Budan?"

Lucky shrugged again. He didn't answer.

The sun set and the people in the compound appeared and disappeared moving like wraiths in the firelight. A shriek startled them all as some boys ran in from the dark. Simon guessed they had returned later than their curfew.

A woman grabbed the one closest to her and walloped him hard as he squirmed in her grip trying to avoid the hand aimed at his backside. The fortunate youngsters darted away and kept a safe distance while the old chief laughed. A torrent of words poured out in between his guffaws and Lucky translated that he was highly amused that the young scoundrels had stayed out too long when there were dangerous predators around. The women, they were always worried that a lion or leopard might attack their children or they might disturb a hippo on its nightly forage to eat.

The little lad broke free and raced over to the party sitting round the fire. He babbled, gesticulating with his arms, acting out his story to the villagers who'd gathered round to listen.

"They have returned from the camp," Lucky whispered. "The Chief sent them off to spy out the land. They have been gone for two days and the women were worried. He will be able to tell us how things are."

Despite the hiding he'd received, the lad recovered much faster than Simon expected. His mother, or maybe it was an aunt, had beaten him hard, slapping him around the head and boxing his ears. A few minutes later, he was eager to share his news and revelled at being the centre of attention as he rattled out his story.

It was frustrating for Simon, and he had to be patient and wait until Lucky translated for him. The boy illustrated his experiences by waving his arms and pantomiming events.

At last, he ran out of breath and Lucky turned to Simon.

"The soldiers who were there to protect all the important people are dead. The camp is surrounded by men. The boys do not know where they come from or what they want. I think they must be from Budan. This is not good, Simon."

"No, it's not." Despite his orders to disrupt the negotiations if he could, it didn't include carnage on such a scale. "Are the diplomats alive? Is Ian Fleming safe?"

"The children don't know. I doubt if they can tell one from another. He tells us that the men outside have guns and big rockets and there are a lot of people inside the *boma*. The camp has a large fence all around it but they could not get close enough to see inside."

"Ask him how close we can get to the camp tomorrow."

Lucky nodded but had to wait because their young narrator had got his breath back and was off again, the words spilling out as fast as he could utter them.

Some of the other adventurers crept closer and added bits until they ran out of words and fell silent.

Simon had a dozen questions to ask. How many people were in the camp? How many were holding them hostage? Had the children seen the President? Was he still alive? Had anybody escaped?

The numbers were impossible to guess. The children couldn't count beyond five and they'd only seen one car leave, which Simon guessed was the burned out one belonging to the Chinese. They hadn't made it back to Apatu. The children had not seen the President. The only concrete information was they had seen a white woman walk out of the camp, but it didn't mean anything to Simon; any of the diplomats could have taken secretaries with them.

Lucky, Trident, Bones and Simon talked late, planning to leave in the early hours of the morning to recce and assess the situation. Simon wasn't sure how he felt when he realized that the village men would accompany them as well.

It was past midnight when Simon fell onto the sleeping mat in one of the huts. He was too tired to worry about the scrabbling in the rushes above him, the odd small creature scurrying across the floor, or the roar of the lions far away on the hunt. The moment he closed his eyes, he fell fast asleep dreaming of Amie who he imagined was safe miles away in Durban.

37 PLANS TO ESCAPE

Ben Mtumba was also awake long after midnight. His plans for a successful auction were in tatters. Kirimu had agreed they would all have a long talk the next day, politicians and diplomats, and make plans to break out – and then what? They had tried that already and it was a disaster. The foreigners survived but they lost a driver and one of the aides. If Ben was honest, he didn't trust any of them. His Right Honourable Finance Minister and closest friend, Kirimu Nashele, looked him in the eye – always a bad sign – and told him that it was not his fault, and he had no idea who was keeping them hostage.

If it was only the Togodians who were held here, it wouldn't be as bad, but they were locked in with international representatives from North Korea, the United States, Britain and Russia. Their governments would go crazy when they heard, and Togodo would be a country to avoid at all costs. The mining wouldn't be the only project hit. Every other development planned or in progress would be affected too. It was a disaster. Nothing made sense and the thoughts swirled round in his head. If it was the local tribesmen, why not send a delegation asking for reassurances that they would get a share of the profits? Did they want to negotiate with the remaining diplomats and sign their own agreements? If that was the case, why kill off two of the countries willing to pay money to excavate the minerals? They would gain nothing if they were left under the ground. Perhaps for now it didn't matter, for the auction was not going ahead. They needed to concentrate on escaping and getting back to Apatu to restore order.

Ben didn't rate their chances of surviving and returning to the capital very highly. The only private vehicle they'd had in the compound was shot up and useless. The limousines still parked outside were not built for speed or rough terrain and the army vehicles had been commandeered by the enemy and driven away. The few Africans left, his cabinet ministers and bodyguards might slip out and make a run for it through the bush, but most were used to city life and wouldn't last long. As for the soft diplomats, he doubted they'd make it further than a couple of miles, if that.

There was a scratching at the front of the tent.

"Yes?"

It was Royal Papele, the Foreign Minister, or possibly ex-foreign minister. He poked his head through the flap.

"It is the British man, Mr Ian Fleming, he wants to talk with you, Your Excellency."

Ben sighed and nodded.

Ian appeared behind Papele and squeezed inside.

"Mr President," he bowed his head.

"Come, sit."

Ian perched on a camp stool and cleared his throat.

"And what do you have to tell me?"

"Mr President, all is not lost."

Ben's eyebrows shot up.

"Really?"

"There are a few difficulties, I grant you, but there is a way out."

"You are planning to dig a tunnel?"

Fleming gave a wry smile. "Not exactly, but we do need a plan. I'm sure you'll agree."

"Yes, but I am loath to put foreign diplomats at risk. I don't think they will cope with the walk back to Apatu, do you?" Ben let his eyes slip to Ian Fleming's paunch. "And, much as I hate to admit it, my cabinet ministers have led a very easy life these last few years."

"You have a point, but we can't sit here and do nothing."

"It may be the safest thing to do. The terrorists did not kill the ambassadors when they tried to escape. They must have a reason for letting them live."

"I for one am not happy with the idea of doing nothing – sitting and waiting. We don't have huge stocks of food and we have no idea what poisoned your soldiers."

"Their food was mixed with parts of the Naked Lady Euphorbia Tirucalli."

"Pardon?" Ian's eyes opened wide.

"That's the Latin name. We have many names for it, the Firestick plant, Finger Tree, Milk Bush. Every part of the plant is poisonous."

"How can you be so sure?"

Ben looked irritated. "After seeing the symptoms, it was obvious: the vomiting, purging, delirium and death. Even the sap is an irritant, it burns the eyes out making you blind and the skin blisters as if the victims had been boiled in oil."

"So, it's not something we can catch?" Ian was

relieved. He had seen the horrific symptoms too, and they had terrified him.

Ben gave him a nasty look. The man was only concerned for his own safety and nobody else.

"How did they manage to contaminate the food?" Ian persisted. "The perimeter was heavily guarded. Was it put in the food?"

"Does it matter? They did it and it won't help us to know how." Ben stood and paced to and fro inside the small tent. "They could have ground it and mixed it with the mealie meal in the sacks. Easy to do. The point is that someone infiltrated the camp despite the stringent security – unless they were here all along."

"We have to make an inventory of what food and equipment we have left, see how many men are fit, and plan a counter attack or at least, break out."

Ben slumped back down into his seat again. "Do you realize how many insurgents there are out there? We're not even sure how many are armed and what arms they have. We're surrounded."

"But you've faced worse odds before."

"Before, I had the backing of an army, my cell phone worked and I could call on reinforcements. There is no signal here." He paused, not about to admit to Ian Fleming that he couldn't count on any of the armed forces left in the capital. And all of his previously trusted aides were here and equally incarcerated.

"We have four diplomats with their two side-kicks, plus you, Mr President and your four ministers and bodyguards."

"Yes, they have two each and I have four."

"Do you know if any of the soldiers survived?"

"I believe there are six in total."

Ian Fleming thought for a moment. "So, with the doctor and the nurse, we have thirty-seven inside the camp."

"We need to bury the bodies soon, or it will not be only the people outside we have to worry about," Ben said at last. "The decaying bodies will make everyone sick. It is of great urgency."

"It's gruesome, but if we get a few of the corpses outside the fence which is still intact, then we might attract predators and that will harass our attackers."

Ben looked at Ian Fleming. The man was ruthless but he had to admit his idea might work.

"And while they are distracted, we can arm ourselves and get ready to mount a counterattack," Ian continued.

"We have a few guns from the late soldiers."

"That's not all we can do. Have you ever made a Molotov cocktail?"

"That's where ya'll been hiding," Edward Keller said as he pushed his way into the tent. "Mr President, I really must protest about this disgrace with myself and my country being attacked. We have diplomatic immunity, and I demand you make those goons out there aware of it. Do they realize who they have stuck in here?"

"They know it's a band of important people, but they won't give a damn about your diplomatic immunity even if they understood what it meant," Ian snapped back.

"About time they were told then. I'm lodging a complaint at the highest level to those back home about this total debacle and the way America's representatives have been treated."

"Now is not the time, Keller," Ian growled at him. "In case you hadn't noticed, it's possible that none of us will survive to complain to anyone. Save your diplomatic speeches for and if we get back to Apatu. The important thing now is to get out of here alive. There are men on the other side of a rather fragile fence who are trying to prevent us from leaving."

"Yeah, well," Keller's face burned red in the gaslight. "This ain't what I signed up for."

"None of us did, least of all Togodo's president. There'll be time for recriminations later. We need an escape plan now, or a way of neutralising those outside."

Keller glared at Ian but made no reply and sank down onto the President's bed.

They were joined by the other diplomats who slipped in one by one. The other attachés were useless. They'd occupied comfortable chairs behind desks and pushed paperwork all their working lives. Coming on safari was horrendous for them and well outside their comfort zone. The same could be said of Mtumba's cabinet members, though they were probably more ruthless. The bodyguards could be relied on and were probably better trained than Togodo's soldiers. At most, Ian could count on twenty people to be effective and, at a pinch, Amie. Where was bloody Amie? He hadn't seen her for hours, or that Gaga woman who'd organized this disaster. They must be in camp somewhere. He sighed, probably hiding out under their camp beds swapping cooking recipes. He'd go search for her in a while.

The North Koreans took no part in the discussions but sat quietly to one side while their interpreter whispered what Ian hoped was an accurate account of the conversation.

Vladimir Petrovnikov chewed his fingernails, throwing workable ideas into the plans now and again. Ian recognized a trained agent and was glad he wasn't the only one, since all Edward Keller could do was huff and moan about how they'd landed in this situation.

They came up with a workable plan which had minimal chance of success but was the best they could do with the little resources they had.

The offensive was arranged for dawn.

38 AMIE'S JOURNEY

Amie kept up a steady pace as she journeyed towards Apatu. The thought of taking refuge at Mrs Motswezi's orphanage kept her going, and if that wasn't possible then she would find Sohanna Reddy at the hospital and stay with her. She'd had enough of this cloak and dagger life. All she had ever planned was to marry Jonathon, have two children, buy a house on the new estate not too far from her parents and her sister Sam, and settle down to Saturday shopping trips at the mall and planning overseas holidays in the sun.

Instead, she'd been dragged out to Africa, embroiled in a civil war, attacked by terrorists, found and lost her foster daughter, Angelina, become a widow, and had been highjacked by the British government and forced into spying for them. To add to her misery, just when she'd found a man she adored, he'd taken off for London and she hadn't heard from him since.

She was past anger, past raging at the world and the injustices she'd suffered. That would get her nowhere. But the sheer fury that came with the anger had reached its zenith and had nowhere left to go and might get her through the next few days.

She thought back to the journey from Apatu. They had spent at least ten hours in the truck and had probably averaged 60 kilometres per hour which made the distance 600. At four miles an hour times six she could cover 24 miles – but she was confusing kilometres with miles. Her calculations were wrong; she'd never been great at maths. Concentrating on how she'd get by allowed her to forget about the discomfort of tramping through the bush with water bottles stuffed in her backpack weighing her down. *Face it Amie*, she thought *it's a bloody long way, but once I hit the main tarred road I might be able to hitch a lift.*

What then? She mused as she plodded on in the brief twilight. If she got to Apatu, could she find a way of escaping? Maybe it was overly dramatic to think SIS or MI6 would bother to look for her. She was an incompetent spy and of little use to them, and she had no secrets to spill to the enemy. She'd been over-reacting: too hysterical and emotional. *No excuses*, she told herself, *for being pregnant.* Once she'd had the baby she would leave Togodo, leave Africa, and make for Europe. In the meantime, there would be plenty of places she could hide out and live a quiet life. Criminals did it all the time and dozens of them never got caught. But that was stupid. She needed to jump on a plane, or hitch a ride over the border, to Budan, and take a plane from there as soon as possible. That way she and baby could travel on one ticket. She smiled at the thought of getting two for the price of one on an airline.

Her decision was made, but her passport remained a problem. Ben had got those illegal ones made in Apatu, but she had no idea where. She'd dumped it once SIS had given her a new, legal one. She would try the British Embassy first to see if hers was still there. She could make up a story about Ian sending her back early with instructions to fly out. What were her chances of walking into Apatu before any of the delegates returned – or maybe none of them would.

Much as she disliked Fleming, she didn't wish him dead and that Vladimir Petrovnikov was dishy even if he was pushy. A picture of Simon flashed into her mind. Should she contact him? Yes, of course, but not before she was somewhere safe, and she'd take it from there. She didn't have to tell him where she was, and she couldn't expect him to give up his career to go and live with her in some far-flung land. Despite the nonsense the soppy romance stories fed you – you cannot live on love alone. What was it her mother used to say? 'When poverty flies in the window, love flies out of the door.' She giggled, remembering her mother quoting that once to her sister Samantha when she dragged in an unsuitable, scruffy, unemployed young man barely surviving on benefits and declared she was in love.

The sun was below the hills and it had become dark which was the most comfortable time to travel. But animals were on the hunt. It would be wise to find a place to sleep and wait until first light.

The bush was dense in places where the parched vegetation had grown between the rocky outcrops. Amie's preferred place of rest would be in a tree, but only a few of them were much taller than she was. She'd have to climb one of the *kopje*s and huddle inside a rock crevice.

It had been late in the afternoon when she'd left the camp and she didn't think she'd travelled far, but she felt much safer outside the *boma* than inside it.

The dew was falling and made the rocks slippery as

she scrambled up towards a crack she hoped was unoccupied. She balanced on a narrow ledge, pushed her rucksack into the space and felt for her bush knife which she used to cut off a nearby tree branch. She tied it on to the handle of the knife and poked it into the crevice, waggling it from side to side to see if she disturbed any creatures living there. Nothing rushed out and she couldn't hear anything.

She cut down some thorn branches and wedged them in the opening in front of her to protect her from enquiring noses. It wouldn't be comfortable but she could catnap long enough to get her strength back for the next day's hike.

The night was punctuated by the roars, snuffles, squeals, and shrieks of pain typical of areas in Africa where few men lived and the animals were left undisturbed. Amie sat with her legs hunched in front of her and her head resting on her knees as the night passed. Every two hours, she rose to flex her cramped muscles before huddling back behind her little barrier of thorn spikes. She treated herself to a couple of mouthfuls of water, saving most of it for the harsh heat of the day. She had to make it last.

She had yet to find out if it had been a mistake to take off alone, but it was crazy waiting to be killed. If she'd told Ian maybe he would have looked after her and they could all have escaped. But that wasn't practical at the time. Either way, her conscience bothered her in the early hours of the morning. She didn't sleep well and her stomach kept cramping, and the baby was kicking. What message was it trying to convey this time?

You do understand I'm trying to save both our lives,

don't you baby? I am trying to do the right thing for us.

As the light of the pre-dawn illuminated her surroundings, she crawled from her refuge and stretched. She was getting too old for this sleeping rough. She rummaged in the backpack and wrenched the top from a can of cold meat. It looked unappetising, but she dug into the tin scooping pieces out with the end of her knife and washed it down with a few swigs of water.

Observing the landscape, she caught her breath as she watched a family of giraffe meandering sedately below the rocks. If they were aware of her they did not appear to be bothered. They stopped to stretch their necks and curl their blue tongues around the prickly acacia trees. It was a marvel that the sharp spines didn't bother them. Two young calves danced around, darting between the long legs of the adults, reaching to suckle milk from their mothers. They were Amie's favourite animals. She liked them because they were seldom aggressive, though a kick could kill a man if he got too close. Amie stayed where she was content to keep her distance. It was terrible to think that the graceful creatures were on the verge of the endangered list. They had no horns suitable for medicine, their flesh was seldom coveted, even by the tribesmen, and they were of little economic value to anyone except as tourist attractions, yet their numbers were declining by the year.

The giraffes wandered off and the sun had risen well above the horizon. Amie hadn't made up her mind what to do. The sight of the animals reminded her how much she loved this continent with its vast open spaces and unique wildlife, and even many of its loveable people. What was she thinking – was she going to run away and hide out in

Europe? She would hate to end up working at a resort bar catering to drunken holidaymakers, and worrying if her child was in safe hands while she struggled to earn enough to pay for rent and food. She would be looking over her shoulder in case SIS came looking for her, too. Her imagination ran riot. She'd be arrested at work, unable to get word to the babysitter. Her only son or daughter would be terrified after being taken into care and forced to face an uncertain future while believing he or she had been abandoned.

So, she was just a coward. She ran away and left Ben, Ian, and Gaga and all the others behind to fend for themselves. It was irresponsible; more than that, it was cruel. *Shit,* she thought. *I'll have to go back, who am I kidding? But I'll stay on the outside. I'm not going back inside the compound.*

It was easy to slide down the smooth surface of the rock where she dug a hole in the sandy soil big enough to bury the empty can. She filled it with earth before putting it in the ground, hoping it wouldn't attract an animal as the sharp edges could easily slice through a tongue and wounds went septic very easily in the wild.

It was time to set off on the long hike back to camp. How could she help those held inside? Would it be possible to send in information about the attackers on the outside? Whoever they were, they were serious and they had no qualms about taking lives. She would have to be careful and think back to the training she'd had on surveillance and concealment. Of course she'd do it all wrong, but at least she'd have tried. What a nuisance a conscience is and why did she have to be bothered by it? At least with going back for them, she could feel good about herself before they shot her to pieces. That was a comforting thought. She didn't want to explain to her child that she had run away and left her friends to an uncertain fate, by leaving them to die.

She retraced her steps and approached the camp from the west, keeping a sharp eye open for any dangers from animals and people. She stopped often to ease the cramping in her stomach. *It must be that tinned meat*, she thought as she edged round a particularly large termite mound. *The meat was part of the rations for the soldiers and several of them had died. No,* she reassured herself. *The can was sealed, no holes in it so I'm sure it was fine. Just a touch of indigestion Amie, don't be such a wuss.*

39 THE PRISONER

Not so far away as the crow flies, Simon also approached the camp but from the east. The chief reassured him it was only half a day's walk, but despite all that clambering around the Welsh valleys, after the first couple of hours he struggled to keep up with the village men whose feet appeared to skim over the ground. Several of them were elderly, but agile, wearing old, ill-fitting sports shoes while others were barefoot. The skin on their soles worn thick and hard from daily contact with the earth. He envied them their resilience, but that wasn't unusual. The rural Africans always made him feel inadequate. He could change a car tyre, wire a fuse, even construct a swimming pool, but when it came to survival skills after being stripped of modern conveniences, he was woefully lacking.

They moved in a straight line to begin with, but then they zigzagged to avoid detection. Simon looked at Lucky who put his fingers to his lips before putting them next to Simon's ear. "They may have soldiers a long way from the camp as look-ins."

Simon smiled. It would be unkind to correct Lucky's English, but his meaning was clear. They had no idea who their enemy was, how many there were, or where they came from.

The village kids were playing a version of touch,

laughing, giggling, and shrieking when one of them landed a punch or a poke from the long sticks they carried. Simon could only surmise that their presence would not be seen as a threat by the terrorists, they were only children and could not be expected to contain their exuberance.

The adults slowed their pace and were almost creeping from bush to bush looking around them. Simon hung back. As the only white man he did not blend in as well with the rest of the crowd.

The sun beat down relentlessly, its rays burning through his shirt causing the sweat to trickle down his back and chest. It bothered him as it meandered over his skin and however many times he scratched, another point of irritation flared up somewhere else. The perspiration poured down his forehead, stinging his eyes and causing him to blink and rub his face on his sleeve. The Glock 17 Lucky had handed him from the supplies dug into his back. He didn't want to be seen carrying it, and the only place to put it was in the waistband of his trousers.

The cicadas sounded louder than express trains, butterflies floated past and the scurrying in the undergrowth alerted them to creatures on the ground. Hadedas flew overhead, their honking drowning out everything else.

As they topped a rise in the land, they saw the camp. It was quiet. They were too far away to see details inside the *boma*, but there was no movement. Some army trucks were parked outside the perimeter fence, and a dozen Africans were relaxing against them, their voices floating over the still air. A few more were patrolling near the gate.

"What are they waiting for?" Simon whispered to

Lucky. "If they attacked the camp yesterday, why not finish the job? Are they waiting for more back up?"

Lucky shrugged his shoulders, a habit that irritated Simon.

The chief said a few words to Lucky and then disappeared through the bushes.

"What did he say?" Simon asked.

"They are going to capture one of the soldiers, take him back to the village and find out what these terrorists want and who sent them." Lucky smiled. The idea obviously met with his approval.

There was nothing for Simon to do so he wandered to a rock and sat down. The situation was chaotic. Despite his instructions from London to disrupt the auction, it had been blown apart before he arrived. Now he was unsure what action to take. He should make an effort to save Ben Mtumba, and his cabinet. Not to mention Ian Fleming, Her Majesty's representative, but he didn't know which side the hostage-takers were on. And the only way to find out was to ask.

"I want to go back to the village," he told Lucky quietly. "I need one of you to come with me."

"We will all come; the people in London told us to stay with you all the time."

"I need to talk to my head office."

It was late in the evening when they reached the village. Simon accepted a cup of tea from one of the Chief's wives before he unlocked the truck and retrieved the satellite phone.

There were too many trees and huts to get a good line of sight, so he walked out of the village looking for an open space. He felt exposed as he scrambled up a rough *kopje* and looked around. Opening the case, he took out the phone, extended the antenna and connected to London.

He explained the situation in a very few words and asked for instructions. Through the encryption, the voice at the other end sounded robotic. He guessed they were a little shocked by the news and after some deliberation they told him to wait and see, but take no firm action. He was ordered to report back in 24 hours. If the villagers got any information from a captured soldier, he was to find out as much as he could before a decision could be made.

Well that was bloody unhelpful, he thought as he switched off. *Bloody bureaucracy. Basically, do nothing, although what one man can do against half an army was limited.*

He was angry with his bosses. They were alarmingly vague as to what role he should play and what their intentions were about the auction, the President, and any members of his cabinet. Why had they dragged him all the way over here? He had no defined role, except that of derailing the auction if he could. But he was here on the outside, and Ian bloody Fleming was right there on the inside as far as he knew. They had told Simon the reasons for sabotaging the auction, but did it mean Ian had been kept out of the loop? Fleming was their man in Apatu for heaven's sake. Did they distrust their own government representative? There were always too many questions and never enough answers.

He was hot, itchy, the early evening mosquitoes were buzzing around his ears and he was worried sick he'd not been able to contact Amie. He had no idea if a satellite phone only connected with other phones of the same kind and had been instructed not to use the phone for any other purpose than to contact London, but he was past caring. He dialled her number. *Please answer, please answer*, he muttered as he listened to the crackles and pops coming from the handset. There was no ringtone, no message, and no bloody answer.

He walked back into the village his arrival coinciding with the return of the hijacking party. They dragged their prisoner with them.

The poor man was in an appalling state. His face was covered in blood and the way he dragged one leg behind him suggested it was broken. He whimpered, and shook his head from side to side as the men propping him up hauled him into the centre of the village and allowed him to fall in a heap close to the fire.

Simon watched from the sidelines. He suspected the interrogation would not be gentle, but he wasn't prepared for the brutality he was about to witness. The captive was hit again and again, questioned mercilessly, thumped, pinched, kicked and shaken. One eager interrogator put a steel bar into the fire and drew it across the man's cheeks causing him to howl in agony before passing out. He fainted several times, but someone was always ready to throw a bucket of water over him.

After half an hour, Simon turned away sickened by the cruelty. The prisoner's torturers barely gave him enough time to answer their questions before they rained more blows on his broken body.

Simon tried to block out the screams and moans. He didn't want to be here; he wanted no part of it. The auction had been abandoned and that was his job over and he would tell London that tomorrow. In the meantime, he was stuck here for another 24 hours and he hated every moment of it. What kind of example was this for the village children? Simon realized that he hadn't seen the youngsters return with the rest of the party. Where were they? Perhaps they'd sneaked in without him noticing them. He hoped they could neither see nor hear what was going on in the middle of the village compound.

At last, even the torturers got tired, and they dragged the remains of the soldier into one of the huts and crowded around in a circle waiting to be fed. The women passed out plates piled high with meat and gravy and more bowls of pap. They all set to, moulding the maize meal porridge with their fingers before dipping the balls into a communal plate. Tin mugs of frothy beer passed from one to the other as they relaxed, pleased with their night's work.

The sight of the watery stew, the unwashed, grabbing hands and the men's excitement over the torturing persuaded Simon he was not hungry. He waited until they had finished before asking any questions. They were in high spirits as a result of the adrenalin rush from the savagery they had performed and witnessed. It turned his stomach to think of it.

A light touch on his arm made him look down to see a young African girl her face shining in the firelight from the grease she wore to prevent her skin from cracking. She was wearing traditional clothes, a short skirt of *Kitenge* material and a beaded top which rested over the top of her firm young breasts.

She smiled and handed him a plate and spoon and then

giggled at her boldness and ran away into the darkness. How old was she? Not a day over fourteen, Simon guessed. He went to join the men and squeezed in between Lucky and Bones on the wooden bench set out for the visitors. He was feeling sick but put on a brave face. It was difficult to smile and be civil to the men who'd acted with such savagery.

The women showed no emotion when they carried out another pot of stew and topped up the communal plates. In the half-light, it was impossible to identify the contents, and the smell was not enticing to anyone used to western cuisine. Simon took as little as he dared without offending his hosts, indicating his stomach was bad. The men roared with laughter at his pantomime showing them he was not well. He bent over his plate and his throat clamped and his stomach lurched every time he tried to swallow.

As the last plate was cleaned, the women reappeared holding more gourds containing their home-brewed sorghum beer, the froth bubbling on the top as it continued to ferment. Simon stood and made an excuse about a bathroom break to avoid refusing the drink. Not only was his stomach churning, but he didn't like the beer. The locals might be used to it, but half a mug would be enough to put him flat on his back for days.

He felt the African night around him, the rustling leaves and the far away sense of movement, unseen and unknown. He remembered Amie saying that she could feel the earth move beneath her feet. For the first time in the darkness of the bush, he experienced those age-old drumbeats rising from beneath the ground and resonating through his body. Maybe she had a point, after all. How he wished he could see her, talk to her, and hold her. He wanted to hold them both, Amie, and the child they had created together.

The shouts and cackles from the men gathered around the fire were increasing as the alcohol took hold. Simon wasn't in the mood to join them, and he would have to walk past the crowd to get to the hut that had been allocated to the visitors, so he ambled over to the Jeep, pushed back the front seat, and settled down to get as much sleep as he could. He foraged in the glove compartment, finding a stale energy bar which he wolfed down, it was a pleasure to connect with something familiar and tasty. If they thought he was being unsociable, he would make an excuse about not feeling well and hope they would accept that. He closed his eyes, trying to block out the sight of the poor wretch they had dragged back into camp and wondered if he was still alive.

The dawn chorus woke Simon even before the sun had risen to heat the land, rocks, inhabitants, and the air. He was stiff and sore from sleeping in the Jeep and wondered how long the men had been carousing the night before. He hoped they would have some answers about the situation at the camp and how many people had been killed.

Chief Lgego didn't seem too concerned about the battle raging not so very far from his village, and it was still difficult to guess whose side he was on. Lucky had told Simon this village was firmly on the side of the government, but was that true?

He climbed out of the vehicle, stretched and strolled over to find a quiet place to empty his bladder, but as he meandered back towards the huts, he disturbed one of the villagers who had his head stuck under the open bonnet of the Jeep.

"Hey! What do you think you're doing?" he shouted hurrying towards him.

The man stood up with a horrified look on his face.

"Ah, no harm, no harm. I was just looking, just looking. See, a very fine engine, very fine indeed."

Simon didn't believe him, he knew guilt when he saw it. Was he trying to disable the Jeep to make sure they couldn't leave?

"I'm sure you've seen plenty of engines before," Simon snapped, grabbing the bonnet before the villager could let it drop. He peered at the engine but couldn't see if anything had been tampered with. He'd ask Lucky to have a look before they tried to start it and possibly get a second opinion from Trident as well. You couldn't be too careful miles away from civilisation.

Cries inviting him to come and join them for breakfast rang out from the village. He slammed the bonnet down and locked the Jeep. Simon nodded to the inquisitive man indicating they should go together. He'd keep an eye on him for now, and the other eye on the transport. It was getting that he didn't know who to trust, if he could trust anyone at all

.

40 AMIE IN TROUBLE

Now that Amie was returning to the *boma* to spy out the land and see how she could help, she experienced a feeling of euphoria. She tried to make a plan as she retraced her steps. Could she creep up on the enemy and dispose of them one at a time? If they thought everyone was safely inside the *boma*, they would not be expecting an attack from outside. However, the one drawback to that was she'd already left one soldier incapacitated and realized with a shock that she hadn't stopped to check if she'd killed him or only put him out of action.

Yet another black mark for this very bad spy, she thought. If he had recovered, he could give a very exact description of his attacker and the element of surprise would be lost.

The baby must have been worried too, because after the first real kicks she had felt the day before, the little human growing inside her today had football boots on and was practicing own goals for the World Cup. She had to stop and take deep breaths, as the discomfort became worse and worse.

She had not gone more than a mile when her back ached too. She sank down on a handy boulder and rested. If she found it difficult to walk, it would be impossible to accomplish anything or to help anybody when she got near the camp. Before she could even start asking herself, yet again, if she was doing the right thing, she firmly closed off that part of her mind. No, she'd made her decision, and she would stick to it. She couldn't live with herself if she walked away.

She broke the seal on the second bottle of water and took a swig, pleased that she hadn't wasted any, but during the day she would sweat and need more to drink. She hadn't seen a river, or even a waterhole, but that may have been a blessing as it would have attracted animals and the water could have contained parasites and diseases. Apart from the boulders left scattered like a giant's discarded toys, the land was flat as far as the eye could see in all directions. The tall *kopje* in the distance that backed on to the camp was one of the few landmarks for miles around.

She struggled to her feet and walked, this time with more purpose, but possibly less concentration because instead of heading towards the camp and the imprisoned diplomats, she struck off at the wrong angle, mistaking another rocky outcrop in the distance for the one near the camp.

She was putting more distance between herself and those she wanted to rescue.

Amie trudged on for hours, certain she was going in the right direction. She had to take frequent rests to ease her aching back and the constant battering from inside her tummy. No one had warned her that unborn babies could be so active. How pregnant was she? The doctor she'd consulted in Durban hadn't been specific. He'd given her a brief examination, confirmed she was having a baby, and said it was early days. He had told her to book an appointment to see him again in a month's time.

To take her mind off her aches and pains, as she marched, Amie ticked off the weeks on her fingers. Not only was she indecisive, her maths were sadly lacking as well.

Ouma Adede had told her she was having a baby when she and Simon stayed in Apatu for a few days before their idyllic holiday on Mauritius – then they returned to work in Durban – she saw the doctor, was it four weeks later? It must have been another five at least before Ian abducted her. She scowled and wondered if the doctor had noticed she'd not been back to see him. There was no free medical service in South Africa unless you were destitute, so most people had medical insurance.

She had worked with Gaga for ten weeks planning the safari. The figures swirled around inside her head as she counted and recalculated the sums. Every time she got a total, she counted again and each time the answer was different. With all the preparations for the safari, she hadn't made time to visit the hospital or see a doctor. How stupid was that? At the final reckoning she was possibly four or maybe five months. One look at her distended stomach would have told the world that she was a mother to be, though she had concealed it well with her voluminous shirts.

That's the story of your life Amie, she berated herself. *One stuff up after another.* Would life ever be normal? Not if Ian Fleming ever had his way. But Ian Fleming might not survive the safari. For the first time, maybe, there was a light at the end of the tunnel.

She trudged on under the blazing heat of the sun with her clothes sticking to her back, the humidity was higher than normal, and the sweat poured off her. She was forced to take refuge in the shade while she dug in her backpack and grabbed a t-shirt which she wound round her head. *Not the latest in fashion*, she thought but it relieved the burning feeling as the sun beat down on her.

Fluffy clouds floated across the sky, occasionally obliterating the sun which lowered the temperature for a few precious moments. Her feet were aching but they didn't bother her as much as the pain in her stomach.

She looked around, realising for the first time that she was not going in the right direction. She should have seen the camp in the distance by now. The far hills looked no closer, and one jumbled pile of boulders looked much the same as the rest scattered across the open plain. None of them looked like the tall sheer-sided *kopje* behind the camp. She peered at the sun and checked her watch, calculating the angles with the time and the shadows to get a sense of direction. She was definitely heading the wrong way.

Another bolt of pain shot through her, and she sank onto her knees. She was scared, lost and quite possibly in trouble. She rested until the pain eased off and then clambered to her feet to set off again, this time veering off to the left. There were no tracks to follow, no habitation that she could see, and so far, she had not met anyone, even the wildlife was scarce. She paused to take a swig of water and it took all her willpower not to drain the whole bottle. She had to make it last, but she felt weak and dizzy. She would have been better staying in the camp, after all. Even if she found it again, she would be in no condition to attack the soldiers or help those inside in any way.

She continued on, putting one foot in front of the

other, counting them, pushing herself to take at least another five hundred steps before stopping.

The heaving pains in her stomach weren't getting any better, if anything they were more frequent, and her feet screamed, her legs ached, her head thumped from the drums playing inside it, and the landscape waved and tilted with every step.

She stumbled on, past caring which way she was going, there would be a road or a track somewhere soon she told herself. I just need to keep walking.

The grass was higher towards the centre of the vast open landscape, it came up to Amie's waist and posed further dangers. If predators like lions were resting in the shady vegetation, she wouldn't see them, but she had no option but to continue her trek, and try to get back to the safari camp.

A movement to her right made her pause. It was a buck, a kudu she thought, as the air created mirages in front of her eyes. It was racing for its life pursued by a cheetah, capable of running at 80-120 kilometres per hour in short bursts, and the wild cat was racing flat out. The kudu was tiring, its curved horns lowered. It could only cover the ground at 70 kilometres an hour and it was unusual to see them out on the open grasslands; they preferred the dense woodlands. For whatever reason, Amie could only stand and stare at the life and death drama unfolding before her as the buck raced to escape.

As suddenly as it started, the battle ended. The cheetah took a leap forward and the horns disappeared from view. The chase was over. While Amie felt sorry for the poor creature, a small part of her was relieved as the cheetah was unlikely to attack her now it had just killed its next meal. Amie knew they are solitary animals that fiercely defend their own territory, and she was unlikely to meet another one.

She steered away from the kill and cut away to the left. If she'd known how close she was to the camp, it would have given her renewed energy, but the tall rock piles hid it from view.

The baby kicked again, hard and fast making her gasp. She bent over double, breathing deeply, the earth swimming, the air enveloping her, the sky sloping at a weird angle as she slid to the ground. It dawned on her that she might be in labour, but it was too soon, it wasn't her time. *Please don't let the baby come early*, she whispered. She burst into tears and rocked as her body was wracked with painful contractions.

She didn't have the strength to get to her feet, and she slumped on the ground, unable to move as the pain washed over her in waves. She was alone, helpless, and scared.

41 INERTIA

Inside the *boma* conditions were deteriorating. The previous night everyone agreed they would go on the offensive at dawn, but the sunrise had come and the fierce rays beat down on the earth and no one had done anything. It seemed the idea of action sometime in the future was fine, but action now, didn't have the same appeal. There was no offensive, not just yet.

Instead, just after dawn the repaired *boma* gates flew open and an unruly group appeared and raced through the camp grabbing every weapon they could find. The guns had been collected and stored in the kitchen areas and the hostage-takers swooped in and grabbed the lot before anyone could stop them. Ian counted six of them, none in battle fatigues, but they looked strong and capable. All the time they were ransacking the camp not one word was spoken and they communicated with arm signals, the sign of trained troops. They may not have look like a conventional army, no two individuals were dressed the same, more scruffy vagabonds than troops, but they were well co-ordinated and impressed Ian by how disciplined they were and how quickly and methodically they moved.

At a signal from the leader, they exited the *boma* with the weapons and the gate slammed shut leaving the occupants stunned.

Once they had their equilibrium back, the remaining diplomats and the ministers shuffled into small groups arguing about what to do. Some were determined to break out and smash through any guards outside while others believed it was best to sit and wait to find out what their captors wanted from them.

There was no way of getting word out or sending for help. The cell phones didn't work and no one volunteered to sneak out and take a message to Apatu. Who could they trust to send?

Samuel Suma, the Minister of Sport and Blessing Ochido, Minister of the Interior, were as scared as the rest. While they had planned to assassinate the President on this trip, they had not foreseen being attacked by a third party and neither of them wanted to take charge in the middle of the chaos. If they could fade away unnoticed into the background they would. For now, Ben had their support and if they came out of this alive, they could take full credit and blame the 'late' president.

Ben Mtumba called a council meeting, but nothing was decided. No one agreed on any course of action. If there were any decisions to be made, the President must take them. He had ultimate responsibility for the lives of everyone.

A meeting held between the remaining four superpowers didn't come to any conclusion either. The North Koreans were impossible to understand. Their chief interpreter was in shock, shaking from head to foot and almost catatonic.

The British, Russians, and even Edward Keller, were made of sterner stuff. Loud arguments broke out as one idea after another was proposed and discarded. They retired to the far corner of the large marquee to make plans for action of some kind.

The American was all for busting out.

"Y'all see we can't sit here and wait to be blown to bits. I say we blast our way out."

"With what?" Ian Fleming asked him calmly. "Yes, we could do that if we had the guns the poisoned soldiers won't need now. But if you remember, the terrorists rushed in and removed those."

"Yeah, well we should've hidden them better."

"Believe me, they would have found them, they searched everything." Ian was scathing, but he told the truth. No inch of the *boma* had been left undisturbed, as the soldiers ripped open diplomatic cases, investigated under beds, pawed through the supplies and ransacked the kitchen. They even removed every knife they found.

"We must find a way to fight back. I never thought I would think like an American," Vladimir's tone suggested he didn't have much regard for the Americans, "but we cannot sit and hope they will leave us alone."

The North Korean ambassador whispered to the translator who spoke up. "North Korea thinks we should wait. The men outside left the food for us, so they must want us alive. If we attack them they may kill us."

There was a stunned silence as everyone looked at Hyeon Park, sent to the auction on behalf of the Democratic People's Republic of Korea. This was the man representing the country that was threatening to rain nuclear bombs on the United States. North Korea defied the rest of the world and was testing larger rockets. They held marches with hundreds of thousands of soldiers through the streets of the capital. Now they advocated a passive reaction.

"Y'all may have noticed," drawled Ed Keller, "that in the democratic way, it's a vote of three to one that we don't sit here like a bull sniffing cows."

His words were met with puzzled looks from the Russians and the North Koreans.

"We have to get our butts out of here and fast."

"Has anyone got any idea what the bloody hell that bunch outside are waiting for?" Even under these circumstances, Fleming thought to brush the dust off his trousers.

"I think they wait for instructions, maybe? Or at least to talk to the President. He speaks their language. We don't." The Russian's words made sense.

Outside, their captors were doing nothing. They hung around, patrolling the perimeter, shouting and making threatening gestures to anyone walking too close to the thorn fence. None of the captors were guarding inside the *boma*, so the prisoners were free to mingle, help themselves to food and generally behave as if everything was normal – except that it wasn't.

The earlier bluster from the diplomats fizzled out as they argued as to what to do. *It's a miniature replica of any large international conference*, thought Ian Fleming, *no one could agree on anything and in the end, nothing was decided.*

By the middle of the day, Ben, who didn't have to get agreement from any of his ministers, took action. He summoned everyone to the tent.

"We all agree this situation is untenable," he said, pausing to allow the North Korean translator to translate. "It's time to take stock of what few resources we have, and to deal with the bodies inside the *boma*."

"Fling them over the fence," Keller called out.

"That's what I have decided to do," the President replied. "We are in this together, so we must work together. It doesn't matter if you are an important diplomat or a bodyguard, so let's forget status and titles for now. I need a group of six men to remove the dead. I need another group to make an inventory of the remaining food and water, and a third group to search the camp for anything we might be able to use as a weapon. Maybe there is something that was overlooked. Finally, I need a volunteer to escape and go back to Apatu to summon help."

His remarks were met with general murmurs of approval but no one stepped forward to volunteer for any particular duty.

Ben sighed. He had hoped the men would organize themselves, but it now fell to him to select the people and to allocate their tasks. Ben paired his own men with the foreigners in the hope it would help them work as one team.

Ed Keller, Ian Fleming, and Samuel Suma were instructed to list the supplies and work out a schedule to ration what they had. One of the North Koreans, Vladimir Petrovnikov, and Blessing Ochido were on corpse detail. Despite the bodies being dumped in a heap to one side of the compound, and covered in blankets, the flies were buzzing around and creeping through the gaps to take advantage of their unexpected windfall. The smell of rotting flesh permeated the far corners of the camp and those designated, who were less than enthusiastic, wrapped anything they could find over their noses as they began their gruesome task.

Attracted by the stench of rotting flesh, the vultures were gathering overhead, the braver ones swooping down in the hope of slicing off a lump of dead meat before they were chased away.

It was none too soon. The creatures were getting bolder by the minute and less inclined to take off when the men shouted and screamed at them. They skittered out of reach, fluffing their dark brown feathers, and revealing the black skin on their heads and necks, while black eyes and curved beaks of the same colour glared at their opponents. The African white-backed vulture is not a foe to be ignored. A bird's head comes up to the waist of most men, their wingspans nearly as wide as a lorry and they weigh as much as a cannonball. As a species, they are revered by many Africans who believe it is bad luck to kill them. Hopefully, they might cause problems for the men outside guarding the camp.

After much discussion, they decided they would lay the bodies on a blanket with a man at each corner and catapult the deceased over the *boma* fence. It took several attempts before they got into their stride all the while battling the swarm of blowflies angry at being disturbed.

When the American and the British ambassadors, with a reluctant Minister of Sport trailing behind, investigated what remained of the food, they were horrified to discover that the gas to the freezers had run out and much of the food had spoiled. The spare gas was stored outside the *boma,* a sensible precaution at the time, but it was out of reach, and it was too late to save the food that had gone off. As Ian tried to remove a pack of butter the wrapping squelched in his hand and it poured out like thick soup.

"I guess we're in a heap o' trouble here," Ed remarked as he sniffed at a carton of milk and wrinkled his nose. "This sure is no good either."

Ian glanced up at the makeshift shelves.

"There's a few cans of meat and fish, but the vegetables are rotten and smell. They'll attract vermin. It looks as though we've precious little left to feed thirty-seven men." Ian surveyed the spoiled food.

"Ya think that's what they plan, to let us starve to death?"

"I know as much as you do," Ian snarled. "Stop asking me damned fool questions I can't answer. You want to know if that's their plan, then go and ask them yourself."

"No need to get yer feathers ruffled. We're all in this together an don't yah forget it."

Keller was right. They were all in a fix and this was not the time to squabble among themselves.

"We better collect all the rotting food and get that outside the *boma* as well, though it might be better to stuff it all inside the fridges and freezers to stop it smelling."

"Yeah, might come in useful as weapons though." Ed sniggered. "We could go down in history as the first to defeat the enemy with decaying cabbages and carrots."

Despite the seriousness of the situation, they both burst out laughing at the thought.

"Thirty-seven hungry men," Ian repeated, "and the women. Have you seen Amie anywhere?"

"Can't say that I have, nor that little black lady that was running around making sure everything was going to plan and y'all was happy."

"I'll search for them." Ian strode towards the door of the kitchen tent. "It shouldn't take me long."

He walked out into the blazing hot sunshine. Squeezing his eyes against the glare, he systematically searched every corner of the camp. He looked in tents, skirted round the corpse detail, and even poked his nose into the latrine areas. Checking to see he was not being observed, he even glanced into the tents allocated to the Ministers and diplomats, although there was nowhere to hide inside the small canvas shelters.

Since they were all in the same fix and protocol had gone out of the window, Ian popped his head into Ben's tent to ask if he knew where Amie was. Two steps in from the entrance he paused. The Englishman had never seen an African, whose face was almost white.

"What's the matter? What's happened?" he asked reaching out to grab Ben's arm but the man shook his head.

"Have the terrorists sent demands? Are you ill?"

The only response was a shake of the head as Ben collapsed on his camp cot.

Ian didn't know what to say; he was at a loss for words. He'd never seen a man as frightened as the one in front of him. The President was quivering like an aspen leaf. Ben took a breath and looked up.

"I have been cursed," he whispered and opened his hand to show Fleming the skin pouch he'd found under his mattress.

Ian's first thought was to tell him not to be so stupid,

that curses had no power. Poison yes, but if Ben was referring to a small bag stuffed with herbs, bones and hair, it could have no effect on his health as long as he didn't believe it. He was so lost for words that all he could do was enquire again if Ben knew where Amie was.

The President shook his head and stared at the scrap of skin he clutched so hard it was turning his knuckles white.

Dumbfounded, Ian backed out of the tent. This put them all in greater danger. Ben was now useless as a leader and uniting force. Who would replace him? Kirimu? He may have been the choice at an earlier point, but he'd shown precious few leadership qualities and Ian had his doubts as to how malleable he might be if the UK supported him as the next President. Watching him on this trip, Ian didn't trust him an inch.

Amie was missing and Gaga and Ngonicansaga were nowhere to be seen either. A chill ran down Ian's back. In all the chaos of the explosions and attack had the soldiers taken them? Women as spoils of war was a common practice the world over. Amie might be both stupid and irritating – and a woman – but she did not deserve to be raped and tortured.

42 HYENAS

Amie's hand shook as she attempted to unscrew the cap off the water bottle. An everyday task was now a major battle. It came loose and she lifted it to her mouth. Her arm shuddered as another huge contraction gripped her body. It took her by surprise and the plastic bottle spun out of her hand and fell on the ground. She watched as the precious liquid poured out and soaked almost immediately into the hard, dry African sand. She made a desperate effort to reach over and grab it, but another contraction caused her to grip her belly instead. She would have burst into tears but another sensation made her gasp in horror. Her waters had broken. The baby was coming. Too soon. It was much too soon.

She was frozen to the spot, sitting on the damp ground unsure what to do. The contractions eased up which gave her some relief, but the shock, and fear pushed her into a state of stupor. She wasn't able to think and she blacked out.

When she came to, the landscape was still undulating. Despite the t-shirt wrapped around her head, she could feel the sun's heat radiating down on her. She was no longer sweating, her tongue was swollen and the inside of her mouth was bone dry.

She was hallucinating. One moment she sat alone, leaning against a small granite mound with the wide valley spread before her devoid of life. Then she was joined by several small brown creatures covered in spots. They swirled before her eyes like a surrealistic ballet. Four of them sat and stared at her while the fifth paced slowly to and fro, coming a little nearer at each pass. Five pairs of large black eyes fixed on her, five sets of brilliant white teeth gleamed from long snouts below two round furry ears. The pale grey spots on the sloping back of the patrolling beast told her it was a pack of hyenas. Were they real or were they a figment of her imagination? Amie couldn't decide. Either way she was helpless against them.

No. She had a gun, the AK47 she'd taken from the soldier, if she could reach it. Would a sudden movement cause them to rush in and attack? If she shouted and waved her arms it might frighten them away. Her brain refused to function and refused to instruct her arms to scare them and send them off. There was no movement except the silent pacing of the matriarchal pack leader as her feet paced backwards and forwards.

The stench of the creatures, habitually feasting on decaying meat, reached Amie's nose and spurred her into action. She couldn't just sit there and wait to be torn apart. She battled to stay focused. The bandolier of bullets was wrapped around her body but the rifle lay a couple of metres away on her right and she would have to move to reach it.

She took a deep breath, held it and exhaled, the air rasping in her parched throat as she leaned over and stretched out her hand. The alpha creature gave a high-pitched whine. If it was a signal to attack, none of them moved.

Amie's fingers scrabbled in the dust, stretching the

tendons and muscles as far as she could. The tips of her fingers were almost on the hot metal and she felt the heat radiating from it. She leaned further but she was only able to touch the barrel. To pick it up she would have to get closer.

She kept her movements as smooth and as slow as she could, not wanting to give the animals an invitation to attack. She leaned her right hand on the hot earth and put her weight on it and then heaved herself towards the gun.

The lead animal came closer, sniffing towards the damp patch Amie had exposed. It whined again. Hyenas are unfairly labelled as cowards. They are capable of taking down a fully-grown beast like a lion or a domestic cow if they put their minds to it. If there was no carrion to clear up, then this species of nature's rubbish collectors would hunt live prey.

Amie saw the landscape tilt again and knew if she didn't do something soon she would black out and it would be for the last time. Of all the situations she'd been in before, this was the worst. She took another deep breath, shot her arm out and dragged her aching body towards the gun.

The matriarch of the pack sank down, its belly brushing the sand and crept deliberately forward.

In a last desperate effort, Amie grabbed the gun which was red hot. The metal seared her skin, she could not have let go of it if she tried. She ignored the pain on her palm and swung back toward the animal swiping as hard as she could. The butt connected with the side of its head flinging it backwards. It gave a high-pitched howl and somersaulted, landing on two of the hyenas that failed to get out of the way in time. They turned and snarled at each other, snapping at legs, noses and backs before retreating. Blood ran down the side of the maimed creature, exciting the rest of the group. They crowded in and licked at the sticky red liquid, working themselves to a frenzy.

Amie watched in horror. She had to get away or shoot them all. She heaved herself into a sitting position with her back against the boulder and peeled her hand off the gun barrel removing layers of skin. She pulled the t-shirt off her head and wrapped it around the injury and, taking aim, she sent a bullet flying into the melee of fighting animals. They turned tail and fled and within seconds they were gone, their shrill, high cackles, much like human laughter, echoed across the wide open plain.

Amie assumed once they had calmed down and licked their wounds they would be back, just as soon as they plucked up enough courage. They knew instinctively she was wounded, lying there helpless, and it was only a matter of time before they came back to claim their meal. How long could she keep them at bay?

She exhaled and lay back exhausted but her body gave her no rest as the next contraction threatened to tear her apart. She choked back a sob and tears ran down her face, she was too dehydrated to produce much fluid.

She closed her eyes, willing the pain to go away but instead it got worse. It was one way of helping her to stay awake for if she fainted now she would never wake up. She took a deep breath and remembered no more as darkness descended and the sights and sounds of the wilderness faded to black.

43   A LOCAL AFFAIR

Simon smiled at the lady who handed him a tin plate indicating he should eat. Looking at the unappetising offering of what appeared to be beans and corn, he imitated his hosts' custom and ate with his fingers.

The elderly woman, who was one of the Chief's wives, wore a faded floral dress with a matching kerchief over her head. She put her head to one side and raised her eyebrows. She wanted to know if he liked it.

He smiled again and rubbed his stomach with his free hand and nodded.

She relaxed and smiled, her teeth shining white in her lined face. She looked old but had probably not seen more than forty winters, her skin baked dry in the sun was deeply wrinkled.

Lucky strolled over and sat next to him on the wooden bench.

Simon glanced at him.

"Headache?"

"Bit, but I have had worse."

"Can you remember what they found out yesterday?" Simon knew it was rude to get straight to the point, but his curiosity was killing him. There was no sign of the prisoner and he hoped they would not need to repeat last night's brutality.

"Yes. I came to look for you but I could not find you."

"I had things to do – for London," he said, adding weight to his excuse. "So, what's the score?"

"We still don't know how many are alive inside the *boma*, but some have been killed. They have thrown bodies over the fence and the men outside have had to bury them; they were not pleased." Lucky chuckled.

"Who are these guys and what do they want?"

Lucky laughed again. "He told us everything we wanted to know."

"Which is?" Simon sat back as if he had all the time in the world. Africans did not like to be rushed and Lucky was going to string this out as long as he could. He took out a penknife and cleaned his nails pretending a nonchalance he didn't feel.

"It's complicated," Lucky enunciated slowly. "There are two, how you say sides, parties?"

"Factions?" Simon supplied.

"Yes, that is it. Two factions. One is from Budan. The M'untus there are claiming the minerals for themselves."

"But we're miles inside Togodo." Simon waved his arm towards the far distant hills barely visible in the early morning mist. "Budan is on the other side of those mountains isn't it?"

"Yes," agreed Lucky, "but when the colonial powers drew the borders and carved up Africa, they chose mountains and rivers where one country started and the next began."

Simon nodded. He knew the long-held myth of how a young prince, later to become Kaiser Wilhelm II of Prussia, complained to his grandmother Queen Victoria that she had two snow-capped mountains in Africa while he had none, so she bequeathed him Mount Kilimanjaro as a birthday gift. The truth was the British gave up the mountain to German Tanganyika in exchange for the Sultanate of Zanzibar which seemed a fair exchange, a mountain for a coastline. Either way, it was a typical example of how the western powers designated borders without a thought to the tribes and cultures who'd lived there since the birth of man.

"Budan is claiming this part of Togodo. They want the minerals and all the foreign countries to come and pay the money to them."

"It makes sense. I can see their reasoning," Simon replied wishing Lucky would get on with it. "So Budan sent soldiers to disrupt the auction?"

"Yes, and to kill all the people of course."

"Of course," Simon nodded.

"But they are not alone."

"Oh?" Simon looked up in surprise.

"No, they have help here from more M'untus."

"From Togodo?"

"Yes. They want a country only for M'untus all one tribe. They want their president Muwaba to rule our country as well as Budan."

"But who, who in Togodo is working with Budan? And why?" Simon stopped. He should take it one question at a time.

"The man did not know. He was not an important man and does not know everything. He is from Budan and he should not be here." Lucky stood, his face was angry as he grabbed a couple of beers from the back of the Jeep. He knocked the caps off on the footplate and returned to sit next to Simon passing him one.

Simon didn't usually drink beer at breakfast, but he didn't want to interrupt Lucky's story. Finding out what the man knew was like pulling teeth. He nodded his thanks and waited for his colleague to continue.

Lucky took several agonising swigs before he rested the bottle on his knees and continued.

"All the filthy dog told us was there are people in Apatu who want President Ben Mtumba out, because for them he is a dirty Kawa." To emphasise his point, Lucky spat in the dust before taking another swig of his beer.

"But the Kawas, with the help of some Luebos, took back power in the second war." Simon hoped his praise would help Lucky's story along.

"Yes, but there are some bad Kawas in the government who will fight their own people while they pretend to be loyal. Maybe President Muwaba, has promised they will be in charge."

It all sounded complicated to Simon and did not make sense. Why ally yourself with a man who wanted to take over your country? If you were the same tribe yes, but against your own people?

"We should kill all the dirty M'untus and remove them from the face of the earth." Lucky spat the words causing Simon's heart to sink. It was genocide by any other name. It wouldn't be the first time it had happened in Africa, nor would it be the last. The Matabele in Zimbabwe were targeted for years and the stories out of Rwanda were beyond belief, with the brutality and carnage as the Hutus systematically eliminated the Tutsis.

"So, what are the plans now, Lucky?"

"We go to fight them. Chief Lgego is preparing the

villagers." Lucky grabbed Simon's arm and pointed to where a crowd of men were digging a large grave.

"Did the soldier die?" Simon asked.

Lucky gave him a strange look. "Yes, he is gone, but …" he paused and laughed. "You think they are digging a grave for him?"

"Well, yes."

"No. They are getting their guns. They will not take time to make a grave for a M'untu from Budan. No, they will leave him for the vultures."

Lucky had lived in England, spoke the language well and was an intelligent man, yet his tribal roots ran deep and his loyalty to them was absolute.

Simon stood up and walked over to where the village men were digging. Lucky was right. As he watched, the men pulled canvas wrapped bundles out of the ground. There was laughter and back slapping as they uncovered their haul.

"Amazing," muttered Simon, looking at the huge pile of guns, grenades, pistols, hand-held rockets and ammunition they uncovered. He watched them unearth an RPG, a rocket-propelled grenade. These guys were serious.

"Chief Lgego has prepared well," Lucky spoke in his ear. "He is a wise man – because he is a Luebos," he added as an afterthought.

"Amazing," Simon repeated.

Lucky raised his eyebrows. "No. There is not a village in Africa that does not have a store of guns like this, though maybe this is extra big."

"All buried?"

"Until they are needed."

"When do they plan to attack the *boma*? Are they are going to free the President and all the diplomats?"

"They are still talking." Lucky swung round to indicate where the chief was seated outside his hut with his men.

Simon was alarmed to see they were quaffing copious amounts of the local brew. Would they be in any fit state to fight?

"I think tonight," Lucky added. "The dogs will not be expecting us. It is going to be a glorious fight."

Shivers ran down Simon's spine. No fight was glorious. He had to contact London and tell them what was happening. He needed to find out what they wanted him to do. He retrieved the case from the jeep and was about to walk over to the highest point on the local hill when Lucky grabbed his arm.

"If the villagers see you using the phone there will be trouble."

"But why? Don't they understand I must speak to my chief?"

"This is no business of London. This is African business. Try to talk to your bosses there and the villagers will kill you. They will think you are warning the President or even the M'untus. They don't know you so they can't trust you."

Lucky yanked the case away from Simon and put it back in the vehicle, locked the door, put the key in his pocket and walked away.

Simon stared after him. What would he do now? All at once these friendly villagers did not seem as friendly as before and he was vulnerable.

44 NGONICANSAGA

A lone vulture circled overhead looking down at the prone figures on the ground. Neither was moving, neither looked threatening. One was a hyena, the other a white girl, though the bird wasn't consciously aware of this, all it saw was food. It circled once more and was on the point of swooping down when a movement caught its eye. Something was approaching. It flapped its wings and rose higher – waiting.

A hand on Amie's shoulder from behind shook her out of her stupor. The hand gripped her and was shaking the top of her arm back and forward.

"*Kuamka, Kuamka,*" Wake up.

Amie groaned. As she regained consciousness the pains returned. She'd prefer to slip into oblivion, back into the black, comforting darkness.

"*Kuamka, Kuamka,*" the voice repeated with a sense of urgency. "*Wewe ni shida,*" You are in trouble.

Still there was no response from Amie except for a couple of moans.

"Amie. Amie."

The sound of her own name had the desired response. She opened her eyes and looked straight into those of the young girl she had first seen in the coffee shop in Apatu, and again in the *boma,* the one brought by the government minister.

"You," she exclaimed. "What? What?" A vicious bolt of pain shot from her belly to her head as her body got ready to expel the baby.

"You hurt?" The girl looked puzzled, "there is problem?"

"I am, I am losing my baby." Amie's words came out garbled, her swollen tongue reducing her words to gurgles and grunts. She wept and screamed as another pain left her gasping.

"Baby?" repeated the girl as she frowned then looked round as if trying to see a baby.

"No, no I am pregnant," Amie gasped between waves of sheer agony.

The young girl hesitated. Maybe she didn't know the word pregnant? Amie pointed to her legs, "Baby," she said. "*Mtoto.*" The words croaked in her dry throat, it was impossible to talk.

With a cry the girl threw down the bag she'd slung over her shoulder and brought out a bottle of water. She held Amie's head and let the liquid trickle into her mouth. She knew enough not to let her patient have too much too quickly. She looked enquiringly at Amie before lifting the over-sized t-shirt and running her hand lightly over her bump. The stains on Amie's cargo pants told her the waters had broken.

With Amie on the point of falling unconscious again, she leaned forward and slapped her hard on the cheek.

Amie's eyes shot open and she gasped to find her cargo pants being ripped down followed by her panties. Through a blurred haze she tried to follow what the girl was telling her to do. It wasn't necessary to know. Her body was instinctively programmed by nature thousands of years earlier. It knew what was needed now was to birth the child.

Amie lay back, though it seemed the girl wanted her to sit up, stand and crouch down, but she didn't have the strength. Her cries alternated between the waves of pain as the contractions got stronger. She was so far out of it that she didn't even react when she felt small fingers probing up inside her, wriggling, exploring. The agony went on. Nothing mattered, nothing at all but getting rid of the baby and the pain it was causing. She ceased to think as the world swirled around her in a pink and grey fog. The girl took the bottle out of her bag and gave Amie more sips of water.

Time lost all meaning. She was unaware that the sun had passed its zenith, that the wind carried the rancid scent of the hyenas approaching, or that the vulture feasting on the carcass close by, had now been joined by several of its flock, all screeching and squabbling over the putrefying flesh.

Like all mothers the world over, animal and human, Amie was fixated on giving birth. The recurring bolts of pain did not let her faint, but from feeling woozy, her brain cleared, her senses sharpened and she was able to focus and help her rescuer.

"No, wait," the girl raised her hand, she didn't want Amie to push.

"I must. I must."

The girl shook her head violently, her shiny black curls glistening in the sunshine. She jumped up and walked to and fro searching the ground. For a moment Amie thought she was leaving her but then she heard her pulling on a plant. She tore it out by the roots and peeled long strips off the stem. She braided them into two lengths of string and waved them towards Amie with a smile. Amie didn't understand what she was trying to tell her, then she felt the girl's small hands below but couldn't see what was happening.

The girl prodded Amie's belly hard with her fingers and then looked at her. "Now. Now. *Kushinikiza.*" She paused for a moment her face crumpled in thought. "Push," she shouted and laughed. "Push. Push."

Amie pushed and pushed again, each time her body contracted she gave another push. When she was least expecting it, the baby shot out and the young girl flew backwards in an effort to stop it landing on the ground. Amie fell back exhausted but couldn't understand why the labour pains continued. Was something wrong? Wasn't the baby born yet? With her last ounce of strength, she struggled to raise herself on her elbows.

The girl was rifling through Amie's bag, and held up the knife she found. She opened a blade, spat on it and used her homemade string to tie off the umbilical cord in two places before cutting it apart.

"Is my baby ok?"

One look at the girl's face told Amie all she needed to know.

Silent tears ran down the dark brown face as she cradled the blood and mucus-soaked bundle of flesh in her arms. Then, to Amie's horror she began to smack and thump the small body, she shook it hard, over and over, she held it upside down. There was no response.

"No, no! You will hurt it," Amie screamed

The girl put her ear to the baby's chest and listened, then, shoulders drooping, she shuffled over and handed Amie her new-born son. His features were perfect, his little hands with their tiny nails and cute toes, the mop of fair hair already drying on his head and the pair of grey eyes, just like Amie's which stared out at a world and saw nothing.

Amie lay back wracked by dry sobs. The little body was perfectly formed but not quite the length of her hands and as light as a feather. He was born too soon. Even with the best medical facilities in the world, Amie realized his chances of survival would have been uncertain. She curled her hands round the tiny body and pressed her lips to his head. How could something as small as that, have caused her such discomfort and pain, and now such heartache?

The young girl roused her and urged her to move. While Amie had begun her grieving, her visitor had been busy, cleaning up the afterbirth, and was now nudging her to her feet indicating they should move. Amie had heard tales of women labouring in the fields, moving into the shade, giving birth, bundling the baby into a blanket tied on their back and immediately going back to work. She'd never really believed them but this girl expected her to get up and walk now.

"You were at the camp." Her words were lost in her parched throat and the African offered her the water bottle. She drank greedily until it was snatched away.

She hoisted Amie to her feet, supporting her as the bereaved mother swayed in time with the tilting landscape.

Her vision cleared and she saw the reason her friend wanted to go. The hyenas were closing in again.

Amie leaned against her midwife and pulling the gun up to her chest she let off a round towards the animals. She didn't hit anything her aim went far wide but they scattered at the noise and the recoil sent her flying backwards.

"You are the girl Kirimu brought with him?"

"Yes, I am Ngonicansaga – Ngoni."

"How can I ever thank you, Ngoni?" Amie didn't get to finish as she was pulled roughly away from the scavenging animals slinking closer. For a moment, she thought Ngoni was going to urge her to leave the body of her child behind. The girl pointed to her nose and then back at the advancing hyenas. She was saying they would leave an odour trail and the animals would follow but Amie shook her head. She could not leave her baby to be torn apart by the creatures.

"We will go a safe distance and then bury him," she sobbed.

With the gun in one hand, the baby in the other and Ngoni holding fast to her arm they shuffled away. Glancing behind, Amie could see the hyenas challenging the vulture flock who took to the air, large black wings forming an umbrella over their disturbed lunch, filling the air with their angry hissing.

The pair stumbled over the ground, weaving around the tall termite mounds some as tall as a man. Twice, Amie sank to her knees and each time Ngoni dragged her back on her feet and urged her on.

When she considered they had gone a safe distance, she pushed Amie down and gathered some rocks that were scattered over the valley floor. The sun-baked earth was too hard to dig, and the only protection they could give the small baby was a rock cairn.

Amie sat and held her son close. He had never breathed, not moved, and yet only yesterday he was kicking furiously inside her as if he knew something was wrong. If she'd stayed in Apatu could she have saved him? She would never know. She was overcome with guilt. How could she tell Simon? Thoughts of him were too painful right now.

Ngoni held out her hands.

Amie shook her head violently. This was something she had to do herself, yet she couldn't let go. She rocked, hugging him tightly to her and fiercely resisted Ngoni's efforts to take the child.

The girl lost patience. She got angry and shouted at Amie in her local dialect. "You have more babies, but this one is late," she spat, seeing only stupidity in this white woman who was putting both their lives in danger.

Amie gave herself a shake. Ngoni was right. The smell of death could attract predators from miles around, and until she'd had a good wash, even she was a walking invitation to dinner. She scrambled to her feet and wrapping the t-shirt round the small body she laid him on the ground.

"I don't believe in God anymore," she whispered to it, but I christen you Simon Junior and Raymond after my father. She licked her finger and drew a small cross on his forehead, allowing a few tears to fall on his face before covering it over.

Ngoni rummaged in her bag and brought out a cloth stained with blood.

"What?" began Amie, then realized that the African had brought the after birth which in their custom needed to be buried with the baby to ensure its spirit remained at rest.

Ngoni piled the stones as quickly as she could, maybe in case Amie changed her mind and tried to reclaim the baby. Amie gathered two sticks and bound them together in the shape of a cross and pushed it down between the stones.

"Rest in Peace," she whispered. "You are the second child I have lost but I will never forget either of you."

If Ngoni was unfeeling and callous, Amie couldn't complain. She was bent on them both surviving and picking up the gun she thrust it into Amie's hands, hung her bag over her shoulder, and led them away from the makeshift grave.

As they slogged towards the mountains in the far distance, Amie looked back, but saw no sign of the scavengers.

They walked in silence for a long time, one foot in front of the other. Amie was sore and uncomfortable but she found an inner strength she didn't know she had. Every pace took her one step away from the danger they left behind and further away from the child she had just delivered. She had no idea where they were going but blindly followed the young African as they hurried along the valley.

45 INDECISION

For the first time in his life, Ian Fleming was at a loss. He had no idea what to do. The son of wealthy parents he'd led a privileged life, school at Harrow, then Oxford University followed by an easy passage into the diplomatic service, all part of the 'old boy' network. He rose quickly in the ranks, served in several countries, two before this one in Africa, and this was not his first safari. Never before had there been such chaos, nor had his life been in such danger.

He wandered around the camp and paused, leaning against a gum pole which supported the main gate. A few people were wandering aimlessly around, but most were hiding in the shade of their tents. No one had taken charge. The President was a basket case, whimpering about witchcraft nonsense and when he'd approached each of the ministers, instead of eagerly jumping into the breach and taking command, they backed off, saying they couldn't possibly usurp their beloved President. Strange, since one of them must have purchased the evil little bag that threatened death, but no one was admitting to it. Were they waiting for Mtumba to die before taking power? Ian couldn't understand it.

He thought about taking charge, but as a diplomat and a white man he thought his chances were slim. Every action he'd ever taken was in service of Her Majesty's

Government and his aims were clear, put Britain's interests first. Right now, he didn't know what was best for Britain, but he dearly wanted to save himself. He did not want to die in this godforsaken, baking hot hell hole, hacked to death before being abandoned in an unmarked grave – or left as food for the scavengers.

The other diplomats were of no use. They all came from similar backgrounds and were more bluster than action. No one was prepared to work together. They'd gathered to talk three times and no consensus could be reached on what to do. Some were for sitting tight and hoping they'd be released. Vladimir wanted to fight back, but was reminded they had no weapons and if they upset their captors they might turn nasty. No one would even consider making Molotov cocktails. The North Koreans and Ed Keller argued that the men outside must be waiting for someone. Only Ian and the Russian were keen to make another attempt at escaping. The others were half-hearted about it but there was no agreement on how much of the scarce supplies they could take and none of them were trained in bush craft and would die of dehydration or attack by wild animals.

Ben was the driving force that could galvanize them all into action, but he was now useless, huddled in his tent attended by his two bodyguards and refusing to talk to anyone.

So, they sat scared and vulnerable, waiting to be picked off – one by useless one.

Looking through a gap in the plastic grass fencing, Ian saw that their captors weren't doing anything either. They were lazing around the vehicles, smoking and laughing, totally at ease. It was a boost to their ego, he thought sourly, to have a whole bunch of important foreigners under their control.

They were running out of supplies and had cut back to the bare minimum; it was the one thing they agreed on, but there was only enough food and water left for two more days.

He had to talk to Ben again. It was the only thing he could do, but he didn't rate his chances.

46 SIMON SIDELINED

Simon watched the villagers prepare. They made half-hearted efforts to clean the guns but loaded them with a lot more enthusiasm. They were in a merry mood, laughing and joking, pushing each other around, and hyped up. Without doubt they were looking forward to the bloodshed and the thrill of the battle.

"You do not come with us," Lucky announced appearing suddenly at his elbow. "They do not want a white man involved in their battle."

"I was planning to stay in the background."

"No. If the enemy see a white man they will not believe these brave warriors are true Africans. This is an African battle and nothing to do with any other country. This is not the white man's land." Lucky was emphatic.

"Except my fellow countrymen are stuck inside that camp, so it has plenty to do with me and I am not the only white people. Have you forgotten the French, Russians, Americans and the Asians are all in there as well?" Simon was angry. He certainly didn't want to fight, but an extra gun would be useful and he wanted to be there to ensure these villagers didn't turn on the captives and allow their bloodlust to get out of hand. They were an undisciplined, unruly force.

Simon was also unsure which side this village was on.

Despite assurances from Lucky that Lgego was an ardent supporter of President Mtumba, he'd had no proof. Perhaps their plan was to hook up with the terrorists and massacre everybody inside the *boma*. If that happened, he wanted to be a witness. Somebody needed to tell the world what really happened.

"You stay," hissed Lucky.

"Look," Simon tried to reason. "I know you are African, but you are also working for the British Government too. You owe us some loyalty."

"I am an African first," Lucky replied. "I may do a little work for your embassy, but these are my people." He turned and walked away.

Simon stared after him not sure what to do.

By the time the ammunition had been liberated from its hiding place it was time to eat, and to Simon's dismay, that included gallons of the local beer. *These men will not be in a fit state to fight anyone* he thought, *what were they thinking? If the troops guarding the camp were trained soldiers this mob would be mown down in seconds.*

Chief Lgego must have had the same thoughts as he stood up and made an announcement which was met by cheers from the half-drunken men.

"The Chief has told them they must sleep now and tomorrow before the sun rises, they go to fight." Trident had to shout in Simon's ear to make himself heard.

"Is Lucky going with them?" Simon shouted back.

Trident thought for a moment and replied, "Yes, I think so."

So much for sticking to me like glue, thought Simon.

"Trident?"

"Yes Boss?"

"I've left something in the Jeep and I need it. Can you get the keys from Lucky please?"

"Yes Boss, of course."

Simon hated using the man as an errand boy, but he was sure that Lucky wouldn't give the keys to him. He would follow the villagers at a safe distance tomorrow and if necessary, the truck would allow him to make a fast escape. He hoped he had enough fuel to reach Apatu if he had to drive all the way back. He might also be able to rescue some of the prisoners if the debacle turned into a wholesale massacre.

Simon held his impatience in check as one by one the men rose to their feet and staggered to their huts to sleep off the beer before setting off the next morning.

A few of the women were seen flitting in front of the fire busy tidying away the left-over food, pouring back the remains of the beer and chasing off the odd child who was still awake.

Trident slipped the keys into Simon's hand before he too disappeared into the dark corners of the village where the firelight didn't reach.

Simon pretended to go to bed but lay awake until he was sure everyone was asleep. He crept out and opened the door of the jeep removed two jerrycans of fuel and topped up the petrol tank. He moved as silently as he could, but the smell of petrol permeated the air and any moment he expected Lucky to come to reclaim the keys. He breathed a sigh of relief as the last drop dribbled into the tank before he replaced the stopper and stowed the cans in the back. It was all he could do for now. He crept back to his mattress in the guest hut and before settling down, he stuffed the car keys down his underpants and smirked in the dark at the accusations he could yell if anyone tried to take them away from him while he was sleeping. He closed his eyes and drifted off thinking of Amie safe in Durban and of the child he couldn't wait to welcome into the world.

47   NGONI'S STORY

The clouds skittered across the sky blocking and unblocking the sun like vast venetian blinds swishing backwards and forwards. It was a relief to walk in the shade and Amie plodded behind Ngoni without noticing where they were going. She was past caring. All she could think about was that small face just before she covered it for the last time. Her guilt was overwhelming. She had been selfish, so careless of the life entrusted to her, taking it all for granted that she would give birth to a happy, healthy child like so many millions of women the world over.

In rural Africa, it was common for a woman to have a child every year and there were always dozens of bare bottomed, snotty-nosed children running around the villages. These hardy ladies gave birth with no fuss. Sometimes the baby did not survive and there was much weeping and wailing as it was buried before the stoic acceptance that life goes on. If there was any depression following a still-birth or an early death, no one discussed it. Life went on and the next day brought the same tasks as the day before.

Amie tripped over a pile of Kigelia fruit that had dropped from the parent tree. Up to two feet long each weighed up to fifteen pounds and the long sausage-shaped pods were favoured by baboons, bush pigs and porcupines. Her boots slid from under her and she landed heavily on the ground.

"Ngoni, wait," she cried.

Ngoni came back to help her to her feet.

"Not far now," she said. "It is close."

"What is?" Amie realized that she had no idea which direction they were heading.

"You see. It is good," and with that, Amie had to be satisfied.

She struggled on, taking more care, and the odd sip of water helped clear her head. It seemed impossible that only a few hours ago she had given birth and here she was trekking across the valley floor.

Ngoni stopped and pointed to the long grass in front of them. She pointed to her eyes and then her ears, warning her companion to be vigilant.

Amie did not need to be told twice. She knew that long grass could conceal any number of predators and volunteered to go in front. She was carrying the gun, but Ngoni shook her head and picked her way through the lush undergrowth. A little way in, she stopped and turned to Amie with a bright smile and pointed.

There, almost hidden between the long rushes on either bank was a river. The abundant vegetation was the only sign it was there.

Ngoni pantomimed washing, but Amie didn't need to be told twice. Keeping a sharp lookout for crocodiles, the river looked too narrow and overgrown for hippo, she stripped off and immersed herself in the cold, clear water. A jacuzzi in a five-star hotel would not be as welcome as this. The feel of the fast-flowing water soothed and cleaned her, and Amie took the opportunity to rinse out her clothes. She ignored the wisps of blood that floated away from her diluted by the water. She had no idea if that was normal so soon after a birth, but there was nothing she could do about it. She thought of asking Ngoni, but she didn't want to worry the girl who might take fright and run away, so she kept the knowledge to herself.

Upstream Ngoni re-filled the water bottles. Seeing Amie gyrating, as she struggled to put on the wet garments that refused to slide over her skin, she burst out laughing. Even Amie had to grin.

Leaving the river, they pushed through the undergrowth until they were back on the dusty plain.

Ngoni paused, then turned.

"Where we go?" she said at last.

"I was going back to the camp. To help," Amie replied.

Ngoni nodded.

"But you ran away too Ngoni?"

"I follow you," she replied simply.

"But I didn't see you." Amie realized that it would have been easy for the girl to track her while keeping well out of sight. She looked up at the clouds scudding fast across the sky. "The cave?" she suggested putting her hands together against her ear with her head on one side in the universal sign for sleep.

Ngoni nodded and pointed the direction to take.

"I try to … member … my English words," she said with a smile and set off at a brisk pace.

They reached the crack in the rocks where Amie had

spent the previous night at dusk. The clouds stretched as far as they could see and the temperature had dropped. It was a tight squeeze for both of them but the thorn branches were undisturbed and it only took a few minutes to pull them back in place to guard the entrance.

Ngoni pulled a bottle of water out of her backpack and shared it between them and Amie wrenched open a can of corned beef and they sat in silence taking it in turns to eat chunks of the meat off the end of the bush knife. For dessert Ngoni produced two chocolate energy bars from the bottom of her bag and offered one to Amie. She smiled and on impulse, put her arms around the young girl and gave her a hug.

"Thank you," she murmured. "You saved my life."

The young girl stiffened for a moment then relaxed and hugged Amie back.

"You … are … welcome," she said slowly and they both giggled.

"I'm Amie." Amie patted her chest. "But of course, you know that. "And you?"

"Ngonicansaga, Ngoni."

"Pleased to meet you." Amie grinned as she held out her hand and shook Ngoni's. "You work at the palace?"

Ngoni sat in silence for a moment, trying to recall the correct words in English. When she spoke, it was slow and she pronounced the words carefully as if she might give the wrong information.

"I make the floors to be clean and the …" she flapped her hands, mentally searching "the chairs and tables."

"You always live in Apatu?"

"No," she shook her head. "When small in village, the same village as Mr President."

"So, you know Ben?"

If Ngoni was shocked Amie called Togodo's President by his given name she didn't show it. She nodded her head vigorously. "I know well, at school." She raised her hand trying to explain her point.

"He was older than you?"

"Yes. I not go to school every day."

"That's a shame." Amie had heard this story so many times before.

"When my mama is late then I must care for the children."

"You were the eldest, the firstborn?"

Ngoni nodded. She gave herself a shake and it was if all the words in her second language poured into her head and she talked in stilted English, rarely stopping to take a breath.

"I have many little ones to care for, but mama was sick a long time. She was very thin, and the villagers were angry. They said she bring the sickness to the village, so they burnt down our house."

Amie gasped. Was there no end to the cruelty among people?

"What did you do?"

"We must make a new house away from the village and it was hard. A long way to walk to get water. The small boys they are bad. They do not as I tell them. They do many bad things." She sighed. "*Kulikuwa na mvua.* It rain the day Ouma Adede helped me dig a grave for my mama."

Amie gasped. "You know Ouma Adede?"

The girl nodded and smiled. "Yes, she was in our village also. But then she went away to be a sangoma."

There was silence for a few moments before Ngoni continued. "She was my one friend. Then Kirimu come and say I must go to the city. But I have the children to care for. I said, 'No, Kirimu I cannot go.' Then he get so angry and tell the families to take the children to their huts and then he put me in the car and drive me to Apatu."

"The Finance Minister? He was the man talking to you in the coffee shop in the Grand Hotel? I saw you there."

Ngoni nodded. "Yes. He has want me for a wife a long time."

"But you don't love him."

"No, he is a bad man. He is not kind."

"You love someone else, don't you?" Amie had no idea what prompted her to ask such a question; it was so impolite to delve into private African matters.

Amie saw tears run down the young girl's cheeks before she put her head down to hide her emotions. She gave her another hug and told herself not to enquire further into the poor girl's life. She had been insensitive and unkind.

They sat in silence. Amie shifted, trying to relieve the pains that were shooting through her body, but there was not a lot of space in the small rock crevasse under the overhang.

They listened to the sounds of the African night: the occasional bark of a hyena, the cicadas in a nearby Iron tree, the squeal of a small mammal taken by a night owl, a lion roar, and the far distant rumble of thunder.

Neither of them remembered falling asleep, but when Amie opened her eyes it was already daylight. She was stiff and sore, her behind was numb and Ngoni was slumped against her, with her head in Amie's lap. She hated to disturb the girl, but nature was screaming and she had to relieve herself.

Scrambling out of the cave, pushing the thorn branches out of her way she glanced round before looking for a bush to hide behind. *Silly really*, she thought, *Ngoni was with me when I was lying with my legs splayed wide open yesterday, but now I'm looking for privacy for another natural function.*

After a breakfast of corned meat, followed by a shared tin of sardines, they considered what to do. Trying to get to Apatu would take days, even if Amie was fit. She looked back towards the area where she'd given birth and thought how far it was to the city. Going back to the camp was their only real option, but they would hang back and take stock before rushing in.

There were a couple of dozen men, maybe more, captive inside the *boma* and who knew how many fully armed men surrounded them outside. Amie didn't think that two women armed with one AK-47 would be much help.

They set off across the valley floor, dark rain clouds hovered above, and they wondered what they would find when they reached the camp.

48 COUNTERATTACK

Simon had no idea what time it was when he was woken by the villagers' noisy departure. His watch battery had given up and he would only be able to judge the time by the sun – only there was no sun. Poking his head out of the hut doorway all he could see were thick grey and black clouds blanketing the sky from one horizon to the other.

The village resembled an abandoned playroom, only instead of toys, there were gun wrappings fluttering in the breeze, tea mugs abandoned, plates left unwashed on the ground, empty gun cartridge boxes littering doorways and stools lying at odd angles.

It puzzled Simon that he saw no women or children. One very old man sat outside a hut puffing on his pipe, but when Simon called out to him he either could not or would not reply to his questions. Had everyone gone? All the men? The women and children could be hiding. There was no one to tell him. He knew Lucky went with the men, but Trident and Bones had disappeared as well.

Simon shrugged, it would make his escape easier. He washed his face and hands in a bowl of water he found perched on a chair, grabbed some dry stale bread to put something in his stomach and risked a mouthful of last night's beer. It tasted foul and Simon spat it out to the amusement of the old fellow watching him. He walked over, intent on asking him again to explain the deserted village, but as he approached, the old man leaned on his knobkerrie with one hand and reached over with the other and very slowly picked up a plastic bottle of water and offered it to Simon. Even here in this remote place, the tentacles of modern civilisation spread out to provide clean, potable water – and a non-biodegradable hazard.

He thanked the old man, and twisting the top off he drank. When he offered it back, the man shook his head and motioned for Simon to finish it. Simon bowed his thanks and for good measure put his hands together as in prayer as a sign of respect. Then he made for the Jeep. He wondered if the old man would shout or try and stop him, but he placidly puffed on his clay pipe and watched.

Simon unlocked the door and climbed in breathing a sigh of relief when the engine kicked first time. He waved as he drove out of the village and turned in the direction of the safari camp. He'd planned to follow the tracks, convinced that so many footprints would be easy to follow but he hadn't planned on the breeze that kicked up the dust and wiped out the indentations. Still, he was confident he wouldn't get lost. The GPS worked, and if he missed the camp altogether he would make straight for Apatu and hopefully, some sanity.

He stopped to examine the ground. He was on the right track. They had passed this way. He reckoned it would only take him an hour to get close enough to the battle scene and then find somewhere to conceal the vehicle before he approached on foot.

Even before the camp came into view, the sounds of gunfire came floating in through the open car window. The tat, tat, tat of automatic rifles followed by explosions. He slowed and parked in a grove of acacia trees, and tucking his pistol in his belt he walked closer to the action, guided by the clash of the battle.

Amie and Ngoni also heard the gunfire as it echoed across the valley. They stopped and stared at each other. Ngoni was stricken, terrified that the man she loved was inside the *boma*. They hesitated for a few minutes then began to approach more slowly from the north.

The heavens opened, and the rain came down in torrents. The raindrops bounced on the parched earth before slowly sinking into the sand as more and more water drilled down relentlessly on the thirsty earth. Soon the ground was turned into a thick mud. From the south side of the camp, Simon's feet squelched in the ground that had become a slurry of red sludge. It sucked at his boots as he struggled to turn around and take refuge in the Jeep he'd just left. As he lunged towards shelter, his hair and clothes became soaked and stuck to him while the excess rain ran down his back.

Ngoni tugged Amie's arm and pointed to a slightly curved rock where the wind had eroded the base leaving an overhang. It would give them some protection. They ran for it, throwing themselves under the shelter out of the downpour. Hailstones shot from the sky, hard and painful as they rained down, stinging the bare patches of skin when they landed.

Amie dug out her large plastic poncho and they

huddled together for warmth, the baking temperature had plummeted to 15 degrees; it was cold in comparison to the previously hot day. Neither of them could stop shivering.

The storm raged and lightning bolts zigzagged across the sky and speared the earth. The thunder rumbled, deafening them. Amie blocked her ears and squeezed her eyes shut. Nature had gone mad. A fork of lightning cleaved an acacia engulfing it in flames. The rain lashed down and the thunder roared overhead, drowning out the gunfire.

Opening the car window for a moment, Simon listened but heard no sounds of fighting. He could imagine the chaos, the men sliding about in the mud, the driving rain obscuring their vision hampering both sides. He was anxious to know how far the battle had progressed, but for now he could do nothing but sit and wait. The rain was so dense he couldn't see two feet in front of him. He'd intended to contact London as soon as he got closer to the action so he could give an accurate report, but there was no chance of getting through now, not with all this rain.

* * *

The captives huddled together inside the marquee. There was safety in numbers and no one wanted to be on their own. They woke early that morning to the first shots, which sounded too far away to have come from the men guarding them. They'd raced out of their tents, eager to see who had come to their rescue.

"Deliverance. At last." Ed Keller threw his arm round Ian's shoulder.

"Not necessarily," Ian said, as he shook off the overly

familiar American. "Whoever they are, they're just as likely to break in and blow us all away as take us to their embassy and give us tea. I wouldn't celebrate just yet."

"Glass-half-empty-type," Keller huffed. "The good old US of A won't stand by and see their people in trouble. I tell ya, they'll be ready to protect us."

Ian turned to look at him, eyes wide open. "You really think anyone in the States knows what is going on? I doubt news of this debacle has got as far as your Embassy in Apatu."

"Have faith man. They'll be on the alert because they haven't heard from me."

The sound of men outside attacking the riff-raff on the other side of the fence cheered him up and no surly English type was going to put him down. He practically bounced like a child on Christmas morning.

Vladimir Petrovnikov joined them. "Who are they?" he nodded towards the sound of the battle raging outside.

"We have no idea," replied Fleming. "But it seems to be coming from both sides, so I think we are safest in the middle of the camp." As if to prove him right, a bullet came whistling over the perimeter fence making them fall flat on their faces.

An almighty crack of thunder followed the bullet, and the rain came down. They scrambled and ran for the safety of the main tent.

Ian ducked under the long table and grabbed a tablecloth, no longer white, and dried himself off. The scene was so ridiculous he almost burst out laughing. Huddled under the trestles, were the remnants of the diplomats representing six nations that had expected to wine, dine and then bid for permission to mine and export precious minerals. Gone was the veneer of power and presence. They were closeted with the President and his ministers, cowering behind dirty white tablecloths. They were soaked through, covered in mud and shaking. It was impossible to judge whether they shook from fright or the sudden cold, but they resembled a crowd of scared schoolboys waiting for someone in authority to tell them what to do.

Ben Mtumba, President of Togodo, was in no position to take on that role. He sat on the ground, his shoulders hunched, rocking gently to and fro with a stricken look on his face. His cheekbones were more prominent, his hands claw-like and his hair had flecks of silver in it that hadn't been visible two days earlier.

He really must believe this cursing nonsense, Ian thought not for the first time. The unquestioning belief in the powers of the witch doctor was as powerful as any medicine, or poison. He knew that no common sense 'pull yourself together' talk would get through to Ben. Africa was in the grip of primeval powers the west would never understand. He sighed and shuffled as far away from Keller as he could. The boorish American was just one extra burden to bear.

The ferocity of the rain halted the battle. Both sides fired wildly at each other, not sure what they were hitting. The villagers ducked behind trees and termite mounds, popping up to let loose a volley in the direction of the *boma*. It was chaos as they slithered and slid on the slimy mud. Several fell, shrieking in pain as bullets slammed into soft flesh.

While the terrorists took cover among the vehicles, bullets bounced off the surrounding trucks, and the gas bottles brought to power the fridges and lighting at night. Two of them exploded wounding many of the terrorists.

Limbs were ripped off, intestines torn open and people dropped where they stood. Soon the dead and wounded from both sides, littered the ground and shrieks of pain were heard over the rumble of the thunder.

The perimeter fence offered some protection but was no real deterrent against the armoury. Three of the bodyguards received fatal wounds and the North Korean envoy was hit in the leg. Samuel Suma, the Right Honourable Minister of Sport, lay bleeding next to the table. He would not live to see his beloved football stadium built, nor award further contracts to his friends and relatives. He would never know that when he left on this ill-fated safari, his wife gathered the children and moved in with her lover several hundred miles south of Apatu.

As stray bullets pierced the tent walls, they moved the tables into a makeshift shelter, enclosing the sides and putting one on top to serve as a roof. The only person to sit and do nothing to help was Ben, who was lost in a catatonic world of his own. Ian had no idea what was likely to happen if any of them got out of this alive.

As suddenly as it started, like a tap in the heavens being turned off, the rain stopped. There was silence before the cries of the wounded floated from both sides.

The villagers launched their final offensive. Simon saw them manhandling the RPG, sending it through the air in a loud whoosh of grey-white smoke, aiming not for the insurgents but for the vehicles parked neatly together beside the fuel containers and the gas bottles. The explosion shook the earth as the vehicles disintegrated, with pieces flying through the air like shrapnel, except, Simon noticed with amazement, two of the diplomatic cars. They had been lifted off their wheels and flung several feet skywards then fell and settled down with a thump. It was impossible to see the full extent of the damage through the smoke and flames.

The captors scattered, racing from the attack, shouting to each other, and like wraiths they disappeared through the smoke leaving their dead and wounded behind.

It was over.

The villagers whooped and swooped down on those still alive, kicking them, clubbing them with their guns, screaming questions and insults at them before dispatching the remaining injured with bullets to the head.

Simon watched in horror, unable to tear his eyes from the carnage as the villagers dispensed their own form of retribution. He saw Lucky, Trident and Bones joining in the general melee, kicking and shrieking with the rest. The sight sickened him and he turned away, jumped out of the Jeep, and heaving, sent the stale bread he'd eaten earlier into the mud.

It was impossible to look away for long, almost as if he had no will of his own. Simon watched the villagers cautiously approach the gates of the *boma* which, throughout all the onslaught, had remained firmly closed. His stomach churned as he crept nearer, sheltering behind the slim trunk of a yellow-barked fever tree.

Chief Lgego banged on the gate with his knobkerrie and shouted to the prisoners inside. He waited for an answer but none came. He motioned to his men to break open the gates and they rushed to demolish it. The crowd filed inside, guns pointed from side to side as they disappeared from view.

Simon shifted to where he could see inside the camp. He watched the men approach the large white tent in the middle. They froze for a few moments, looking to their chief for guidance. He nodded and one of them flung open the flap.

The hostages were taken out, dazed and wounded, with several of them on makeshift stretchers fashioned from the once-white tablecloths. Simon let out a breath of relief when he saw Ian Fleming walk out unaided, two other white men accompanied him, but it was impossible to say what nationality they were. From the contingent of six countries, it looked as if only half of them had survived. There would be hell to pay on the world stage as a result of this.

Simon waited until they were all out before walking over to join them.

"Ian?"

Ian Fleming gave a start and peered at Simon. "Simon Peterson? What the hell are you doing here?"

Simon couldn't say he'd been part of the rescue party, so he ignored the question and steered him towards the Jeep. The other two men followed as Lucky ran over.

"What …?" he began.

"I'm driving them back to the village to clean up and get some food and water and then I will take them back to

Apatu." Simon spoke firmly and with as much authority as he could. Visions of the brutality he'd seen his earlier companions commit swirled around in his head, and he was desperate to distance himself from them. All he wanted right now was to stay close to his own countrymen and their allies from a world he understood.

Lucky nodded. "The Chief is going to take the prisoners back to the village." He pointed over to where they were starting the only army truck to escape demolition and the two diplomatic limousines. They were herding the survivors and injured aboard and filling the gaps with their own dead.

Without saying a word, Fleming, Keller and Petrovnikov climbed into the Jeep as Simon turned the key and pulled away. He'd get them settled in the village then contact London to bring them up to date. He wanted to find out why Ian Fleming had not been party to the order to disrupt the auction for the mining rights and get further instructions.

49 THE DESERTED BOMA

The girls squeezed as far back as they could under the overhang but the shelter it offered them didn't keep them dry. They huddled together watching the hailstones bounce off the ground, turning the reddish-brown earth white and they shivered. It was as cold as Amie remembered winters in England, a sharp contrast to the hot African sun normally beating down and baking the earth.

When the rain ceased, they watched miniature rivers flowing past their feet. In a few hours new grass shoots would poke green spears above the ground changing the colour of the landscape.

"I don't hear the guns any more, do you?" Amie asked. There had been one enormous explosion followed by total silence.

Ngoni shook her head her damp curls bouncing.

They sat like statues, fearful of what they would find or who they might meet when they left their refuge.

Amie fished inside her bag for water, angry at herself for not remembering to place an open bottle out in the rain to catch the downpour. The river was now some distance away, and they only had one bottle left between them. They feasted on sardines and scooped baked beans out of the tin with their fingers, savouring the tomato taste.

"We can't stay here Ngoni. We must go and look."

They crept out under a brooding grey sky which threatened to drench the land again at any moment.

Amie's body protested, her stomach ached, her legs were stiff and her back screamed at her after sitting hunched up for so long. She was aware she was bleeding and that frightened her. The smell of blood which was now staining her pants would attract predators, and they needed to get back to the camp as quickly as possible.

Ngoni turned and threw her arms around Amie and gave her a hug. It brought tears to Amie's eyes. Whatever they found, they would do it together.

Gathering the bags and the rifle they walked towards the camp. This time there was no mistaking the large rock which had formed the rear of the *boma*. Amie couldn't believe how stupid she had been to mistake another outcrop for this one, it was by far the largest in the wide valley and the only one with sheer sides.

They were not far from the *boma* when Amie stopped so suddenly that Ngoni bumped into her. She saw the remains of a body partly hidden under some of the smaller rocks. The legs and arms were hacked off. It was too small to be any of the guests and as Amie bent down and turned it over she gave a cry.

Little Capitan had not died from the puff adder's bite. A cruel human being had butchered the defenceless child. Why hadn't the doctor, or at least the nurse cared for him? Predators stripped a carcass, they did not cut off limbs and leave them next to the body, and they only killed to eat. And wild predators did not cover bodies with rocks. Whoever had done this had done it out of spite. She choked back a sob not helped by Ngoni who put her arms around

Amie. The sympathetic gesture was enough to bring more tears. It was a sad sight but there was nothing they could do for him. Amie laid a few branches over the small body but it was only a token gesture and she knew it was a waste of time. There were no rocks nearby but it felt as if she had done something.

They were not the first to arrive at the battle scene, nature's scavengers were already dining. The vultures were stripping the flesh from unprotected faces, squabbling over the eyeballs – their favourite delicacy: a pair of jackals circled on the edge of the carnage nipping in to grab what they could and the hyenas were back.

Amie unslung the gun and kept a sharp eye open for any animals coming too close. If there were lions or other large cats in the area they might be tempted to join in the feast. A gunshot would scatter them and keep them at bay for a while; but they would return as soon as they built up enough courage.

The gates to the *boma* were hanging open at odd angles, one of them swinging in the wind. As they picked their way inside, they were forced to step over a body. Amie recognised one of Ben's bodyguards.

They worked their way down one side of the fence line, searching the tents. They were all empty, but whoever had stayed here had left all their possessions behind. Amie saw bags and cases, and clothes hanging on the improvised rails. Sleeping bags and bedding were thrown to one side, the mosquito nets hung limply from the roofs, shoes were abandoned. The small bedside tables held books, empty mugs, toothbrushes and toiletries, paper, folders and files. It flashed through

Amie's mind this was a Mari Celeste scenario in a safari camp not a ship at sea.

The kitchen area was deserted, but tidier. The fridges had run out of gas and when Ngoni opened one, the stench made her jump back and slam it shut. There was only one more place to look, the large marquee in the centre. The size of the tent, towering over everything else was threatening. This was where they would have taken refuge. Amie hesitated by the front flap. Was she about to see Ian Fleming's sightless body? While she had little love for Her Majesty's choice for this safari, she dreaded seeing him lying there lifeless. What of that American, and the French envoy she'd last seen drinking and laughing with other diplomats? And Ben? Was Ben in there? So many people she had known and grown to like, if not love, had lost their lives.

Side by side they pushed their way in. The conference tables formed a fortress arranged in a square where they must have sheltered. Spent cartridges crunched beneath their feet and there were patches of blackened flooring, possibly where grenades landed. They walked to the back, but the only bodies Amie saw were people she did not recognize.

She slung the rifle over her back and bent down to pick up some papers left lying on the floor, when she heard noises outside. She glanced over to Ngoni who'd heard them as well. Amie nodded towards the barricaded tables, it was the only place to hide.

Hidden from view they crouched low and listened. Amie could feel her ears flaring as she tried to identify the sounds. She turned to Ngoni.

"People or animals?" she whispered.

Ngoni put her head on one side. "People."

A sharp giggle came from the other side of the canvas and a high-pitched voice called out.

Ngoni's head shot up. "Children." she hissed. She scrambled out from behind the upturned tables and shot out of the tent. Amie followed more slowly.

The group of ragged children froze and stared at the girls. One ran out of the *boma* when Ngoni shouted at him. He stopped and turned. Another child ran round the side of the marquee and skidded to a halt.

He was holding a rifle and it was pointing straight at them.

50 BEN BEWITCHED

The Jeep bounced and slid over the wet earth as Simon drove back to the village. His questions swirled round but none of his passengers had anything to say. He wondered if they were temporarily shell-shocked or partly deaf from the RPG explosion, but apart from Ian asking Simon what he was doing here, there was complete silence.

Word travelled faster than the returning warriors, for as he drove into the village, Simon saw the women clearing up after the storm. The fires outside the huts were lit, the pots on the boil and the children were all back and running around jumping in puddles and throwing mud balls at each other.

Parking up beside the farthest hut, Simon turned to his silent passengers and considered asking them what they wanted to do. The villagers would bring all the survivors back here and he would help in any way he could. He only had one vehicle, but it had enough fuel to get back to Apatu, and space for four passengers.

Then he reconsidered. The last thing Simon wanted was for Ian Fleming to take charge, so he took advantage of their shocked state to announce what he was prepared to do. He would wait until everyone had returned and get the full picture and then leave for the city.

A little while later two of the diplomatic cars arrived in the village. It was difficult to believe they could survive such an onslaught and made excellent marketing points for future armoured cars.

It was hours before the men on foot came in. Simon counted three makeshift stretchers carrying the wounded and was surprised there were not more.

The women rushed over and the wailing began. Now they knew who had survived and who was *late*. The men were more interested in their food than in mourning the loss of friends and swaggered over to sit by the cooking pots calling out for food and beer. The wounded were carried into one of the huts.

Simon was uncomfortable beside his silent companions, but when the limousines drove in, the doors on one didn't open and no one got out.

"Is the President safe?" Simon directed the question to Ian in the back seat making deliberate eye contact with him.

Ian's head jerked up. "He's alive, but he's not functioning."

"What do you mean?"

"He's been cursed. He believes he's going to die and there is no way of stopping it." Ian snapped out of his own stupor as he talked rubbing his ears hard to get his hearing back. He spoke slowly, but he was reverting back to his normal self and his voice became stronger with every sentence. "President's aged ten years in the last couple of days. Unbelievable. The whole bloody thing is one big bloody stuff up."

51   AT THE MERCY OF CHILDREN

Ngoni gasped and took several steps back careening into Amie who stood frozen just outside the tent flap. If there was anything more frightening than facing a man with a gun, it was facing an unpredictable child with a gun.

Amie took a deep breath and gently pushed Ngoni to one side as she faced the ragged mob which had gathered in front of them and took a step forward.

The AK47 never wavered in the small hands as the lead child barked at her.

"He says not to move," Ngoni whispered from behind. "Amie, they will kill us." She whimpered.

"I am friend," Amie said taking a step backwards. "Not an enemy," she added and forgetting the rifle she had slung over her own back, she held up her hands in surrender.

The barefoot leader, he was about ten years old at most, and wore torn blue shorts, and a faded red checked shirt missing two buttons, shouted some more.

Amie didn't dare move. "What is he saying?" she asked Ngoni.

"He says to …" Ngoni searched for the words. "He says to give him gun."

Keeping her hands in view and moving slowly, Amie began to pull her arm through the gun strap before lowering the muzzle and pointing it at the ground.

The boy motioned for her to put it down and step away.

Two of his followers leapt forward, both eager to get their hands on the weapon. One got hold of the stock, the other the muzzle and they tussled and fought for it.

The sound of the shot rang through the air, disturbing the predators that had closed in again. The hyenas fled and the vultures and other raptors took to the air.

One of the boys screamed and fell, blood pouring from his chest.

Without thinking, Amie dashed forward and cradled him in one arm and with the other she threw her knapsack down and fished inside for a spare t-shirt which she used to put pressure on the wound.

"Help, Ngoni," she called, not even thinking to look and see what the little band of armed youths was doing. "I need the box in my bag, you know the one you used when I …" she choked up before she could add 'when I had my baby'.

Ngoni grabbed the first aid kit, and Amie bandaged the wound. It was not as bad as she'd feared. The bullet had gone right through the child's body, in the flesh close to the armpit so she didn't think it had damaged any major organs.

A cry distracted her and she looked up to see another ragamuffin soundly cuffing the leader who was holding the gun, only now it was shaking. The new arrival looked round and peered at the girls.

"Amieeee!" he shrieked. "Amieee." He raced to her dropping the spoils he'd gathered from the abandoned tents and wrapped his skinny arms around her waist.

"Zeebee." Amie was astonished. What was he doing here? She ruffled his tight curls and patted his head.

"Amieeeee," Zeebee grinned at her, patted her arm, and gave her another big hug, before looking down at his fallen comrade.

Ngoni rattled off words in Swahili to him, explaining what had happened and he nodded vigorously. He patted his comrades face and then ran back to the leader and cuffed him again, boxing his ears until Amie begged him to stop. If the situation had not been so serious, she might have burst out laughing.

The deposed leader in the blue shorts reluctantly handed over his gun, and Zeebee waved it in the air triumphantly.

Amie saw one of the other boys creeping closer with an eye on her rifle which had been flung to one side. "Leave it!" she shouted at them. If at all possible she was not going to donate it to any child.

Zeebee slung the gun over his shoulder and walked back, eying Amie as she tied the final knot in the bandage. She dug out a Paracetamol and forced it between her patient's lips before standing up. "Can you find out where this crowd are from and what they are doing here? And what has happened to the people that were inside the *boma*?" she asked Ngoni.

Ngoni did not need telling twice.

At first, the children were reluctant to reply but once one broke the silence, the others raced over gabbling and trying to outdo the others as they waved their arms and pantomimed their stories, all talking at once.

There followed a rapid conversation of which Amie

caught maybe one word in twenty. The questioning went on for some time. The youngsters were deferential to this young black girl who grilled them as if she'd been recruited into the KGB. She fired questions at them like verbal bullets.

Amie was frustrated, she couldn't understand a word. She sank back to the ground feeling dizzy and waited patiently.

One of the little lads ran off and returned with water. He handed one bottle to Amie and the other to Ngoni.

At last Ngoni turned to Amie. She spoke slowly and carefully, pausing between words as she remembered them.

"They are in the village of Chief Lgego, and their men have killed the bad guys here."

"The bad guys?" Amie's eyes opened wide. "Do they mean the diplomats, the men from Apatu and the President?"

Ngoni put her head on one side and the staccato words shot back and forth again.

"I think they kill the bad men outside." She waved her arm to indicate the *boma*.

"Where are the men who were inside the camp?"

More dialogue followed.

"They take to the village of Chief Lgego."

"Will they take us there?"

Ngoni nodded her head. "But there is a problem."

"What? Is it miles away?"

"Only half a day."

When Amie heard this, she groaned. Half a day could be anything from a couple of miles to a couple of dozen.

"That is not the problem," Ngoni said.

"So, what is?"

"Zeebee is frightened you tell his father he has a gun."

"Is that all?" She pointed to the child. "Zeebee, I not tell your father."

It was irresponsible, but they had no time for messing about. She shook her head as Ngoni rapidly translated.

Zeebee shrugged his shoulders, grinned at Amie then shouted to his 'men'.

Ngoni dragged a sleeping bag from the nearest tent, and they put the injured child in it. With a comrade at each corner, they walked out through the gates of the *boma* and began their trek to the village.

The flat ground made the walk easy-going, but before long Amie flagged. She struggled to keep up with the youngsters who were full of energy and bouncing around all over the place, teasing and playing some form of tag as they zigzagged along. They showed little concern for their fallen playmate who groaned each time his carriers dumped him on the ground to change places.

Amie tried to sip at her water but she was seriously dehydrated, that, combined with her miscarriage, had weakened her. She had lost a lot of blood and she was still bleeding. Waves of nausea washed over her, her head thumped and she felt cold one moment and hot the next.

Ngoni kept pace by her side, supporting her elbow and relieving Amie of the weight of the rifle by slinging it over her own back.

The horizon kept tilting, the termite mounds, many of them earth hillocks as tall as a man, shifted and the ground refused to remain steady. It was like walking over earth tremors and each step took an effort. She tried counting her footsteps. She picked nearby landmarks, a large stone, a short acacia bush, a fallen tree branch from a Leadwood tree and used them as targets to aim for. She was weak and angry with herself. This is what came of being a pampered westerner; the local people were tough and in comparison, she saw herself as weak. *Amie, the great spy*, she thought, *was now at the mercy of a young African girl and a ragtag bunch of children. If Ian Fleming ever got to learn about this, she would never hear the end of it.*

The children didn't know who had been rescued or killed. There were many mutilated and burnt bodies around the auction camp so it had been impossible to identify them. She would have to wait until she reached Chief Lgego's village, if it was the same village and if she was able to walk that far.

52   AMIE IN TROUBLE

Simon grabbed the case containing the satellite phone and went to the hill where he'd got a clear signal before. He dumped the case on the ground, and opened it and was on the point of taking it out when a hand shot out and stopped him. He looked up to see Ian Fleming staring down at him.

"You were going to call London." It was a statement rather than a question.

"Yes, I haven't been able to log in for a couple of days and they'll be wondering what's happened."

"No need to let them know what a fiasco this has been. They will be looking for someone to blame, you do realise that?" Ian looked desperate.

"Well they can't bloody well blame me. By the time I arrived, there were armed guards around the *boma* and there wasn't a thing I could do about it."

"I'm not suggesting you act like Superman, but let's wait until we sort out the position here before getting them involved."

"I have my orders, Ian." Simon shook off Ian's hand and went to grab the phone, but Ian got to it first and, to Simon's horror, he twisted away and smashed it on a nearby rock."

"What the bloody hell do you think you're doing? What the fuck have you done?"

"I'm making sure that when we contact London from the embassy in Apatu we have all the facts. Now they can't advise us to take any damn fool action when they don't understand what's going on, and we can't be blamed for not 'doing as instructed'."

"Oh, that's bloody marvellous, and how do I explain how the phone got wrecked?"

Ian smirked and shrugged his shoulders. "I'm sure you'll think of something. Stuff gets damaged when you're in the middle of the bush. It could have been stolen, happens all the time in Africa."

Simon seethed. He had no idea who could pull rank between Ian and himself, but did it matter miles from nowhere?

"We'll turn in a full report from the embassy when we get back to Apatu, something that will make them happy."

"Suit yourself." Simon stood up and kicked the case. "You can tell them a pack of lies, but I want to see exactly what's in that report before it leaves your desk."

Ian threw an arm over Simon's shoulder. "Oh, course you can. Remember, we both work for the same boss."

"I'm beginning to wonder about that," Simon murmured.

They turned at the sound of frantic shouts from the cluster of huts. They saw some boys racing into camp screaming at the tops of their voices.

"What's going on?" Ian looked angry. "One thing after another. What's happened now?" They ran back to the village.

The children were jumping up and down, each trying to tell his story and pushing the others out of the way as they tried to get the attention of the adults. The racket brought Chief Lgego out of his hut. One loud word from him was enough to silence the excited youngsters. The Chief pointed to one of the boys and waited for him to explain.

The child gabbled until the Chief motioned for him to stop. He barked out a command to the men standing next to him and then beckoned Fleming. Simon followed close behind.

The Chief's interpreter listened carefully. "The boys have two of the women from the camp," he said as the Englishmen reached the door of the hut. "But one of them is sick, very sick. The Chief has sent men to bring them."

"Women, that must be Gaga and Amie," Ian exclaimed.

"Amie. You mean Amie is here? My Amie?" Simon took an abrupt step backwards. "What's she doing here? I thought she was in Durban."

Ian eyed Simon's confusion, enjoying his discomfort. "No, she's been here all along. We flew here together and she was working with Gaga Medwewe to organize this fiasco."

Simon felt the rage course through his body. "You mean we have a missing foreign national from our own service and you didn't think to mention it?"

"No need to get tetchy. Good thing you didn't get through to London, your news would be outdated. Listen Simon, you haven't been through the hell we have in the last few days. I presumed the women were dead. It'll be in my report."

Simon balled his hands into fists and walked away

before he gave way to his anger and punched the man. He set off at a run after the villagers who had raced off on their instructions from the Chief. He caught up with them as they were improvising a stretcher for Amie who lay on the ground half propped up by Ngoni who cradled her, rocking to and fro, whispering soft words in singsong Swahili. She was bleeding. Had she been shot? Simon saw the blood staining her cargo pants and groaned.

The men rolled her onto a blanket and with one at the front and the other to the rear, they carried her back to the village. Simon walked alongside trying to talk to her, but the men were keeping up such a rapid pace and the blanket swayed so wildly from side to side that it was impossible. Not that she could have responded. She was out cold.

Simon couldn't get his head round the fact Amie was here, in Togodo when he thought she was miles away. Why had Ian dragged her back here? It wasn't just to organize a safari camp in the bush. No, he'd have a more devious plan in mind.

Ian looked at the body on the blanket and glanced at Ngoni.

"Where the hell is Medwewe?" he barked. "I thought Amie and her took off together." He grabbed Ngoni by the arm. "And who the hell are you?"

The girl hung her head and whispered "Ngonicansaga, Sir."

Simon pushed Ian away. "For heaven's sake man, stop behaving like a bloody idiot and mind your manners. Upset the Chief and we'll all be in trouble."

Ian glared at him but backed off wandering away muttering under his breath.

The villagers crowded round the makeshift stretcher jostling and pushing as they tried to see the girl. One of the wives of the Chief took charge and pointed to a hut. The men disappeared inside and came straight out to make space for the women and Ngoni, but when Simon tried to join them the women shouted at him and flapped their hands and roughly manhandled him as they shoved him away. He got the message. This was women's work and no place for a man.

He paced the village with questions tumbling over in his head. How ill was Amie? Was she going to die? How would he live without her? The blood – had she lost their baby? He could accept that, only if she lived. In his despair, he prayed to a god he didn't believe in.

The rest of the day dragged on. It had been late afternoon when they'd brought Amie back to the village and now the sun was setting. The light from the cooking fires illuminated the ghostly figures and the smell of cooking floated through the air. The women called to each other as they stirred the pots and the men sat in groups talking and puffing on their pipes. The children were nowhere to be seen, and Simon wondered where they were; he hadn't seen them melt away into the darkness.

He went to the hut where Amie lay but, time after time, they shooed him away. The Chief's wife was a formidable adversary, as broad as she was high and, short of felling her to the ground, there was no way Simon could get past her.

He went back to the Jeep to collect the flashlight and the first aid box and handed them to the two women who guarded the door. He constantly asked what was happening, and how she was, but he did not understand a word they said. Chief Lgego and a few of the men spoke a smattering of English but none of them offered to translate and the official interpreter was nowhere to be seen.

The diplomats had settled on chairs near one of the cooking areas, and if they were making plans, Simon didn't care. He could only think about Amie.

The limousine containing the President sat like a large black, predatory vulture on the edge of the village. One of the women took food and water to it. The door opened, hands reached out to take the offerings, and then the door slammed shut. Simon wasn't sure who was in the car – Ben for certain and possibly one of his bodyguards and maybe a couple of his government officials. He hadn't met any of the Ministers and no one was making introductions.

There were a few men in crumpled suits who'd arrived in the second diplomatic car, but they kept to themselves, and didn't communicate. They huddled and whispered incessantly and barely acknowledged the villagers when they fussed round them offering food and drink. They did not eat in the communal area with everyone else.

An ululation announced the evening meal. The families appeared from all directions and gathered in a large circle as tin plates were passed round. It did not look appetising, but Simon forced down some of the watery stew and the maize meal pap which he balled in his fingers. He refused more than half a mug of the local brew. He wanted to keep a clear head.

Inside the hut on the far side of the compound, the women

fussed over Amie. They bathed her head with a cool cloth, washed her, and assessed her bleeding.

Ngoni watched them with tears in her eyes. In the short time she had known Amie, she had grown very fond of her. She admired the strong young woman who made her own decisions, showed great bravery, and cared so much for others. When the young boy was shot, she didn't stop to think about her own safety and rushed to help him. Ngoni wished she was as brave.

The women mixed bottled water with a little salt and plenty of sugar, like the health visitor in the nearby town had shown them, and spooned it into their patient to re-hydrate her. They sang, low and rhythmically, and when she came round, they offered her a bright green mash which they pantomimed would make her well and strong again. She fell into a deep sleep.

If the occupants of the President's car got out to answer calls of nature, they did so under cover of darkness when the fires had burned down low and the people were asleep. At some time in the night an engine started, and in the morning, only one car remained.

"Hey y'all, did you hear one of the cars take off? It sure ain't here no longer." Ed Keller stood looking at the space where the second limousine had been.

Ian Fleming ducked his head down as he came out of the guest hut. "No, didn't hear a thing. Wonder who went and who stayed?" He leant against the remaining car and tried to peer through the windows but the heavy tint only reflected back his own face. He knocked on the door and even tried the handle but it was locked.

"Bloody weird," he mumbled. "I can only think Mr

President is sitting in there frightened to death and waiting to die."

"Never seen anything like it my whole life." The American frowned. "These folks really believe all this shit?"

"Believe me, they do. I've seen it happen before. There's no rhyme nor reason as we understand it, but to them it's very real."

Just then Ian saw Blessing Ochido washing his face and hands in a bowl of water one of the women had put on a tree stump.

"Let's see what his Right Honourable the Minister of the Interior can tell us."

Ochido looked up in alarm as he saw them approaching and would have ducked back into the nearest hut if Keller hadn't stopped him.

"So, what's going on then?" he almost shouted at the terrified minister. "Who left last night?"

At first the African said nothing. He glared at them and looked down at the ground, shuffling his expensive Giuseppe Zanotti shoes in the dust. He shrugged then started as Keller gave him a good shake.

"Stop pissing on ma' boots. We been through enough shit on this bloody safari nonsense. I want answers, and I want them now."

Ochido shrugged again. "Nashale, Suma, and Papele."

"And why would the cabinet ministers take off? Is the President still sitting in the other car?" Ian pointed to the lone limousine which looked totally out of place parked on the edge of the rural village.

"Possibly," was the only answer they got.

"And why leave you behind? Why didn't y'all go with them?"

Ochido refused to answer. He looked miserable, his shoulders drooped and his hands flapped.

Keller let go of the minister's arm and watched him walk away. "That's odder than an Armadillo eating a banana. It ain't looking so good. Might be planning a coup, do ya' think?"

"Probably," Ian sighed.

"Well I intend to hightail it out of here and get back to my embassy as soon as possible. Where's that fellow with the Jeep?"

"For once we agree," Ian gave a wry grin. "I'll tell him we leave in ten minutes."

Fleming found Simon hovering outside the hut, waiting for news of Amie. Still no one had told him how she was.

"There you are Peterson. We're about ready to leave. Don't want to overstay our welcome with the Chief. We've accepted his hospitality long enough. And these people can turn nasty on a sixpence. We'll be ready in ten minutes." He turned as if to walk away, but Simon's words stopped him in his tracks.

"I'm not going anywhere."

"You bloody well are. You're going to drive me and the other diplomats to Apatu."

"I'm not leaving until Amie can travel with us."

"Now look here, Peterson, you'll take us back right now and that's an order."

"I don't have time to argue about seniority or who can and cannot give who orders, but I'm telling you I'm not leaving without Amie."

"For heaven's sake man don't be such an ass. This is government business, not some bloody ambulance service. We'll get her back later, send a car for her."

"No." Simon walked away, feeling in his pocket for the keys to the Jeep. He'd locked the doors, so if Fleming was intent on hot wiring it, he'd have to break into it, but he doubted if the man knew how to hotwire a car.

Amie opened her eyes. She was weak and listless reminding her of the other time she'd woken, in another hut many miles away, when she was on the run from war-torn Apatu. The darkness swirled and dipped, the fog came and went, and then Ngoni's face came into focus.

"Where am I?" she croaked.

"Safe, in village."

"I, thought … I thought I saw Simon. Is he here?"

Ngoni frowned. "Simon?"

"Yes, a white man, he was not in the *boma*."

The girl shrugged her shoulders. "I not know, I do not see. I here with you."

"Please. Please can you go and ask?" Amie struggled to sit and stretched out her hand to grab Ngoni's. "Please ask if he is here. Bring him to me." She sank back down exhausted by the effort.

Ngoni blinked in the bright sunlight and shaded her eyes. She couldn't remember who had been in the *boma*. Kirimu Nashele told her to stay in his tent. He'd instructed her to remain out of sight and speak to no one. She jumped when a white man gripped her shoulder.

"Have you been in there with Amie?" he indicated the hut behind them.

Ngoni nodded.

"Is she alive, will she live, how sick is she?" The words tumbled out making no sense to the girl, but she guessed this was Simon.

"You Simon?" her voice was so low he almost didn't hear her.

"Yes. I'm Simon."

"Yes, she want you."

Simon didn't wait to hear more but barged into the hut, ignoring the cries of protest from the women. He stared at Amie, not believing his eyes, then he rushed forward and took her in his arms,

Amie burst into tears. The women tried to pull Simon away, fearing he was frightening her, but she cried out. "No, leave him. Simon I can't believe you're here. How …"

"Long story," he smiled down at her. "As long as you're safe and well."

"Yes, I'm much better, but the baby's gone." The tears flowed down her cheeks. "I'm so sorry Simon. I lost our baby," she choked through the sobs.

"It wasn't your fault," he murmured raining kisses on her head, then her cheeks and then her lips. "As long as I have you, nothing else matters."

While Simon held her, refusing even to move as the women offered her more green mash, they caught up on events since Durban. Amie felt well enough to giggle when he told her of his fitness runs in the Welsh valleys, and he gasped at her account of how the hyenas gathered when she was miscarrying the baby.

"Are you sure that Ben is still in that car, afraid?"

"As far as I know, yes, and there is nothing anyone can do about it."

Amie looked thoughtful. "I have an idea. I think I know what to do."

53 RETURN TO APATU

By the following morning. Amie had recovered enough to travel. Simon drummed his fingers on the steering wheel blocking out the complaining from the back seat. He'd insisted that Amie travel in the front where she'd have more room and that sorted out the pecking order of the disgruntled diplomats each of whom claimed to represent the most important country on earth. He smiled at his feeble attempt at diplomacy. Fleming was furious to have Amie usurp him as the superior ranking official by taking his rightful place in the front seat.

Amie waited for Ngoni. She'd expected it to take a while and guessed Simon and the others would be getting very impatient.

Half an hour later, the girl scurried into the village clutching a bundle. The poor thing looked terrified. Amie took her hand and whispered words of encouragement. It looked as if Ngoni would refuse, then she nodded and walked away.

Amie ambled over, not bothering to hurry.

"Get a bloody move on," Ian shouted.

"Oh, wait, I didn't say goodbye to Mtala. She was one of the ladies who looked after me." Amie turned on her heel and disappeared around the corner again.

Simon thought Fleming was going to have a fit, when

he repeated that he was not leaving without her, though he couldn't understand her strange behaviour.

It was an age until Amie reappeared, and this time she eased herself into the passenger seat, smiled and told them she was ready. She leaned over and whispered to Simon who nodded. He turned the key and drove out of the village. He was disturbed they were leaving Ngoni behind. Yesterday, Amie had been insistent they take her back as well, today she didn't even mention it.

"I'm surprised you're leaving your little friend behind," Ian Fleming remarked from his cramped position wedged in between Edward Keller and Vladimir Petrovnikov.

His sarcasm was ignored.

"Can't you go any faster than this?" asked Keller.

"Yes, but we need to hang back for the other car. Travelling in convoy will be a lot safer. The bad guys might be hanging around."

Looking behind they saw that the other limousine was following.

"First stop, the hospital," Simon announced leaving no room for argument. "I think you'll agree it's best the Togodians do not see their revered President in his present catatonic state."

There was silence from the passengers.

The journey back was painfully slow, the Jeep had to wait for the limousine. The armour plating and soft suspension made it unsuitable for the rough terrain, but once they hit the tarred road, they made better progress.

"What the fuck are we going to do when we get back?" Ed Keller asked no one in particular. "There'll be chaos, but I guess the hospital will put his Excellency to rights."

"Not a chance," Ian replied.

"Come on man, at least the Apatu medical facilities are not too bad. Sure, they'll inject him with something, bring him back to life in no time."

Ian Fleming shook his head. "Ed, you don't know Africa at all, do you? Once cursed you die, it's as simple as that. It's over for Ben Mtumba and we just have to hope that any takeover will be peaceful."

"So, which of the monkeys is his deputy?"

Ian glared at him in the mirror and Amie turned around from the front seat with a look of horror. "How can you work in an embassy and not know who was who in the host government, and how could you describe them that way?"

Keller was such an odious man.

"I guess we'll liaise with Kirimu Nashele," Ian muttered and smiled.

Dusk fell as they drove into the hospital grounds. An orderly came out while Simon went off to find Sohanna Reddy, the matron. To her disgust, Amie was pushed into a wheelchair and taken to the accident and emergency department while Ben Mtumba was whisked away out of sight. The glimpse Amie had of him was heartbreaking. He had to be helped out of the car, picked up like a baby and laid on a stretcher. His eyes were wide open, but there was no expression on his face as he stared into space.

As soon as Amie was settled and Simon returned, she asked him to find Ngoni. He tried to dissuade her, but she said it was urgent and became agitated when he was in no hurry to do as she asked. He was also to find out where Ben was.

Hooked up to two drips, one fixed to a wall bracket, Amie ground her teeth in frustration. She was exhausted after the journey, but refused to let herself fall asleep. It seemed an age before Ngoni arrived.

The young girl was distraught, and whispering in Amie's ear, she shook her head. Amie smiled and squeezed her hand before Ngoni left, exchanging a few words with Simon on the way out of the ward. He came over, grabbed a plastic chair, and sat down at Amie's bedside.

"What was that all about?"

Amie ignored his question and changed the subject. "What's been going on? Tell me the news."

"First, how are you feeling?"

"Much better. I've no idea what the village women gave me, but it helped. Do I have to stay here?"

"Yes. I won't let you leave until you're quite well, but they tell me you only need another twenty-four hours."

"It can't be soon enough."

"Amie, about the baby."

"Are you worried about my mental state, Simon?"

"Yes," Simon looked down embarrassed.

"Don't be. I'll mourn him, but I've been in Africa long enough to become a little fatalistic. If he was not meant to live, then so be it. I didn't do anything more strenuous than if I'd been back in London, well, not much really, and to survive here you need to be born strong and healthy. I can accept it, but it hurts."

"That's a relief to hear. I know women can go … well, odd."

"Simon, as long as I have you, I can cope with anything."

He leaned over and gave her a hug, pulling at the cannula which made her shriek. Other patients looked up and glared at him, and a nurse hurried over as Simon and Amie burst out laughing.

"You still haven't told me what's going on in the world."

"I have no idea. I heard someone mention the streets are quiet and most of the shops are shut."

"It's not Sunday, is it?"

Simon glanced at his watch. "Damn battery went. No, I think it's Wednesday."

"I hope there isn't going to be more trouble."

"I wouldn't be too sure."

The following morning, Amie received a surprise visit from Ian Fleming. He was the last person she wanted to see. He didn't bother to bring any grapes, flowers, or even a book, but that didn't surprise her. Ian wasn't a flowers sort of person. He walked in peering at the various beds until he spotted her and marched over.

"Better?" he asked.

"Yes, thank you. I'm hoping to get out today."

"Ah, good."

"Simon's heard that it's gone quiet outside."

"Ah, Simon. Yes. But never mind him, there is trouble brewing. It seems your friend has caused an uproar."

"Friend? Which friend?"

"That Gaga Medwewe. She and Kirimu have holed up in the palace, surrounded themselves with troops and announced that since Ben Mtumba is no longer alive, Kirimu is in charge."

Amie gasped. "Gaga and Kirimu? Since when?"

"Since the night before last."

"Now I remember, Gaga disappeared as soon as the safari camp was attacked. She must have come straight back to Apatu."

"I suspect that Kirimu was going with her but got caught up in the fighting before he could leave."

Amie groaned and leant back against her pillows. "Please don't let this be another coup. Ben is an excellent president. He cares about his country and the people."

Ian's eyebrows shot up. "You still believe that, Amie? How naïve you are. These leaders are all the same the moment they get into power."

Amie glared at him. "Ben's different," she snapped. "You forget how well I know him."

"Yeah, sure. Well, I just came to say as soon as you're out of here, report back to the embassy."

"Yes, sir." Amie put as much sarcasm into the two words as she could, but Ian probably didn't notice as he stood up, turned and walked briskly out of the ward.

A few minutes later Ngoni crept in carrying Amie's backpack which she dumped on the bed. "You need?" she asked.

"I'm not sure what's in there," Amie rummaged around inside.

"Is it true that Kirimu and Gaga are in the palace and telling Togodo they are in charge?"

Ngoni nodded her head then smiled. "You right. I see Ben better like you say."

"And?" Amie shuffled forward in the bed.

"It is good now."

"It worked?"

"Yes." Ngoni looked happier than Amie had ever seen her. She wrapped her arms round the girl and squeezed tight.

"He has, like you," Ngoni pointed to the drip over Amie's bed. "One day, two?" Her face fell and the light went out of her eyes. "Maybe Ouma Adede …"

"Trust me Ngoni, I will make it right. I promise you. Goodness, look."

Standing in the doorway to the ward was the renowned witch doctor herself.

Amie waved to her. Coke bottle tops clinked from the bracelets around her wrists and ankles as the lady approached. It didn't matter how many times Amie met her, she always felt an aura of awe and power and felt small in her presence. She smiled at her.

Ngoni wasn't smiling. She was terrified until the older lady looked at her and laughed.

"I see you Ouma Adede. I am happy to see you," said Amie.

"But this little lady is not," the witch doctor pointed to Ngoni.

"She is frightened you will be angry." Amie held her breath waiting for the reply.

Ouma Adede said, "No. How can I be angry? She has saved a very valuable life. She does not know that what she has done will make a big change in her life."

54 DEBRIEFING

Sir Humphrey sat beneath the portrait of Her Majesty and tossed the bottle of designer water from hand to hand. He placed it on the boardroom table and pulled his electronic diary out of his pocket. He'd see Simon Peterson first. He pressed a button under the table.

Simon entered the dungeon and at Sir Humphrey's nod, he sat down.

"Fully recovered from your Welsh escapade?"

"Yes, thank you, Sir. I certainly feel fitter."

There was a long silence broken by the question he'd been dreading.

"So, why didn't you keep in touch? I understand you didn't even return the satellite phone."

Simon squirmed on his chair. It was never a good idea to drop a colleague in it, yet he didn't want to drop himself in it either. "It got broken Sir. Unusable."

"I see." Another long silence. "Would it help if I told you that London was worried Fleming was over eager in his support of Kirimu Nashele? That we considered you might have Ben Mtumba's best interests at heart?"

Simon breathed a sigh of relief. Maybe London had a better understanding of the situation than he'd thought. "It was never mentioned, but I suspected Ian didn't know the contents of the Decker report."

"No, he didn't. We kept that close to our chests, on a need to know basis."

"And the other diplomats?" Simon hesitated to ask.

"Not a whisper."

"And the President?"

"Need to know only, Simon." Sir Humphrey smiled, he wasn't giving anything away.

"If I have this straight, Fleming was to go up there and bid for Britain, along with the others, but you wanted me to disrupt the auction. I don't understand."

"Exactly. But in this case, it wasn't necessary. I understand by the time you arrived all hell had broken loose."

Simon nodded and sat back in his chair. It was all a bit convoluted for his liking, but then secret services the world over never played it straight.

"We knew what the other players were after, but our biggest worry was why Fleming dragged Amie all the way out here and placed her so close to Ben. Has she mentioned anything to you?"

Simon was back in the hot seat. He sighed. "She told me he hinted that Ben was expendable and that she had the impression he had a preference for Nashele, the Finance Minister, to head up Togodo."

Sir Humphry didn't reply.

"He told her to stay close to Ben and find out what she could, especially about the other bidders."

"The village under Chief Lgego, are they loyal to Mtumba?"

"Yes, I would say so. They were upset when he went into a catatonic state after being bewitched."

"Which puts another dimension on the situation." He abruptly changed the subject. "I understand you put in for field work then cancelled it?"

"Yes, Sir. I was – we were – expecting a baby, and planning to get married. A stable job looked a better option."

"Still the case?"

"No. Amie lost the baby."

"We are talking about Amie Fish?"

"Yes." Simon was unsure about being honest but relaxed when he saw Sir Humphry smile before asking him to send his fiancée in.

Amie stepped into the dungeon wondering why the representative from London wanted to see her. She hadn't played much of a role in the disastrous auction which had not even got off the ground.

"Amie Fish?" Sir Humphrey stood up to shake her hand. "Take a seat."

"Thank you. I honestly can't tell you very much," in her nervous rush she didn't wait for him to ask questions. "The villagers told us that the people who attacked the camp came from Budan and the M'untus were the tribe involved."

"The same tribe of villagers where you stayed?"

"No, Sir. They are Luebos and very peaceful, but I now understand they had a large cache of weapons and they went to liberate the camp. But I didn't really know all this, as I was ill, and I got it all from Simon, Sir." Amie ran out of steam.

"And what's all this about a witch doctor?"

She stared at him in horror. Where had he heard about that? He'd think she was a total nutcase.

Sir Humphrey laughed at the look on her face. "My dear, don't look so distressed. My grandparents had a farm in Kenya, on the slopes of Mount Kenya in fact, and although I don't remember visiting too clearly, I've heard all the tales and I know being cursed was, and still is, very real to the African people."

Amie relaxed. "You know then that someone cursed Ben, sorry I mean the President. It was probably one of his ministers though no one knows who. His fear was so great he just sat there waiting to die, it was awful. He just stayed in the diplomatic car for ages and then we discovered that Kirimu Nashele had raced back to Apatu probably to take over."

"But the fact he was being overthrown wasn't enough to snap Mtumba back into the land of the living?"

"No. I met Ngoni when I was … in trouble. We spent the night together in the bush and she told me that my friend, Ouma Adede, the most famous witch doctor in Togodo, and Ben and Ngoni had all lived in the same village as children. Ngoni had had a hard time and Ouma Adede had been her only friend. I suggested that Ngoni tell Ben that she had the power to lift the spell because Ouma Adede had taught her stuff."

"But she hadn't?"

"No, not at all. Ngoni was really scared, but I persuaded her to lie to Ben. She gathered a few leaves, berries and bones, and then chanted a bit to fool him into believing he would recover. She was worried and scared it wouldn't work and she was also terrified that Ouma Adede would curse her for pretending to have the power."

Amie paused for breath then continued. "But in the end, it was fine, because the witch doctor approved. I think it helped that Ngoni was in love with Ben which goes right back to when they lived in the village. Kirimu also came from the same kraal and he's in love with Ngoni and furious that Ngoni doesn't love him. He dragged her on the safari to seduce her and then make her his third wife. So, it was all a bit of a mess."

Sir Humphrey nodded. "It certainly was. It still is. We have Nashele holding hostages in the palace, and Ben is in hospital. Matters are very unstable."

"You, Britain I mean, you think Ben makes a good President, don't you?" Amie blurted out before she could stop herself.

"As far as we can tell. Yes. For now he has our full support, but we won't be bringing in the troops to support his claim to the Presidency. They will have to sort that out for themselves, I'm afraid."

Sir Humphrey stood up. "I think that's all for now. If I think of anything else before I fly back, I'll let you know."

They left the dungeon together, and Amie went to find Simon. As she had hoped, he'd moved into her little cottage in the embassy grounds.

The moment she walked through the door he took her in his arms, caressing her hair, dropping gentle kisses on her face and neck, guiding her gently to the bed.

"How I've missed you and worried about you."

"I was angry, then worried, then angry all over again," she muttered as he removed her t-shirt. She reached out to unbutton his shirt but was interrupted when there was a loud banging on the door.

Amie groaned, pulled her shirt back on and went to see who it was. Tanya waited outside and pushed a note into Amie's hand as she rubbernecked to see what was going on inside. She pointed to the scrap of paper. "I was just coming back from the chemist, but they were closed and this weird looking lady with all kinds of strange things in her hair said you must have this immediately. She was most insistent."

Amie looked down at the scrap of dirty, crumpled paper and nodded.

"Thank you, Tanya. We'll see you later?"

Tanya reluctantly took a step backwards and left.

Amie uncurled the note from Ouma Adede and read it to Simon.

Ngoni taken to palas you must rescu.

Amie gasped. "Simon, we must do something."

"Go to the palace? You must be mad."

"Probably, but I'm not going to sit here and do nothing, Simon. Ngoni saved my life. I have to try and save hers."

Simon got up from the bed and sighed. "Oh, God here we go again. Why is it that the right thing to do is always the hardest? Listen Amie, for once we'll work together and I'll be keeping an eye on you. Who knows what we're up against?"

55 CHAOS AT THE PALACE

Amie searched through the drawers flinging out the contents in all directions.

"What are you looking for?" Simon wondered who would clear up the mess.

"My pass. When I was working at the palace I had a pass for work. I'm hoping it will get us in."

"You think the guards will allow us to walk inside with all this going on?"

"It's worth a try. You got a better idea?"

Simon ran his fingers through his hair. "No, I guess not, but two of us on one pass?"

Amie paused in her search and eyed him up and down. "I was going to suggest the boot, but maybe the floor in front of the back seat covered with a blanket might be better?" she giggled.

"I'm not amused." Simon sat on the bed wondering how he could get her to change her mind.

"You won't talk me out of this. You wouldn't leave a friend in danger. Not when she'd saved your life."

"I'm not sure what you think we can do."

"Simple. Find her and get her out."

"You sure she wants us to drag her out? Maybe she's in cahoots with Nashele and wants to marry him."

"Believe me, she doesn't. I saw them together in the

Grand Hotel. He was bullying and threatening her. She loves Ben."

"Ben's already married."

"Simon. Really. Wives are collected in bundles in Africa and you've not met Mathilda."

"Mathilda?"

"Ben's English wife, a hellcat on high heels. I wouldn't like to tangle with her. Awful woman." Amie squealed as she pounced on the pass and waved it triumphantly. "I sure wish I still had that AK47. I wonder what happened to it?" She picked up her 9 mm Glock 26 and pushed it into the waistband of her cargo pants.

"It'll be buried by now."

"What?"

Simon checked his own Smith & Wesson and the knife he had strapped to his ankle. "Never mind, long story. I'll tell you later. I guess you want to leave right now?"

But Amie was already out of the door.

"Don't forget the blanket," she called back.

There was no one on duty at the carpool so Amie opened the cabin door and lifted the keys off the board. She found the mini she had used before and drove out the back entrance of the compound where Simon jumped in the back seat clutching the blanket.

The roads were strangely deserted. Most of the shops were shut and there wasn't a pedestrian to be seen, even the minibus taxis were absent.

"I'll take the long way round, and go in from the back. The guards know me and it's our best chance of getting inside."

"No heroics, Amie. We grab Ngoni and get out, promise me?"

"Agreed, promise. I've no intention of getting mixed up in a political power play. Ben's safe in hospital, and it's for him to sort out when he's well enough."

Simon saw the three-metre-high pink painted wall that surrounded the home and offices of the presidency. It was topped with electrified razor wire and video cameras, though he'd be surprised if they worked.

As Amie drove up to the gate, Simon ducked down and pulled the blanket over himself. It was a tight squeeze and he wished she'd chosen a larger car.

Amie's hands were damp and she felt the sweat trickle down her forehead and run into her eyes. She gripped the steering wheel so tightly her knuckles turned white and she had to concentrate on keeping her hands from shaking as the guard ambled over. She turned to him with a smile, but he just stared at her.

She waved the pass hanging round her neck. "Hello. It's me again, here to see Gaga Medwewe."

The guard didn't respond.

Amie's heart sank. It wasn't going to work. Should she have asked for Kirimu Nashele or even Ben?

The second guard wandered over and Amie repeated who she was and taking a firmer line she added. "Hurry, Gaga Medwewe wanted me to come at once and you are delaying me!"

After hesitating for what felt like hours, the second guard pushed the gate open and Amie drove in as fast as she dared, not stopping when she caught the wing mirror on the gatepost. She parked as close to the back door as she could and hissed for Simon to follow her up the steps. The guards hadn't even glanced in the back of the car so maybe, just maybe this would work.

She pushed open the door surprised to find it unlocked and they slipped inside. To her relief, the hallway was empty, but they'd only taken a couple of steps when another guard appeared. He wasn't one of the palace staff, he wore an army uniform. Amie used the same excuse, waving her pass in front of him. "…and this," she indicated Simon, "… is one of the diplomats I've been told to bring to meet the Right Honourable Nashele."

The man pulled out a radio, but before he could press the call button, Simon stepped to the side and gave him a chop to the neck. The soldier crumpled to the floor.

"Shit," hissed Amie. "That's blown it."

"What was I supposed to do?" grumbled Simon as he grabbed the man under his armpits and looked around for a suitable place to hide him.

Amie opened the door to a utility room and helped Simon drag the body inside. They were in luck. The packed storeroom had floor to ceiling shelves stacked to the roof. There were tools, spare light bulbs, stepladders, stationery, toilet rolls and a variety of supplies necessary for palace maintenance. Amie pounced on a packet of plastic ties, and helped Simon secure the soldier's hands and legs. Simon manufactured a daisy chain from the ties to secure him to a pipe attached to the wall.

"Must be a good sign," Amie whispered as she stuffed the soldier's mouth with a cleaning rag.

"God knows how many germs are on that," Simon observed with a wry smile.

"You think I should find a cleaner one?" Amie looked at the filthy rag she'd found on the floor.

"Nah, don't bother. Let's do this and get out of here. The place gives me the creeps."

"So, you don't want a nice big palace like this when we're married?" Amie teased, opening the door and peeping out.

"Get serious, we may not live that long."

They followed the corridor past Amie's old office and the deserted canteen. Amie wondered if it was true that Kirimu Nashele had taken over the palace. It could have been a piece of fake news which wasn't uncommon these days.

"Where to now?" whispered Simon.

"No idea. This is the only part of the palace I've been in, except for the Versailles ballroom."

"The what?"

"You'll see. Well maybe. The stairs, we'll try up there." Amie bounded up the red carpet on the wide marble staircase. They found more offices, but these were larger and well furnished, for ministers and their secretaries. They opened the door to a large empty council chamber. The seats, each one with a desk in front, were arranged in a semi-circle facing the largest chair mounted on a dais.
Simon drew his gun and nudged Amie to do the same but she shook her head.

"No. I'll bluff it out first," she whispered. "Gaga is a friend."

"Was, you mean."

They scuttled down another passageway and skidded to a stop when they heard voices that were coming closer.

Simon tugged at Amie's shirt and they crept backwards and in through the nearest doorway. They were back in the council chamber. The voices came nearer and the door opened.

Amie dived under the largest desk on the podium, burrowing back as far as she could while Simon hid behind the long velvet drapes hanging either side of the windows.

Several people shuffled inside. Amie recognized Nashele's voice barking orders and murmurs from the people with him, but she couldn't decide how many of them. They talked rapidly but not in English. To her horror she saw a man's legs approaching, inches away from her face. If he sat down and stretched his legs forward, he'd kick her. She took a deep breath and pinched her nose. The dust was swirling and she had to stop herself from sneezing. She could hear the blood coursing around her ears while her heart thumped in her chest. Her right leg was crunched up at an odd angle and she bit her lip to take her mind off the pain, but she dared not move.

The voices rose and fell, a few people left the chamber and more arrived. Amie's leg grew numb but she remained still, wedged in the confined space under the president's podium. She had no idea where Simon was.

After an age, the legs in front of her moved away, the door opened and the people left, their voices fading down the corridor. She wriggled and slid out, sitting on the floor massaging her dead leg. She stretched her arms and staggered to her feet only to come face to face with Gaga Medwewe.

"Gaga, I've found you." She said the first words that came into her head and gave her friend a huge smile.

Gaga did not smile back. She was holding a gun and it was aimed at Amie.

56 SHATTERED MIRRORS

Amie blinked. She couldn't believe her eyes. It was so incongruous that her happy, smiling friend in her pastel coloured polyester suits, who was so earnest, so unsure, and so approachable, was now threatening her with a firearm.

"Gaga," she spluttered "put that down, you're frightening me." She took a few steps back and sat down in one of the seats in the semi-circle, aware that Gaga had seen her crawl out of her hiding place.

"Why are you here?" Gaga did not smile, nor did she lower the gun.

"I came to find you of course," Amie bluffed. "I was worried about you. You'd disappeared from the camp, and I thought you were dead. Then I heard you were in the palace, so of course I came. What's the problem? Why the gun?"

Amie leaned back in the councillor's seat and spread her legs as if she hadn't a care in the world. She wasn't sure Gaga would fall for her story, but it was the best she could think of.

"You came to find me?"

"Of course. Why else would I come? I was puzzled why the streets are so empty and there is no one in the offices, but I guess it's a public holiday?"

"Holiday?" Gaga frowned. "No, no holiday, a new government. A new future for Togodo."

"Pardon?" Amie played dumb. "I have no idea what you mean. I've been sick, lost the baby," she sighed hoping this would soften her friend's attitude, "and haven't the faintest idea what's going on. What's happened?"

"You do not know?"

"Know what Gaga? Tell me."

"We have a new president now. President Nashele, a great man and it is the end for your friend, Ben Mtumba. It was planned even before we go north."

"Goodness," Amie did her best to keep calm. "Well that's nothing to do with me. I understand you have to do these things sometimes. It is your country."

"Yes, my country."

"So, you knew about this? Kirimu, sorry, President Nashele arranged all this?"

"We did." Gaga relaxed and boasted. "Who do you think put the Milk plant in the soldiers' mealie meal? And who called the men to come and attack the camp? I did all that. Me. President Nashele has agreed with the North Koreans, who will mine our valuable resources and it will bring great wealth."

I bet he has, thought Amie. *And I doubt the people will see any of this great wealth.* "Gaga you have come such a long way in your life, you must be so proud." She thought a little flattery might go a long way.

"Oh yes. My mother cleaned houses. I cleaned houses. And soon I will be the first lady in Togodo. I have come a long way, yes a very long way."

"Doesn't the new president already have a wife?"

Amie knew the moment she said it she'd put her foot in it.

Gaga's face darkened, she raised the gun and held it steady. "She is not important, and he will soon get tired of Ngonicansaga. She will not keep his interest for long."

"I've no idea where she is either. Is she here in the palace?"

Before Gaga could reply, they were startled by loud, shrill, high pitched screams.

Gaga rushed to the door. It flew open knocking her backwards into Amie who was close behind her. Amie reached round the plump body and tried to take the gun away. Gaga resisted but was distracted by the screams from a distraught Mathilda – she was trying to escape the clutches of a soldier who ran in after her.

There was chaos. Simon jumped out from behind the curtains, grabbed the soldier round the neck and rendered him unconscious. Amie and Gaga were in a desperate struggle to get the gun, and Mathilda just screamed and screamed.

Amie's arms were aching with the effort of holding the struggling Gaga who was strong. It was like trying to uproot a hundred-year-old oak tree. Amie balanced on her left leg, bent her right knee, and drove it into Gaga's plump leg. The African tilted and lost balance. They fell to the floor causing the gun to go off. The sound of the shot in the confined space of the council chamber reverberated and made Amie's head spin and her ears ring, yet she was aware that the screaming had stopped.

Footsteps and shouts from outside announced the arrival of more guards, and Amie knew they would be outnumbered. She tried to wriggle from under Gaga who now had her pinned to the floor, still holding the gun. She tried to see where Simon was but the circular seating obscured her view.

The door flew open with a crack and boots clattered on the polished wooden floor accompanied by arguing voices. Then one of them began to laugh and several more shots rang out.

"What is going on?" Amie thought it was Kirimu's voice.

"The white bitch, Mr President, we have sent her to heaven." The statement was followed by roars of hysterical laughter, hand clapping and foot stamping. Taking advantage of the raucous noise, Amie resumed her struggle with Gaga. She'd loosened one arm and was pressing a hand over the woman's mouth to stop her from shouting out.

"Come." One pair of feet left the chamber followed by all the rest.

Amie twisted Gaga round and managed to drag herself on top the woman, pressing her head hard against the floor. Amie pushed down as hard as she could.

Amie was losing strength but still clinging on, her arms were locked tight, her muscles screaming, her back aching and her head thumping. She felt someone tugging at her and another pair of hands attempted to pull her off her prisoner. She resisted until Simon hissed, "Let go, I've got her."

Amie released her hold and levered herself up. She massaged her arms and rubbed her back. She'd been so intent on stopping Gaga from firing the gun that she hadn't had the opportunity to draw her own handgun.

She watched as Simon's greater strength easily pried

Gaga's finger off the gun, hooking out the finger that was still on the trigger. He handed the rifle to Amie and dragged the woman off the floor.

She turned and spat at him, hate in her eyes. "You will pay for this," she raged, spitting the dust and dirt out of her mouth. With Gaga unarmed, they let their guard down for a moment and she took off, moving faster than either of them expected. She raced out of the council chamber screaming at the top of her voice. They ran after her.

"Kirimu. Kirimu," she shrieked "Help. Help."

The new president appeared at the end of the long corridor. He lifted the gun in his hand and fired three shots into Medwewe's body. He turned and walked away without glancing back.

Simon and Amie skidded to a halt on the plush red carpet.

Amie's instinct was to rush to the woman's aid, but Simon pulled her back and they almost fell back into the council chamber where she tripped over another body. "Did, did you see that? Simon, he just killed her!"

"She was no longer useful. She would never fit the bill as first lady. Is this the former president's wife?" He pointed to Mathilda spread-eagled on the floor.

Amie looked at the corpse. As beautiful as ever even in death. Her long blond hair framing a perfect face, the long legs, slender arms, polished fingernails, if it were not for the blood seeping out of her chest and her large almond-shaped sightless eyes that stared at nothing, Mathilda could be asleep. The expression on her face was strangely peaceful, and Amie's heart ached for Ben. She turned to Simon.

"We didn't kill her, did we? When the gun went off?"

"No. The soldiers shot her when they rushed in."

Amie wasn't sure she believed him. Mathilda had stopped screaming before the men ran in shooting, but it would never be proved, no autopsy would be held and no ballistics match to identify which gun had taken her life.

"What now?" asked Simon. "Where would they be keeping Ngoni?"

"Most likely in the presidential suite, though I have no idea where that is. This place is enormous."

"Upstairs," Simon suggested as they peered out to see if the corridor was clear. They retraced their steps and darted up the first flight of steps they came to leading up to the third floor.

"This looks more like it," muttered Amie as they peeped into an opulent drawing room. Slipping inside she barely had time to notice the tasteful sofas, occasional tables, chairs and expensive paintings on the walls. After the carnage downstairs, it was a haven of peace and quiet and luxury living.

The lounge led into a dining room dominated by a long highly polished yellowwood table laid for twenty people, with silver cutlery, bone china plates set around a central display of flowers in filigree holders.

"Gracious," said Amie stopping to stare. "It's like a stately home in England."

"Stop gawking," Simon hurried her on.

One room led into another: an informal sitting room, a study, a dressing room, until finally, the last room opened into a bedroom the size of a small farmyard.

Ngoni lay on the four-poster bed with her ankles and wrists securely tied. Her eyes lit up when she saw Amie.

It took a matter of moments for Simon to cut through the cloth strips and they helped her to her feet.

"*Asante. Asante*. Thank you. Thank you."

Amie took her arm. "We need to get you out of here," she whispered. "Kirimu is running the palace."

"Do you know the quickest way out?" Simon was more practical.

Ngoni nodded and darted back towards the dining room. They followed.

The soldiers were everywhere. They had to double back as they ran down corridors looking for a way out. They managed to get as far as the second floor when they were caught between noises coming from both directions.

Simon flung open a door and hustled the girls inside. Footsteps walked past, voices shouted, shots were fired, there was a full-scale battle going on right outside the door.

"Ben," whispered Ngoni in astonishment.

"Is that his voice?" Amie kept her voice low.

Ngoni nodded.

The noise was horrendous. The screams from the wounded, the shrieking orders and guns set to automatic, firing, over and over as the battle raged past.

Silence fell and Simon peeped out to see if the coast was clear. They began to run, but by now Ngoni was so rattled that she took them the wrong way and they found themselves at one end of the hall of mirrors. Simon's mouth fell open, so this was the fake Versailles ballroom Amie had told him about.

From the middle of the wall, on the left a door burst open and a dozen soldiers backed in firing as they retreated. The fusillade of shots smashed into the floor to ceiling windows on the far side and the defenders fired back, shattering the mirrored walls. Glass flew everywhere, catching the light and cascading down like broken rainbows. Bullets hit the glass chandeliers and created tinkling music as they were blown apart. It would have been beautiful if it wasn't for the carnage. Wounded men fell, writhing in agony, their boots carving furrows in the polished parquet floor now painted in blood.

"Let's get out of here," Amie said. She was the first to recover and the three backed up the way they'd come and raced down the nearest staircase to the ground floor. They met no one and breathed a sigh of relief as Simon flung open the back door and ran to the car. They gasped for breath as they dived into the Mini and did their best to look calm and normal, as they approached the back gates. Amie hoped they'd be left open but they were firmly closed. She drew up and beeped the horn. There was no response from the other side and the guard house on the inside was deserted.

Simon hopped out and ran to open the gate. It took an age, as the rusty metal gate inched open little by little. The girls tried not to panic, Ngoni looking behind to see if anyone was chasing them.

The moment Amie judged she could drive the Mini through she put her foot down, damaging the other wing mirror. The car was moving as Simon grabbed the door handle and leapt in, leaving the gate wide open behind them.

"Where to now?" Amie asked. "Do we smuggle Ngoni into the cottage at the embassy?"

"I go to Ouma Adede," Ngoni said from the back seat.

"Show me the way," Amie replied.

Ngoni directed them to the edge of town and one of the informal settlements that looked vaguely familiar. "Here," she said as they approached a side road. Amie stopped the car. The path between the shacks was too narrow to drive down and she was unsure of the mood of the people to even try. Simon moved his seat and Ngoni scrambled out.

"*Asante*, Amie. I find you, at the embassy, yes?"

"Yes. We will go there now. Are you sure you'll be safe?" Amie was worried about leaving her. If Kirimu won the battle, he might come looking for her.

"I am safe. Ouma Adede will put spell on Nashele and he will not win. Ben will win," Ngoni said simply and walked away.

"I wish I had the basic uncluttered beliefs of the Africans," sighed Simon. "So fatalistic and accepting of what life brings."

"A land where life is cheap and can end in a heartbeat," Amie replied as she turned the car round. "Now we need to work out what we're going to tell them at the embassy. I think we're in hot water again. I'm not sure how we'll talk our way out of this one."

57   LAST DAYS

Amie nodded to the guard on the back gate, and parked the Mini. She got out and looked ruefully at the broken wing mirrors.

"Think they'll dock my pay for the damage?" she asked. Then shrugged. "What am I saying? I probably won't have a job after this."

As they walked back to the cottage, Amie felt guilty. It didn't matter if she was fired, but she'd dragged Simon into a situation that was none of his business and the diplomatic service was his career, his life. She dreaded to think what Ian Fleming would say about their latest escapade.

Amie put the kettle on. She needed her coffee, everything else could wait.

Simon flung himself on the bed. "It will be interesting to see how understanding they are."

"They don't expect me to behave normally," Amie spooned in the coffee. "They know I'm a very bad spy and not particularly good at following orders." She added the sugar, milk and boiling water. "I'm sorry I dragged you into it, but you didn't have to come. I would have gone on my own."

"I know and that's why I was right behind you. Now you can come and say thank you properly." He smiled as Amie approached the bed.

The summons to the dungeon came a few hours later. As they walked in, Amie was relieved to see Sir Humphrey and no sign of Ian Fleming.

"Take a seat."

Amie perched on the edge of her chair. It was impossible to read her boss's face. Simon went to the opposite side of the large table and sat down.

Sir Humphry strolled across the room juggling a water bottle. "Would either of you like to tell me a little more about your palace adventure?"

Goodness, thought Amie, *he's on the ball. What has he heard and so quickly!* She jumped in before Simon had a chance to open his mouth.

"It was all my fault, Sir Humphrey," she said, running her sweaty hands down her cargo pants. "I heard that Ngoni was being held prisoner and I went to rescue her. She saved my life and I couldn't leave her to be mauled by that odious Nashele. He's been chasing her since they were children, but she loves Ben and is loyal to him, and she saved his life as well, and as the British are behind Ben, I'm sure you would have sent me to do exactly that. We didn't get involved in the fighting, though, all we did was grab her and drive her out safely. And you can't blame Simon, he was afraid to let me go on my own and he knew he couldn't stop me, and so I got him into it. And Ngoni is out now safe and sound and we didn't interfere in the battle at all." Amie ran out of steam and sat rigid waiting for the response.

Sir Humphrey kept them waiting as he paced the room, tossing the water bottle hypnotically from one hand to the other. "I think that may well be the longest sentence I've ever heard. Don't you ever take a breath woman?

"I can see your motivation, and I admire your loyalty. It is lucky for you that the army stayed loyal to Mtumba and he's still in power. If the tables had turned, the British government would have been put in a very awkward position."

"Ben's ok?" Amie jumped out of her seat, an enormous smile on her face.

"Yes. Peace has been restored, though I'm sorry to tell you that both Kirimu Nashele and Gaga Medwewe have been killed."

Simon shot a look at Amie who picked up the message.

"Oh, I'm sorry to hear that. Gaga was a good friend."

"To you maybe, not to the president. She was in it from the start with the Finance Minister."

"Really? I expect Mathilda is relieved." Amie's eyes opened wide. She dared not look at Simon who was digging his fingernails into his palms to stop himself from laughing out loud.

"Another casualty of war, sadly."

"So, everything is back to normal?" Simon said before Amie said too much.

"As far as we can tell. That's enough for now." Sir Humphrey changed the subject. "And Amie, since you've recovered so quickly and had a recent experience in event management, I'm putting you in charge of organizing Her Majesty's Birthday celebrations, to be held here in the embassy grounds. All the ambassadors, wives, etc. etc. The usual thing."

It looked as if Sir Humphrey was about to dismiss them, but Simon jumped in. "Sir, what news on Lucky, Trident and Bones? What side were they on?"

"Frankly I can't tell you. I haven't heard any news of them since they were sent to meet you off the plane."

"They were in the village when we left, so I just wondered."

"I suspect we can rely on them in the future, unless you have information to the contrary?"

"No, not really. I had my doubts but nothing concrete."

"Let's leave it there for now then."

Amie was kept busy arranging the birthday celebrations. On the day, the garden to the rear of the British Embassy looked lovely, with portraits of the Queen and Prince Philip, red, white and blue flags and fairy lights strung in the syringa trees. Patriotic music played in the background. The tables were laden with food and waiters hurried about with trays of drinks and snacks.

Amie played hostess to Sir Humphrey, welcoming all the Commonwealth ambassadors, and doing her best to avoid Edward Keller whose booming Texas accent could be heard telling everyone about the wonder of the Lone Star State. She also kept her distance from Vladimir Petrovnikov whom she heard asking for vodka.

Ben arrived late. It was the first time she'd seen him since he'd been wheeled into the hospital. He approached her across the bright green, manicured Kikuyu lawn, coaxed into life by throwing gallons and gallons of water over the scorched earth.

"Amie. My friend Amie," he said taking her hand in both of his. "I must introduce you to my new first lady, but I think you have already met?"

Amie looked at the shy, but radiant Ngoni standing by his

side. She was dressed simply in the colourful red, green and blue traditional dress of Togodo. She gave Amie a warm smile and stepped forward. For a moment it looked as if she was about to give her a big hug before she remembered her new status as the wife of the President and stepped back. It reminded Amie that she'd been so busy she hadn't thought about her own wedding. It was time to start planning.

"Yes. Ngoni and I know each other," Amie replied shaking her hand.

"You organized this function?" Ben asked.

"Yes. I had plenty of practice." Amie laughed and then she couldn't resist it. "Are you suggesting I organize another auction for the mineral rights?"

"Minerals?" Ben's eyebrows shot up.

Amie was confused. "Yes, all that stuff under the ground, up north."

"They didn't tell you?" It was Ben's turn to look puzzled. He dropped Amie's hand and pulled her to one side away from the crowd.

"Tell me what?"

"The so-called Decker report was a fake. Your government told me months ago."

"Are you saying there were no minerals? Nothing?" Amie couldn't believe what she was hearing.

"Nothing worth digging out of the ground."

"And you knew that and still arranged the safari and an auction?"

Ben smiled. "It was an excellent opportunity to find out who I could trust and who was prepared to put up a little pre-bidding cash."

"And the rights to mine – nothing?"

"Hefty payments, which will fund many improvements for Togodo. Suma might get a football stadium named after him after all."

"But when they start mining and they find nothing?" Amie couldn't get her head round Ben taking money from all the countries that had attended the auction, and more for the pleasure of watching them dig only to find nothing of value. It would cost them millions to set up the operation.

Ben smirked and shrugged his shoulders. "They can afford it," he replied. He bowed his head and excused himself, turned back to Ngoni and went to greet Sir Humphrey.

Amie raced over to Simon. "Did you know?" she demanded. "Did you know about the … what is it, Decker report?"

Simon had the grace to look ashamed. "Need to know only, Amie," he whispered in her ear. "Why do you think they sent me in to break up the party?"

"But, Ben's signed the rights and now some poor country is going to be duped."

"That wasn't part of the plan Amie, but I don't have to remind you, this is Africa."

Amie gazed across the lawn at the elite society laughing and drinking and then at Ben. Would she ever understand the mindset of an African, even one she thought she knew so well? *No, maybe I'll never understand, but it's still a land and a people I can't help but love, and I always will.*

<<< O O O >>>

ACKNOWLEDGEMENTS

No book is ever produced by one person alone and Savage Safari was a massive effort by many different people – there were times I wondered if it would ever be published. I would like to thank the following people – Dave Cantrell, Valerie Poore, Frank Parker and Colin Pryce for going the extra mile and patiently correcting all my mistakes. Last, but certainly not least my long-suffering husband, you are my inspiration, my proof reader, book formatter and sounding board.

ABOUT THE AUTHOR

Lucinda E Clarke has been a professional writer for almost 40 years, scripting for both radio and television. She's had numerous articles published in several national magazines, written mayoral speeches and advertisements. She currently writes a monthly column in a local publication in Spain. She once had her own newspaper column, until the newspaper closed down, but says this was not her fault!

Five of her books have been bestsellers in genre on Amazon on both sides of the Atlantic awarded several medals and certificates and previously, she won over 20 awards for scripting, directing, concept and producing, and had two educational text books published. Sadly, these did not make her the fortune she dreamed of to allow her to live in luxury.

Lucinda has also worked on radio – on one occasion with a bayonet at her throat – appeared on television and met and interviewed some of the world's top leaders.

She set up and ran her own video production company, producing a variety of programmes, from advertisements to corporate and drama documentaries on a vast range of subjects.

In total she has lived in eight different countries, run the 'worst riding school in the world', and cleaned toilets to bring in the money.

When she handled her own divorce, Lucinda made legal history in South Africa.
Now, pretending to be retired, she gives occasional talks and lectures to special interest groups and finds retirement the most exhausting time of her life so far; but says there is still so much to see and do, she is worried she won't have time to fit it all in.

© Lucinda E Clarke
 Spain 2019

To my Readers

If you have enjoyed this book, or even if you didn't like it, please take a few minutes to write a review. Reviews are very important to authors and I would certainly value your feedback. Thank you.

Why not sign up for Lucinda's newsletter for special offers, competitions, news on other authors and new releases. http://eepurl.com/cBu4Sf Subscribers get a free book and the exclusive serialized back stories to the Amie series.

Web page: lucindaeclarkeauthor.com
Facebook:
https://www.facebook.com/lucindaeclarke.author
Email: lucindaeclarke@gmail.com
Blog: http://lucindaeclarke.wordpress.com
Twitter: @LucindaEClarke
I love to hear from my readers.

Also by Lucinda E Clarke

Walking over Eggshells

The first autobiography which relates Lucinda's horrendous relationship with her mother and her travels to various countries.

The very Worst riding School in the World (free)

Who in their right mind would open and run a riding school when they can't ride, are terrified of horses, with no idea of how to care for them and no insurance or capital. Add to that two of the four horses are not fit for the knacker's yard Yes, that would be me.

Truth, Lies and Propaganda

The first of two books explaining how Lucinda 'fell' into writing for a living – her dream since childhood. It began when she was fired from her teaching job, and crashed out in an audition at the South African Broadcasting Corporation. In a quirky turn of fate, she found herself writing a series on how to care for domestic livestock; she knew absolutely nothing about cows, goats and chickens. And it all continued from there.

More Truth, Lies and Propaganda

Tales of filming in deep rural Africa, meeting a ram with an identity crisis, a house that disappears, the forlorn bushmen and a video starring a very dead rat. You will never believe anything you watch on television ever again.

Amie - African Adventure

A novel set in Africa, which takes Amie from the comfort of her home in England to a small African country. Civil war breaks out and soon she is fighting for her life.

Amie and the Child of Africa

As Amie goes in search of the child she fostered before the civil war broke out, she encounters a terrorist organization with international connections. She is not alone, but one of her friends will betray her.

Amie Stolen Future

In one night, Amie loses everything, her home, her family, her possessions and her name. She has nowhere to turn, but she has no freedom for other people now control her life and if she does not obey them, they will not let her live.

Amie Cut for Life

A look and listen mission turns out to be more sinister as Amie is left to rescue four young girls who are destined for the sex slave trade with a horrifying twist.

Samantha (Amie backstory)

A light comedy as Amie's sister ventures overseas for the first time with her boyfriend Gerry – if it can go wrong, it goes wrong.

Ben (Amie backstory)

Ben's story of his passage into manhood and the beginning of the civil war in Togodo.

Unhappily Ever After

The real truth you've never been told before. In Fairyland, Cinderella is scheming on how to get a divorce with a good settlement from King Charming, and the other royal marriages are also in dire trouble. This year's ball is approaching, along with a political agitator hell bent on rousing the peasants into revolting against their royal masters.

Reviews

*That Lucinda E Clarke can write and write well is not in question. This memoir left me breathless at times. She writes of her adventures, misadventures and family relationships in an honest but entertaining manner. I wholeheartedly recommend this book, (**Walking over Eggshells**) buy it, delve in and lose a few days, well worth it.*

---

*This book was written with such consummate skill. I have enormous admiration for Lucinda E Clarke as an author. She not only knows how to write an edge-of-the-seat, well-constructed story that would make a brilliant movie – she does it using beautiful, spare, intelligent, and amazingly descriptive language. By the time I got to the end of 'Amie' I felt as though I'd been to Africa – seen it, touched it, smelled it, heard it... loved it and hated it. Everything that is the truth of the country is there in this book. Can I give it six stars please? It deserves it. (**Amie an African Adventure**)*

---

*Lucinda E. Clarke takes the reader on another fast-paced African adventure full of suspense and twists and turns. The characters are so well developed that I felt as if I was watching a movie while reading this wonderful book. Mrs. Clarke both entertains and educates the reader about the African experience. The story never lags and quickly pulls the reader in this new adventure. (**Amie and the Child of Africa**).*

What a great book! I have so enjoyed this and love the tongue-in-cheek, self-deprecating humour with which Lucinda Clarke relates her experiences. It's quite fascinating to read how she becomes involved in writing and broadcasting, and also really interesting to realise how much easier it was to get in touch with decision makers in the days before the digital onslaught. Either that or Lucinda is being overly modest and making it look simple! I loved the descriptions of her early experiences in Libya - both funny and frightening. And of course, there are lots of memories for me here as I moved to South Africa in the early eighties and always listened to Springbok radio. The style is easy and fluid, and I have enjoyed every page, riveted by the quantity of writing she managed to do without any previous knowledge of the subjects. Amazing. For me, this is the best one of Lucinda's yet in terms of keeping me pasted to my Kindle! I've read two of her other books before, and I'll definitely be reading the sequel to this one! **(Truth, Lies and Propaganda)**

I picked this one up purely on the basis of how much I enjoyed reading the first book and I was not to be disappointed. Lucinda E Clarke is one of those writers who can tell a story effortlessly in a way that just carries you along with her adventures. I have to say she is fast becoming one of my favourite authors. The book revolves around a period of her life as she returns to work in Africa and she uses her natural writing ability to not just recount events but to entertain along the way. Her skill is not in telling extraordinary tales but in making often ordinary real life stories come to life and it is in the smaller details of each story that I often found myself most enthralled. I cannot recommend this book and indeed the previous one highly enough. If your next book purchase is from the pen of Lucinda E Clarke you will have made a wise decision indeed. A thoroughly deserved 5 stars out of 5 from me. **(More, truth Lies and Propaganda)**

The author's imagination and humour are combined to create a story that makes your smile or LOL from beginning to end. It is a rollicking pantomime of dry wit and well-described imagery that works exceptionally well. Highly recommended. **(Unhappily Ever After)**

An excerpt from: **Amie - African Adventure**

They came for her soon after the first rays of the sun began to pour over the far distant hills, spilling down the slopes onto the earth below. At first the gentle beams warmed the air, but as the sun rose higher in the sky, it produced a scorching heat, which beat down on the land with relentless energy.

She heard them approach, their footsteps echoing loudly on the bare concrete floors. As the marching feet drew closer, she curled up as small as she could, and tried to breathe slowly to stop her heart racing. No, please, not again, she whispered to herself. She couldn't take much more. What did they want? Would they beat her again? What did they expect her to say?

There was nothing she could tell them she was keeping no secrets. She knew she couldn't take any more pain every little bit of her body ached. How many films had she seen where people were kicked or beaten up? She'd never understood real pain, the real agony even a single punch could inflict on the body. Now all she wanted was to die, to escape the torture and slide away into oblivion.

The large fat one was the first to appear on the other side of the door. She knew he was important, because the gold braid, medals, ribbons and badges on his uniform told everyone he was a powerful man, a man it would be very dangerous to cross. He was accompanied by three other warders, also in uniform, but with fewer decorations.

They unlocked the old, rusty cell door and the skinny one walked over and dragged her to her feet. He pushed her away from him, swung her round and bound her wrists together behind her back, with a long strip of dirty cotton material. She winced as he pulled roughly on the cloth and then propelled her towards the door. The others stood back as they shoved her into the corridor and up the steps to the ground floor.

She thought they were going to turn left towards the room where they made her sit for hours and hours on a small chair. They'd shouted and screamed at her and got angry when she couldn't answer their questions. This made them angry so they hit her again.

She'd lost track of the time she'd been here was it a few days, or several weeks? As she drifted in and out of consciousness, she had lost all sense of reality. Her former life was a blur, and it was too late to mark the cell walls to record how long they'd kept her imprisoned.

This time, however, they didn't turn left. They turned right at the top of the steps and pulled her down a long corridor towards an opening at the far end. She could see the bright sunlight reflecting off the dirty white walls. For a brief moment, she had a sudden feeling of euphoria. They were going to let her go!

She could hear muffled sounds and shouts from the street outside. It was surreal there were people so close to the prison going about their everyday lives. On the other side of the wall, the early morning suppliers who brought produce in from the surrounding areas were haggling over prices with the market stallholders, shouting and arguing at the tops of their voices. Not one of them was aware of her, of her pain or despair. Even if they *had* known, they wouldn't give her a second thought. Why should they care? She didn't belong here. Only a few years ago she'd never heard of them or their country. The sounds drifting over the wall that were once so foreign had become commonplace, then forgotten, and now remembered. She was aware of the everyday bustle and noise of the market, goats bleating, chickens squawking, children screaming and the babble of voices. But all these sounds could have been a million miles away, for they were way beyond her reach.

Hope flared briefly. Her captors had realized she was innocent. They'd never accused her of anything sensible, and she still didn't know why she'd been arrested. She knew she'd done nothing wrong. Her thoughts ran wild, and she tried to convince herself the nightmare was over at last.

All the doors on either side of the corridor were closed, as they half carried, half dragged her towards the opening in the archway at the end. The closer they got, against all reason, her hopes just grew and grew. They were going to set her free. She was going home.

As they shoved her through the open doorway, she screwed up her eyes against the bright light, and when she opened them, it was to see they were in a bare courtyard, surrounded on three sides by high walls. As she looked around, she could see there was no other exit leading to the outside world.

Then she saw the stake in the ground on the far side, and brutally they dragged her towards it. She thought of trying to resist, but she was too weak, and there was too much pain. It was difficult to walk, so she concentrated on putting one foot in front of the other, determined not to give the soldiers or police or whoever they were, any satisfaction. She would show as much dignity as she could.

The skinny one pushed her against the post, took

another long piece of sheeting from his pocket and tied it around her chest, fixing her firmly to the wood. She glanced down at the ground and was horrified to see large brown stains in the dust.

Not freedom; this was the end. She squeezed her eyes shut, determined not to let the tears run down her cheeks, but the sound of marching feet forced her to open them again. She saw four more men, all dressed in brown uniforms, with the all-too-familiar guns who had lined up on the other side of the courtyard opposite her. They were a rough-looking bunch, their uniforms were ill fitting and stained, and their boots were unpolished and covered in dust.

She was trembling all over. She didn't know whether to keep her eyes open to see what was going on, or close them and pretend this was all a terrible dream. She was torn. Part of her wanted it all to end now, but still a part of her wanted to scream, 'let me live! Please, please let me live!'

The big fat man barked commands and she heard the sounds of guns being broken open as he walked to each of them handing out ammunition, then with the safety catches off, they shuffled into position.

To her horror, she felt a warm trickle of liquid running down the inside of her thighs. At this very last moment, she had lost both her control and her dignity. They had not even offered her a blindfold, so she closed her eyes again and tried to remember happier times, before the nightmare started. Briefly, she glanced up at the few fluffy white clouds floating high in the sky as the order to fire was given.